WORLD WAR II

MEDITERRANEAN THEATER

✦ 1943 - 1945 ✦

Bologne

YUGOSLAVIA

ITALY

Adriatic Sea

Rome

Cassino

Anzio

Foggia   Bari

Naples   Tara...

Salerno

Tyrrhenian
Sea

Michael

British Naval Officer

Palermo

Messina

SICILY

...n

...nis

Sea

MALTA

The White House

Eden Barrowman

HOME AGAIN AT LAST

HOME AGAIN AT LAST

A WORLD WAR II NOVEL

JERRY BORROWMAN

Covenant Communications, Inc.

Covenant Communications, Inc.

Jacket design and endsheet map by Jessica A. Warner, © 2008 Covenant Communications, Inc.
Cover painting *No Trains Today* by Stan Stokes © The Stokes Collection, www.stokescollection.com.
Endsheet sketches of White House and British officers © Eden Borrowman.

Published by Covenant Communications, Inc.
American Fork, Utah

Printed in Canada
First Printing: April 2008

15 14 13 12 11 10 09 08   10 9 8 7 6 5 4 3 2 1

ISBN 978-1-59811-531-4

In Memoriam—N. Winn Allen
1951–2005

Beloved brother, uncle, and friend. My brother-in-law, Winn, filled our lives with joy and laughter by sharing his time and his good nature. We traveled much of the world together, learning from him how to celebrate other cultures and to relish and savor the time we have on earth. His untimely death from cancer at age 54 has left us bereft, but his memory lives forever in our hearts.

We love you, Winn, and we think of you every single day. Congratulations on a life well lived.

Marcella, Jerry, Scott, Jeffrey, Steven, and Kelissa
Hilary, Eden, and Maya

***

Dedicated to Geneva Borrowman

My mother has been a lifelong supporter who takes particular interest in my writing. She has read all my manuscripts before publication to correct the grammar and spelling. She is a person who finds great joy in service to others and has been a blessing in the lives of her family and friends. As a master school teacher for forty years she helped more than a thousand first and second graders to find their place in the world and to feel secure in her love. Even today, at age 90, she serves as her ward Scout Committee Chairman, working directly with the boys as she helps them qualify for advancement. Her vitality, curiosity, and energy are an inspiration, and we hope she'll live at least as long as her mother, who made it to age 105.

ACKNOWLEDGMENTS

In the course of getting this story ready for publication I had a number of friends and family who were kind enough to read this book in manuscript form, offering their encouragement and ideas. I specifically wish to acknowledge the efforts of Val Johnson, a professional editor and friend, who did a line-by-line edit of the manuscript, as well as my wife, Marcella, for her unique insights on the storyline.

Other readers include members of our immediate family—Kelissa, Scott, Hilary, Jeff, and Eden Borrowman. Evan Rowley was also extremely helpful in his comments and suggestions. My thanks to Rick Justesen, Aldin and Shirley Porter, Evan Liddiard, James Dye, and Paul Decker.

I'm also pleased to introduce you to the remarkable artistic skills of my daughter-in-law Eden, who did the inside cover drawings.

I also want to thank my editor, Kirk Shaw, and all the other folks at Covenant Communications who worked so hard to bring this book to you. Most of all, I want to thank my readers who have made the effort of writing this series so worthwhile. Thank you!

Part One

INVASION OF ITALY

Chapter One

PROTECTING AN AMERICAN

Felixstowe on the English Channel—1943

"Lieutenant Carlyle, please wait!"

Michael turned and smiled at the sound of Commander Prescott's voice. With a crisp salute he asked, "Are you commanding today's mission, sir?"

"I am. It's been a long time, Michael. How have you been?"

Michael was thoughtful for a moment, even though it was a casual question. But he couldn't help but think of his crew and all they'd been through together. "We've done all right, sir." Michael had served under Prescott when he was new to the motor torpedo boats, and there was no one in the service he respected more. Under Commander Prescott's tutelage, Michael had qualified for his own command in a different service area and they hadn't been together since. "What about you?"

"I'm getting old. My body hurts, my brain hurts, and I find I have no patience for incompetent superiors."

"Me too, sir." Then realizing the implication of what he'd just said, he quickly added, "Present company excepted, of course."

Prescott laughed. "Don't count on it, Michael. Once we get out there today you may very well think I've gone 'round the bend—just another doddering old fool in command of the fellows who know what they're doing."

"I doubt that, sir. But speaking of which, what's so special about today's mission that they've brought in the number one commander in the group to take us out in broad daylight on a Sunday afternoon? I'm not sure I know how to drive a boat in anything other than moonlight and the glow of oil fires."

"It is a little different, isn't it? Of course I think that you'll start to see an increasing number of daylight missions now that we have increasing air control over the Channel. As for today, there's a special courier coming in by corvette. My guess is that they're bringing in some kind of technology that needs to get to London from the States as soon as possible, but that it's too heavy for an aircraft. So, our job is to fend off the E-boats that we expect to attack."

"E-boats? They'd come out in daylight?" In the first three years of the war it seemed like Germany had an unlimited number of aircraft to throw against Britain, but with the Nazis now tied up in Russia and the Mediterranean the Royal Air Force finally had the means to send aircraft out to attack any German patrol boats that dared to venture out during daylight hours.

"From what I gather, there must be spies in New York that gave the Germans information about this particular courier, and they've been doing their best to attack it all the way across the Atlantic. Now that the corvette has made it to home waters, the E-boats and whatever aircraft fighters they can send out from Belgium are the Germans' only hope to sink it. Our intelligence indicates that they've decided to take the risk." Prescott scowled as the image of the corvette sinking within a few miles of London formed in his mind. "And wouldn't they love that—to put it down right here in our front yard."

Michael nodded thoughtfully, his brain quickly conjuring up the various ways the Germans could attack. Like the Allies, the Germans had both gunboats and torpedo boats. The German boats' German moniker was "Schnell Boot," meaning "fast boat," but the Allies knew them as E-boats. The British boats were called MTBs (Motor Torpedo Boat). At only seventy-two feet in length, the British boats generally had a crew of thirteen.

The German boats were almost twice as large and could match their speed, but were not as maneuverable. Most of the battles between the two fleets took place at night when aircraft were grounded, the most effective time to bring a convoy through the narrow English Channel. The goal of both fleets was to use their small size and rapid speed to close in on much larger enemy ships, like a troopship or supply ship, and put a torpedo in its side before the bigger ship could take evasive action. Then the small boats would zip out of range and attempt to disappear into the darkness.

But as English trade had increased under the convoy system, the battles had increasingly become the Germans attacking English-related shipping. Which meant that the British boats fighting off the Germans were kept busy.

Today's battle would be more complicated than usual since they'd not only have to engage the German Navy but also the German Air Force. That would make for a pretty dicey battle scene, which Michael would rather avoid.

Michael sighed. It didn't matter what he wanted, since this was going to be the German's show. In the end his crew was either up to the task or not. They'd been together long enough that he had full confidence in their abilities. Now it was up to chance whether they'd be hit by a random aerial bomb, surface fire from a gunboat, or well-aimed torpedo, but hopefully, none of those.

Michael and Prescott had been walking at a rather crisp pace and were now approaching the depot ship where the small boats were resupplied after their nightly missions into the Channel. There Prescott would brief Michael and the other boat captains under his command on the specifics of the mission.

"Well, whatever they're hauling on that corvette had better be important. I'm supposed to have dinner with Jules Ellington and my family tonight, and my mother will be extremely unhappy if I'm late."

Prescott cocked an eye. "Ellington? Our commando friend that did his best to get you killed in France?"

Michael nodded. "The very same."

"Then with any luck we'll all get torpedoed so you won't have to listen to him drone on and on. I'd just as soon shoot myself as sit through a dinner with him."

Michael laughed. He knew that many in the regular navy found Jules's bravado as a commando to be off-putting. But they'd been friends since prep school and Michael found his droll humor quite refreshing, particularly since Michael himself wasn't really that quick on his feet. "Well, my parents like him. And I need him tonight since he can always cheer them up when I have bad news to deliver."

"Bad news?"

"I assume you've heard about my transfer?"

"Ah. Yes. In fact, that's the main reason I requested you bring your boat 'round for today's mission. Maybe I'm getting sentimental at the ripe old age of twenty-eight, but I just wanted to have one last mission together before you go off to more temperate climates."

"I'm very glad you did, sir. I really don't know why I have to go, but I guess that's the way the service is. An officer does what he's told."

"You'll do great down there, Michael. Our loss is their gain."

"Thank you, sir." This was always the awkward moment when there really wasn't anything else to say. "Well, it looks like we're here. How many boats are going out?"

"Six. Apparently that's all the king's navy can afford today. Besides, we should be getting some fighter protection, but that's not really ever enough, so we'll have to be on our toes. Perhaps you could come through with one of those award-winning maneuvers of yours that has gained you such notoriety."

Michael blushed. Having earned the Distinguished Service Cross in earlier action, he'd been invited to Buckingham Palace to receive the medal personally from the king, with the prime minister looking on. And then Prime Minister Winston Churchill, a friend of Michael's father, had requested a ride out on Michael's boat, which caused no small stir among the flotilla once it became known. It was all quite embarrassing to Michael.

"With all due respect, sir, we both know that you've earned more medals than I could ever hope to—you just haven't been recognized properly."

Prescott sighed. "I knew I shouldn't have said that to you. Sorry. Notoriety is more of a burden than a blessing, isn't it?"

"More than you'll ever know."

"Well, let's go onboard the tender and I'll give you and your peers our orders for the day. Should be exciting." Michael's countenance brightened immediately. The thrill of battle was addictive and he found himself relishing the thought of a fight in the daylight.

* * *

The best part of any mission, naturally, was shutting the engines down after returning to port with all members of the crew safe and healthy. But the next best part for Michael was when he could give the order for *MTB-982* to go to full speed ahead. The only real protection a person had on a torpedo boat was its speed, since the chine wood hull was vulnerable to just about anything the enemy could throw at it. The metal shield around the bridge did offer some protection from machine gun fire if they had to engage the enemy up close, but it was useless against the enemy's deck guns.

"Full speed ahead," he said easily and thrilled as the three powerful, American-built Packard engines roared to their full potential with a great cloud of blue exhaust smoke billowing out from the stern of the boat. As the boat started hydroplaning, the bow lifted up and out of the water, creating the sharp bow wave that gave rise to the phrase, "a bone in the teeth."

"Care to take the wheel, sir?" Michael turned to his first officer, Joseph Carver, and shook his head. Everyone on the boat knew that Michael loved to control the helm, but today he would need his wits about him, and he didn't need the added distraction of conning the wheel. Besides, they had a new helmsman who needed the experience.

"I don't think so, Number One. I'm going to go down to my cabin for awhile. Call me when we approach the rendezvous or before if anything out of the ordinary comes up."

"Yes, sir!" Carver said. "Should be about an hour to an hour and a half, depending on how the seas are running."

* * *

"Bad turn in the weather, isn't it?" Carver said. In the time it had taken to traverse the sixty miles to reach the rendezvous point, a squall had set in so they had rain slickers on and the boat battened down.

Michael scanned the ocean for the enemy. "A very bad turn. All aircraft have been grounded and gray skies make for a gray ocean, which is the perfect hiding place for a gray E-boat. They'll be upon us before we hardly even know they're there."

"But the corvette can outrun them, can't it?"

"Yes, if it can get past them. But if they're able to angle in on it from the east it could be a sitting duck. Apparently whatever the thing is that the Americans are carrying is quite fragile, so they don't have a lot of latitude to maneuver or take evasive action."

"Signal from the flag officer, sir. Corvette has been sighted." The signalman then gave the coordinates.

"Thank you, Mr. Renton." Instinctively both Carver and Michael turned their powerful binoculars to the spot and identified the sleek little corvette as it sliced through the water. A corvette was the next-largest ship in the navy from the torpedo boats. This one looked to be about 1,500 metric tons and approximately 100 meters in length. American ships always had something of a different trim than their British counterparts, but it was still a beautiful little ship. Compared to a torpedo boat, which was about one-fourth the size, a corvette was made of metal, had fairly heavy deck armament, and was able to do a transatlantic crossing as part of a convoy screen, in concert with the larger frigates and destroyers. It was ideal for courier duty since it was so fast and agile. In enemy waters it could move close in to shore to avoid detection from the sea.

Michael gave the order to the helmsman to close the distance. Prescott's plan was to set up a screen with his six boats, putting the corvette between his boats and the English shore. That way the Germans would have to get past the small boats before they got a shot at the corvette.

At forty knots it didn't take long for them to take up their assigned position at the head of the screen. Prescott had put his own boat in the center so he could pivot to whatever danger presented itself. Even if an attack came up from behind, Michael was to stay on post at the front of the column, just in case the Germans intended to trap them in a pincer movement—an old trap. All the escort boats in a group would be drawn into a battle at the rear, leaving the corvette vulnerable to a second attack from the front, but Prescott was far too experienced to let that happen.

As they approached the Americans, Michael waved at the officers stationed on their bridge. He decided he liked protecting a ship this size since it was so much closer to their own in size. On the one occasion when he'd been involved in escorting a battleship through the Channel, it felt like he was an ant scurrying around a fat old cat. The men on the bridge of the battleship were hardly even visible, they were so far up in the sky.

"Sir! Possible enemy sighting!" In the months he'd worked with Renton, Michael had come to marvel at Renton's eyesight, as well as his ability to detect even the slightest aberration on the horizon.

Michael couldn't remember a single time he'd made a false sighting, which was an extraordinary accomplishment indeed.

"Range and position?"

Renton gave it to him. It was off to the southeast, just as Prescott had anticipated, and Michael quickly trained his glasses in that direction. All he could see was choppy black water, punctuated with whitecaps.

"I'm not seeing it, Renton."

His signalman, who doubled as a lookout when not sending signals, came over and angled Michael's shoulders slightly. Straining his eyes, Michael still didn't see anything.

"There! Did you see that?"

Michael wished that he had seen something, but he hadn't.

"There it is again!"

This time Michael did see. It was the Germans, all right.

"Battle stations!" Michael rocked the lever that sounded the Klaxon horn. He loved doing that. "Make a signal to Prescott and let him know what we've sighted."

"Yes, sir!" Renton replied.

"How many?"

Carver peered through his binoculars. "Five, six . . . make that seven."

Michael shook his head. "Seven to seven, if you count the corvette. The odds are against us." The odds were against them because it only took one German torpedo to win the battle, while the British had to successfully destroy, damage, or deflect all seven of the German ships. Since the British had six torpedo boats to the German's seven, they couldn't go one-on-one against the Germans. No matter what they did, there would be one boat open to make the strike on the corvette.

As he thought about it, Michael decided it was a little bit like soccer, with just one goalie facing down the other team's strikers. If even one opponent player gets past the defensive screen to get a shot off, the chance of a goal is relatively high.

"Particularly if the goalie has limited motion because he's protecting something."

"Pardon?"

"What?"

"I just thought I heard you say something, sir."

Michael laughed. "Just thinking out loud, Joseph. Trying to get the battle scene clear in my head." By this point they were streaking through the water at flank speed—he'd ordered his engineer to run the engines past the red line to get all possible speed. They couldn't keep that up for long or it would overheat the engines, but right now the goal was to get the corvette out in front of the Germans since it had the speed to outpace them if the torpedo boats could foul the German's line of attack in a stalling action.

"Of course it's all for naught if there's another attack force up ahead. In that case we're driving the corvette right into them." This time Carver didn't bother to ask. He'd been in battle with Michael often enough to know that he was constantly evaluating the scene, looking for vulnerabilities, seeking out opportunities.

As they drew within six hundred yards, the German boats fanned out in an awesome display of seamanship. The goal was to draw the six British boats into chasing a particular target, leaving the corvette vulnerable to attack.

"Bear port twenty degrees," Michael ordered calmly. At least it sounded calm. His heart was racing at this point. One of the German boats was trying to cross the bow of the corvette so it could get between the Americans and the shore, which would be disastrous since the Germans could then attack the corvette from two sides. Michael knew that taking this fellow out was his only concern right now. He'd have to leave it up to Prescott to figure out what to do with the other six German boats.

Speaking into the tube that went from the bridge to the engine room, Michael said, "We're going to need to keep this speed for a while longer, chief. We've got a hotshot trying to cross the bow and we've got to get in its way."

"We're doing all right, sir. Another five minutes at least."

Five minutes didn't sound like a lot, but Michael knew that in battle it meant everything. The problem with this battle was that everything was being done in daylight. It would be very hard to get a torpedo off that the Germans couldn't avoid. Since they only had four it would be easy to get themselves completely disarmed except for deck guns unless he was careful.

"Looks like our angle is good, sir. We should cross between the German and the corvette. What do you plan to do then?"

"They'll start firing on us shortly—in fact I'm surprised they haven't done so yet. They're going to try to force us to veer off course, so I want to keep heading straight for them. If they turn, we turn; if they slow down, we don't. I want to head straight for them no matter what they throw at us."

Carver nodded grimly. "Your American game of 'chicken' again?"

Michael had been born in America and held dual citizenship. Even though the family moved to England when he was ten, he still had a lot of memories from America, which often proved a source of amusement to his fellows in the Royal Navy.

"Chicken it is. Assuming we don't get blown out of the water by our predictable course, we'll fire a torpedo spread once we get close enough so that he can't turn his way out of it. It will be tricky."

Michael observed Joseph licking his lips—his way of showing anxiety.

There was a flash of light on the bridge of the E-boat, followed rather quickly by a dull thud from across the water— the sound of the deck gun firing. "It's taking our range." A large waterspout popped up behind them on the starboard side.

"Starboard five," Michael said quietly into the helmsman's ear. At this point he was standing right next to the young man so he could communicate his desires instantly. The boat immediately shifted to the right. To Carver's amazement it was just what was needed to hold them true to the slight course change the German boat had taken as it sought to reposition its guns for the next salvo.

"Open fire with the deck guns!"

Carver gave the signal and the Oerlikons opened fire. While not heavy enough to sink a German E-boat, they were certainly powerful enough to knock a hole in the bridge or to destroy an enemy gun if they hit. At the very least it kept the enemy gunners off balance, which was crucial at a time like this when Michael was setting up a torpedo shot. The air was immediately shattered by the "pom pom" sound of the guns opening fire. By now they'd closed the range to the point that the German boat would either continue pounding them or it'd break away and try to get a new angle.

"Stand by tubes one and two!" Michael watched as the men prepped the torpedo tubes. "Joseph, would you go down there and personally supervise? Hanson is still new and these shots have got to be precise."

Carver immediately left the bridge to go down to the forward deck.

There were three or four flashes on the enemy's deck and Michael instinctively braced for the expected blow. The Germans didn't disappoint him. This time two columns of water shot up at the stern, but a third hit so close to the port side that it lifted the hind quarter of the boat up and out of the water. A great spray of water cascaded down on the deck, drenching everyone as they picked themselves up from the fall precipitated by this unexpected distraction.

"Damage report?" Michael called down to the gunners on the aft deck.

The two men looked up with astonished eyes and raised their hands to indicate that it didn't look like there was anything. For the terrific concussion it had made, the shot had apparently fallen into the water without hitting the boat.

"Make ready to fire!" Michael shouted while simultaneously ringing down to the engine room to slow the engines to two-thirds. He hadn't forgotten the five-minute warning from the engineer and it had all been used up now. Slowing the boat would also give them a steadier platform from which to fire.

The Germans realized that they'd failed to cut the corvette's bow because of Michael's interference and were now fully cognizant of the risk they'd accepted in trying to make it. The two boats were close enough to each other that Michael's crew could hear the alarm bells sounding on the German ship, which indicated that there was going to be a very sharp, high-speed turn, and that every German onboard had better be grabbing hold of something to steady himself if he hoped to avoid being thrown overboard.

"Which way is it going to turn?" Michael said through clenched teeth. The Germans still had a chance to turn away from Michael's boat and attempt to get seaward of the British again to make another run at the corvette. Or they could turn directly toward Michael to force him out of the way, maybe even with the thought of ramming the smaller boat. Michael watched carefully for any indication of the Germans' intention, but there was nothing. Then he saw the slightest movement at the stern of the ship—so slight that most people would never have noticed.

"All slow!" he roared. "It's coming towards us. Set up a narrow spread, Mr. Carver. Fire now!"

"Fire one! Fire two!" Carver said with authority, even though he was probably every bit as scared as Michael. By this point the German boat still hadn't revealed its intention, and if Michael was wrong the two torpedoes would be wasted. If he was right, they were set to explode at such a close range that if they hit the German boat, the *982* ran the risk of being showered with debris and perhaps even crashing into pieces of the wreckage.

After giving the order to fire Michael subconsciously braced himself and was rewarded for doing so when, upon releasing the compressed air that fired the torpedoes from the deck, the ship recoiled from its launch. Just as he felt the second torpedo leave the boat, Michael ordered, "Full speed, hard aport!" Now it was his turn to get the heck out of there.

"It turned towards us!"

Even though Michael had looked away momentarily he was pleased to hear Carver's voice. He was grateful to have made the best choice. Of course the German still had a chance to avoid getting hit if it was able to complete the turn before the torpedoes reached it, since the profile of a ship heading straight forward made for a very slender target. But in his mind Michael knew the German boat wouldn't make it. As fast as an E-boat was, it wasn't as fast as a compressed-air torpedo. Michael estimated that at least one of the torpedoes would hit the German about two-thirds of the way through its turn.

"Brace for impact!"

It was a good thing he gave that order—not because of their torpedoes, but rather because the German gunners somehow managed to get a shot off, even in the act of the ship turning. It may have been a desperation play, but the gunners' shell tore directly across the bow of the *982* as though the shot had been perfectly planned. Michael looked on in horror as the shell tore one of the deck guns right off its mounting. There was a sickening ripping sound as the decking was torn up, mingled with the cursing of the men who were thrown off their feet as the boat lurched from the force of the impact. Michael's first fear was that the gunner had been killed along with his gun, but then he saw that the young man was thrown back on his haunches a few feet away. Apparently he'd been moving away from the gun to get some more ammunition. This young fellow would have a great story to tell when he got back to port.

In the next moment there was a tremendous explosion as the first torpedo found its mark. By now the *982* had completed its turn and was on a new heading that was taking them closer to the corvette, so to look at the German boat, Michael had to physically turn and look over the stern to see the cataclysmic results of the British torpedo on the shattered hulk of the E-boat. The torpedo had caught the Germans at midship, which happened to be where the ammunition bunker was situated, and the explosion of the torpedo had been quite subdued in comparison to the magazine blowing up. The German ship was torn apart by the two explosions, and the ocean's surface was already littered with debris and bodies. Michael hated that sight more than anything in the world.

"Nice work!" he shouted to his crew and was gratified by their cheer. "Damage report?"

Joseph came bounding up the steps. "We've got some serious hull damage where the gun was torn loose. But nothing below the waterline."

"The engines?"

"The chief tells me that they've got some sunlight down there, but the engines are fine. You still have full power if you need it."

Michael looked up and mouthed a silent prayer of thanks. "Well, we lived through that one. Let's take a shot at someone else. Can you identify a new target?"

"Yes, sir . . ." Joseph replied, "looking."

The scene in front of them was really quite unique. The storm had picked up so that everyone was being rained on. The corvette was bounding through the water at top speed, its bow lifting up and out of the water with each collision with the growing waves. But it was holding steady on its course, which meant that for the moment they hadn't spotted any torpedo trails. He could see the other British boats in the group engaging the enemy.

"Where's the striker?" He was worried about the one extra German boat that would not have an MTB on its tail.

"There it is!" Carver shouted excitedly. "Standing off to the side, waiting for an opening it can get through."

Michael quickly turned his glasses to port and, sure enough, there was an E-boat just sort of lying out there, still ahead of the corvette and not engaged with any British boat. That was Prescott's work. Somehow he'd managed to simultaneously engage a German boat while keeping himself between the extra German and the corvette.

But the striker was picking up speed—it must have thought it'd found a way through. It was obvious that the German would have to make its move quickly or let the corvette get past it. Working out the math in his head as quickly as he could, Michael gave the order to go back to flank speed while simultaneously giving a new heading to the helmsman. The young man was proving himself very adept in his handling of the ship and Michael made a mental note to compliment him when it was all over.

By this point the corvette had gotten involved and Michael watched in fascination as its deck guns came to life. The first target was the E-boat that Commander Prescott was engaging. From the look of Prescott's boat, as well as the German, they were both struggling. The first two shots from the corvette missed, but the third managed to hit the E-boat on the aft deck. A great shower of splinters erupted into the air, and Michael knew immediately that that boat would pose no more threat. Prescott also knew it because he immediately turned his attention to the same boat that Michael was pursuing. The E-boat commander now had to worry about two torpedo boats converging on him, which reduced his range of operation significantly. Fortunately, the other four German boats were now astern of the corvette so that the British simply had to run blocking maneuvers to keep them off the corvette's tail. If Michael and Prescott played their cards right they could end the battle very quickly.

Prescott didn't waste any time. Apparently he was disgusted with the Germans because he didn't wait for a good firing situation. Instead, he sent two torpedoes into the water in a fairly wide pattern, which forced the German to turn directly toward Michael in an attempt to get out of the way.

"Tubes three and four, prepare to fire!" Michael shouted excitedly. "Let's send out just one, just to keep our German friend in the lane for Prescott's torpedo." Michael called down the coordinates and gave the command to fire. There was the whooshing sound, followed by the splash of the torpedo as it hit the water, and then the trail of bubbles that showed its progress as it started on its path of destruction.

"He's got nowhere to go," Michael explained to the helmsman. "Can you see that if he takes action to avoid our torpedo he goes right back into the path of Commander Prescott's? If he tries to avoid Prescott's, then he's going to get clobbered by ours."

"How did they allow themselves to get in such a pickle?" the young man asked. Michael was amused by his use of the word *pickle*.

"Through bravery. With the other ships astern of the corvette, it was the only one left to get a shot off at the corvette. In spite of the risk, they decided to make a run for it. Now they're going to pay with their lives." The victory was thrilling, but the thought of brave men dying was still sobering.

"Look, it's launched a torpedo at us."

Michael turned quickly. "Two of them. But they're in a fairly wide spread." Michael felt his hands trembling as he tried to decide what to do. If he veered in either direction he ran the risk of getting hit. If he stayed where he was, the German would be right on top of them when their own torpedoes hit, and there could be collateral damage.

"Mr. Carver?"

"I say we stay right here."

Michael smiled. Carver's judgment had improved consider-ably with his experience in the war. "I agree. All ahead slow." The ship dropped speed immediately, the bow dropping back into the water.

Often Michael turned away at the moment of impact, particularly at night since the flash of the explosion could leave him with night blindness, but now he couldn't help but watch. With three torpedoes running against it the German was in a fatal position. Michael was suddenly startled when the German boat seemed to stall dead in its track. Michael couldn't figure out how the captain could have executed the maneuver so precisely. By bringing the boat to a dead stop, he ran the chance of having all three torpedoes run right past him.

"That is amazing!" Michael turned to Joseph. All Joseph could do was nod in agreement. "Do you think he's going to get away with it?"

"I dunno. I hope not. We only have one more torpedo." The thought that the Germans still had a shot at their target was very discouraging.

By this point they were barely moving so they could miss the German's torpedoes, which streaked past them on a converging course with the corvette, but the American ship noticed their track and quite easily took evasive action.

"I think we're going to miss." Carver said.

But Renton proved to have the better eyes once again. "I don't think so, sir. I think that second torpedo from Commander Prescott is going to catch her in the nose!" Sure enough it did. Prescott's first torpedo ran harmlessly ahead of the E-boat while the *982's* ran even further away on the portside, but Prescott's second torpedo managed to nick the front edge of the bow, exploding in the process. The crew cheered as the front of the E-boat was lifted decisively up and out of the water. As it settled the smoke obscured the damage and for a moment Michael expected the captain to order it to make headway. That would have been crazy since it was inevitable that there had been damage and any forward motion would simply thrust ocean water into the cavity of the ship.

The captain immediately started backing the boat, even as the bow started to sink forward. "She's done for!" Renton said.

"But still dangerous. Look at those men on the guns." The crew turned at the sound of Carver's voice and watched in disbelief as the men on the aft gun deck carefully raised the barrel of their gun and fired two rounds in the direction of the corvette. As Michael's eyes followed the trajectory of the German's shells up and across the sky it became obvious that at least one of them was going to hit the bigger ship.

"Prepare to fire number four," Michael said grimly. Just moments earlier he was planning to issue an order to rescue the Germans in the water, but now it was clear that they were still a threat; the German boat had to be put down. Since Prescott had turned to help chase off the other three boats it was up to the *982* to finish the job.

"Tube loaded and ready sir!"

"Then fire!" The last of their torpedoes left the ship and Michael grimaced as he heard the anguished cries of a handful of Germans in the water. Many had started to abandon ship. He hoped, somehow, that at least some of them would survive, but it wasn't likely. The shock wave created by a torpedo going off in the water was likely to crush all of them, even though they had safely exited the ship.

"Let's go see how the corvette is faring," he said quietly. With that they streaked off toward the corvette. "We'll come back to see what's left once we know our American friends are safe."

It took perhaps five minutes to close on the corvette. The German shell had damaged the upper deck, but the Americans signaled that the damage was superficial.

"Hard aport!" Michael ordered and they returned to the scene of the second German boat. All was quiet now. The ship itself had slipped beneath the waves and there was no noise coming from the debris field.

"Stupid, brave fool," Michael muttered. "His one extra shot was amazing—and it cost him the lives of everyone onboard."

"Signal from flag, sir. Mr. Prescott asks that we take the lead on getting the Americans into port!" The remaining German boats must have turned tail and ran once they saw that the attack was thwarted.

"Acknowledge. And tell him congratulations."

Once again, against poor odds, Prescott had brought his charge safely through the English Channel under the direct line of fire of the Germans. He really was the best there was.

Michael looked down at his watch and sighed.

"Mr. Renton, would you signal the corvette that we intend to make best time possible?" Renton responded in the affirmative.

"Sir?"

Michael turned to Carver. "Believe it or not I have to go to a family dinner tonight. Like we always do in situations like this I'll have to put the best possible face on the day, when in reality it was carnage. Our own ship is torn up and from what I hear at least two other British crafts are damaged. Fortunately, no one was killed from what I understand, although we have a number of wounded." He turned and looked back to where the German ship had gone down. "The same can't be said for all of them."

"Still, there are a lot of American families who won't have to get a black-edged telegram."

Michael nodded. "And that's a good thing."

Chapter Two

SEPARATION

London—April 1943

"That may be the finest Sunday dinner I've ever had. Thank you, Lady Carlyle."

Claire Carlyle smiled at the handsome young man who had joined them for dinner.

"You're quite welcome, Captain Ellington. It's nice to have people to share it with."

"I'd prefer you call me Jules, ma'am. I'm afraid these military titles don't really fit me very well."

Claire smiled again. "All right then, Jules. I'm glad you enjoyed the meal."

"Perhaps you could give me the name of your cook?" He said this while trying to sound as innocent as possible.

"Give you the name of our cook?" Michael Carlyle almost snorted. "And watch you try to steal her? You don't really take us to be that naive, do you?" When Ellington feigned incredulity, Michael continued. "Besides, we rather have a lock on this one. My mother cooks our Sunday meals, and I promise that she's not going to go to work for you!"

"Why Lady Carlyle, I don't believe I've ever been cooked for by a member of the aristocracy." He cocked his left eyebrow. "Except, I suppose, for the occasional piece of toast from my mother . . . but she usually burns it."

"You're rather incorrigible, aren't you, Captain Ellington?" Claire replied.

"Oh, dear, it's back to Captain Ellington. I've put my foot in it yet again, haven't I? But how is it that you do it so well? Is cooking a hobby?"

"It was hardly a hobby when I fed the whole family every meal." She saw the young man's consternation. It occurred to her that he had never contemplated the thought of a family cooking for itself. "I'm an American, you know, and an unusually common one at that. When Philip and I first started our family in Salt Lake City, the last thing we could afford was a cook. I'd grown up sharing in kitchen responsibilities, so it's all very natural for me. It was difficult to give up that part of the nurturing process when the family moved to England so Philip could claim his title. I miss being the one to provide for my children." She straightened her apron, suddenly feeling a bit self-conscious. "At any rate, Sunday is the one day of the week when I take charge, and the family seems to like it."

"As do the servants," Michael added.

Jules Ellington nodded appreciatively, for once at a loss for words. Claire's suspicion was correct that the thought really hadn't ever crossed his mind that parents would cook for their children. It was another one of those charming aspects of Michael Carlyle's life that puzzled Jules, yet intrigued him.

Jules settled back contentedly in the plush leather armchair that sat up to the dark mahogany dining room table in the Carlyle's dining room. Carlyle Manor was a century-old English country home situated on an estate of several hundred acres southwest of London. In some regards it was very much like the home he grew up in, although a bit more grand in its chandeliers and public rooms. As a viscount, Lord Carlyle was further up the pecking order than Jules's father, particularly since he was a minister without portfolio in Winston Churchill's War Cabinet. But the Carlyles were very relaxed about such things so

Jules never felt uncomfortable in their home. Glancing around the room, he decided he needed to try something else to stir things up. He was convinced that to simply allow conversations flow naturally would be a dreadful bore.

"And when you and Michael marry, are you going to cook Sunday dinners?" Jules asked Karen Demming with a mischievous look on his face.

"Marry?" Michael's face flushed immediately.

But before he could say anything further, Karen rather easily replied, "The nature of Michael's and my relationship is none of your business, Jules, but you'll be surprised to know that I like cooking. Our cook has been sharing some French recipes with me. They're delicious, and he says that I'm getting quite good at it. Of course I'd never submit myself to the critique of the heir to the Ellingtons but I'd be pleased to cook for the Carlyles. Perhaps I could cook something simple to add to the Sunday dinner . . . on a Sunday when you're not here."

"Oh, now that really hurts," Jules started to reply, but he was interrupted by Claire.

"We'd be delighted to have you cook for us. Do you have plans for next Sunday?"

Philip Carlyle intervened. Since Michael's breakup with his recuperation nurse, Marissa Chandler, who had cared for him after he was injured in a battle off the English coast, Michael and Karen had become great friends and spent nearly every weekend together when he wasn't on duty. While Philip and Claire had speculated about the possibility of a marriage, nothing had been said publicly by Michael or Karen. Which made Jules's comment clearly out of order—a trademark of Jules's.

"So, Jules, anything you can tell us about the Special Forces—something to give us hope for the eventual outcome of the war?" He turned to face the young man squarely and was struck by his rugged good looks. At barely twenty-three years of age, Jules and Michael both looked far older than their years. Yet with three and a half years at war, Michael was already in command of a torpedo boat, and Jules had risen to the rank of captain in the Royal Navy Commandos. The war had forced both young men to grow up quickly and to assume roles and responsibilities that would normally take half a lifetime to secure. Philip sighed at the thought of their lost youth as he asked the question of Jules.

"I'm afraid the outcome of the war is still classified, sir. As far as I know, it remains in the realm of divine providence. There is some excitement developing down in North Africa, and there's talk that they might need my services there. General Montgomery undoubtedly needs me to pull things out for him." Jules flashed a devilish smile.

"You really are impudent, aren't you?" Philip said, only half in jest.

"I think I prefer Lady Carlyle's characterization, sir. 'Incorrigible' seems a bit more friendly."

"Let's move to the drawing room, shall we?" Philip suggested.

Philip started to rise, but before he could make it to his feet Michael asked him to sit back down for a moment. In the present circumstances of the war, any invitation to a serious conversation was enough to sober anyone pretty quickly.

"What do you want to tell us, Michael?" Claire asked anxiously.

Michael's countenance darkened. With his wavy brown hair and earnest features, he always seemed overly serious—almost the exact opposite of Jules Ellington. Jules and Michael had met at an expensive private school when the Carlyles first moved to England. Later, after the outbreak of war, Jules was also the individual that Michael had gone on a clandestine mission with that had led to Michael's injured neck. As part of the citation that earned him the Distinguished Service Cross, Michael had rescued the unconscious Ellington in spite of his own serious injury after they had successfully secured a set of German ciphers from the French resistance.

By this point, a year and a half later, Michael and Jules had become fast friends who spent as much time together as the war would allow. That their personalities were quite different seemed to add to the strength of their friendship. Whenever they both happened to be in London at the same time, they'd find a way to spend some time together, often dropping by Philip's townhouse in the fashionable Queen Anne district of London in the heart of the political center of the city.

Philip was pleased with their association, since Jules was able to cheer Michael up when the weight of his responsibilities as an MTB captain seemed to weigh him down. Jules had that rare type of ebullient personality that the more infamous British eccentrics were famous for. While most Britons were rather serious and steady, they also loved the odd character whose sense of humor and devil-may-care attitude allowed him to hide his anxieties behind a façade of nonchalance. Jules, with his muscular build and wavy hair, was that type of person.

Philip turned to face Michael, his own anxiety level rising. "Well, son, what is it? You do seem subdued." He noted the anxious look on Karen's face as well.

"Yes, sir," Michael said nervously. "It's just that it was something of a bad day out there . . ." He regretted saying that instantly since he didn't want to have to explain about the skirmish with the Germans. So before anyone could press him, he continued. "It's just that with all this talk of North Africa I thought I should tell you that I've received orders to ship out to the Mediterranean. They're sending a small flotilla of torpedo boats down there to run raids on the African coast and to take advantage of our position at Malta." He dropped his gaze when he saw his mother's alarm and Karen's dismay.

"Probably getting set for an invasion of Sicily," Philip said quietly. When both Jules and Michael looked at him in alarm, he laughed. "It's hardly a secret that Sicily is situated squarely between North Africa, where we're finally gaining an advantage over the

Germans, and Italy to the north, where we obviously want to gain a foothold on the Continent. So I'm not giving away state secrets to speculate that you may be needed for action in that area."

"Yes, sir," Michael said quietly, not entirely reassured about the propriety of his father's comments.

"But that means no more Sunday dinners! We simply can't have that. You'll have to tell the Lords of the Admiralty that you can't go," Claire said in a voice filled with mock indignation. Philip knew that it was her way of masking her fear at the thought of Michael being transferred so far from home. In this case her anxiety was undoubtedly exacerbated by the fact that their second son, Dominic, had died in North Africa not many months earlier. He had taken his own life after making the decision to turn away from battle and being charged as a deserter. His death had been a devastating blow to the family, from which they'd hardly had time to recover.

From which we may never recover, Philip thought. Now it was as if the entire continent of Africa was a place of dread for them, and the thought of Michael going there was stressful to Philip— though of course he wouldn't say so.

"That's why I wanted Jules and Karen to come over today," Michael said. "I thought perhaps they could drop by occasionally to keep my seat warm. But now it appears as if he's going to try to steal my thunder by going to the Mediterranean Theatre as well." He turned and gave Jules a stern look. "I'm not sure I like that, since I seem to find my life in danger each time we get near one another."

"Oh, really, Michael! I missed that car by at least two feet on the way up here from Dover. You certainly can't hold that against me. After all, the girl on the sidewalk was so devastatingly beautiful. If you weren't so serious all the time, you'd have seen her too." He smiled his roguish smile. "Or perhaps you're past looking at girls." He was careful not to glance at Karen, even though a very subtle smile played across his face.

Michael shook his head but chose not to take the bait. "It's lucky I didn't see her, or I couldn't have grabbed the wheel and saved your sorry life yet again."

Claire shushed both of them. "Of course Jules is welcome to come anytime he likes before he ships out—particularly on Sundays. And I hope Karen comes out frequently. But we'll get by until you both come home again." Her voice started to choke, so she fanned her face with her hand to mask her concern. Michael rose to comfort her, but she waved him back. "It's all right. They need capable men down there, and it's right that you should go. We'll miss you both but keep you close through our prayers."

Michael gave her a hug. When they finally broke the embrace, Philip asked, "How long before you leave, son?"

Again Michael cleared his throat uneasily. "Tomorrow. I transfer down to Southampton, and we'll be incognito after that. I can send letters, but they'll be very generic."

"Tomorrow?" Claire was indignant. "But that means you won't get to see Grace!" The look on Claire's face was serious this time, and both Philip and Michael could picture her calling the Admiralty. "This is the first weekend in months that your sister hasn't been here on Sunday, and now you go and tell us something like this. She'll be heartbroken."

"I didn't know until just last night as I was leaving the base," Michael said defensively. "A courier came chasing me with the orders. And then I had to go out on a mission today and honestly, Mother, I didn't have time to even clean up properly, let alone get permission to place a call. Please tell Grace I'm sorry."

Philip moved over to give Michael a hug. The two men held each other tight. It was in Philip's nature to provide emotional support to people, having served as a Church of England chaplain in the First World War and later as a leader in the LDS Church. Yet after the thousands of hours of counseling he had given people through the years, he had finally reached the conclusion that the best support of all was no more complicated than a good, firm hug. It was as if the combined emotional energy of two people rejuvenated itself so that both the giver and the receiver were strengthened. Right now he needed some rejuvenation. "We'll miss you, Michael." He wanted to say more, but that was all that came out.

At just this moment the family's little tableau was disturbed by an obvious clearing of the throat—a young male throat. "Pardon me, but it seems like this conversation has somehow turned away from me, the natural center of attention. I find that rather distressing." The three Carlyles looked up to see Jules feigning an emotional wound, and they burst out laughing.

"Oh, Jules." Karen harrumphed.

"We are bad hosts, aren't we?" Claire moved over to give Jules a hug, and when she wrapped him in her arms, he gave the others a wry smile from around the back of her head.

When he held on a bit too long, Philip moved over to cut in. "That will do quite nicely, Lieutenant."

Jules shook his head ruefully. "If I must. It's at least several weeks until I leave, so perhaps next Sunday I could join you and Karen? It would be nice to be here without Michael so we can have a really interesting discussion. And that way I could trap Karen into fixing one of her French delicacies."

Michael shook his head in mock disgust. He had counted on Jules acting like this. It was why he invited him in the first place. He wanted the banter to soften the blow of his transfer. As usual, Jules had come through perfectly. His ego made it a certainty.

"We'll be pleased to host you again next Sunday," Claire said warmly. The crisis of the transfer was over. At least now they could play a board game of some kind and laugh on Michael's last night at home.

Later, when Jules offered to give Karen a ride home and then return for Michael, Karen and Michael told him to shove off in unison. Jules smiled and said that he could find his own way home if that's the way they felt about it.

Philip and Claire watched with mixed emotions as the young couple drove off into the darkness. "It's a bad time to form relationships," Philip said quietly. "I'm afraid it too often leads to despair in times of war. Better to wait until it's over."

"But how do you explain that to the heart?"

Philip smiled and put his arm around his wife as they closed the door.

* * *

The Prime Minister's Residence, Number 10 Downing Street, London—April 1943

After more than fifteen years as a member of the House of Lords, Philip found it surprising that he still felt a sense of awe at being invited to the official residence of the prime minister. Although his official duties had often brought him to this place, the number of times he spoke with the PM were quite limited and always a bit intimidating. Over the centuries, from this house the empire had been won through the unusual but very practical alliance between British businessmen and the military to enforce British authority around the globe. More recently it was from this place that the great appeaser Neville Chamberlain had finally yielded authority to Winston Churchill, who had the passion and the inspiration to lead the British people wholeheartedly to war. As Churchill himself had characterized his fiery rhetoric, it was up to him "to give the roar to the British lion!" Now, with America as an ally in league with the nations of the British Commonwealth, the tide of war had at last shown some encouraging signs with the British victories at El Alamein in North Africa.

"Viscount Carlyle. It's good to see you." Philip looked up and saw the prime minister's personal secretary. "It will be just a few more minutes. Please make yourself comfortable."

"Thank you." Philip settled into one of the plush chairs in the anteroom of the prime minister's office and wondered how many notable people had sat in this very chair. *Viscount.* The word had such an odd ring. Viscount was a middle rank of the aristocracy, superseded by earl and marquess, and followed by baron. Of course all were subservient to the royal family, which used the titles of duke, prince, and king. Still, with just a relative handful of noble families out of the many hundreds of millions of British subjects around the world, his title placed him in a small and extremely exclusive group of people whose inherited wealth and rank gave them preference politically and socially.

As if we did anything to deserve it. Philip's great-great-great grandfather had done something of note by serving with such distinction in the military that the king had awarded him the Carlyle estate south of London along with his noble title. Through pluck and ambition, several of Philip's later forebears had added to the family fortune by developing coal mines in Wales into power companies and other business enterprises that enabled the family to collect royalties and income from numerous sources. The best part, from Philip's point of view, was that he was free to pursue a career in politics while leaving the management of the estate largely in the hands of his business managers. It was a well-established British tradition that the noble families "sacrifice" their time to public service.

Now Philip had an important but mostly anonymous role in Churchill's administration. It was a reward, perhaps, for Philip's loyalty to Churchill in the politically dark years between the First and Second World Wars. Churchill was often out of favor with the government for his outspoken criticism of both Nazi Germany and the Allies' unwillingness to enforce their rights under the Treaty of Versailles. Churchill had warned the world that there would be a terrible price to pay for allowing Hitler to set himself up as a dictator, but few in France, England, and America wanted to listen. The horror of the Great War was still too fresh for the nations to even consider another conflict, and so Germany was largely overlooked right up until the moment the German dagger was thrust into Poland. Nazi treachery finally forced the nations to take action on behalf of their wounded ally.

"The prime minister will see you now." Philip shook his head slightly to clear his thoughts.

"Thank you." He stood and was ushered into the office. There he saw Churchill smoking his customary cigar while a group of military leaders bustled their papers together to leave. When they'd cleared the room, Churchill came from behind his desk to shake Philip's hand.

"Philip! A long overdue pleasure. I don't think I've seen you since that glorious day when your son took me out on his torpedo boat. What a grand adventure that was." Churchill's eyes danced as he recalled the experience.

"Yes, sir, I believe that's right. In spite of the fact that we work in the same buildings, our comings and goings never seem to quite coincide, do they?"

Churchill shook his head. "It's a tragedy, really. There are so many people I'd like to spend time with, but there's always so much going on." He motioned for Philip to sit down, pulling up a chair so that their knees were almost touching. Continuing, he said, "Well, I'd like this to be one of those times, but I find myself behind schedule yet again, and I'm very likely to be abused by my secretaries if I don't move things along."

"Certainly," Philip replied.

"It's like this, Philip. You've done an extremely credible job in your role of minister without portfolio in overseeing our credentialing system for the Cabinet War Rooms. Aside from that one instance that was out of your control, I'm not aware of a single breach of security." Philip's face colored as he remembered the attack that had almost cost him his life at the hands of George Cook, a German sympathizer who was a member of the Lords.

"No, sir. I think the staff has succeeded quite well, all things considered."

"Yes, well. It strikes me that we're underutilizing your talents now. With the system well regulated, I don't know that we need a member of the Cabinet to supervise it anymore. Would you be all right if we asked you to give it up?"

After the Cook incident, Philip had expected this and had been surprised that he'd been left on as long as he had. The truth was that even though it was the Civil Service who had broken protocol by allowing Cook into the ultrasecret war rooms, it still fell to Philip as the political overseer for the breach of security. Because Cook was in touch with the Germans, the breach could have ended with a direct German attack on the facility. As the nerve center of the entire war effort, with the prime minister himself often in the rooms, who could calculate the potential damage had they succeeded?

"I'm certainly willing to yield the position. Thank you for giving me the chance to be part of it." In spite of his very best effort, there was something of a catch in his voice. He hated that but was powerless to stop the emotion. Relieved of this responsibility, he would return to the Lords, where his days would be spent fighting over mostly silly things, like giving rubber-stamp approval to minor government appointments and such.

Churchill looked at him with searching eyes. "Philip, we're not demoting you. We need your unique talents in another area. That's all this is about."

"What?" Then quickly trying to collect his composure, he said, "I mean, how may I be of service?"

Churchill sat back and took a long draw on his cigar. "It's the Americans. Hundreds of thousands of them. Eventually millions. That's the problem."

"The Americans. How are they a problem? I think they're a rather useful ally."

Churchill laughed. "Useful, yes. Obnoxious and pushy, too."

"Sir?"

"Look, Philip. My mother was an American just like your wife and children. You lived in America and understand their exuberance and zest for life along with their remarkably pragmatic get-things-done-right-now attitude. But as we gear up for a cross-channel invasion, we're going to have thousands of them arriving on British soil every week. We have to set up camps for them, find entertainment, and most of all keep them from riling up the local citizenry. As they land on these shores with all their cash and youthful vigor, it would be easy for our people to feel that we're being invaded after all. We need to do something to manage the whole affair."

"I can certainly see that you're right about that, sir. The Americans are an energetic group of people and would happily take over the whole country if we'd let them."

"Precisely. So what do you propose we do about it?"

"Me, sir? Why ask me?"

"Blast it, man, we've been through that. You've lived with one foot in each place, England and America. I've set up a staff to develop a set of plans to accommodate them, including everything from food and housing to sewers and nightclubs. We need to create diversions to absorb their energy while we gather enough strength to secure those blasted French beaches. The Americans and Russians want us to invade right now, but I'm fighting them on it. I don't want to do anything until we're fully prepared. The last thing I need is to have an invasion repulsed. That would be a disaster beyond measure that might force us to negotiate with the Germans, and I simply won't accept anything other than a total and unconditional surrender." At this point he was drawing rather heavily on the cigar while working himself into a fervor. "So the point is that we're likely to have these people here for upwards of a year. It's vital that we're prepared to handle them."

"So what role do you have in mind for me, sir?" At this point Philip's stomach was churning. "I don't really have experience with this sort of thing."

Churchill relaxed. "Not to worry. I'm not asking you to take charge of anything. It's just that I need someone with Cabinet credentials to act as one of my representatives on the various committees that meet to discuss and organize matters. You and I think alike on many issues, so I'd be far more at ease if I could get your personal report on how things are going. And of course you are free to offer your suggestions and help wherever it seems to make sense to do so. Is that something you could do for me?"

Philip relaxed. He knew how to sit on government committees. As a member of the Lords, he had done little else. The Lords' primary legislative function was advisory in nature. It was more through their power of persuasion that the Lords had an impact, so he could certainly exercise the same kind of leadership in this situation. "Of course I can do that. Thank you for thinking of me."

"Oh, you won't be thanking me when in the midst of one of those interminable meetings that you'll be attending. But I'll rest easier knowing I have an informed set of eyes and ears acting on my behalf."

The two rose, and Philip accepted Churchill's firm grasp, grateful that he was being given a new chance to serve his country.

"By the way, sir . . ."

"Yes?" Churchill said suspiciously.

"I like the Americans. It will be good for the country to have them shake things up a bit."

Churchill laughed. "I think so too, Carlyle. If we survive it!"

Chapter Three

TUNISIA

Bone, Tunisia—April 1943

As Lieutenant Michael Carlyle found his way down the gang-plank of the troop transport that had brought him once again to the coast of North Africa, he was embarrassed to find himself a bit wobbly. Severe storms had buffeted the lumbering old tub as it struggled against headwinds on its voyage down the potentially hostile coast of France and Spain. Even worse, a number of U-boat warnings had forced the captain to take a wildly erratic zigzag pattern in spite of the fact that doing so sometimes put them parallel to the waves instead of perpendicular, hammering the boat mercilessly—a sure recipe for seasickness. Like the others, Michael had marveled at just how wide an arc a hammock could swing as the ship rolled from side to side, always leaving the uncomfortable suspicion that the ship would simply turn turtle and never right itself. But always at what seemed the last possible moment, the roll would start to the other side and the troops below decks would find themselves swinging in the opposite direction while desperately trying to maintain their balance and the contents of their stomachs. Fortunately for Michael, as a naval officer he'd been allowed to go on deck where there was some fresh air.

He'd even been invited into the wheelhouse on a couple of occasions. "And how does this compare to previous ships you've served on?" the first officer had asked cheerfully, knowing full well that the comparison was likely to be unflattering. Fortunately, Michael was wise enough not to mention his first ship by name. He'd served as a junior officer on the *Hood*, the flagship of Britain's fleet, sunk by the German flagship, *Bismarck*. The loss of the *Hood* had been devastating to morale and, since British naval officers were a superstitious group, it would have been considered bad luck to talk about the *Hood*.

Instead, Michael simply said, "While it's not quite as impressive as the bridge of a battle cruiser, I like your ship a great deal. You can give me a smaller ship any old day. Not so stuffy and formal." He smiled. "Take the motor torpedo boats, for instance. They're a lot more fun than the big ships and a great deal more maneuverable." The fellow had laughed with him, which helped Michael divert his thoughts from the *Hood* and all the memories of the friends he'd lost when it went down.

The thing that had attracted Michael to the navy in the first place was ships, and he tended to love them all—big, small, fast, lumbering—they all had their unique charms, and he'd enjoyed the experience of traveling on the transport ship, if for no other reason than he'd know better than to volunteer for this type of duty in the future. But now the voyage was over and Michael was in Africa. As he reached the bottom of the gangplank, an earnest-looking young man approached him and said, with an uncertain voice, "Lieutenant Carlyle?"

Michael steadied himself as he looked at the young sublieutenant who greeted him with such a crisp salute. *How is it possible that they can find someone who looks even younger than me?* Impossible as it seemed, this fellow looked like he was still a freshman in high school.

"And whom do I have the pleasure of meeting?" Michael asked.

"Sublieutenant Jeremy Jenkins, sir. I've been posted to your boat, and First Officer Coleman asked me to meet you."

"Ah! Well then, Mr. Jenkins, I'm very glad to meet you. How far to our berth?"

"It's about a thirty-minute drive since we're moored on the other side of the harbor. But Mr. Coleman thought you might like to be taken to your lodgings for something to eat and a chance to stow your gear before going out to the boat." At this the sub looked a bit nervous for fear the captain would think him too forward. The likely explanation was that the first officer wasn't fully ready for the captain to come onboard so had told Jenkins to find some way to stall him.

"Let's take Mr. Coleman's advice. Perhaps you could take a little extra time to show me around the base?"

"Yes, sir!" The young man's relief was obvious.

Eighteen years old at best, Michael thought. *Yet he may be the difference between life and death when we get into action, so don't underestimate him.*

Climbing into the waiting automobile, Michael barely had time to close the door before the local African driver popped the clutch in such a way that a spray of gravel caused curses from the dockhands even as Michael's head was nearly snapped off his neck. It was so unexpected that he couldn't help but let out a yelp of pain—a reminder of the mission he'd accompanied Jules Ellington on when a German soldier tried his best to break Michael's neck before Michael had been forced to kill him. Even now, nearly a year later, he still had trouble with his neck and sometimes had to wear the leather collar the doctor had given him to immobilize his neck and protect it.

"Are you all right, sir?" Jenkins asked anxiously.

"It's nothing . . . just an old war wound. Is this the way they all drive?" he said just as their car missed a huge truck belching a black cloud of diesel smoke by perhaps two inches. The driver of the truck cursed at them in an unknown tongue, and Michael winced again as his driver called back with equal ferocity.

"Welcome to Africa, sir!" At that, both Michael and Jeremy Jenkins broke out laughing.

* * *

"For those of you still new to Africa, you will have to abandon your escort way of thinking and adapt to the realities of this assignment. I know that's difficult for some of you." Given that Michael was the only one who was still "new" to Africa, even after a month in the area, it was easy to figure out who this comment was directed at.

In what he thought was an inaudible whisper Michael couldn't stop himself from responding, "Aside from the threat of boiling to death here while freezing to death there, the only meaningful difference is the quality of command . . ."

"What was that Carlyle?"

Michael stiffened instantly. "Nothing, sir, just going over your orders in my mind." He did his very best to keep his voice even and his gaze steady. Commander Billingham had exhibited a strong dislike for Michael almost since their first meeting, and subsequent encounters had served to reinforce his antipathy. Fortunately, Michael had muttered quietly enough that he was certain that no one could have heard what he said.

Billingham looked as if he might press the issue, which caused Michael to do some quick mental thinking of what he might say in reply, but at the last moment Billingham scowled and said, "Then kindly do your thinking without engaging your mouth, and spare the rest of us your interruptions."

"Yes, sir!"

Michael heard the other torpedo boat captains shift uneasily in their seats. While Billingham had rebuked each of them at one point or another, no one seemed to irritate him as much as Michael, and the commander's constant harangue of the newest member of the group made everyone uncomfortable.

Billingham surveyed the group one last time before growling, "If no one has any questions, then you're dismissed. Good hunting!" No matter how many people he'd belittled in the course of a briefing, he always ended with a strong "Good hunting!" as if that small boon to morale settled everything.

As the briefing broke up, the small group who played up to Billingham formed a huddle around him. The others made their way toward the gangplank of the small ship where the briefing had been conducted.

"You really need to watch what you say, Carlyle, no matter how much he provokes you. You could get yourself arrested for what you mumbled today."

Michael turned and looked at Jeff Smith in alarm. "What do you mean? No one could hear what I said."

"You're not as subtle as you think. I could certainly hear it, and I suspect some others could as well. Most of us choose to cover for you, if only to avoid hearing Billingham chew you out. But even he has friends, and someday someone is likely to inform him of your insubordination."

Now Michael did panic. *Insubordination* was an extremely strong word, tinged with legal ramifications. In every previous assignment he'd been thought of as overly uptight and loyal to a fault—that's certainly what his brother Dominic used to accuse him of—so to hear this word used in reference to him was a genuine blow.

There was only one thing for Michael to do at this point, and he moved immediately to make things right. "I have to beg your pardon, Lieutenant. I certainly meant no disloyalty. It won't happen again." Even though he and Smith had served for approximately the same length of time, Jeff Smith was his superior based on service points and age. Besides, he was a well-respected torpedo boat captain and could make a big difference in how Michael was perceived by the others in the fleet. He needed that sort of ally.

Smith sighed. "It's all right. You can relax. Everybody knows that he provokes you, and it makes all of us want to say something. The burden is on you, though, not him."

Michael shook his head as they walked. "I don't know what I've done to make him dislike me so," he said. "I've tried to be respectful, I carry out his orders precisely, even when I think independent action would yield better results, and I do my best to avoid him whenever possible. Yet he goes after me."

Jeff laughed a humorless laugh. "You really don't know?"

"No . . . should I?"

Jeff shook his head as if in unbelief. "Well, if it isn't obvious to you, it certainly is to everyone else. I can't believe you haven't figured it out."

"Call me a little stupid," Michael said with a hint of irritation. "Or maybe it's one of those British things I missed when I was a child."

Rather than take umbrage at this comment, Jeff replied quite seriously. "That may be the case. With your American background you may not appreciate just how galling it can be to someone like Billingham to have a first-generation Navy man earn the Distinguished Service Cross along with other citations. Particularly someone as young as you. Add to that his jealousy of the naval fleet defending the Channel, where he thinks he ought to be, and you were doomed before you ever got here."

"Are you saying I'm in trouble because I did well in the Channel Ports?" Michael was incredulous. "Or that I'd be better accepted if I was mediocre?"

"Well, it does sound pretty bad when you put it like that, but yes, that's probably the case."

"But I didn't do anything to draw attention to myself. Nothing that you or Billingham wouldn't have done in the same circumstances."

Jeff laughed. "You don't need to apologize. It's just the Buckingham Palace reception they threw for you and, you know, meeting the king. For someone with such a proud old name as Billingham, it's just a bit too much. You're simply too prominent for his taste."

Michael sighed. "I can never tell if it's a British thing or a military thing. Either way, it seems like you're sized up and judged before you even get a chance to speak for yourself." There was more than a little bitterness in his tone, perhaps caused by the rather abrupt termination of his relationship with the beautiful young nurse Marissa Chandler earlier that year for much the same reason.

"Ah, well," Jeff said. "So it is, whether you like it or not."

"So what do I do? I don't want to spend the rest of the war in the doghouse."

Jeff shook his head dubiously. "Yes . . . well, when it comes to someone like Billingham, the best thing is to just do your job and studiously avoid the temptation to react when he goads you. Putting up with an irascible commanding officer is a naval tradition that goes well back into the days of sailing ships. So it's time to exercise your stiff British upper lip. There. Glad that's out of the way. Now I have to wreak a little mischief on Lieutenant Kennedy."

"Lieutenant Kennedy—what did he do to you?"

"Oh, it's for two reasons, really. First, he boxed me in while we approached port the other night and forced me to take the tail end position, even though it wasn't my spot in the queue. Second, I think it's time we give Commander Billingham someone else to be angry with in addition to you—might take a little heat off you for a day or two. Care to join me?"

"So you're the infamous practical joker?" Michael said with awe. Even in the short time he'd been in Africa, he had seen some tricks played that were absolutely stunning in their deviousness.

"Oh, don't be silly," Smith said. "I'm an amateur compared to your first officer, but I can still give it out pretty good once in awhile."

"Coleman is responsible for the mayhem?" Michael was truly perplexed at this revelation.

Jeff Smith burst out laughing. "Of course he is. That's another reason you're always in trouble. Even Billingham has figured that one out. You mean you really didn't know?"

Michael shook his head with a look of disbelief. "I guess I am a country bumpkin. I'll probably never figure out this wacky culture." The thought that his own first officer, who never even cracked a smile, was responsible for all the jokes just seemed beyond imagination.

"Well, time's wasting. Are you in or out?"

"What are you planning?"

"Oh no you don't. You either say yes or no, sight unseen. I don't want you backing out for lack of courage."

Michael furrowed his brow. The thought of getting Billingham upset with another captain was awfully tempting. "He really did box you out of your rightful spot?"

"With no remorse or conscience."

"Then I'm in!"

Jeff Smith laughed delightedly. For the first time in a month, Michael felt like he was among friends. Perhaps it had been his fault all along for being so stiff and aloof. Now that he knew how things were really played, perhaps he could change his image. At least it was worth a try.

Chapter Four

A NEW ROLE FOR CARLYLE MANOR

London—May 1943

Soon after Germany started indiscriminate bombing of London early in the war, Carlyle Manor had been converted to a convalescent care facility for civilian members of the LDS Church injured in London. Situated safely in the country southwest of London, the grand old estate had been a place of refuge and rehabilitation. But of late, the German attacks had abated considerably, with a corresponding reduction in the number of people who needed assistance, so much so that they were down to just five residents from more than twenty just a year earlier. Accordingly they had released all but one of the nurses, and it looked like even her usefulness might soon be coming to an end. Of course it was a volunteer enterprise, and the lack of patients was a good thing, but it still left Claire with the prospect of little to do with her time if they stayed in the country, as Philip preferred. Philip had called a family meeting with Jonathon and Margaret Richards as invited guests. The couple were English-born friends who had spent most of their adult lives in Utah, eventually becoming naturalized American citizens. At the outbreak of war, they had returned to England as special representatives of the LDS Church to offer what aid and comfort they could to the Saints since all missions had been suspended and contact with General Authorities of the Church was difficult.

To set the proper stage for the discussion, Philip started with a prayer and then launched directly into the idea that had been forming in his mind since his meeting with Churchill. "I need to share a conversation I had with the prime minister." While this would cause quite a stir in most British households, Philip's relationship with Churchill went back many years to the pre-war days when Churchill had pushed for the government to do something to constrain Germany's rearmament, often to his own political detriment. Even when most of the ministers shunned Churchill, Philip had been one of those in the House of Lords who had supported him, even going so far as to share insights with him about how members were reacting to the intelligence that was received in that body. Since those days, Philip had enjoyed an easy, if infrequent, dialogue with his old friend.

"As you undoubtedly know, there will be a continual increase in the number of American soldiers who are billeted here in England in preparation for an eventual cross-channel invasion of the Continent. What isn't well known, and what you must all keep confidential, is that it may be more than a year before such an action takes place. I think you can imagine the potential disruption to British society of having more than a million young men on our shores for such an extended period of time, to say nothing of the effect on the soldiers' morale at living in temporary quarters in a foreign land."

Jonathon laughed. "Americans can be a rambunctious bunch, can't they? I hope we can accommodate all of them."

"As it turns out, that's the reason that I invited you here tonight. The government does have extensive planning for housing, food service, even recreation. In recognition of my American connections, the prime minister has asked me to assume a role as an informal liaison with the groups that are responsible for all that."

"Congratulations!" Margaret said. "You're obviously the

perfect man for such a job." The others agreed.

Philip cleared his throat. "Yes, well, it turns out that I'm not the only one with American connections. Grace and Claire are native-born Americans, and the two of you are naturalized Americans. Really, I'm the least qualified in this group."

"But dear, you're the only one who's a member of the War Cabinet." Claire said.

"But that's just the point, dear. I can certainly do my little part to help in the grand scheme of things, but mixed in with all of those hundreds of thousands of young men will be a small group who are members of the LDS Church. It seems to me that between us we could come up with something special to help that small group with the inevitable cultural shock they'll experience in the military. Since more than a few will be stationed in this area, I thought we might put the old place to yet another useful purpose." He paused and lifted his shoulders in a slightly exaggerated shrug. "And that's about as far as I've got in my thinking. Is there any merit to the idea?"

At first he was disappointed by the silence that followed, but he shouldn't have been. Once the idea had time to sink in, everyone started talking at once, and the discussion became an enthusiastic free-for-all as one potential opportunity after another revealed itself. Finally, Grace brought order to the chaos by demanding that everyone slow down so she could write a list of the best ideas, as well as potential problems to overcome. In time the list of positives included weekly firesides at the house; an informal study-group program for those who could attend; dances with local girls aside from the USO clubs that the American military would establish; visits, when permitted, to the bases themselves to conduct Sunday church services; and letters to the soldiers' families back home to reassure them that their soldier was all right. The last item was suggested by Margaret, whose son Trevor had been assigned overseas in the First World War until his life was ended in aerial combat.

In the "obstacles" column, as Grace labeled it, there were also numerous entries such as transportation to and from the house; permission for the soldiers to leave the base; and permission for us to go on the base.

"You were a chaplain in the last war," Claire said to Philip. "Can you use those credentials to gain access to the bases?"

"I was a chaplain for the Church of England, dear. They're not likely to reinstate my authority now that I've left the established church. Besides, I can gain access easily enough with my government credentials, but we'll have to look into what all of you can do. Of course, much of it will be up to the Americans, so for now let's concentrate on turning the manor into a haven for as many as we can."

"It's a fine thing for you to do, Philip," Jonathon said earnestly. "I'm sure your home will bless many lives. But I have another idea. Were you aware that in America the Church leaders have started a program very much like this adjacent to the campuses of secular universities? They're called Deseret Academies, and the students who participate love having a chance to study the gospel in a university setting since it helps to maintain their spirituality throughout the week. Just think how much more important it is in this environment as these young men prepare to face mortal dangers. It's very generous. They could also invite their friends of other faiths to come along and enjoy the camaraderie."

"All in all, it's a wonderful idea, dear, and we're behind you one hundred percent."

For his part Philip felt as if a great burden had been lifted off his shoulders, as he now had the considerable talents of his family friend and mentor, Jonathan Richards, to help with the young men of the Church who would be coming to England.

Chapter Five

FROM ARMADILLO
TO ALGIERS

Ardentinny, Scotland—May 1943

"If we could trouble you to wake up, Mr. Ellington, it's time for you to go jump in the lake."

Jules rolled over and covered his head with the trousers he'd been using as a pillow.

"Begging your pardon, sir, but the commandant said it was rather urgent." This was delivered in a monotone that was clearly intended to infuriate, and it succeeded.

"Ohhh—blast you, Miles! You like this part of your job, don't you?" Jules considered this an insult.

But his steward simply smiled and said, "Perhaps if I hadn't been up for the past hour getting your hot cocoa ready . . ."

Jules sat up and rubbed his eyes before growling, "If you were in my private service, you'd be sacked in an instant—you know that, don't you?"

"Certainly, sir. And what a disappointment it would be. To think that all my life has brought me to this pivotal moment where I get to wake up twenty-year-old officers who stay up too late at night. Personal service has been good to me—no question about that. What would I do without it?"

"Oh, for heaven's sake! I'll get up. Taking a twenty-mile hike and fording an icy cold river in the rain will be a joy compared to listening to you blather."

"Mission accomplished then," and Miles moved on to the next cot to repeat the ritual with his next victim.

It wasn't always like that. When out on bivouac, the trainees had no stewards to wake them. In spite of Miles's attempt to make it look like they were soft, the truth was that the young men of the Royal Naval Commandos were among the most elite forces in the military, bearing the responsibility of being first to land on a hostile beach and to secure a path through the minefields for the Army troops to follow. No one was in better physical condition.

On this occasion they were at His Majesty's Ship *Armadillo*—a so-called "stone anchorage," which was really the Royal Naval Commandos' training camp in Scotland near the small village of Ardentinny. Naval tradition demanded that men always serve on a ship, even if it was a wooded campsite miles from the sea. Thus the preface HMS *Armadillo*. Jules and others in his commando group had returned to the site of their initial training for additional specialized instruction they would need in the upcoming Mediterranean operations.

As Jules struggled his way out of the building to the muster area, he did his best not to curse at the infernal rain that soaked the place in an almost continual drizzle this time of year. "My friend Michael Carlyle tells me that there are places in America where it hardly ever rains, and you actually get to see colors other than green! Do you suppose he's daft or a liar?"

"And what makes you think he's either?"

Jules turned to face Roger Cummings directly. "Because there's enough green here to cover the entire planet two or three times over! I'm so sick of green I can't stand it. I'm glad when I get a cut to my arm or leg just so I can see the color red. I don't know how much more of this I can take."

"A pleasure to see you on this bright, cheerful morning, too!"

"Bright morning indeed," Jules grumbled. "Bright takes a large orb called the sun, and it's obvious that it has little interest in Scotland or in warming me."

"Are you gentlemen quite through?"

At the sound of the commander's voice, Jules straightened up and stood at attention. "I have good news for you today. In addition to your good fortune at not having been awakened at 0300 for night marching, we're going to pass on our customary ritual of the endurance course today." There was a ragged cheer from the assembled men. "Instead we're going to practice our barbed-wire drill and telegraph-pole tossing. Then in the afternoon, following a leisurely lunch, the beachmaster will take you by lorry to one of the moors, where you'll practice arm-to-arm deep-water drills." The cheers were replaced by groans.

"Yes, Mr. Ellington?"

"I'd like to volunteer for the barbed-wire drill, sir. Since everyone is accustomed to walking over me anyway, it only seems appropriate."

"Feeling a bit picked on, Mr. Ellington? Well, I'm sure we can give you plenty of practice lying on the wire. Now grab your kits since you're not likely to get back before 2200 or so." Then to add insult to injury, "And do have a good day in His Majesty's service."

"I'm not sure it's safe to be seen with you," Roger said quietly. "Volunteering for the wire? You're the one who's daft— not your American friend."

"It's really not so bad. Call me thick-skinned or something, but it's a lot easier lying down on the barbed wire and letting you blokes walk over my body than forging the trail. At least it gives me a few moments to lie down."

"But doesn't it hurt?" Roger had never been given this duty. The thought of lying face down on a pile of barbed wire seemed loony to him.

"Surprisingly it doesn't. The wire absorbs the impact of the people running across you, and by landing straight on the barbs they don't tear you as would happen if you tried to move through the wire. By the time everyone's tramped across my back the wire is pretty well flattened so that it's a cakewalk for me to follow."

Roger shrugged his shoulders and then hoisted his kit onto his back. "It's the telegraph poles that I dread. Hefting one of those things up to your shoulder and then tossing it in the air to transfer it to the other shoulder—that hurts!"

"I don't have any labor-saving ideas for that drill. It seems that lugging telegraph poles ought to be up to the Royal Corps of Signals."

By this time they'd arrived at the truck, where they first tossed in their tools and kits, all of which weighed more than forty pounds, and then climbed into the back of the truck for the ride up to the parade grounds. Both Jules and Roger coughed involuntarily as a great cloud of smoke roiled up from the exhaust of the truck, coating the men in a blanket of smoke and fumes.

The commandos were vital to the success of any invasion—whether it be the beaches of North Africa or the expected assault on Italy. Eventually they would be the first to land on the beaches of Northern France when the time came for a cross-channel invasion. As such, the commandos probably faced the greatest dangers of any group in the Royal Navy. They also had the satisfaction of belonging to a very small brotherhood whose success could directly influence the course of the war.

By 1500 hours, they'd spent the morning executing drills and enjoying the cold lunch that had been promised to them, and now found themselves unloading onto a forsaken beach for the most dangerous duty of all.

"I hate this," Roger said with excitement. It was the nature of the job that the most demanding exercises were also the most exhilarating. In this case the task was to form up with arms extended to the shoulder of another commando on either side and to create a string that would wade out into the water as far as the group could go before the outermost man was about to drown. As a general rule they started with the shortest man toward shore, the tallest far out in the water. The only exception was that the assistant beachmaster usually considered it his duty to take his place in the deepest part of the water. If he was shorter than the men next to him, it put him in real peril of drowning.

Once the string was fully extended, the goal of the maneuver was to march on a course through the water perpendicular to the beach, searching for hidden obstacles that could damage or sink a landing craft. This task was as hazardous as it could get, since in real combat conditions they could easily be seen by the enemy on the shore, who could easily fire at them. They also ran the risk of stepping on a mine and being blown up. It was a vital duty, though, to protect the main landing force. Practicing in the icy waters of England would be quite different from the warm waters of the Mediterranean, but it was the best they could do under the circumstances.

By the end of the day, they returned to the *Armadillo* exhausted.

"I'm sure that combat is worse than this, but right now a bullet to the head doesn't sound so bad," Jules said as he stripped the wet wool clothing off his body. All the exercises they completed were done in full dress, which meant they had spent most of the day cold and waterlogged.

"I'd disagree with you if I had the energy," Roger replied, "but it takes too much effort to talk. Particularly because tomorrow we will practice throwing ourselves out of the back of a lorry traveling thirty to forty miles per hour."

"Oh, good, I've been hoping for that for so long now." Amazingly, Jules's sarcasm grew sharper with fatigue. "Bet I can get more cuts and scrapes than you!"

"You're on, Ellington. I don't think you're half clumsy enough to pull it off. Of course tomorrow will tell the tale . . ." With that they both fell into their beds and were asleep in a matter of moments. They didn't see Miles come quietly into the room to put an extra blanket over each of them. It had been a long day for everyone.

Chapter Six

AN ITALIAN SUBMARINE

Bone, Tunisia—May 1943

"The air is so stifling here." Michael wiped his brow with a white handkerchief and then smiled ruefully at the amused look on his first officer's face. "What? You never sweat, Mr. Coleman?"

"Most certainly I do. It's just that May is so much more pleasant than the summer months that are yet to come. If you're having trouble now, I can only imagine what you will be like then."

Michael sighed. "Two years on the English Channel undoubtedly thickened my blood to the consistency of peanut butter. There were nights I was so cold from the humidity that it felt like my bones had turned to permafrost. Now I complain of being too hot. Ironic."

Michael stared silently into the moonlit water for a time. It had been easier for Michael to understand his first officer since his chance conversation with Jeff Smith. In retrospect, it was clear that David's seeming indifference in their first month together was just caution, fed by the fear that Michael was nothing more than an uptight, by-the-rules sort of person. *That is generally true, but there's more to me than that.* David had lightened up considerably after Michael helped Smith set up Kennedy. He smiled at the thought of the prank.

In one of those odd coincidences where two people are
thinking of the same thing at the same time, Coleman broke the
silence. "I was just thinking about Lieutenant Kennedy as he
burst in on Commander Billingham in the middle of dinner
with the admiral. It had to be excruciatingly embarrassing when
he asked about the 'urgent' summons that ordered him to interrupt Billingham regardless of what he was doing."

Michael laughed. "It was a cruel thing to do, but certainly
well executed."

"I haven't dared ask you about something, but it's driving me
a bit daft not knowing . . ."

"What?"

David turned to make sure no one on the crew was within
earshot. Michael followed his gaze, although he wasn't really
worried about being overheard since he would give nothing vital
away no matter what Coleman asked him.

"Well?"

"What I want to know is just how much you had to pay that
rating to take the phony message to Kennedy telling him that he
was wanted urgently at HQ? I mean, he had to know Kennedy
would be all over him when the trick was found out."

"Five quid is all. A very small price to pay to help a friend
get revenge."

"Five quid?" Coleman said this with a twinge of awe in his
voice. "How did you ever pull that off? The job was easily worth
four or five times that."

"And you'd certainly know the fair market value of a practical joke, from what I understand. People tell me you are the
master."

Coleman was completely taken by surprise at this unexpected twist to the conversation and squirmed uncomfortably
before attempting to respond. Even in the moonlight, Michael
could see that his face had reddened as he lamely started to
reply, "Yes, well . . ."

"Not to worry, David. As long as your pranks don't land the boat in trouble, I'm not your babysitter after hours."

"Thank you, sir."

"But as for the quid, it turns out this fellow was due to ship out later that evening. So there was no risk to him at all. Besides, it seems he'd fallen victim to one of Kennedy's pranks a few weeks earlier, so he was happy to participate."

"Well, it certainly turned out well. Kennedy busts up the commander's party, Ambrose Billingham looks like a fool in front of the admiral for not knowing why he'd summoned one of his best boat captains, and Smith and his accomplice come off scot-free. A nice piece of work."

Michael nodded in affirmation. *And not only that, but Billingham has ignored me for more than a week.* While it had become known pretty quickly around the base that Michael was party to Jeff Smith's practical joke, no one had any inkling that he had any other motive in doing so than helping Smith get even for Kennedy muscling in front of him while coming into port. The last thing Michael needed was for Coleman or anyone else to suspect that he was trying to deflect Billingham's negative attention away from himself. So far things had gone perfectly, with Michael getting credit for being in on the joke but with no ulterior motives suspected.

As to staying out of Billingham's line of fire, there had been only one close call two days earlier when Billingham found a small rip in Michael's uniform that Michael hadn't spotted in time. Michael had tasted the salty hint of blood from biting his lip when Billingham sarcastically dressed him down for it, but he managed to squeak out a simple "Yes, sir" without adding any other incriminating words to the response. Jeff Smith had congratulated him later on his restraint.

It was getting easier for Michael to remain calm now that he was starting to gain some friends and supporters in the group of torpedo boat captains. He was feeling good about his own crew.

So for the moment at least, Billingham was nothing more than an annoyance that he had to put up with occasionally while in port.

Michael heard a vague sound somewhere to port. "I want quiet on the ship," he said sharply. Coleman stiffened and passed the order along to the crew. Although they'd been resting some five miles off the coast in relative silence anyway, the ship suddenly became totally silent. No one dared even ask what to listen for until Michael said very quietly, "I'm quite sure I heard a mechanical sound off to port. Metal against metal."

Even with everyone attentive, nothing was sighted or heard. After perhaps three or four minutes, Michael was about to dismiss it when there was a fairly pronounced clanging sound far off in the distance. All heads turned in the direction of the sound, but no one could see the source. The night was cloudy, and it was quite dark this far from any human habitation. The lack of all human activity also explained why the unnatural sound of metal seemed to carry so easily across the water. "I hear it now, sir!" David whispered. "Any idea what it is?"

"I can't tell you what it is, but I can tell you what it's not. It is definitely not one of our torpedo boats. We have no hatches that make that kind of sound. And it's not a battleship, since its wake would have swamped us already . . ."

"Nice sarcasm, sir."

"It could be a German E-Boat or destroyer, but we'd almost certainly have heard the sound of their screws churning through the water. That pretty much leaves just one thing."

"A submarine?"

Michael nodded. "A submarine. And since the Allies don't have any subs working actively in these waters, it has to be Italian or German."

"But what would they be doing this close to shore?"

"My guess is that they've been sent to provide protection for a German resupply ship making its way along the coast. They've learned to stay close inshore to confuse any of our ships equipped with radar."

Coleman whistled softly. "I didn't know they did that. Our only encounters with supply ships have been farther out to sea on the direct line from Italy to Africa." Michael could tell that Coleman was trying to decide whether to be impressed or skeptical.

"It's something we learned while patrolling off Belgium. The Germans have to balance the risk of having their silhouette spotted against the shoreline or remaining somewhat protected from radar. Out in the open water, it's harder to find them visually, but they're subject to a full 360-degree radar sweep. It's a devil's choice for them, really."

"So, what do we do?" asked David.

Michael was about to say that they should ease towards the sound with the electric motor so as to not draw attention to themselves, but before he got the words out, he was interrupted by young Jenkins, who whispered, "It's 0400, sir. You told me to alert you so we can return to base in time."

"Belay that," Michael said firmly. "I'm not about to leave when I've got an enemy contact this close."

Coleman reacted immediately. "Sir, permission to speak freely?"

"Of course."

"Commander Billingham will be furious if you don't return at your appointed time. You know how he values an orderly return to port. 'Each boat to return in its proper sequence at the appointed moment to show the other slackers around here how the job should be done!' If you mess with his routine, you'll be back in the doghouse."

"Believe me, lieutenant, I don't want to disappoint Commander Billingham, since I know as well as anyone how exquisitely painful he can make life for someone who muddles up his plans. But we were sent here to engage the enemy more than to look good on parade, so I'm exercising my prerogative and will report that we were engaged at the moment appointed to return." He turned and looked directly at Coleman. "Will you back me up in that even though shots haven't yet been fired?"

Michael looked at the reluctance in Coleman's eyes. In the short time they'd been together, there had been no active engagement with the enemy—just endless hours patrolling at sea, always to return home at precisely the appointed hour, even if that meant leaving key passages unguarded during the times the Germans were most likely to pass that way. In fact, the scuttlebutt in the officers' wardroom was that the Germans had figured out the British pattern and had arranged their own arrivals and departures to avoid detection. This had been terribly frustrating to the crew but especially to Michael.

Coleman finally smiled. "Absolutely, sir. We're in active pursuit of an enemy combatant, which may lead to action. It would be most unwise to break off contact." And to make his point truthful he switched on the electric motor so that the seventy-two foot boat started to slip quietly through the water in the direction of the sound.

Michael nodded. "I'm glad I can count on you, David. It may be a phantom we're chasing, but better that than another return to port with nothing to show for the fuel expended. Pass the word among the lads that we're on the lookout for a submarine—my guess is Italian. When we find it, we plan to engage with surface guns until we can get a good bearing with torpedoes. Anyone not manning one of the main guns should be given a machine gun, since it's likely to get ugly once we make contact."

"I'm afraid some of them may wet their pants, sir, since this will be their first action."

"Let's hope not. One more thing—it's vital that we maintain silence while doing all of this. If we make the same mistake they did, like dropping something on the deck, that submarine will disappear beneath the surface faster than a cannonball dropped in the water."

"I understand, Captain," and then David slipped down the steps at the back of the bridge to personally pass the word to each member of the thirteen-man crew.

Minutes passed in silence with no other sound from any direction. Michael worried that the almost imperceptible sound of their battery-powered electric motor had given them away and that even now the submarine was slipping below the surface. That would be the most frustrating of all, since he'd get chewed out for being late with nothing to show in return.

Still, Michael's hope didn't die easily, so he continued to strain his ears until he could hear the sound of his own blood pulsing through his eardrums. He was so focused he nearly jumped out of his skin when there was a sharp, metallic sound directly at his own feet. Even though it was impossible that it could be the enemy, it still took his brain a moment to sort it out since all thoughts had been focused on hearing a sign from the submarine.

"Sorry, sir!" Jenkins whispered nervously. "I dropped my compass."

In one of the little acts that distinguish a leader, Michael suppressed his natural reaction to chew the lad out and instead simply reassured him that it was all right. "I'm glad you did that since we don't have to worry about who is going to make the first noise now. It's kind of like getting the first scratch on a new automobile—it makes you crazy until it happens, but once you get over the grief of it, you can relax about the automobile after that. Rest easy, Jenkins. If the Italians run from the sound of a compass, they're not worth fighting anyway."

"Thank you, sir!" The relief in the young man's voice was evident.

At this point Michael thought it advantageous if the Italians had heard Jenkins's mistake, since the sound of a submarine preparing for a crash dive would instantly reveal their position. But there was nothing. After another ten minutes, Michael was starting to second-guess himself. That's when he was startled a second time by Jenkins, who shouted, "Sir, dead ahead!"

Michael jerked his head up and saw an ominous dark shape move into view. As the hair stood up on the back of his neck, he shouted, "All astern! Quick, Chief, I need full power now!" His shout was accompanied by startled voices on the enemy ship shouting in an unfamiliar language. "It's not German," Michael cried, "and it sounds something like French, so let's go with Italian."

As the three powerful diesel engines roared to life, Michael pushed the levers for full power reverse. But it was too late. Just as the propellers started clawing at the water, there was a sickening crunch as the bow of the boat lifted up. While there was very little chance that their wood-hulled torpedo boat would damage the metal frame of the submarine's deck, their own hull was at great risk. But no matter their own condition, there was no time to lose in checking for damage. They had to get away from the submarine as fast as possible, since a typical submarine had a crew complement of at least seventy men compared to their thirteen. This was not the time for a boarding party.

Unfortunately, some of the men lost their footing, and for a moment Michael was afraid that someone would go overboard. That would complicate things immeasurably. Somehow, though, everyone managed to hold on, and they started pulling back from the now lively Italian submarine at breathtaking speed.

Of course it wasn't fast enough to outrun bullets, and the Italians were quicker to their guns than the British. Michael instinctively ducked behind the metal screen as he heard the sound of bullets whizzing past him.

"Return fire!" he shouted, frustrated beyond measure that his men had apparently frozen in the face of the danger. "Fire at will to keep their heads down!" He was gratified to see David

Coleman slip down off the bridge once again to take personal charge of the forward guns. In a matter of seconds—a rough measure of eternity when under fire—he heard their own six-pounders come to life as his forward gunners got their wits about them. Soon they were joined by the sound of their own machine guns, and in a matter of moments it was an all-out crossfire.

The noise was incredible, following so closely on the heels of total silence. The rapid bursts of fire from both sides were too fast to process so that the battle became continuous noise, punctuated occasionally by the more powerful blasts of their heavy gun. Fortunately the submarine had not yet brought its own cannon to bear, or the battle would have been over in an instant.

Miraculously, they were quickly putting the required distance between the two craft when there was a new sound, the one Michael hated most in the world. It was the dull thud of a bullet smashing into a human body, inevitably followed by a yelp of pain. Michael looked down from the bridge to see that one of their gunners was writhing on the deck. Fortunately, Coleman was there in a flash and dragged the man back and behind a covering piece of metal. David looked up and caught his eye. "It's a wound to his leg, sir. I think he'll be all right!" Michael felt a rush of relief but realized that the odds were still very much against them.

"Hard astarboard, Mr. Jenkins. Mr. Coleman, I need a damage report. Are we seaworthy?"

"Superficial damage only, sir. Some leakage in the bows, but it's well contained." There was a kind of mad exuberance to Coleman's voice.

"All ahead, engines slow." Michael steadied himself as the ship changed direction and pulled hard to the left. "Mr. Coleman, join me on the bridge!" Coleman came bounding up the steps. As the sound of the engines quieted down, Michael could hear the Italian equivalent of a Klaxon horn sounding the signal to dive. It was a risky move for a submarine this close to shore, but the collision had obviously scared the wits out of the Italian commander at least as much as it had Michael's crew.

"What are you going to do, sir?" David asked breathlessly.

"Whatever we do, we've got about sixty seconds to make it happen, or the opportunity will be lost." Michael's mind raced as he thought of the possibilities. They could try to set up for a torpedo run, but with the Italians in the act of diving, it would be a difficult shot at best. It would be extremely difficult to set the correct depth at which the torpedoes should run. Another alternative was to charge back in and try to damage them with their surface guns, but the chance of a crippling shot in the darkness was even more remote.

"There's just one option," Michael said to himself.

"Sir?"

"Here's what we're going to do. I want you to take the wheel, David, and head directly for the enemy submarine. Fire a star shell so you can see their angle of descent. And bring us forward of their position so I can fire off our two depth charges. Once our charges are up and in the air, get us out of there as fast as you can, or we'll be blown to bits by our own attack. I wouldn't normally risk it, but it's our only chance to get them."

Coleman shouted to the gunners, "Fire a star shell at this bearing." It took him a few moments to calculate the angle of fire, which he called down. This time, the crew was ready, and the shell was up and in the air in seconds. When it exploded, they were temporarily blinded by the flash, but then the entire night sky seemed to fill with a ghostly sort of light that illuminated the entire area. As it was designed to do, the star shell seemed to hang in the air as if suspended by cables from the stars.

Once his eyes adjusted, Michael looked in the direction where the submarine had been and sure enough, there it was in the distance, a menacing presence off to starboard. As Michael watched, he saw the last officer clear the conning tower, and with a great blast of air a cascade of water was thrown up into the night sky as the water doors of the submarine were thrown open to take on water as part of the dive.

"That's it, then, David. Calculate your line of travel and get us there fast. I'm going to set the depth charges for thirty feet. It will take them almost a minute to drift down that far, so put us far enough in front for the charges to fall. Any questions?"

"No, sir. I'm ready."

"Good. I'm going down now to set up the attack. Give us a countdown to when we're in position. I'll launch the first one, then give us a quick turn to port, and we'll fire off the second one. I'm assuming they'll be in a shallow dive for fear of hitting the bottom, so if we get it even close to right we've got a good chance of hurting them."

With that Michael turned to leave the bridge. "Good luck, sir!" It was obvious that there was anxiety in Coleman's voice, but there was nothing Michael could do about it now. He simply had to come through, or all was lost.

Bounding down the stairs, he raced to the port-side torpedo launcher and stood next to the gunnery officer. "You're in charge here, Stowell, but I'm available to back you up if needed. Here's the plan . . ." and Michael quickly repeated what he had told Coleman.

As he finished, Stowell said, "Thank you, sir." In spite of all the drills they'd done, there was still hesitation in the man's voice. First combat was always frightening, no matter how much practice a soldier had under his belt.

"You'll do fine, Stowell. Just follow protocol, and it's going to work perfectly."

"Yes, sir." Stowell attempted a smile, but he was too nervous.

In all the twisting and turning it had taken Coleman to bring the boat around, Michael had lost his bearing on the submarine. Everything was happening so quickly. It had probably been just three or four minutes since they'd stopped shooting, but it seemed like hours. The star shell was fading a bit now and no matter where Michael turned, he couldn't see the submarine. All he could do was hope that Coleman had kept track of it.

"We have a solution, sir!" There was a triumphant sound in Coleman's voice. "Prepare to fire your first charge in thirty seconds, starting now." Although he didn't want to take the responsibility away from Stowell, Michael couldn't help but audit the scene to make sure all the settings were correct. They were, so he relaxed a bit. It was insane to fire so close, but opportunity knocked so very infrequently in these parts that it was worth the risk.

At ten seconds Coleman started the countdown. At the count of two, Michael stepped back and watched as Stowell licked his lips and then pulled the cable that released the pin holding the powerful spring catapult. With a twang the depth charge was up and into the air. Michael instinctively braced for the turn to port, was gratified to feel the shift in direction, and then heard David start the next ten-second countdown. A moment after the second charge was launched, he said, "Nice job, Stowell," and then braced himself as the ship lurched forward at full power in a hard turn to starboard. He had to fight the torque of the turn to make his way up the steps to the bridge.

From what he could tell, Coleman had done a terrific job. But the look on his first officer's face was anything but satisfied. With both their depth charges now in the water, this was their one and only chance of success, and that knowledge weighed heavily on his first officer.

"Well done, Mr. Coleman!"

Coleman turned and looked at him with evident anxiety.

"Don't worry, David. Another thirty seconds and we'll know if we found them. Hit or not, you handled yourself very well."

He could see that Coleman wanted to say something but

couldn't get any words out. As a habitual mental counter of stairs and steps and things, Michael couldn't help but count the seconds since the depth charges had been fired. The number in Michael's mind was now in the fifties—meaning fifty seconds since the first launch—so he turned and looked to the spot where the expected explosion would take place. *Fifty-seven, fifty-eight, fifty-nine, sixty.* When nothing happened, his stomach tightened up, and he replayed the scene of watching Stowell arm the depth charge in his mind to make certain that they hadn't fired them off incorrectly. Before he could visualize the arming sequence, there was a deep rolling sound in the water followed by a massive disruption in the surface of the ocean and then a giant waterspout as the hundreds of tons of water displaced by the explosion of the depth charge forced its way up to the surface, prompting a spontaneous shout from the crew.

"All right, let's hope we struck pay dirt. Twenty seconds to the next one." Of course he was already doing the mental countdown for that charge. The sound of the second eruption brought another cheer. Now they'd have to pay particular attention to see if any debris or other signs of a successful attack came to the surface.

"Bring us around, Jenkins." Then to the entire deck crew, he said, "Keep a sharp eye for any signs that we got a hit. Look for debris, listen for sounds of a ship breaking up, or watch for an oil slick. It's got to be a big one since subs often send debris up through a tube to try to convince the surface ship they got a hit when they didn't. Report anything you see to me immediately!"

Now it was Michael's turn to feel the anxiety. In order to confirm a kill they had to be fairly quiet in the water, but if the submarine had survived and had any maneuvering room at all they might be setting up a torpedo attack on the boat even at that moment.

"Keep a sharp eye out for torpedo tracks as well!" He always hated the waiting.

The problem with depth charges was that the surface ship seldom had an accurate enough bearing on the submarine to get a direct hit, and the further away the depth charge was from the submarine when it detonated, the greater the chance the submarine could withstand the damaging effect of the shock wave. A submarine chaser with a large inventory of depth charges can spend many hours attacking a submarine before they either get a kill or give up, because the odds of the submarine making an underwater escape make it unprofitable to continue the attack. A torpedo boat doesn't have such a luxury, since it carries just four depth charges at most.

On this trip they had just two, so, at this point the attack had either succeeded or failed. There were no other possibilities. All of these thoughts passed through Michael's mind as he waited to see the results of their depth charges. Fortunately, it wasn't a long wait. One of the gunners suddenly shouted, "Over there, sir, at 0400!" Michael and David both turned and were thrilled to see a large boiling motion in the water, perhaps two hundred yards away.

"That's got to be them, doesn't it, sir?"

"It's them all right, but I can't tell what's happening for sure. Perhaps it's a late rupture in their hull." Turning to Jenkins, Michael said, "Take us towards that spot, all ahead slow."

"Yes, sir!"

Michael felt his hands sweating and wiped them against his trousers. His mouth was dry, and he wished he had a large glass of water.

"There, sir," one of the men shouted. "I think I see men on the surface!" Michael strained his eyes but couldn't see anything in the darkness.

"What are your orders, sir? If there are other Germans or Italians in the area, they're almost certain to come after us."

Michael turned and looked at the faces of his crew members, all looking to him for guidance. Clearly some wanted to get out of there while they could, but he knew that others would despise him if he left men floundering in the water.

He'd learned in battle that there was very little time for decisions once events were under way. Acting purely on experienced instinct, he said, "I don't believe there are any other ships in the area. We need to take survivors onboard, even if it nearly swamps us. I don't want any more blood on my hands than necessary. Prepare the nets." Coleman acknowledged his order.

Turning to his gunnery officer, Michael said, "Fire another star shell, Mr. Stowell. Since the last one didn't bring any help or any enemy, a second isn't likely to hurt us, and if there are men in the water, we need to see them."

"Aye, sir." Stowell said this with a mixture of anxiety and relief in his voice.

"And Stowell, I want all our deck guns disabled before a single enemy sailor is brought onboard. There's likely to be a lot more of them than there are of us, and I don't want them taking over the boat. Once the deck armament is neutralized, I want half our men to stand guard with automatic weapons while the others assist the prisoners onboard. Keep the Italians in two groups, one forward, one aft, and all out in plain sight on the deck. If we can't fit them all on deck, then they'll have to take the extra men on their laps. Everyone has to sit with his legs out in front of him, hands where we can see them, and no unusual movement. Understand?"

"Yes, sir."

"Good. Before anyone comes on this ship you make them strip their clothes off in the water until they're down to their Skivvies. Check for weapons. If anyone refuses to surrender a weapon, shoot him immediately. We can't take any risks of anyone else on our crew getting wounded. Any questions?"

There were none, only a surprised bunch of British sailors who were seeing their captain in a whole new light.

"By the way," Michael called to his crew as the ship moved in among the survivors, "congratulations on a first-rate job!"

At that Coleman shouted, "Three hurrahs for the captain!" which was immediately met with the jubilant voices of the crew.

* * *

It took nearly half an hour to collect the sailors in the water. With no one speaking Italian, it took some odd gestures to convince them to take off their clothing. Michael's French had enough in common with Italian that he was able to shout to them through a megaphone in words they eventually understood. While most were resentful, none made any move to resist. Toward the end of the loading, one of the Italians acted kind of peculiar, and when it was clear he was hiding a weapon, a crewman shot him. After that there was no more trouble from any of the other survivors, and they quickly formed into the groups Michael had ordered.

As the overloaded boat made its way back to port, Michael found a couple of the enemy sailors who spoke French, and so he asked some basic questions about their ship, the fate of their captain, who they claimed was killed in the attack, and where their homes were in Italy. It seemed to relax both his own crew and the enemy crew to hear the captain speaking to the prisoners in a calm voice. The French-speaking prisoners indicated that the second depth charge had destroyed their ship. Apparently the first had caused some minor damage in the forward torpedo room, but just as they were abandoning the room to seal it off, the second depth charge exploded within a few feet of the conning tower, cracking the sub open like a dropped watermelon, and water came cascading into the control room. The entire bridge party perished, only giving the men in the engine room and sleeping compartments a chance to scramble up and out the emergency hatch. They were falling so quickly that some drowned while trying to reach the surface.

With the torpedo boat fully laden by the extra bodies—some thirty men—and the bow damaged by the collision, they had to travel very slowly back to port. Michael kept radio silence in case there were any other enemy ships in the area. It was well into the morning by the time they came cruising into the harbor.

"Get ready, sir, for the reaction."

"I don't know what you're talking about, Coleman."

"I suspect you do, sir. When we round that next bend, the whole fleet is going to come out to see our little collection of prisoners. You'll be the talk of the base before we even tie up."

"You are awfully prone to exaggeration, David. You really should be more circumspect." It delighted Michael to say that to a native-born Brit, since it was always the Americans who were accused of being emotional.

"Right, sir. Good advice." David shook his head slightly but held his tongue.

In the end, David was correct. As they made their way past the various ships on the docks, there was first a look of astonishment on the faces of the sailors who happened to be on the decks and then cheers as they made their way to their moorage. Michael was inordinately proud of his men for rigidly holding their positions guarding the prisoners no matter the potential distractions from the other ships. Of course everyone in the crew did their best to make it appear like it was nothing, just a regular night's work, but Michael couldn't help but feel relieved when the ropes were secured and the prisoners were handed off to the port authorities for guard.

Once clear of these entanglements, Michael first arranged for his one wounded man to be taken off by the medics and then ordered the rest of the crew to gather so he could address them.

"Well done, men. You comported yourselves very well for our first real combat. While we were a little slow on the uptake after the collision, all in all you did a credible job. Now that we know where our weaknesses lie, we'll drill more carefully in order to do better the next time."

He smiled at the crew. "Now, let's tidy up and get ready for repairs. Since it's likely we'll be held in port for a few days, Mr. Coleman will arrange for appropriate shore leave. Try not to spend all your money the first day out." The crew laughed and then started chatting excitedly as they stood down.

Michael felt terrific inside.

* * *

Michael stood quietly at attention waiting to be acknowledged by Commander Billingham. He'd been there for a good three minutes without a single glance from his commanding officer. *Keep your composure . . . keep your composure.* He forced himself to breathe slowly.

Finally, with a rather obvious sigh, Billingham looked up. "Well, Carlyle. I see you finally decided to show up. I've just finished reading your written report."

Michael inhaled sharply. Of course the reason he showed up at this hour was that he had gone straight to the hospital to check on his men and then to sign off on the Italian prisoners as was required, but Billingham knew all that. Rather than react, Michael knew it was better to say nothing at all than to say anything at this point.

"Yes, well. I understand that you finally saw a little action last night. Of course you were out of position and overdue when it happened, which potentially jeopardized the entire flotilla. Then you hazarded your ship and crew by taking on prisoners even though you were still in open water and exposed to enemy dangers. Through negligence you had a collision with the enemy ship. I'm afraid that one will take a great deal of explanation to the board of inquiry."

"Board of inquiry, sir?" Michael was flabbergasted. His was the first ship to see any action in nearly a fortnight. They'd killed an enemy submarine, saved more than two dozen men . . .

"This indicates that your seamanship clearly leaves something to be . . ."

At this point the sound of the door being flung open behind him startled Michael so badly that he almost jumped out of his skin.

There was a broad laugh. "Sorry about that, Carlyle. I just received the news that you were here and wanted to congratulate you personally."

Michael swung around at the sound of Admiral Chadwick's voice.

"Sir?"

"Absolutely outstanding. This will do more for morale around this base than anything that's happened here in the past three months. To kill an Italian submarine while your own boat was damaged and with only one casualty—not fatal I understand—well, it's just magnificent. Congratulations, Lieutenant!"

"Thank you, sir," Michael stammered. He'd become so angry at Billingham that it was difficult to adjust his emotions to this new situation.

"Yes, well of course there was the issue of the collision, which will require a board of inquiry." Both Michael and Admiral Chadwick turned at the sound of Billingham's voice. It seemed incredible that he would push the point just now, but Michael decided it was very much in his character.

"A board of inquiry?" Chadwick replied in a perplexed voice. "I don't really think that's necessary. Do you, Billingham? After all, the boat made it back in one piece; Lieutenant Carlyle obviously handled the situation with extreme daring and control, and he brought about a rather marvelous victory."

"Well, I suppose . . ." Billingham sputtered.

"Of course we need to congratulate you as well, Commander Billingham. This reflects great credit on your leadership. To have one of your captains act with such skill and pluck surely speaks well of your unit."

Why you sly old devil, Michael thought to himself. *You know exactly how to protect me from Billingham without having to issue any orders whatsoever.* In spite of himself, Michael couldn't help but suppress the tiniest of smiles.

"Yes, well, of course we're very proud of *MTB-620*. Obviously, its crew was well trained when Lieutenant Carlyle arrived."

"Yes, yes, of course. Still, this has to be almost as exciting as your action in the Channel Ports, eh, Carlyle?"

Michael had never grown to love a man as quickly as he had this one. "Every bit as exciting, sir. Perhaps more. I've never had occasion to be quite so close to the enemy, and it was all a bit hair-raising." Michael thought it best not to talk about the time he'd done hand-to-hand combat while on the secret mission with Jules Ellington.

"Well, sorry to interrupt, Billingham. I'm sure you were in the midst of reviewing this very successful mission with Lieutenant Carlyle when I burst in. I'll leave you both to it. By the way, Carlyle, perhaps you'd join me for dinner one night this week. I'm sure some of the other ships' captains would like to get a firsthand report about your adventures."

"I'd be honored, sir."

"Good! I'll send a formal invitation by courier once I know my schedule. Of course you'll join us as well, Commander?" He didn't even wait to hear from Billingham before he was out of the room, the door slamming shut behind him. So fast and furious was this encounter that Michael temporarily lost himself.

"Please stand at attention, Lieutenant!"

Michael's mood immediately darkened as he snapped to attention. "Yes, sir. My apologies, sir!"

Billingham sat down heavily in his chair. "At ease, Carlyle." Michael relaxed ever so slightly. "Well, it's obvious that the admiral is content to leave the mission as is. Politics being what they are, it makes sense for the navy to relish your little victory. And you will be a hero for a few days." He looked up and smiled an insincere smile. "So I add my congratulations to those of the admiral."

"Thank you, sir."

"That will be all, Carlyle."

"Yes, sir." Michael saluted and did a crisp turn to leave.

"Oh, Carlyle—just one more thing!" Michael turned to face Billingham, a sense of dread in his stomach. "Just remember as you regale the many dinner guests you'll entertain in the next few days—the dogs in this unit wear *my* collar. Do you understand?"

"Yes, sir. Of course, sir!"

"Good. Now leave me."

Chapter Seven

HELP FOR THE HOMESICK

Carlyle Manor, Southwest of London—June 1943

"Excuse me, Sister . . . I mean Lady . . ." The young American soldier's attempt at conversation stammered to a stop.

Claire smiled. "Sister Carlyle will do nicely. What can I do for you, Lieutenant?"

The young man replied, "You can call me Brother Williams, for one thing. Or Michael. It would be good to hear that for a change."

Claire had one of those rare smiles that had the ability to single-handedly light up a room. At five-feet-eleven, she was taller than most British women, and her dark hair and piercing brown eyes betrayed her intelligence. Nearly everyone found her attractive, with a sense of poise and grace.

In the present circumstance she responded immediately to the young man's cheeky response, replying with a grin, "Turnaround is fair play, isn't it, Brother Williams?" She turned thoughtful for a moment. "Perhaps I will call you Michael, though. That's the name of my oldest son, who is off in the Mediterranean. It feels awfully good to say the name." Her smile had faded, and all those in the room could see the emotions that this small encounter had brought out in her.

"So do we all get to drop our military titles?" another young man asked hopefully.

Claire brightened immediately. "Only with me, I'm afraid to say. It wouldn't be seemly for you to not show proper regard to your military superiors, Private Knowles. But it was a nice try."

The boy's shoulders slumped in mock despair while the others in the room gave him something of a triumphant look. "It was worth a try, though, wasn't it?" The obvious goodwill these young men felt for each other was refreshing. As Claire gazed around the room, she was struck by how young most of the half dozen men looked. While four of the six were from Utah and Idaho, Lieutenant Williams was from Southern California and Private Knowles from Arizona. There were two lieutenants, two corporals, and two privates. In any other circumstance, they would hardly pass a word among each other. Yet here in the safety of Carlyle Manor they were able to relax as brothers in the gospel, and the relief it created among them to be with like-minded individuals was almost tangible. While no one could ever fully find the words to express what the phrase meant precisely, everyone who had experienced it knew exactly what it meant to "feel the Spirit in the room." Tonight the Spirit was very strong indeed.

"So tell us some more about your son, Michael. What exactly does he do in the British Army?"

Claire settled down into one of the velvet-covered wing chairs that sat close to the fireplace. Even though it was summer, there was an unusual chill to the damp air, and she had allowed one of the boys, *young men,* to light a fire. There was always something comforting about a fireplace, particularly in anxious times like these. This group of young men were all part of a Special Forces unit that was among the first to arrive in England and who would face some of the most demanding and dangerous assignments when the invasion of Europe ultimately arrived. Even Claire knew enough about the military to realize that at least one, perhaps several, of these warm-hearted boys from America would not live to see their families again. So even though it made her anxious to think about her Michael in his tiny little boat in the Mediterranean, she accepted the responsibility of talking about him now so that she could build a bridge of trust with the young men who had given up a trip to the local dance hall on a Friday night to join her here at the Manor. Philip was supposed to be home an hour earlier but had obviously been delayed, so she'd been filling the breach as best she could but wished he'd show up to help her.

"Well, he's the captain of a motor torpedo boat in the Royal Navy. Even though he's no older than any of you, we've been at war much longer than America so that he's seen action for more than two years." She debated momentarily whether to brag about her son and his many accomplishments but decided against it. Perhaps the Americans would assume that it was all part of the false splendor that seemed to attach to British nobility, and the last thing she wanted was to create any distance at this point.

"Can you tell us about any of his battles or exploits?" the senior lieutenant and by far the most serious member of the group asked.

"Well," she smiled, now free to abandon her earlier reticence, "while Michael has limited what he tells us for security reasons, he has shared one or two things that you might find interesting." With that she proceeded to regale them for the next thirty minutes with some of the stories Michael had shared with her. The group seemed to relish it, and Claire found that it lifted her spirits to sense the respect they felt for what he was doing. *Who knows, perhaps it will give them courage when they face the perils of battle.*

Just as she was running out of things to say, she heard the cheerful voice of her daughter, Grace, who was coming out from the city with her father. Claire sighed in relief as she thought of Philip and Grace helping her with the entertainment.

"Sorry we're late!" Grace said brightly as she came in the room. "Daddy got caught in the hallway with the prime minister, and you know how distracted that always makes him."

The effect of this small revelation was not lost on the group, and in just a matter of moments the conversation had turned from Michael to what it was like to know and work with Winston Churchill, what it was like to be a member of the House of Lords, and so forth. For her part, Claire excused herself to go to the kitchen to supervise the dinner that had been prepared, relieved to be out of the spotlight, yet oddly grateful that she'd had that brief time alone with the boys. She realized that they would always be boys to her—perhaps they would become her boys for a brief period. That prompted her to go back into the parlor and interrupt Philip to make certain that he would get the addresses and names of each of their parents so she could write them a letter to report on their boys' adoption into the Deseret Academy.

After answering some of their questions about what it was like to be British, Philip begged their permission to share a gospel thought, followed by a marvelous dinner. The evening ended with everyone gathering around the piano to sing while Grace played happily away at both gospel tunes and contemporary songs. The group probably would have stayed all night except that the sober young lieutenant finally declared that they had to leave immediately or they'd all be declared AWOL.

"I think I can help avoid that," Philip said. "Why don't we all go out to our livery, and I'll give you a ride back to base. Cutting out the bus trip will save a good thirty minutes."

As they each gathered their things, they managed to individually come up to say good-bye to Claire. When it came to Private Knowles, he stuck out his hand as the others had done, but then leaned in to give Claire a hug. She accepted it happily, and with a new protocol established, each of the others came back and gave her a hug as well.

"It seems they miss their mothers," Philip whispered in her ear as he stepped out behind them into the darkness.

"And I know just how their mothers feel, so it's good for both of us." Claire held Philip's arm for just a moment. "Thank you for thinking of this. I think it means the world to the boys, and it is certainly good for me. I hope that even more will come next week."

"Be careful what you wish for." Philip smiled. "There should be approximately four or five thousand LDS boys coming through here in the upcoming months. That's an awful lot of mouths to feed."

Claire straightened up and looked at him. "Ah, but we know how to feed at least five thousand with a handful of loaves and fishes, don't we?"

Philip laughed and gave her a hug. "I love you, my dear."

* * *

The Mediterranean

> *. . . so in spite of myself I find I still miss you. I know we agreed that I should date, but the truth is I have no heart for it. Marissa says I'm a lost cause and boring, but then she's always thought I'm boring. I can only take comfort from the fact that she said as much about you. I take it as a positive that we have that in common. At any rate, here I am in London with no one but my girl friends while you're out there somewhere in the Mediterranean. Perhaps you don't feel as I do, but the truth is that I'm lonely and wish you were here. It makes me wish they'd hurry up and invade the Continent just so this awful mess can end—but then that will involve so many casualties, and I don't want that. So I'm all mixed up. Well, enough rambling. Please write whenever you can. Those fragile scraps of military mail are the highlight of my day. Love, Karen.*

> *P.S. I had lunch with your parents in London last Sunday. Your mother somehow managed to save up for a beef roast. It was delicious! They miss you too.*

"Are you all right, sir?"

Michael blushed at Jenkins's question and hurriedly folded up the letter and stuffed it into his pocket. He felt it crumple as he did and instantly regretted that he hadn't been more careful. But he didn't want any prying eyes to see that he was every bit as lonely as Karen.

"I'm fine, Jenkins," he said a little too brusquely. He thought about saying something more to undo the harshness, but decided it was better to leave things as they were. For his part, Jenkins suppressed a smile, pleased that his captain had someone who was important to him.

Chapter Eight

INVASION OF SICILY

The Island of Malta—July 1943

"And that, gentlemen, is our objective for the next two weeks."

No matter how hard he tried to focus on what Commander Billingham was saying, Michael couldn't help but be distracted by the man himself. Short and stocky, he was at least fifty pounds overweight, had fleshy jowls that supported a wide and often sneering mouth, narrow green eyes, and prematurely gray hair. His ruddy complexion made it appear as if he were always angry about something, and in all the time Michael had known him, the man had never shown any sign of a sense of humor. *In fairness, he dresses impeccably, is always punctual and pointed in his remarks, and doesn't waste time.* His clothing really was superb. Rumor had it that he'd requested a tailor to be transferred from England, but that was only hearsay. Regardless, he must have hired someone—perhaps a local person—to look after his uniforms, because they were always crisply pressed and fit him like a glove.

And he does know naval protocol. While many of Billingham's decisions were frustrating, one could hardly fault them on traditional grounds because they came right out of the regulations. *Except that in a dynamic situation like battle, one needs initiative and flexibility.* Billingham was definitely not flexibile.

"Am I boring you, Mr. Carlyle? Are my instructions unnecessary for one of your skill and qualification?" Michael jumped at the sarcasm as his thoughts raced to find a response.

"Not at all, sir. I think what you said about three boats patrolling together is perfect for the situation. Our landing troops need flexibility to adjust their line of attack, and this way we can provide whatever support best meets their need." He breathed a quiet sigh of relief to realize that his subconscious mind had apparently been paying attention, even when his conscious thoughts were wandering.

"I'm so glad you approve, sir. I can rest easy now, knowing that my orders have been confirmed by our most junior captain."

Michael winced. *He got me anyway—but at least not for inattention.*

In the past his face would have burned at this rebuke, but it didn't seem to matter anymore. When the flotilla first learned that they were to be transferred from the mainland of Africa to the island of Malta, he had hoped against hope that Billingham would stay put and that the much-admired Commander Robert Allan would lead them in Malta. Allan was in overall command of all the torpedo boats and gunboats at Bone and was really the one responsible for the group's success. Michael felt he could learn a lot by serving with such a man. But it wasn't meant to be. For the time being, Allan was staying in Bone while Billingham and other flotilla-level commanders moved their groups to Malta. *So it's still his tune I must dance to.* Michael stifled a sigh.

Realizing that Billingham was after him again forced him to concentrate on what his esteemed commander was saying. But it was all so useless that before long his thoughts started to wander again as he thought about their new moorage. Malta had long been a British base of operations, extending all the way back to the Age of Sail because of its perfect location due south of Sicily. At the outbreak of the current war, it had been extremely difficult to defend the island while the Italians and Germans reigned supreme in Africa, along with their air cover to immediately swarm any sorties out of the island. But with Axis reversals on the African continent and the subsequent withdrawal of many of their forces to Italy, it was now much more practical for the Royal Navy to operate out of Malta as they prepared to support the assault on Sicily, the large island off the southern tip of Italy. Intelligence indicated that resistance would be fierce as the Germans and Italians consolidated their lines back onto the southern side of Europe. While the defeat in Africa must have rankled the always proud Germans, it greatly strengthened their strategic position to concentrate their forces in Europe.

"Any questions!" The change of tone in Billingham's voice brought Michael out of his reverie yet again. He was always impressed by the fact that Billingham issued the words 'any questions' as a terminating phrase rather than a question. For some reason the man saw questions as an insult—as if they were an indication that he had been less than clear in his briefing. Consequently, few questions were ever asked, which inevitably led to problems when the mission was under way. *But Billingham likes that because then he can blame the captains.* Michael shook his head to clear the negative thoughts and arose with the others as Billingham exited the room.

"So Billingham has decided to take you on again?"

Michael didn't even bother turning to look at Jeff Smith. They had exited the briefing together and were now walking through the heavy summer air back toward their boats. "It was inevitable. During the move to Malta most of Billingham's energy was taken up in the logistics of moving the flotilla so he couldn't really spend a lot of time on little old me. But now that he's had time to settle in, he needs some cheap entertainment." Michael said this with almost no emotion, showing that he'd made some kind of peace with his status.

"Very cynical indeed. I'm impressed. It's so hard to beat down that American optimism that has characterized you in the past. This new spirit of resignation suggests that perhaps you have what it takes to be a British career naval officer after all."

Michael turned to Jeff with narrowed eyes and a turned-down lip. "I suppose I have just enough fight left in me to say that I wish people would stop talking about my American background. I'm as British as any of you. I've lived sixty percent of my life in Britain, went to British schools, attended the Naval College, and served my whole military career in the Royal Navy. I'd be no more adjusted to the American military than you if we were suddenly transferred to their command." He hesitated for a moment. "And . . ." but then decided not to proceed.

"And what?"

"And nothing. Anything I add at this point would just be catty, anyway."

"Oh, please! I love catty comments. They feed my cynical nature. You can't hold back now. What else makes you more British than American?"

"Fine! You asked for it. In addition to all the reasons I've given you so far, there's the fact that someday I stand to inherit one massive piece of British real estate as well as own a significant interest in British industry and mining, to say nothing of our shipping concerns and political obligations. All of which leads to an enormous amount of taxes we pay to His Majesty's government. If that doesn't make me British, I don't know what does!" At that Michael blushed deeply to think that he'd been arrogant enough to mention his position and property.

Looking up quickly he started to apologize. "I'm sorry, Jeff. I really shouldn't have said all that. It's very crass of me . . ."

"No, no! I love it. It proves your point! You really are British—high born no less. I'll do my best to never accuse you of Americanism again!" He grinned mischievously.

Michael sighed. That was exactly the outcome that he did not want to occur. He was proud to be American born, loved the casual mixing of people regardless of their income that he'd experienced as a boy growing up in Salt Lake City, and he felt particularly uncomfortable with the status that he enjoyed as a member of

British aristocracy. Now he'd effectively done what he despised most about the class system—held it over someone. On top of his rebuke from Billingham, which hurt much worse than he would ever let on, this was turning out to be a rotten day.

For once Jeff Smith seemed to sense his distress. "Look, Michael, I'm the one who should be sorry. You're in a tough spot, and I know that you love both of your countries. It shows in everything you do. I honestly think you emulate the best in both societies, not the worst, and I'm sorry that I goaded you into reacting."

That stopped Michael dead in his tracks. The last thing he wanted was to be emotional, but all of a sudden he felt very sorry for himself, and he was afraid he might show it. Since that would be a disaster, he quickly pulled out a handkerchief and pretended to blow his nose. Finally, looking up, he said, "It's just that when Chesry was sent home disabled after our attack on the submarine—well, it all sort of takes a toll. And now Billingham is pestering me again." He resorted to the handkerchief again. "It's just hard, that's all."

"I've got an idea," Jeff said. "There's a terrific little restaurant I found just a couple of blocks from here. What if we jog over, and I'll buy you a drink." He saw the look on Michael's face. "A soft drink then—although I think something stiffer would do you good."

Michael thought about it and decided he really did need time to compose himself before he went back to the boat. Besides, at this point Coleman would be frantic trying to get things in order for their first patrol later that night, so it would be common courtesy for Michael to stay away for awhile.

"That sounds good. Thanks."

"Nothing you wouldn't do for me in the same circumstance, I'm sure. Except that I'll never be in quite the same circumstance, will I? Your life is about as different from mine as a life can be."

"You know, I think I'd like to hear about your life for a change. I'm tired of thinking about my life."

"Well, then," Smith said darkly. "You're in for a sordid tale of adventure on the high seas, black secrets in dark corners, and beautiful women who tempt a man's virtue."

Michael raised an eyebrow.

"And when I'm done with that fable, I'll tell you about my life."

Michael laughed, and the two friends headed off for the restaurant.

* * *

Syracuse on the Island of Sicily— August 5, 1943

Launched on July 10, 1943, the assault on Sicily was a joint operation between the Americans and the British, even though the two groups only worked together on rare occasions. The American Seventh Army, under the command of General George S. Patton, and the British Eighth Army, under the command of General Bernard Montgomery, formed the Fifteenth Army Group with on-the-ground command by British general Sir Harold Alexander. The two armies were also joined by the First Canadian Infantry Division. American General Dwight D. Eisenhower was in command of the entire operation.

Montgomery and Patton immediately viewed each other as competitors and vied for the title of "largest ego" in the war, and in just a matter of days their two campaigns became a race for bragging rights as to who could capture the most territory.

At the outset, the British were to land on the southeast side of the island, while the Americans would land farther north on the western side. The idea was that the two groups would move independently of one another until they reached an eventual rendezvous at the top of the island near the narrow strait that separated Sicily from Italy.

In the first days of the assault, the British landed in Syracuse with very little opposition, but as soon as they started advancing up the eastern coast of the island, they met fierce resistance from some of Germany's most battle-seasoned troops, and the British advance quickly bogged down.

Patton, on the other hand, was harassed by the Germans and Italians from the moment the first Americans hit the beaches. But through a series of bold moves, he was able to advance rapidly after that, capturing great swaths of Sicilian territory as he started moving northeast toward Palermo. Since the British had been assigned the honor of capturing Palermo, Patton was told to stay away but he pleaded his case to Alexander, who relented and granted permission for the Americans to proceed. The political uproar was such that Alexander then sent a cable withdrawing permission, but Patton later claimed that the order instructing him to hold back was garbled in transmission—a fortunate "error" that allowed the Americans to capture this important milestone. His success was a source of great chagrin to the British. After three years in the field, the British felt it their right to claim this prize, given the Americans' belated entry into the war.

The most surprising consequence of the capture of Palermo was that two days later on July 24, 1943, two officers of the Italian Army, acting under orders of the king of Italy, arrested their dictator, Benito Mussolini. As for the motor torpedo boats, they had done their best to guard the Allied troopships in the early days of the Allied landings, but it soon became clear that there wasn't a great deal of threat from the Italian navy, and by the end of the first month of operation, the torpedo boats had precious few targets to engage. Most of the MTB captains shared Michael's frustration at feeling so useless. Now they were back in Malta refueling in preparation for another night patrol.

"Excuse me, sir, but a messenger is coming onboard. It looks like Commander Billingham's man." Michael acknowledged his first officer, who then said more quietly, "Wonder what he has in mind for us this time." Michael just shook his head in recognition of the fact that he had absolutely no idea what to expect.

Just then the young man stepped onto the bridge. "The commander's compliments, sir, and he wishes to see you as soon as possible."

"Thank you. I'll come with you right now, if that's all right. You'll take command, Lieutenant Coleman."

"Of course, sir." David arched an eyebrow, his usual indication of curiosity, but Michael ignored it and grabbed his hat. Stepping off the boat and into the waiting motor car, they were soon off to headquarters, where he was forced to wait more than thirty minutes outside of Billingham's door. Undoubtedly the commander was very busy, but Michael still nursed the thought that Billingham was keeping him waiting on purpose. Finally, the door opened and Billingham's aide beckoned him to enter.

"Sir!" Michael said crisply.

Billingham continued to look at a stack of papers on his desk, then slowly straightened them and pushed them to the side. Finally he looked up with no emotion showing on his face. "Be seated, Lieutenant."

Michael sat down stiffly in the chair across from Billingham. "Against my better judgment, I have a new assignment to give you."

Just as well we get right to the point—no small talk to bog things down.

"It seems that Commander Allan believes you're the right man to launch a sortie against the enemy troopships traversing the strait that separates Sicily and Italy. The Germans realize that they have no chance of holding Sicily, so their goal is to fight a rearguard action to delay our advance on Messina while moving as many troops as possible to the mainland. Of course our boys on the ground will have wasted their efforts if the Germans simply slink out of harm's way. Yet conditions aren't right for much naval action. The thought is that while an attack by our capital ships or destroyers would bring out their large units, perhaps a small group of torpedo boats can slip in undetected among the throng and create some havoc before they fully realize what's going on."

In spite of who he was with, Michael couldn't help but nod and smile. "What a great idea! Are they running these troopships at night?"

Billingham scowled to make it perfectly clear that it was not appropriate for Michael to ask questions.

"As I was saying, your role is to slip into the pack unnoticed, put a torpedo in the side of one of the obvious targets, then slip out and into the lee of a cove. Fuel will be at a premium for such a long mission, so you'll need to proceed with caution until you can work yourself into position to lie low until dusk. You'll be joined in this endeavor by three American PT boats and will be under their command for the engagement. It seems that they're jealous of the British gaining too much recognition, so this is a shared enterprise. Once you've accomplished your mission, you'll return to our base under your own command. It really isn't that complicated. Naturally, I'd have preferred to send a more experienced captain, but Commander Allan was insistent, undoubtedly because of your American connections." He looked up and fixed a steady gaze on Michael. "I suppose he's right, given your mixed nationality."

There was a lot that Michael would have liked to say at this moment—perhaps *shout* was a better word—but he simply pursed his lips and resolved to remain silent, even though this was the natural place for him to respond.

"Well, don't just sit there—do you have any questions, Carlyle?"

"I simply need to know who will give me an operational briefing, sir. Otherwise I believe I can manage this."

"Yes, well, you can see my Number Two for that." Billingham rose. "Do try to make a decent showing for the British Navy,

Carlyle. The Americans are frankly amateurs at this point, so they're lucky that Commander Allan has consented to support them."

"I'll do my best, sir." Billingham dismissed him with a nod, and Michael exited the room.

* * *

"Do you mind if I ask what you're smiling about, sir?"

Michael turned and looked at David Coleman. "Was I smiling, Number One?" And then he broke into an even bigger grin. "It's the Americans. It seems so odd to hear them speak in their loud and boisterous way. I'd forgotten just how uninhibited they are. It's really rather enjoyable to hear their chatter after so many years away."

"So do they think of you as one of theirs or one of ours?"

"Oh, they think of me as British, of course. They see me as hopelessly stiff and formal and no fun whatsoever. When they found out I'm an American by birth, they immediately started calling me 'the traitor' and 'Benedict Arnold' and having all sorts of fun with my British accent. They don't dare do that with any others of our ilk, since it might give offense. But I guess they feel more at liberty with me, since I have something in common with them." Michael was thoughtful for a moment. "Their teasing about my British accent surprises me, though, since my British friends make fun of my American accent. How is it possible to be guilty of both?" He looked at Coleman with a mock puzzled look. David just shrugged his shoulders, preferring not to get put in the middle of this particular question. "At any rate they definitely think I've gone over to the other side. So you see, it all proves that I really am British."

"With all due respect, sir, there are at least a few in our little fleet who also think you're a bit too stiff and formal, even for the British, so I'm not sure those are fair criteria." Coleman said this a bit warily since Michael was, after all, his commanding officer.

"I know. That's the irony of it all, isn't it? I'm almost too British even for the British, let alone the Americans."

"Yet you don't take offense?"

Michael smiled. "Good heavens, no. I am who I am. If I didn't like it, I suppose I could try to change. But the truth is that I am overly serious and idealistic. It's always been like that."

"So what do you think our chances are? Do the Americans have what it takes to pull this off?" Coleman asked.

"I'm not sure. They certainly talk a good talk, but they really haven't been in the war long enough to have a lot of practical experience. Their equipment is top rate, as you'd expect, and I'm quite certain they'll take the initiative. Their commanding officer told me on at least three occasions that I should take independent action whenever the situation called for it. Not at all like we hear from . . ." Fortunately, Michael caught himself before completing the sentence. The last thing he needed to do was cast doubt on their leader in front of one of his officers.

But Coleman finished the sentence for him. "Not at all like we hear from Commander Billingham."

"Of course we shouldn't think that way, David. It does no good. But it was refreshing to hear the phrase 'independent action' again. And it isn't because they're American. We used to enjoy great latitude in the Channel Ports, as well."

"I think it's a disgrace you're not commanding this operation. You have more experience than all of their officers put together!"

"Ah, but they have more skin in the game. They have three boats to our one, and it's their treasury department that's paying the baggage for most of these operations. Britain is borrowing her way through the balance of the war. We ran out of assets and credit a long time ago. That's why General Eisenhower is in overall command, rather than Alexander."

"Still . . ."

"It's all right. I kind of like being just one of the players. If things go wrong, perhaps Commander Billingham will blame the Americans instead of me."

Coleman nodded. "I see. Well, in that case I will gladly submit to their inexperience."

Michael laughed again. Coleman had never seen him like this—it was as if the weight of the world had been taken off his shoulders and Michael was free for the first time since coming to the Mediterranean to relax in his command.

* * *

The Strait of Messina—August 1943

To position themselves for the attack on the German transports, the four torpedo boats had worked their way across the open sea from Malta to the northern coast of Sicily, where they had cruised quietly at night into a position just to the west of Messina. The city was still held by the Germans, and it was obvious that there was a furious effort under way that likely rivaled the evacuation of the British Expeditionary Force at Dunkirk early in the war—except that at Dunkirk the retreating British had faced dozens of miles of open sea and potential harassment from the Luftwaffe, while here the Germans had less than three miles to cross and still held the upper hand in fending off potential air and sea attacks. The strait was so narrow that it would be difficult for capital ships to fight their way in to get in position to tackle the transports anyway. That's why the torpedo boats had to maintain their secrecy to the very last moment and hopefully slip undetected into a favorable position to attack. By staying close to the shoreline, they could fool any radar that might be searching for them.

With the island of Sicily shaped like a giant triangle, the northern coast ran a relatively straight line from west to east. The British had been fighting their way up the eastern arm of the triangle while the Americans had landed rather squarely on the western side where they had first driven northwest. When that was secured, they started moving to the east to close the distance with the British. Both armies were now within striking distance of the city of Messina, which held the key to the fate of more than a quarter million Italian soldiers.

Unfortunately, the Germans had so far managed to organize an extremely effective evacuation plan. Hopefully that would change tonight.

"All right, men," Michael said quietly to his officers and gunnery staff. "In the absence of a countermand, we're going to get under way in another ten minutes. The goal is to move as quietly as possible out into the Channel, where we'll infiltrate ourselves amongst the enemy ships. We're going out in a fan pattern, with the American boats in positions one through three counting from the north. We'll be closest to Messina. Intelligence has been hard to come by, but with the sheer number of people the Germans are trying to move, we expect that the passage between the island and the mainland will be filled with transports, along with destroyers to protect them. In this case the target is the transports. We want to send as many to the bottom as possible so our boys don't have to fight the same soldiers again when we invade the Italian mainland. So I'll need all eyes forward to help us spot ships in the passage, to help sort out destroyer from transport, and to generally be on the alert for opportunities. Of course it goes without question that we need to maintain silence. To help with that we'll go in with just one engine, Chief, but be ready to fire up the other two when the situation calls for it." His chief engineer acknowledged this directive.

"When we get a good trajectory I'll give the order to fire the forward torpedo tubes. We'll immediately turn to port, which will be north at that point, to escape from the torpedo tracks in the water. I'll want us to zigzag a bit, Mr. Jenkins, so their gunners can't get a good bead on us. Can I leave that up to you?"

"Yes, sir!" Michael could sense the anticipation in Jeremy Jenkins's voice, and he was relieved to hear that it was an excited anticipation rather than fearful. Hopefully all the crew felt that way.

"We'll hold off until we're certain of a hit, and then we'll move out to find another target or to support one of our American cousins in their attack, should they need our help."

"Oh, they'll undoubtedly need our help!" one of the men said. "Seeing as how they're likely to fall apart when faced with real battle."

Michael laughed. There was nothing wrong with a little competitive spirit. "We'll leave it to them to do their own laundry when it's all over, but at least we can do our best to see they're not washing their soiled trousers in the salt water of the Mediterranean. It's the least we can do for a friend."

"I say aye to that." The chief engineer always managed to bring the enlisted men around.

"The hardest part of this whole venture is getting ourselves out alive. I suspect that if we're successful, the Germans will think they're under full-scale attack, and they'll send out everything they can find to drown us. I know they'll be disappointed when it turns out to be four small boats, and if they can catch us, they're likely to take their wrath out on us.

"So," he said turning to the chief, "that's when I'm going to want everything these old engines can give. We won't have a lot of fuel left, but even so, I won't be stingy until we're well clear of the area. It's not likely they'll follow us very far once they know they've driven off the threat; they'll want to get back to their ships in case another attack is launched from the east."

"And may I ask if there is another attack group coming in?" Lieutenant Coleman said.

"Afraid not, Number One. It's really too dangerous to try to bring boats up the eastern side of the island, so we're the entire task force for this evening's performance."

"Well, then, we better make a good show of it!" Coleman said with the same kind of enthusiasm that Jenkins had displayed earlier, and Michael knew that they were at the peak of anticipation. It felt good to have morale running so high. Now they just had to do their part and hope that a lucky shell didn't blow them all to smithereens.

"All right then, back to your stations. I haven't heard anything to stop us, so in another two minutes we're going to ease ourselves out and into the Channel. From that point forward I want communication between us as sparse as possible. Good luck!"

Of course they couldn't cheer, but they did all raise their fists in a silent cheer and then moved quickly and easily to their assigned spots on the boat. It was truly miraculous to see thirteen individual men work as one unified creature as they prepared to face victory or death in the darkness of the Sicilian sea.

* * *

The sheer audacity of it all was thrilling. To sneak out into a crowded enemy convoy lane and work their way into the midst of a small armada of troop transports being jealously guarded by E-boats and destroyers took real nerve. In the back of his mind, Michael was convinced that had Billingham been in charge, they would have never been given this opportunity. But with the Americans, it was full speed ahead and "damn the torpedoes," to quote Civil War hero David Farragut. Except that in this case they were going to be the ones to launch the torpedo. Any moment.

The agreed-upon plan called for Michael to position his boat toward the rear of the vanguard on the side closest to Sicily. The lead American boat would launch its attack at the front of the column closest to Italy, which, if everything went as anticipated, would draw the German gunboats forward to engage the

American boat, leaving Michael and the other Americans with a relatively open field of fire. Once all torpedoes were running, their role was to get out of there as fast as possible on the assumption that the Germans would do an about-face and come after them, hopefully taking pressure off the lead American. A bit complex, but it should work.

Although he really didn't need to say anything, Michael couldn't stand the silence, so he spoke quietly to Coleman. "The hardest part will be picking out the targets with three in view and others likely to be illuminated by the light of the blasts up front."

"I'll leave that to you, if it's all right, sir. Right now I'm most concerned about making sure every torpedo finds its way into the belly of one of those transports. It seems incredible to me that so many troops are getting away, with our land forces so close to Messina."

Michael smiled. As he'd gotten to know David Coleman, he was increasingly pleased by his performance. The man had a wry sense of humor and something of a pessimistic attitude, yet he relished a good fight. Those were not bad characteristics to have in an officer.

"There it is, sir!" Jeremy Jenkins whispered.

Michael turned to the left but saw nothing in the darkness. What he'd apparently missed was the single flash of light signaling the attack was under way.

"Did you see it?" he asked Coleman, frustrated that he couldn't verify it himself. It would ruin the plan completely if he were to start out into the shipping lane ahead of the Americans.

"I did, sir. The agreed-upon single flash."

Michael nodded. "Glad I have a reliable crew. Ahead slow, Mr. Jenkins, on a single engine. Prepare to switch to electric at my command."

"Yes, sir!" Michael could feel the excitement in the young man's voice.

Slowly the torpedo boat started moving forward. Michael found himself puzzling over the seeming paradox of how in this nearly moonless night the boat seemed so incredibly large and noisy while it usually appeared small and insignificant when compared to a capital ship or even a small destroyer. Of course the difference was that in most typical situations they weren't trying to hide themselves while slipping in among a dozen enemy ships. Tonight had the added dimension of terror since the odds were at least twenty or thirty percent that the first ship they'd encounter would be a destroyer with enough firepower to blow them out of the water. It was amazing how danger had the ability to focus Michael's thoughts.

Because the strait was so narrow, it hadn't been hard to find the enemy. In fact, the worst thing they'd had to endure was sneaking up the coastline and hiding in the lees of the low hills as they positioned themselves for the night attack. They could never know who was watching from the hills. If even one person spotted them and reported their movement to the Italians, they'd have been sitting ducks for an air attack. That's why they'd moved mostly in the early morning hours and evening, hiding under camouflage nets during the day. It had been nerve-wracking.

But now the wait was over. It was impossible that they wouldn't find targets at this hour of the night. *Even destroyers.* In spite of the destroyer's superior size and armament, a torpedo boat could still hold its own against a destroyer if it had the benefit of surprise.

"Keep your eyes sharp," Michael said needlessly to the bridge crew. The minutes ticked by slowly as they crawled their way into the shipping lane. For some inexplicable reason, they didn't see a single ship on the horizon. The telltale signs of a ship moving at night included such things as a darker smudge against the night sky—smoke from the boilers—or a momentary flash of light as hot embers escaped the soot mesh meant to capture them in the smokestack. It could even be something as simple as a sailor lighting up a cigarette. There were dozens of small mistakes that could betray a ship moving through the water, and after three years at sea, Michael thought he had seen them all. Yet tonight there was nothing—which made no sense at all, given the apparent pace of evacuations.

Not unless someone has warned them! The thought sent a chill up Michael's spine. *But surely they wouldn't have shut down the evacuation—they'd have just sent an attack group out to chase us away!*

The waiting came to an abrupt end as the sky off to port, perhaps two miles distant, burst into flame from a terrific explosion. Whatever the torpedo hit was hot—very hot—because the flash was mostly white in color, not the more usual red and orange that accompanied the explosion of a torpedo.

"What on earth could cause that?" Coleman said in awe.

"Ammunition," Michael replied quietly. "Whoever they hit was carrying a large supply of ammunition along with their troops. Our torpedo must have hit it square on to send everything up at once." Coleman turned to look at Michael, who continued with a grim face. "What a bunch of fools—or, even worse, uncaring idiots—to mix highly explosive ammunition with troops." He turned to Coleman. "No one's going to escape from that inferno. You can count at least one troopship out of the equation. Who knows, maybe they have so many men in uniform they don't have to worry about losing a couple of hundred needlessly." The sound of disgust was strong in Michael's voice.

"But I thought that's what we wanted."

Michael looked at his first officer. "Oh, it's a great thing for us. I wish every single ship we hit were like that—it would make our job a lot easier. It's just that it tells you what kind of people we're fighting that they'd be so careless with their own troops." He finished by shaking his head.

"All right, enough of that," Michael continued. "We need to get ready. Hopefully there will be a couple more explosions up ahead, and then we'll move in. Have you identified any targets, Mr. Coleman?" The task was much easier now that there was light in the distance. Not that the glow of the explosion was bright enough by itself to betray any other ship's position, but rather it gave the chance to spot a ship in silhouette as it appeared as a dark spot between the distant conflagration and their position.

"Three." Coleman pointed first to port and then to starboard. "My guess is that the first one is a destroyer that's racing on ahead to figure out what's going on." Michael watched as one ship clearly increased speed away from them.

"Very good. That means the other two are now ripe for the picking."

"Shall we go to electric, sir?" Jenkins asked.

"I really don't think we need to worry about silence right now, Mr. Jenkins. The Italians and Germans know we're around, and they've all cranked up their engines to the point that they're not even likely to hear Mt. Etna erupt if the old volcano suddenly decides to join the battle. Steady ahead, Mr. Jenkins, all three engines. I want maneuvering power once the others get their shots off."

Michael steadied himself as the ship responded to his command, inching forward under the additional power as they moved slowly toward the leading target.

"Why doesn't somebody else get a fish off!" he said, subconsciously pounding his fist on the metal railing of the bridge. "We're supposed to wait!"

Before anyone could answer him—not that they could answer—there was a bright flash off to port yet again, although this one wasn't nearly as intense.

"Looks like someone else got a shot off!" The exultation in Coleman's voice was gratifying.

"All right then, the shackles are off! Ahead full, Mr. Jenkins. Prepare to attack!" This time he was thrown forcefully backward as the ship lurched under their feet. The wake that he had been so careful to conceal up to this point suddenly glistened in the night as the bow wave rose up almost even with the front of the deck, while the stern wave showed the three distinct trails that reflected the three propellers turning at maximum revolutions per minute. It was always thrilling to feel a torpedo boat accelerate—much more so than any of the capital ships like a frigate or battle cruiser.

"Mr. Coleman, fire torpedoes at your discretion."

"Yes, sir." As a general rule Michael liked to control the battle directly, but since they'd had so few opportunities to engage the enemy since his transfer to the Mediterranean, he thought it extremely important that he use any opportunity available to train his officers and crew.

Michael was surprised that he was able to hear the frantic sounds of sirens blaring to life on the troopship they were quickly closing on, in spite of the roar of their own engines. In a lapse of protocol that would never be tolerated on a British ship, they suddenly saw doors being thrown open with lights blazing behind the men rushing out onto the decks. Of course all the commotion meant that they knew they'd been spotted, even though there wasn't a torpedo running in the water, and that meant the ship's captain had time to adjust course to reduce his profile.

"Anytime, Mr. Coleman," Michael said quietly through clenched teeth. "Anytime you like." He held his breath and looked down to see his knuckles white from his grip on the handrail. *Like right now would be great!*

Just when he thought he couldn't wait any longer he heard Coleman shout, "Fire one!" A moment passed. "Fire two!"

The deck jumped a bit as the ship responded to the sudden loss of nearly a ton of weight as the torpedoes were thrown forward into the water by a powerful burst of compressed air. Michael listened for the sound of the splash and was pleased to hear both torpedoes start running in the water. The worst possible moment for a captain was launching a torpedo only to hear its motor malfunction.

Not this time. Now it's a race between our fish and the troopship captain's evasive action.

Michael studied the two lines in the water that indicated the torpedoes' direction. He then glanced up at the ship to see exactly how the enemy captain was responding to the emergency and was pleased to see that no matter what action the fellow took, it wouldn't make any difference. Barring a failure to explode on the part of the torpedoes, it was inevitable that at least one would hit. All that was left to do was to brace for the impact. Michael almost always failed to turn away from the blast to protect his night vision. He just wanted to see what was happening.

But he did the right thing this time, glancing down to his feet as the moment drew near. It didn't help much since the blast of the first torpedo's explosion was so powerful that the entire night sky flared into full luminescence. Michael counted as he waited for the blast of hot air to wash over the torpedo boat.

"Hard astarboard!" he shouted. "Let's set up for the next attack." Although he didn't need to, he stole a quick look at the ship they'd just hit, fully confident that it would shortly be settling on the bottom of the Strait of Messina. It wasn't the best time to look, as it turned out, since a second blast, some five hundred yards beyond their original target, lit up the sky with another blast that took him so totally by surprise that all he could see was a big round white dot as he closed his eyes.

"What happened?" he heard Coleman shout from the forward deck.

"You missed with your second torpedo, Mr. Coleman! Bad shooting, that. Except that the torpedo kept running and hit a second target that must have been hidden behind the first one. You got two ships!"

He laughed as Coleman looked up at him in astonishment. "Two!"

"Yes, two! Congratulations to you and all the crew!" He was gratified when a terrific cheer went up from the men above the waterline.

"But enough celebrating. If I'm not mistaken we still have two fish left, so let's see what else we can do!"

"Yes, sir!" Surprisingly, that's all Coleman had to say. But he was shaking his head from side to side to indicate his satisfaction.

Of course at this point the enemy ship that had been to their starboard had turned tail and was heading straight back to Messina at full speed, evident from the great shower of sparks that was billowing up and out of the smokestack. While a dead give-away for their position, it also meant that the poor captain was doing everything he could to put on maximum speed to try to get away. Unfortunately, a troopship's top speed of perhaps thirty knots wasn't much compared to the torpedo boat's maximum speed of nearly fifty knots. In the absence of any outside support, the outlook for the troopship in the next duel was grim.

"Perhaps you might consider launching from a little greater distance this time," Michael called down to Coleman. Coleman looked up a bit sheepishly. "I wanted to make sure I didn't miss, sir!"

"Well, you certainly succeeded at that. It's just that I wasn't really expecting a sunburn from the blast." He said this good naturedly so that his first officer wouldn't lose confidence, but he was trying to make a point.

Suddenly there was a bright flash from just above the water-line of the ship they were pursuing.

"Ah, so the prey has some fangs of its own," Michael said smoothly. "Hard to port, Mr. Jenkins." The ship jerked at the command just as a large spout of water went up just off their starboard side.

Calling down to Coleman, Michael instructed, "This one's going to be trickier because they're not going to let us get a good, clean shot off. You'll have to be prepared to shoot with a very short launch window. I'll bring us onto track in another sixty seconds and give you twenty seconds before I have to zigzag. Understand?"

Coleman got a worried look on his face but responded affirmatively. A second shot from the German splashed the entire bridge party with water and forced Michael to take yet another wild maneuver to port. He had to concentrate on anticipating what the German captain would do once they'd launched their torpedoes. Even as big as the troopship was, it could still do some quick maneuvering once the torpedoes were in the water. If they were a submarine they could launch three or even four torpedoes to bracket the fellow no matter which way he turned. But all they had left was two.

"Mr. Coleman! Would you join me on the deck?"

Coleman came running. "Yes, sir!"

"Listen, this fellow's really good. He may be able to outmaneuver us once the torpedoes are running if we don't do things carefully. The natural response is to send the fish out in a V pattern so that if he turns to either side, one or the other will hit him. Problem is, if the V is too wide, he can just stay in the middle. So here's what I propose to do." He pulled Coleman closer so that he could outline his attack. He proposed coming in so close that there was no way to miss. Of course that meant they'd be subject to the enemy ship's fire, including its machine guns. It was very dangerous, but he judged it the only way to hit this ship.

"Can you still give me a twenty-second launch window?" Coleman asked.

"That, but no more. I'll give you some warning before we straighten out the trajectory, but you'll have to be awfully fast."

"Yes, sir." There was a lot of anxiety in his first officer's voice.

"David, you'll do fine. The truth is we're likely to get blown up before you even get a chance to shoot, so there's not a lot of pressure on you."

Coleman laughed. "Well, that's reassuring. Thank you for those inspirational words, sir!"

"All right, then. Get back down there just in case I don't mess it up, and stand ready for my signal."

While Michael had faced a lot of challenges in the Royal Navy, none had been greater than this. It seemed as if the Germans had an unlimited supply of shells for their small cannons, and as if to prove the point, there was a deafening blast on the afterdeck followed by a wave of searing heat, knocking Michael forward and almost over the front of the bridge cowling in what would surely have been a fatal somersault. Fortunately, Jenkins somehow managed to grab him at the last moment.

"We've been hit!" Jenkins shouted into the night air.

Michael whirled around, expecting to see the backside of the boat blown away, but he was surprised to see that while the aft gun and gunner had completely disappeared, the deck was still intact in a gruesome sort of way. The shell from the enemy ship must have been coming in on such a flat trajectory that the force of the explosion was deflected off the back of the deck and out into the water.

"Do we have steerage, Mr. Jenkins?"

"Yes, sir. We still have power, although it's diminished."

Quickly assessing the scene, Michael decided he couldn't possibly follow through on his earlier plan. They had to get rid of the torpedoes now and hope for the best.

"Mr. Coleman, set up a tight spread and fire. No time to lose!"

"Yes, sir!"

He vaguely heard some muffled shouts and felt the familiar shudder as the torpedoes left the deck. And then, to his surprise, he felt very warm and almost cozy. It was such an odd sensation in the midst of battle. At that moment he realized that the back of his head was wet, although he didn't remember getting splashed by the water. He felt his legs buckle beneath him and even heard himself cry out to Jenkins, "I need help," but it all seemed so detached, as if he were watching a movie in which his body was the main character. But surely that couldn't be possible, could it?

Chapter Nine

CONTRIBUTIONS

London—August 1943

"Papa, do you suppose the groundskeeper at the manor has a lathe that I could use?"

Philip put down *The Times* and looked up at Grace from across the breakfast table. "Excuse me?"

"A lathe—you know, a tool to turn metal while it's being machined. Do we have one on the grounds out at the house?"

Philip shook his head and smiled. "A lathe? You'd like a lathe?" Looking up at Claire he said, "And now, my dear, after nearly two decades of raising our daughter, sending her to the finest schools in Europe, having introduced her to the king of England and all his court, she wants a lathe. Well, it should simplify Christmas, shouldn't it?"

"Oh, Papa, you know perfectly well that I'm about to finish my apprenticeship so I can work full-time in the munitions factory. And while I don't use a lathe in the work I do there, I need one to finish the shell casing that I'm turning into a vase as part of my final training. I can always find one at work, but I thought it would be simpler to use one out at the house. But if you're embarrassed . . ."

"Oh, no, my dear, we have an excellent wood and metal workshop at the manor to maintain all the equipment. What's mine is yours—you're welcome to use a lathe, the drill press, or anything else your heart desires." He should have left it at that but couldn't help adding, "Or we'll order a foundry, if you like, so you can really get down to the essentials of metal work."

"That's enough, Philip," Claire said. "I'm very proud that Grace is contributing to the war effort. Princess Elizabeth works as a driver in the Auxiliary Territorial Service, you know, so why shouldn't Grace work in the war effort like so many others?"

"I'm teasing, and you both know it. I'm envious of you for the things you're learning and for what you get to make when you're done. Somehow it feels like a more direct and useful contribution to the war effort than all the paper I shove around and the meetings I attend. So you make your vase and display it with pride. Perhaps you can make them in bulk for us to give as Christmas presents this year. A shell-casing vase is certainly unique."

Grace sniffed. It was one of the happy rituals that she shared with her father. She'd say something serious, knowing full well that in a different context it was amusing. Philip would react to the humor, and Grace would feign being wounded. Her father would apologize, and all would be well until the next time she decided to play the game. They both loved it.

"So on a more serious note," he said, "do you really enjoy the work you do? I'd think it was noisy and grimy and hot—three things you've never been particularly attracted to."

"It's surprising," Grace replied, "but I really do enjoy it. There are very few men, so we don't have to worry about primping and flirting and all that, and everybody is motivated to do their best work so that our boys will be successful when they shoot the horrid things we make. I guess it does feel good to make something tangible, even something like a shell."

"Is it all right for me to ask what type of ammunition you make, or would that be a breach of national security? Jules Ellington about had me arrested when I asked about the work he was doing."

"Jules Ellington is a self-important bore." Grace sniffed. "He's entirely too caught up in himself, so I'd hardly give any credence to what he says."

"Oh, so you like him?"

Grace shook her head. "If you're not going to talk to me seriously, Papa, then I'll just excuse myself right now."

"Don't take offense. I'm just teasing. I really do want to know as much about your work as you can tell me." Grace smiled—the game had been played successfully for yet another round.

"It is kind of exciting, even though it's mindless and boring as a general rule." Grace failed completely to catch the irony in her response. "But we make antiaircraft shells to be fired from ships protecting themselves from German aircraft. I love the fact that the shells are so highly polished and perfectly shaped. Should any irregularity show up anywhere along the assembly line, we reject it. Of course that's where we girls get our one casing to make our vases. The rest are melted down and the process starts over. But the important thing is to not have many rejects. The last thing you'd want is to have a shell blow up and injure one of our lads."

"That would be bad. And what do you do on the line?"

"I operate a machine that seals the top of the shell after the girl before me fills it with the proper amount of gunpowder. Shell after shell after shell—all day long."

"And that doesn't get extremely tedious?" Claire asked. "Or dangerous?"

"It isn't too dangerous since we have strict controls in place to keep us safe. But it does get tedious. Fortunately, there are girls on either side of me, and we're able to chat once in a while, even though it's noisy. I like the breaks and going out to dinner with the others once in a while, too. It's a good job."

"I don't know if you've thought about this," Philip said, "but there's a very high likelihood that the shells that you and your coworkers are making are the same kind that're used on Michael's boat. I'm not saying that any one of your shells will make it to him, but wouldn't it be something if a piece of ammunition that you and your coworkers made ended up saving his life because his crew was able to protect itself from enemy aircraft?"

Grace was very quiet when he said this. She was naturally buoyant and cheerful and loved to banter and talk with anyone. But she was also idealistic, and clearly this thought struck her deeply—so deeply that her eyes welled up as she pondered it.

"Oh, Grace, I didn't mean to make you cry. I was just trying to compliment you."

"It was a compliment, Papa—one of the best I've ever received. I'd never thought of it exactly like that, but maybe I have saved somebody's Michael. Maybe I have made a difference."

"I'm sure you have, dear." Claire and Grace didn't always see eye to eye, but they had always been able to talk with each other, and Claire always seemed to sense when Grace's emotions were running deep. As she looked at her daughter, she could tell that in some inexplicable way, Philip's simple comment had prompted some deep emotional response.

"What is it, sweetheart?" Philip asked when Grace didn't regain control.

"It's nothing . . . it's just that for some reason I thought of Michael, and then I thought of . . ."

"Dominic," Claire finished quietly. Grace nodded her head. Since her next-oldest brother had committed suicide in North Africa after deserting his post, Grace had been extremely tender. Although Dominic hadn't been particularly close to anyone in the family, he was probably closest with Grace, and it was clear that she missed him deeply.

"Do you want to talk about it?" Claire asked.

Grace glanced at her father and saw that the color had drained from his face. "Not really," she replied. "I guess I just couldn't help but think of him, and it makes me sad." She swallowed to suppress her tears.

"I know how you feel," Claire said. "I find myself thinking of him at the oddest times, wondering if he's doing well in the next life, contemplating exactly how he'll work through the problems his death created." Now it was Claire whose voice broke. "I'm sorry I wasn't there to comfort him. Who knows if I was . . ."

Philip inhaled very quietly. He had been with Dominic in Africa and had a remarkably good discussion with his son—perhaps the best of their lives—just after he was charged with desertion. But in spite of that, the charge of desertion was a capital offense and would likely have led to Dominic's execution by firing squad. Instead of face that ordeal, Dominic had chosen to end his own life. The shock to Philip had been severe, and since that night Philip had found it very difficult to even think of his son, and discussions like this made him very uncomfortable.

Claire picked up on Philip's distress as well, so she concluded the conversation with, "I know it's sad, but somehow it feels good not to worry about Dominic like I used to. At least now I know he's safe." She smiled weakly.

An awkward silence followed until Philip cleared his throat and said, perhaps too lightly, "I'm afraid that all of this discussion diverted us from your original question. The answer is still yes, we have a lathe and whatever other equipment you need to make your vase and anything else you desire. Would you like me to drive you out to the manor later this afternoon? I have a meeting, but I'd be glad to cancel it."

"How about we all go out together and I fix dinner?" Claire bit her bottom lip as she said this, indicating that she didn't want to be left alone in the city.

"I'd drive all the way across England and back to have one of your dinners, my dear. Let's make it a date for three PM. I'll let my staff know that only a national emergency could keep me away." He thought for a moment. "No, that's no good since we're always having a national emergency lately. I'll just tell them I'm leaving no matter what's going on. Meet you here at three?"

The girls smiled as he rose, and they each gave him a kiss as he hurried off to complete his work for the day. Then they turned to each other and shrugged, losing yet another opportunity to talk about Dominic and heal their hidden wounds.

Chapter Ten

ATTACKING THE ITALIAN MAINLAND

The Mediterranean—August 1943

The dull roar of the engines seemed to intrude on Michael's dream. He was playing baseball in Salt Lake City and was just about to steal second base. Except that while he was running, his legs felt so heavy it was almost as if he were moving in slow motion. He knew that he had to hurry up, or he'd be tagged out for sure. Even as he labored to make his legs move faster he saw the pitcher turn and smile as he threw the ball toward the second baseman. It was a race now between Michael and the ball—a race he could win if only he could make his legs move faster. But it felt like there was lead in his bones, and he had the terrible feeling he was about to let the whole team down by becoming the third out in the last inning. They would lose the game, and everyone would be hurt if he couldn't respond. "Why won't you move?" he shouted at his legs.

"What was that, sir? Are you all right?"

Michael shook his head at the sound of David Coleman's voice. "What? Where am I?" He opened his eyes frantically and looked up at Coleman. "The Germans! The Strait of Messina. What's happened, David?" Michael quickly surveyed the scene and realized he was in his own hammock onboard the *MTB-620*. Although everything seemed all right, the engines had an unusual growl that didn't sound right.

"Nice to have you back, sir." Coleman smiled at him. "We got the third ship. You were right about the spread; we just barely hit them. But where we hit them is what matters the most—we got the blaggard right in the tail. Blew his stern clear off. He'd made a sharp turn to put himself in the center of the V, but your spread was too tight. Congratulations!"

Michael tried to sit up, but his head swooned at the effort.

"What's our position now?" He hated that he was so completely out of control that he didn't even know where they were.

"We're making our way back to the rendezvous point. You must have been hit pretty hard by that shell that hit the after-deck. After giving the order to fire torpedoes, you passed out. But it was all right. Once the torpedoes struck the target, all resistance from the Germans ceased, and I immediately ordered a withdrawal according to plan."

"Did any escorts try to pursue us?"

"No, sir. I think they were too busy worrying about another attack. From what I've pieced together, there were at least six, maybe seven enemy ships that got hit. And we were responsible for three of them!"

Michael relaxed. What an incredible night. "Thank you, David. I'm glad you were there to take over for me."

"Only for a few minutes. You've only been unconscious for perhaps twenty minutes. I'm afraid the task of explaining to Commander Billingham how your ship got torn up still falls to you," David said with an impish grin, obviously relieved that Michael seemed all right.

"How bad is the damage? What about the men?"

"Not so good. It seems to me that it's pure good luck that we got out alive at all. The German shell must have hit the after-deck and bounced, exploding in the air as it went over the back of the boat. One of the propellers was damaged, so we've shut down that engine. The others may have some problems, too, because it seems like the engines are under unusual strain. The chief says we won't know until we get back to port, where we can send some divers over the side to do a full inspection."

"So the chief is all right? I worried about the men down there."

Coleman was quiet. "The chief's okay, but two of his mates didn't do so well. One just died, and the other is in a bad way. We also lost the aft gunner, so three casualties at this point. And you."

Michael sighed. "I'm sorry about the men. But it could have been a lot worse." He closed his eyes for a moment. Keeping them open seemed to take a great deal of effort. He must have dozed off for a moment because he was startled to feel himself jerk awake. He didn't want to appear as if he were really in that bad of shape, so he said, "What about the Americans? Any word from them?"

"No, sir. Still maintaining silence. We should reach the rendezvous in another sixty minutes. In the meantime I suggest you rest a bit. Doc thinks you might have a concussion."

"Oh, Doc does, does he?" Doc was a gunner who had taken a couple of extra first aid classes. But before Coleman could respond, Michael said, "I think maybe he's right. Since you're doing so well without me, why don't I try to get my brain to fit back inside my skull by relaxing it a bit?"

"Good idea, sir. We'll be fine."

Michael started to relax again but managed to catch himself before he was fully gone. "David!"

"Yes, sir?"

"Thank you!" Before he heard the reply, Michael was back in Salt Lake City. This time, though, he managed to slide into second just moments before the ball smacked into the glove of the second baseman. He smiled to himself as he jumped up, victorious.

* * *

Syracuse, Sicily—September 1943

"Lieutenant Carlyle, what is that thing around your neck?"

Michael was startled by Billingham's voice. Up to this point he'd been sitting quietly at the back of the briefing room next to Jeff Smith listening with the others to the plans for the evening's raids. With the American invasion of Italy at Salerno on September 9, it was now up to the torpedo boats to do their best to protect the various landings that would attempt to widen the small beachhead that had been opened by the Allies.

In the nearly two weeks since returning to port, Michael's time had been occupied by seeing to repairs of the boat, writing letters of condolence to the families of his two crew members killed in action, and trying to recover from the physical trauma he'd suffered from the blast. Fortunately, Billingham had been away at conferences, so this was the first time they had been in the same room since the raid against the German troop evacuation, an exercise that had been thoroughly applauded by both the American and British navies.

"Sir?" Michael said weakly. He'd been so taken by surprise that his voice broke as he tried to respond to Billingham's unexpected question.

At this point all eyes in the room turned to Michael.

"I asked you what you are wearing around your neck."

Michael had to think for a moment before replying. He'd been wearing his leather collar pretty much every day since returning to port.

"It's just a neck brace, sir. I received it after being injured in action off the English Channel. After our encounter with the Germans last month, it seemed prudent to wear it to protect my neck a bit."

Billingham shook his head in disgust. "And you plan to go into battle in such a condition?"

"Yes, sir. I don't really need it—it's just a precaution." It was irritating to have to explain himself, particularly in front of his peers.

"Well, this is a fine mess—an incapacitated officer to threaten the success of the mission . . ."

Although it was against protocol, Michael was so aggravated at this that he fired back, "I'm hardly incapacitated, sir. In fact I'm very much ready for duty, and I would certainly not endanger the mission."

Much to the surprise of everyone in the room, Billingham's eyes narrowed, but he did not shout at Michael. Instead, he said very quietly, "I assume you have medical clearance?" Just as he suspected, this unnerved Michael and threw him on the defensive.

"Medical clearance? I hadn't even thought about it. I'm fine, really. I just wear this because of occasional pain. I'll take it off right now if you like."

"That won't be necessary. You're scrubbed from this mission. I don't want to see you back here until you have medical clearance. In the meantime, your first officer can take your boat out tonight. Unless you think he's unequal to the responsibility of command."

A nice trick—force me to impugn David in order to fight for my own rights. Michael knew he had lost but wanted at least a parting word. "Of course Lieutenant Coleman is capable of command but no more so than his commanding officer."

Billingham's smile turned cold. "That will be all, Lieutenant. We've wasted far too much time on this already. You're dismissed."

Michael stood, his face flushed with anger. But he knew better than to say anything more, for if he started to talk, he knew he wouldn't be able to stop himself, and voicing what he was thinking would surely get him sent to the brig for insubordination. So he simply saluted and then turned and left the room, furious that Billingham had managed to remove him from command.

* * *

Michael entered Billingham's office with trepidation. After their last encounter he'd gone straight to a doctor, who after a cursory examination, had given him a letter of clearance. That was ten days ago. Since then he'd made multiple requests for an appointment with Billingham to get put back on the active duty roster, but his commander had never responded. Finally, he'd left a copy of the letter with Billingham's aide and urged him to bring it to the commander's attention. The young man had looked at him miserably and said that he would, but it was obvious that the fellow didn't hold much hope. Michael wanted to be angry but was grateful that at least he didn't have to meet with Billingham every day like this poor chap. So he left, determined not to let it get him down. Just when he'd about given up hope, he was summoned with no advance notice to go directly to Billingham's office. Fortunately, he was dressed properly, and after a quick stop at a washroom to make sure everything was straight and in good order, he presented himself at the reception desk. "You can go straight in," the secretary said.

His stomach muscles tightened as he saw Billingham look up and scowl when he entered. Billingham's face was more flushed than usual, which didn't bode well. But then Michael caught movement at the periphery of his right eye and turned to see Admiral Chadwick start toward him. His breath caught as he realized there might be hope after all.

"Lieutenant Carlyle," Chadwick said affably. "I trust your neck is doing better. I see there's no brace."

"Yes, sir. It was nothing, really." That was likely to irritate Billingham, but somehow Michael didn't care. "I've been medically certified to return to active duty and am awaiting new orders." He heard Billingham suppress a nervous cough, which was extremely gratifying.

"Well, that's why I'm here. Commander Billingham has been good enough to release you for a series of special missions, although you'll remain under his command."

Of course Michael was intrigued, but for some reason the admiral hesitated.

"Sir?"

"Yes, well, as you know, the new Italian government has agreed to surrender and to aid the Allies as we move north into Europe."

"It should make it much easier to bring pressure against Germany's southern flank." Michael said.

"The problem is that it's not at all certain that the Germans are going to give ground. Italy has little strategic value to them, particularly in the south, but what shaky intelligence we can gather indicates that they plan to slug it out down here and turn it into a full-fledged fight. They probably think it's better to do their fighting as far away from their homeland as possible. So it's likely we'll all be stuck here for awhile as our boys scrap it out with the Germans."

Michael waited as Chadwick paused yet again. A quick glance at Billingham provided no hint of what was coming as the commander simply scowled at him. That clued Michael in to the thought that perhaps Chadwick and Billingham disagreed about what was coming next, which would explain why Chadwick was being so cautious.

"Here's the thing, Carlyle. You've been requested to assist in a number of special missions that involve a great deal of secrecy. You know how just a moment ago I mentioned our shaky intelligence?"

"Yes, sir."

"Well, that's the problem—we have very few connections with the Italians, particularly since Rome is so far behind enemy lines, so we've got to get some people in there to start coordinating a resistance. British Special Forces are going to put some operatives on the ground along with some locals who speak both Italian and English. We've also received an offer of assistance from the mayor of a small town north of Taranto, just inside the heel of the Italian mainland."

Michael pictured the distinctive shape of Italy in his mind and could immediately locate the spot. "Yes, sir."

"The specific location is still behind enemy lines. Of course, the risk is that it's a trap. We have no way of knowing for sure whether these people are genuine or if they are either German sympathizers or acting under coercion by the Germans. So there's a great deal of risk to whoever makes the initial contact."

"And how can my boat help?"

"You'll take care of the landing. It will be at night, and then you'll have to wait off shore for more than twenty-four hours before picking up the landing party at the rendezvous point the following morning. The danger to you is that if it is indeed a trap, the Germans will know precisely where you are and can send in aircraft or even one of their E-boats to destroy you. Since you'll be at the extreme range of your fuel, you won't have any surplus to maneuver. We wouldn't normally authorize it except that the Admiralty itself has concluded the mission is vital."

Michael felt a surge of adrenaline. The risk was obviously very high, and there were innumerable questions like how they could ever get enough fuel onboard to get there and back, to say nothing of what they were supposed to do during the daylight hours when they'd be exposed to prying eyes up and down the coast. But none of that was equal to the excitement he felt. In view of what he knew about Admiral Chadwick, it surprised him that he appeared so hesitant. Michael decided to see if he could tease it out of him.

"You mentioned that I'd been requested for the mission, sir?"

"You have. The operative in charge is a Captain Ellington, and for some reason he's very insistent that he travel on your boat."

Michael smiled. "Ah, Jules . . . I mean Captain Ellington. We had occasion to do something like this once before up in the Channel. It's what caused my neck problem in the first place."

"I see," Chadwick replied, still not as engaging as usual.

"Yes, well, it's highly irregular for a nonnaval person to have such latitude in the first place." Michael turned at the harsh sound of Billingham's voice to see that he had finally risen from his chair. "Normally I wouldn't stand for it, but the admiral felt that we should yield in the spirit of cooperation. Still, I insisted on a number of preconditions."

Michael's stomach tightened immediately, sensing that any conditions Billingham set would be bad for him. "Preconditions, sir?"

Chadwick dropped his gaze and stood silent.

"Yes, preconditions. First, it's impossible for you to get to the spot they've picked out for this operation by yourself, so I've insisted that three boats go, not one. We'll take an abbreviated crew on one of the boats so that we can fit as much fuel as possible both below decks and in barrels on top of the deck. That will give us the chance to refuel. The second boat will act as an escort in case a fight breaks out. Anything less is imprudent."

"But don't three boats increase our chance of being detected?" Michael posed this as a question, not a challenge, since Billingham really was correct about it being too far for a normal fuel ration.

"Whether it does or doesn't isn't the issue. What is the issue is that this is a naval operation, and we need to be in control."

The way he said *we* made Michael cringe, and he turned with something of a desperate look to the admiral. But Chadwick refused to meet his gaze.

"I'll be in command of the operation. I'll travel on your boat to make sure this man Ellington doesn't subvert military protocol."

"He'd never do such a thing." Michael started to protest but was quickly shushed by Billingham.

"The decision is already made, Carlyle. I should have gone out with you months ago, anyway. This needs to be done in a regular way—none of the improvising that has become so *de rigueur* of late. Discipline must be maintained."

Michael had never felt so dismayed in all his life, and it must have shown on his face.

"I think it fair to say that in special operations some degree of improvising may be advisable," Admiral Chadwick interjected.

"Of course, but it should be done by someone with proper authority, not a mere lieutenant."

Michael looked at Chadwick imploringly, but there was nothing he could do. It was Billingham's group and his decision to make. Michael looked back at Billingham, only to see a smug smile that made Michael want to reach out and slug the man.

"It will be our honor to have you onboard, sir."

"Yes, I'm sure it will." Michael was certain he detected sarcasm in Billingham's voice, but there was nothing to say in response.

* * *

Syracuse—September 20, 1943

In the nearly two weeks that had passed since his first briefing on the mission, Michael's life had been a constant buzz of activity as he drilled his crew in how best to land men on an enemy shore at night, worked with Billingham and the other captains at coordinating their efforts, and rehearsed with Jules and his team on the specifics of the operation. He felt great empathy for Lieutenant Tipton, the fellow who was to command the fuel ship, since he would be riding on top of a potential inferno. Besides, as the youngest in the group, he felt Billingham's scorn even more than Michael.

The whole operation was complicated by Billingham's lack of recent experience at sea, which meant that he was often giving contradictory or downright foolish commands. He must have had some consciousness of his incompetence, however, because he had become finely attuned to any hint from members of the group who questioned his judgment. Rather than learn from his captains, however, he simply dug his heels in and insisted that they do it his way, often with unfortunate results. Yet when things went amiss he'd fly into a barely controlled rage while insisting that his orders had been misunderstood and that if they all weren't so incompetent, there wouldn't have been a problem. In some ways he was even more explosive than the fuel on Tipton's boat.

Things were even more complicated by the fact that it took Jules about twenty seconds to size Billingham up and to judge him a fool. From that moment forward he'd teased and badgered the man relentlessly. Because Jules was in overall command of the operation, Billingham couldn't directly contradict him, and while Michael found some satisfaction in watching Billingham squirm, in the long run it wasn't worth it because Billingham was just that much harder on his captains and the rest of the crew. Still, Jules was so quick-witted that he could get Billingham tongue-tied in no time, which left him a blustering and frustrated mess, much to the amusement of the crew. It got so bad at one point that Billingham even appealed to Michael for help, asking, "Can't you do something with that incorrigible man? He really is impossible." Michael knew how painful that must have been for Billingham to condescend to ask for help, so he promised that he'd try.

The result hadn't been entirely satisfactory, with Jules rising up indignantly. "Help that buffoon? You've got to be kidding. The man's an idiot and will likely spoil the whole adventure."

"Yes, but he's my commander, and every time you embarrass him, he takes it out on me and my crew."

"Ah! So that's how it is. Well then, I'll try to do better—but I won't tolerate his mistakes if they put the mission at risk."

"That's all I can ask."

Jules was quiet for a few moments, munching reflectively on a stick he'd picked up off the ground. With head lowered, he raised his eyes to catch Michael's gaze. "And if he says something really stupid, you can't expect me to just stand idly by."

"Yes, I can expect it! If I yielded on this point, nothing would change because he's always saying something stupid!" With that they both burst out laughing, and Jules raised his arms above his head as if to surrender.

"Well, it's a crying shame that he has to come along and spoil what would otherwise be a great lark. I'd secretly planned how I was going to get myself in trouble on shore so you'd have to come rescue me again. I know how your mother likes a good hero story, and I had it all plotted out how we could make you the center of attention again."

Michael shook his head ferociously. "I'd leave you there to rot, you blaggard. It's bad enough I have to put up with Billingham, but the two of you are more than anyone should have to endure."

* * *

West of Taranto, Italy—September 22, 1943

"Finally, we can get some peace." David Coleman said this under his breath, but with a ferocity that indicated he was fully fed up. Still, it was potentially insubordinate, so Michael couldn't ignore it.

"Belay that, Mr. Coleman. I won't have you speak that way of a superior officer."

"Even though it's what you feel?"

Michael turned and fixed his gaze squarely on his first officer. "I said stop, or I'll write you up myself." Coleman huffed and turned away.

After a few moments Michael spoke to break the tension. "At least the landings went well. Jenkins reports that Ellington and the Italian stepped right out of the front of the landing boat directly onto dry sand, so they don't even have wet feet to worry about as they shuffle off into the interior. After the trip up, we should be grateful that all is well so far."

The trip up had been marred by a number of high-profile clashes between Jules and Billingham. In one instance, an aircraft had been spotted far off on the horizon with no possibility for a positive identification. It hadn't even bothered itself to come check them out, which meant it either failed to see them completely or didn't care. Yet Billingham had become a bit frantic, muttering that they should turn back to port rather than risk getting caught out in the open seas. Just as Michael had been about to suggest that perhaps they should wait a bit, Jules had exploded that they were not going to cancel the mission because of some stray bird that had the nerve to fly near their position. Billingham was embarrassed and went off about how Jules could order the details of the landing but not the operations of the Navy at sea. It had been ugly, and everyone onboard was tense because of it.

"I didn't expect it to be so dark," Coleman said quietly. If he was wounded by their earlier exchange, his tone of voice indicated that he'd set it aside. "It was amazing how you and Captain Smith managed to get the boats so close into shore without running us aground."

Michael nodded. One of the greatest consolations of the operation was that Jeff Smith was commanding the third boat. Somehow it gave him a lot of comfort to think that such an experienced and coolheaded fellow was protecting his flank.

Besides, Jeff was somehow able to brush aside the commander's tirades as if they meant nothing, which helped Michael to endure. Responding to Coleman's comment, he replied, "Jeff is a smooth operator. I personally think he's the best boat handler in the whole Mediterranean."

"Present company excluded," Coleman said.

"Oh, I know you're good, David, but I still think Jeff has the edge."

"What?" Coleman said in surprise. "You know that I meant you."

Michael smiled, glad that the earlier tension had passed. "I do. But the point is that we're very lucky to have such capable men to help us if we get in trouble. Even Tipton handled himself exceedingly well on the way down. Maneuvering that poor overloaded boat must be miserable, and yet he's stayed with us through every twist and turn as we hugged the coastline to the rendezvous point. I have a good feeling about all this."

"Captain Ellington is certainly a brash fellow, isn't he? And quite young to be a full captain."

Michael smiled again. "He's a character, all right. But from what I gather, he's earned his promotions. While I don't know everything he's done, I know he's made surreptitious landings in France to help organize for the eventual invasion there. He did some kind of secret work in Sicily before the invasion, and now he's cracking open Italy. While he likes to appear as if he's nothing more than a devil-may-care hobbyist, the truth is he's made of steel."

"Well, I hope he and the Italian fellow make their contact and return quickly to the boat tomorrow night so we can all get safely back in port by the next night."

"Even Commander Billingham couldn't take issue with that," Michael said. David turned and looked at him suspiciously, then just shook his head in recognition of what had passed between them.

Michael took a deep breath. The fall air was fragrant and warm. In the dark silence, it was easy to imagine an Italy that wasn't at war, and he realized why this part of the world was so envied for its moderate temperatures and fertile landscape. It was clearly a place better suited for farmers than warriors. "Just think, David, we've brought the war to the heel of Italy. If Jules is successful, we can help gain a foothold on the European continent itself. In no time we can start climbing our way up to Germany and bring this bloody thing to an end."

"No pun intended about the foot, I assume? The shape of Italy and all that."

Michael laughed. "No pun indeed. But it wouldn't have been a bad one had I thought of it, would it?"

Chapter Eleven

WAITING

London

"We're going out for a drink and a bite of dinner. Care to join us?" Marissa Chandler asked Karen.

"Thanks, Marissa, but no. I've got a date tonight."

Marissa looked at her suspiciously. "You have a date? I thought you'd taken yourself out of circulation for Michael's sake."

"Really, Marissa. You're my best friend, but you don't know everything that goes on in my life."

"So who is it?"

Karen was silent.

"Really, there are no men around here for you to be dating. We all know that. So stop pretending and come to supper with us."

"I have a date with the Carlyles," Karen said sternly. "Not that it's any of your business."

"So you *are* staying true to Michael! I knew it."

Karen shook her head. "You know perfectly well that Michael has made no commitments to me whatsoever. The truth is that I think he's still not over you. And I refuse to become serious with a man who has feelings for someone else. It's just that I like the Carlyles and have accepted a dinner invitation while they're in town. That's all."

Now it was Marissa who sighed. She had been the nurse assigned to help Michael back to health after he was seriously wounded in action in the English Channel, an engagement that had earned him the Distinguished Service Cross. Marissa was beautiful and spirited, and Michael had fallen hopelessly in love. At least hopelessly infatuated. She'd reluctantly agreed to date him when he kept pestering her, but from the beginning she found his lifestyle too boring and religious. Eventually she had broken it off. From her point of view, it was fortunate that Karen, another nurse at the hospital where they worked, had shown an interest in Michael. Whether he and Karen realized it or not, they were perfect for each other.

"Karen, Michael is young and foolish. There was never anything between us, and I made that as clear to him as possible."

"Still, while men come easily to you, it's not as easy for me. You're beautiful and witty and bright, and I'm plain and quiet and boring."

"Honestly, Karen, do we have to go through this again? You're anything but plain, and you can carry on a far more interesting conversation than I could ever hope to with people like the Carlyles. You know history and current events and music and literature—all those things that your upbringing provides you. I know popular music and movie stars and where the best pubs are. None of which would be of real interest to Michael or his family. So you just need to shake him a bit and bring him to his senses." She could see that Karen wasn't convinced. "Besides, the last time I saw him, just before he left for Africa, I can promise you that all he wanted to talk about was you."

That rattled Karen. "He did?" Then she blushed and continued with an attempt at sarcasm in her voice. "I mean, I'm sure he did."

Marissa turned more serious. "It's absolutely true. He stopped by the hospital on his way out of town to say good-bye to you, but you were in surgery and couldn't be interrupted. So he stopped and chatted with me for a few minutes. I promise you that after a bit of awkwardness, the only thing he could talk about was how bad he felt that he had to leave and how he hoped you wouldn't worry too much and how he planned to write you a lot. I think he finally realized what he was doing, and it embarrassed him."

Karen was quiet. "Why didn't you tell me that earlier?"

Marissa laughed. "Because I didn't think about it. It's not like he asked me to give you a message or anything." She furrowed her brow. "Or did he? Perhaps he did ask me to tell you good-bye." She tipped her head to the side. "I guess I just forgot. Sorry."

"That's not very thoughtful."

"Oh, really, just a moment ago you were angry with me because Michael isn't interested in you, and now you're upset because he is? You really should just write him a letter and tell him exactly how you feel."

"And you ought to mind your own business!"

Marissa's shoulders slumped. She'd had enough experience with girlfriends in love to realize that Karen was hopeless.

"Well, at the very least you ought to write and tell him that you'd sooner spend your time with people twice your age than go out with your friends to have fun. If that doesn't inspire him, I don't know what will."

"You could come with me to the Carlyles'. I'm sure they'd be glad to see you."

Marissa raised an eyebrow. "I'm not so sure about that. Lady Carlyle wasn't nearly as thrilled as Michael when he started dating me. I felt her glares on more than one occasion, I can promise you. I'm quite sure she didn't think I was good enough for her precious boy."

"She's not at all like that, Marissa, and you know it. She's a kind and gracious woman."

"Oh, let's not argue. The fact is that I have plans and so do you. And I hope you have a wonderful evening. I plan to have a fun one. So we both ought to be happy."

Karen smiled. "I don't have a date tomorrow night, so perhaps I could take a rain check?"

"Tomorrow night it is. Perhaps you can give me an update on how the upper crust lives. You're my little window into that strange and favored world of theirs."

Karen thought of all the sorrows the Carlyles had suffered with the death of their son, the anxiety they felt for Michael, and the tremendous burdens that Lord Carlyle carried as a member of the Cabinet. She could have chided Marissa for being so prejudiced but decided it would do no good.

"Tomorrow then!" Karen said brightly.

Chapter Twelve

A MISSED RENDEZVOUS

Coast of Italy near Taranto—September 1943

Michael glanced at his watch nervously then glanced up at the shore, hoping to see the flash of light that would indicate Jules had made it back to the point of rendezvous. It had been a miserable twenty-four hours waiting for him. First, a German plane came overhead right at midday, and it was very possible that they'd been spotted, even though all three boats were up close to the shore next to some scrub brush and covered with camouflage netting. The fact that the pilot had made more than one pass had been cause for great alarm on the commander's part, and he'd suggested at one point that they should return to port immediately. Michael had formally challenged this decision and was supported by both captains Smith and Tipton. Billingham had backed down but had spent the rest of the day smoldering. Michael hated the tension and couldn't wait for all this to come to an end. He was certain that Billingham would have a harsh evaluation of his performance, but he didn't really care, since he also suspected that the man would never want to go on a boat with him again after this. That hope was all that Michael cared about at this point. Except that now Jules was late. They had a one-hour window in which the rendezvous was to occur, and they were down to the last five minutes.

"It looks as if your fellow isn't going to make it," Billingham said. Michael bristled at the sound of his commander's voice.

"We still have a few minutes, sir."

"Yes, well, as far as I'm concerned, the mission has failed, and it's our duty to return to port now. You will begin making preparations for an immediate departure." The muscles in Michael's stomach tightened up as he wrestled with what to do. He was praying so hard for Jules to flash the signal that his head hurt.

"Perhaps just a few extra minutes, sir? It doesn't appear that there's any immediate danger."

Billingham turned on him ferociously. "Now listen to me, Carlyle. I've put up with that man's insubordination long enough. He will not endanger the lives of all these men any longer. If you could set your personal feelings aside for even a moment, you'd realize that the reason he's late is precisely because there is danger in this area. If he's been captured by the enemy, they have to know that he didn't drop in from the sky, and they will immediately begin to look for us. So we simply have to leave now! I trust you still know how to obey a direct order?"

"Yes, sir," Michael said. As much as he hated to admit it, Billingham was correct in his assessment. Jules wouldn't be late unless something had gone wrong.

Without observing proper protocol, Billingham then turned to Jenkins and ordered him to signal the other boats to make ready to leave. Normally a commander would issue all orders through the ship's captain, but obviously Billingham was taking no chances. Michael looked back to the shore one last time, a sense of panic rising inside his chest as he thought of leaving his friend alone on the shore.

"Well, let's be off then!" Billingham barked.

Michael turned and looked at David Coleman. Even in the dark, he could see that Coleman was pale. No one wanted to leave, but the rendezvous had been missed, and it was time to go. Yet he could also see from the faces of his men that they would all gladly wait awhile longer if it were up to them.

"Well, then, Mr. Coleman, prepare to make way, all ahead slow." Fearing that Billingham would countermand this order, Michael added, "So that we don't make any unnecessary noise until we're well away from the coast."

"Aye, sir, all ahead slow!"

Just as the engines started to turn there was a flash of light up on the brow of the hill well above the waterline. There was also the popping sound of gunfire at some distance.

"It's them, sir! It's Captain Ellington and the Italian!" Coleman said.

"All stop!" Michael shouted, his heart racing. Even though Ellington and the Italian weren't at the water's edge, it was obvious that they were attempting the rendezvous. "Prepare to lower the boat!" Michael was racing to the back of the aft deck as if to will the boat into the water himself.

He was so anxious that it didn't register for a moment when he heard the command, "Belay that order! All ahead full!"

He turned in a fury on Billingham. "What are you talking about?! Captain Ellington has made the proper signal and is in distress. It's our duty to rescue him right now!"

"He missed the rendezvous and has placed the flotilla in danger. We will leave now!"

Michael turned and looked at the helmsman, who looked at him helplessly. The man had received two contradictory orders and didn't know what to do. He then turned to David Coleman who returned his look through frightened eyes. No one knew what to do, even though it was clear what they wanted to do.

Michael had never felt his heart pound so hard in his chest. Not in any of the battles he had fought had he felt such panic. He had received a direct order and was required by law to obey it. But he also knew that military honor demanded that he assist Jules. His own honor demanded it as well. After just a moment's pause, his heart calmed down, and he felt his hands go icy cold. For better or worse he had made his decision.

"Mr. Coleman, you will obey my order. Commander Billingham is in error. We will not leave these men who have made a legitimate signal. Do you understand?"

"Sir?" Coleman said tentatively.

"How dare you!" Billingham screamed. "This is mutiny. I will not stand for it."

"Mr. Coleman, I will take a boat personally to the shore and attempt to rescue our people. You will give me twenty minutes. If I'm not back by that point, you will submit yourself to Commander Billingham's orders and carry them out with precision. In the meantime you are not responsible for the choice I have made. It is my decision alone. Do I make myself clear?" It was stated as a question, but Michael's tone made it abundantly clear that it was an order.

Coleman hesitated for just a moment, but when Billingham tried to speak, Coleman quickly replied to Michael, "I understand your orders, sir. You have twenty minutes." He then turned to face Billingham directly, as if to make it clear that he would not be obeyed if he didn't allow the twenty minutes.

Michael could sense that the rest of the crew was with him. "Make a signal to Captain Smith telling him what's happening. I want it on record that this is my doing, not that of any member of the crew."

Finally, Michael turned to face Billingham, wondering what he would do. He expected to be blasted by the man, but instead he saw him noticeably relax and then smile. "Very good, Carlyle. You have just earned yourself a court-martial. Mutiny in time of war is the worst crime that one can commit. There are no mitigating circumstances here, and you will go to jail, perhaps to a firing squad." Usually at this point, a commander who has been challenged will offer the miscreant a chance to repent, but Billingham made no such offer now. It was clear that he wanted to bring Michael up on charges.

With a cold and dispassionate voice, Michael replied, "The worst crime you can commit in time of war is to abandon your comrades, particularly when under fire. Now if you'll excuse me, I must be off."

He hadn't thought about how he would get to shore all by himself. He clearly couldn't do it alone. "I will need a volunteer . . ."

Sublieutenant Jenkins stepped forward. "I'd like to go with you, sir."

Michael turned to Billingham. "If I accept Mr. Jenkins's offer, will you promise me you'll hold him harmless?"

"I will not make any promises to a mutineer!"

Michael turned to Coleman. "You'll see to it that Jenkins is protected?"

"Yes, sir."

"Good, then let's go, Jenkins!"

He would have preferred to tie that business down better, but there simply was no time, so he and Jenkins jumped down in the boat and accepted the line when it was thrown to them. "Good luck, sir!" one of the men called. Another added, "We'll be ready to pull you back in." Michael took a deep breath and held on as the little launch tore off through the water at its best speed.

When they arrived near the beach, Michael had Jenkins slow the motor down as he strained to hear anything from the shore. Unfortunately what he heard was the sound of gunfire and a crashing sound in the thick underbrush. "Jules! Jules! We're over here!" he shouted when he saw two dark shapes emerge near the shore. There was a pinging sound in the water as a string of bullets sent up a row of splashes.

"Glad to see you, mate. Sorry we're late!" Jules and the Italian fellow came floundering out in the surf and then dove into the boat, helped by Michael's strong arms.

"Get us out of here, Mr. Jenkins!" Michael was gratified to hear the little motor whine as it spun up to maximum revolutions.

"Do you always have to be so dramatic, Jules?"

Jules didn't laugh. He was breathless from the run, and as Michael scooted closer, he could see that Jules had a bandage wrapped around his arm. The Italian fellow had also been wounded.

"Are you all right?" Michael asked.

"I think so," Jules said tentatively.

"What happened?"

"I don't know for sure. We met with the mayor as planned, but it turns out that there isn't really much he can do. I'd hoped to find a well-established network that could help me get up to Rome on our next visit, but this fellow really doesn't have any useful connections. He just wanted to be on record as supporting the Allies when the landing comes so that he could keep his position. It was a huge waste of time. Then on the way back, we happened across a German sentry who sounded the alarm. I don't think it was a trap set up by the mayor, although I can't be sure. I think it was just bad luck."

"So all of this was for nothing?"

Jules was about to reply when they were interrupted by Jenkins. "Sir! The boats—they're leaving!"

Michael whirled to face forward and was stunned to see the white tail in the water that showed all three boats at full acceleration—and they were heading directly out to sea.

Michael was speechless, but Jules had the presence of mind to let out a few obscenities before getting around to asking what was going on.

"I don't know—Billingham wanted to leave you, but I left Coleman in charge. He wouldn't abandon us." At least Michael hoped he wouldn't. But they were clearly being left behind.

"Off the port side, sir!" Michael turned yet again at Jenkins's new interruption. There in the distance was a single German E-boat making its way directly for them. Now it was clear. Billingham had somehow gained control and ordered everyone out of the area. The four of them were now all alone in the ocean with German soldiers on the shore and a German boat closing in quickly. They were doomed.

"Your boats didn't even put up a fight. Is that normal?"

Michael was humiliated that this question came from the Italian. He tried to think of something to say in response, but no words came to mind. He was both frightened and sickened at what had happened.

"How can he do this?" Jules asked with an air of disbelief.

Michael shook his head a few times as he tried to collect his thoughts and reconcile their new situation. Finally, he let out a small laugh. "At least I don't have to face a court-martial. At least not right away."

Jules and the Italian looked at him, trying to figure out if he'd gone crazy but were startled to see that he was quite serious.

"I suspect we'll have plenty of time for me to explain later. In the meantime I need some white fabric that I can wave. I'd sooner be a prisoner of war than a casualty. With that, Michael unbuttoned his shirt, stripped off his undershirt, and did what every British officer dreads most—he started waving the white flag of surrender high above his head.

As the German boat slowed on its approach, he looked down at Jules with a wan expression on his face. "Not exactly my best day in the Service." And with that he braced himself for what was to come as a prisoner of war.

Chapter Thirteen

PRISONERS OF WAR

Bari, Italy—September 1943

Michael grimaced as the German officer slapped Jules sharply across the side of his head. Jules stumbled and fell to his knees, only to be roughly hoisted back up on his feet by two German thugs who lifted him by his arms. This provoked an anguished groan since his wounded right arm had not been properly bandaged and was soaked in blood. It was obvious that he was in great pain, which made it all the more infuriating that the Germans continued to badger him about the purpose of their mission. If they wanted to pick on someone, why not choose Michael or one of the others who had their full wits about them? That's why they tormented Jules—he was the one most likely to break down in exhaustion and give them what they wanted.

When Jules stumbled a second time, Michael couldn't take it any longer and lunged in Jules's direction to try to protect him. He didn't make it far, though, before the butt end of a German rifle smashed into his face, sending him sprawling to the floor with a bloody nose.

"Why don't you leave him alone?" Michael shouted. "He's injured and needs medical attention. Even an idiot can see that!" This earned Michael a kick in the ribs from the officer conducting the interrogation.

"I know what an idiot is. Hardly a wise thing to call me given your present circumstance." Michael was shocked at the German's good English.

Michael struggled to his feet. "My apologies. But Captain Ellington is wounded. The Geneva Conventions require you to offer medical assistance. He may not survive if you don't." There was a desperate sound to Michael's voice.

"He will receive care. We Germans are civilized people, after all."

While Michael had his doubts about that, he wisely held his tongue. "Thank you."

The officer said something in German to his two aides, and they took Jules from the room, presumably to receive the treatment he needed. Jules managed to catch Michael's eye in time to convey a sense of gratitude. Michael was relieved but knew that the fury of this officer would now focus on him. He mentally braced for the blow to come.

"You are an officer. You will stay with me. These two will go to separate quarters."

"I must protest . . . Sublieutenant Jenkins is a junior officer."

"Don't trifle with me," the German said sharply. "They will go." And with that, Jeremy and the Italian were also taken from the room, leaving the German officer and one enlisted German soldier. Not that it mattered that there weren't more. The enlisted man could easily have played the role of Goliath in a play, and Michael winced as he saw the man flex his arm muscles by slapping a truncheon against his right thigh.

"Ah, you see that Johannes here rather aches to have some fun?"

"I frankly expected better of you," Michael said defiantly. He did not add, "since you're a civilized people."

"Don't judge us too harshly, Lieutenant Carlyle. Our Italian allies have just sold us out, and we now find ourselves obligated to defend their miserable country from your invasion." Before Michael could say anything, the officer laughed. "Ah, to prevent them from being liberated. That's how you would phrase it, isn't it?"

"Now, then, Lieutenant, let's see what we can find out from you. It's obvious that you commanded one of the torpedo boats that left in such a cowardly rush. Frankly, I would have expected more from the British navy."

Michael bit his lip but did not reply. The smile that darted across the German's face made it clear that he'd scored the point he wanted to.

"It must be difficult to be abandoned like this. You, a noble warrior, now out of the war for the duration. Of course, it may be good luck for you since you'll probably pick up the German language in prison that will serve you well when the Fatherland wins this war."

Michael wanted so badly to take the man's bait—to challenge the absurd assumption that Germany would win. With America and Russia in the war as allies of England, it seemed inevitable that the Allies would win eventually, even though the fighting would become more costly as Germany withdrew to more defensible battle lines. But to start an argument now would serve no purpose, so he said nothing.

"Now, let me see," the German said easily. "Oh, I've made a terrible oversight by not introducing myself. Please forgive me." He smiled at Michael. "I am Captain Edwin Mantz of the Kriegsmarine—a fellow naval officer." He gave Michael a crisp salute, which he felt obligated to return. In spite of his inferior position, Michael relaxed a bit, desperately relieved that he did not hear the acronym "SS." He knew enough about the German military to know that an SS officer would not be so charming.

"And you are?"

"Lieutenant Michael Carlyle, Royal Navy." He'd disclosed this numerous times before in the interview, but clearly there was a new tactic taking shape, so he had to go along.

"Carlyle. A very prominent name in England. You're not by chance related to Lord Carlyle, a member of the British War Cabinet?"

Michael's knees buckled, and he felt the color drain from his face.

"So you are related to him! What a delightful opportunity that we should meet like this. It's not often that I get to meet a member of the aristocracy."

"What do you know of Lord Carlyle?" Michael asked tentatively.

"Know of him? I met him when I attended Eton. He came and taught one of my classes. A very impressive person. You should be proud of your father."

Michael did his best not to react, but he knew that his face was far too expressive not to convey that Mantz had guessed his relationship correctly.

"Of course there's not much he can do for you now."

"I wouldn't want him to. I'm a British naval officer, and that alone should assure my safety while in your custody."

Mantz laughed easily. "Of course it does. Still, it is something that we should have so much in common, don't you think? Undoubtedly you attended your father's college."

"I attended the Naval College," Michael said sullenly.

"Ah, a professional. Well, then, you realize that there are certain questions I must ask you. And I realize that all you're required to divulge is your name, rank, and identification number. And we both realize that I will not be content with that answer, which will leave us at an impasse. And then something will have to be done to break the impasse." At this Mantz cast a glance at the brute standing to his left. "So, shall we start the ritual?"

Michael pursed his lips and waited.

"Let's make this easy. It really isn't so complicated. The British and Americans have taken Sicily. You've landed troops on the western side of the Italian peninsula, and soon you plan to invade on our lonely little shore. Your Captain Ellington is a Royal Commando who was sent ashore for a reconnaissance mission, and you were transporting him. Now you are here with very little information that will prove useful to us since the places you can attack are so limited. So it's not as though you hold any surprises. Further, knowing that you might be captured, your commanding officers took great pains to shield you even more than usual from any operational plans aside from the specifics of this failed mission." Mantz clasped his hands contentedly and smiled. "How did I do, Lieutenant?"

"Since you are so confident of your answers, why even bother with me?"

"A very good question. Yet, certainly you can understand that my superiors will want to make certain that whatever meager information you do possess has been fully extracted. After all, we want to repulse your country's attack as efficiently as possible. Each German life is precious."

Michael was bowled over by the man's charm. The fact that he'd lived in England meant that Mantz had a natural advantage in this little "ritual," since he could intuit how Michael would respond. Which meant he knew he would not respond. Yet still Mantz would try.

"The sad part is that you really should have attempted an escape. You were so close, and three British boats to one German should have carried the day. And yet they left you. That is so puzzling."

Michael burned at this. By this point he'd been ridiculed by the Italian and now the Germans, and still he was the one who would be charged with insubordination.

"I'm sure there's a story associated with that. Perhaps you'll share it with me at a future visit." Mantz smiled again at Michael's confusion. "Yes, Lieutenant, that means that we're done for today. I hope you're not disappointed that Johannes didn't get his way with you. Johannes certainly is."

Michael found himself wanting to thank the man, which was about the most stupid thing he could possibly consider. So he stayed quiet again.

"That will be all, Lieutenant. Johannes will show you to your room. I look forward to chatting with you later." At that,

Captain Mantz walked over to his desk and sat down to a pile of papers. Michael turned to go with Johannes. But just as he was about to leave the room, Mantz said quietly, "By the way, Lady Carlyle is a very beautiful woman. An American as I recall."

This so startled Michael that he couldn't mask his expression. To have this man speak of his mother so casually was quite horrifying.

"She accompanied your father both to the class he taught and again at our graduation. Our conversation just brought back memories. It's probably very hard on her now that your father is dealing with so many sensitive issues and is likely away from home a great deal of the time."

Michael should have stayed quiet, but he couldn't let it pass. "I'm sure that I have no idea what my father is dealing with. He certainly has enough integrity that he wouldn't compromise himself by sharing anything with me. Besides, I haven't been home for a very long time now."

"Of course not. Still, when we meet next time I'll have more information about your service." Mantz smiled again and then dropped his eyes back to his papers.

Michael was sick to his stomach. Obviously his father had been very open in the classroom in talking about the family. Mantz was using everything at his disposal to unnerve Michael, and unfortunately it was working. After leaving the interrogation room, Johannes motioned for him to go down a long, dark hall. For a moment Michael had the sinking feeling that perhaps Johannes would take advantage of him here, out of sight. But as they approached the end of the corridor, Johannes shoved Michael roughly to the right and then forced him through a narrow metal door into a gloomy room with a single light bulb hanging from the ceiling. There was no window, and the air was stuffy and oppressive. He listened with dread as the door swung closed on its ancient hinges and then abruptly stopped with a clanging sound. He heard Johannes lock the door and then rattle it a few times to make certain it was secure. And then there was silence.

Michael slumped down on the metal cot, swung his legs up onto the bed, and closed his eyes. He gently rubbed his nose to ease the pain and was startled by how much it had swelled in the fifteen or twenty minutes that had passed since he'd been assaulted. Or was it an hour? Whatever it was, he'd never been so discouraged in all his life.

Chapter Fourteen

A DIPLOMATIC MISSION

Number 10 Downing Street—October 1943

"Philip, I understand there are some problems with our American guests."

"Nothing too serious, Prime Minister. In fact, given the numbers of GIs who have landed, things have gone remarkably well."

"But you wouldn't have requested this interview if something wasn't amiss." Churchill smiled, but it was obvious that he didn't have a lot of time for any banter.

"Yes, sir. The number of Americans yet to arrive exceeds those who are here already. The strain on the local communities to provide services is severe. The problem is that the local American commanders lack discretion to respond to community needs without first seeking permission from Washington. The time involved leads to frustration on the part of our local military and civilian leaders and irritation for the Americans when we show our frustration."

"So what is the solution?"

"We need to get the Pentagon to loosen the reins on their local commanders."

Churchill took a long drag on his cigar. "Do you think, Philip, that in similar circumstances our own people would accuse us of imposing too much interference from London?"

Philip laughed. "I'm sure everyone thinks the home secretaries are meddlesome."

"So why do you think they're so paranoid in Washington that they overregulate in this area?"

"I'm sure that with hundreds of millions of dollars crossing the Atlantic along with their soldiers, they want to keep some control, which is reasonable. But the problems we're speaking of are so modest that they shouldn't cause concern. I can't think of a single instance where Washington has failed to approve the local recommendation. From my point of view, the current situation is simply inefficient."

"So what is it you want from me, Philip?"

"We need someone to have a conversation with the Americans. General Eisenhower is aware of the problem but feels he needs political cover to resolve it. Unfortunately it seems that there's something of a struggle between the civilians at the U.S. Department of Defense and the military leaders at the Pentagon, with each attempting to assert authority. I was hoping you might raise the issue with the American ambassador or through one of your other political channels."

"You're a member of the Cabinet. Why don't you go?"

"Go?"

"To Washington. If the problem is timeliness, I can promise you that my raising the issue with the ambassador, who will raise it with the State Department, who will raise it with the Department of Defense, who will raise it with the Joint Chiefs of Staff, who will raise it with their bureaucracy will simply increase your frustration, not alleviate it. So why don't you go over there and work this thing out?"

"But I wouldn't know where to start. I have no experience in diplomacy."

Churchill smiled. "Perhaps I can help with that. Why don't I arrange for you to meet with President Roosevelt first? After that, I can assure you that the doors of Washington will be open to you."

Now Philip staggered. "The president?"

"You'd like him. A very dynamic fellow."

Philip shook his head. "I should have known that this would come back to me—and that you'd throw me into the deep end of the swimming pool."

"You know how to swim, Philip. I'm not worried about that. Besides, no one understands the issues better than you." He puffed on his cigar for a moment. "Washington is beautiful this time of year. It will do you good to get away."

Philip pondered. It was frightening to think about entering a whole new arena like foreign diplomacy, but also exciting. "I'll go, sir, as long as I can take my wife with me. She needs a trip as badly as I do."

Churchill scowled his famous frown. "I don't know about that. You'd travel on the *Queen Mary* to make a fast crossing, so it would be comfortable enough. But the ship's so fast that it goes without an escort—none of the military ships can keep up. The benefit of that is that she can also outrun any German U-boat, which is her greatest source of safety. But if a U-boat happens to lie in her path, it could be disastrous. Are you sure you want to expose Claire to that?"

"No, sir, I'm not sure. But perhaps you'd leave that up to us. Should she decide to go, we would need your clearance for civilian passage."

Churchill yielded with a smile. "She is adventurous, isn't she? I hope you'll both give my regards to the president. Hopefully Mrs. Roosevelt will be there as well. If so, you'll be in for some of the best conversation of your lives."

Philip grinned. "Thank you, sir. I'll do my best to resolve these issues."

"Don't do your best, Philip. Just do whatever is needed to get the job done."

Philip tipped his hand to his head in a modest salute. "To a job completed, then." With that he excused himself, feeling buoyed in spirit yet again from his brief interaction with Churchill.

* * *

"There's an interesting story to the naming of the *Queen Mary*," Philip said amiably to Claire. They were standing at the railing of the ship as it steamed out of the Port of Southampton on the southwest coast of England. A strong westerly breeze blew in their faces. Philip was always fascinated by this particular harbor because of the ancient stonework fortress that had been built to repel invaders from the Continent many hundreds of years earlier. It just showed that war was something of the natural state of affairs for Europe from time immemorial. The problem in the twentieth century was that the means of killing people had so improved that modern wars killed tens of millions, rather than thousands. It was all a bit depressing, really.

"An interesting story about the ship?"

Philip shook his head, amazed that he'd distracted himself in midsentence. "Yes, the story. As you know, the Cunard White Star Line was famous for naming all its ships in words that ended in "ia," like *Britannia*, *Lusitania*, and *Mauritania*. When they laid this ship down, they wanted it to be the grandest vessel ever built and so wanted a name that would be appropriate for such an impressive ship. So the president of Cunard asked for a meeting with the king to seek his permission to use the name they had in mind. Unfortunately, the words he chose led to a far different outcome than that which he was seeking. After describing just how elegant and powerful the ship would be, he said something to the effect of, 'And so, sir, we'd like your permission to name the ship after the greatest queen in English history.' King George was very flattered and replied, 'Why, thank you; I'm sure my wife will be pleased to have her name attached to the ship.' Of course the king's wife is Queen Mary, not really the greatest queen in history. What the president of Cunard had intended was to name the ship the *Queen Victoria*, to continue the naming convention. But once the king had preempted the name, there was nothing to do but abandon the old convention and launch the ship as the *Queen Mary*. And now we're standing on her deck."

Claire laughed. "I think it's quite romantic that King George would pay his wife such a lovely tribute."

"I wish I could persuade Cunard to name a ship after you too, my dear, but unfortunately Claire doesn't rhyme with either Britannia or Mary, so I'm afraid we're really out of luck."

"What? So what good are you then?" They laughed, happy in each other's company.

"So tell me again how all of this is going to work?" Claire asked.

"Well, first we dock in New York City, where we'll spend a week meeting with our embassy officials, talking with a number of American banks that are lending our government substantial amounts of money, and so forth. And of course there will be time in the evenings to attend some concerts, plays, or whatever else strikes your fancy. My understanding is that New York is still well illuminated at night—not at all like London with our blackout curtains and air raid sirens."

"All right, and then we go to Washington and . . ."

"And you have to bear up under the burden of going to the White House. I know it makes you uncomfortable, but Churchill was insistent. I thought we might get a reprieve when it looked like the president would be out of town, but his trip got cancelled—I think because of his health—so we're on again."

Claire sighed. "I didn't know I was signing up for this when I married you."

"Can you forgive me?"

She squeezed up close to him. "I suppose. You're troublesome but somehow irresistible. Seeing you in black tie and tails at the embassy dinner the other evening . . ."

"Thank heavens my good looks account for something. It makes no sense your infatuation would be based on personality."

"No, certainly not. Now why don't you take me to dinner? It's been a long time since I've been on the *Queen*—is it *Victoria* or *Mary?*—and I'm looking forward to four days of being just a little spoiled."

"A fine idea!" Philip extended his arm, and off they went to the grand dining salon.

* * *

Washington, DC—October 1943

"So, what did you like best about New York City?" Philip asked his wife.

Claire was thoughtful. "Broadway and Central Park. I loved looking at the buildings on Fifth Avenue and Central Park South through the brilliant colors of the fall leaves in the park." She paused. "And Reuben's, of course!"

"Ah, yes, Reuben's on Broadway. That would be for the cheesecake, I assume."

"Not just any old cheesecake, my dear—New York cheesecake— the best there is."

"And the part of our New York visit you liked least?"

"That's easy—the shadows."

"Shadows?"

"Yes, all those tall buildings that don't let light reach the street. I'd hate to spend that much time living in shadows."

"But London's all right?"

"London doesn't have hundred-story skyscrapers, Philip."

"Ah, yes. And what about staying at the Waldorf-Astoria?"

"You know I really don't fit in there. I know we can afford it, but I'm really still a small-town girl. All that fussing around with staff is more annoying than convenient. I'd just as soon make my own bed."

Philip shook his head. She was a hard person to impress. "Was there anything you liked about it?"

"The flowers and the chandeliers—the vase in the main lobby must be six feet tall and filled with the most spectacular flower arrangement I've ever seen. New Yorkers have a great deal of class in that regard."

"So overall you liked our time in New York?"

She nodded. "What about you?"

"The thing I liked best has nothing to do with the city itself, but rather to be in a place where the war isn't threatening. The mood is so different from London. Over there we're all hunkered down and ready to endure the very worst. In New York City people are hardly aware of the war, other than in a theoretical way. And the food! Did you see how much food they have? Even in the poorest neighborhoods the delis and green grocers had an abundance of fresh food. In some ways I envy them, and in others I resent them."

Claire chose not to respond. This was one of the few times when her American citizenship came into conflict with her British residency. It wasn't America's fault that they hadn't been under direct attack, so how else could the people here behave? And wasn't it American farms that had been feeding the British people for the past few years? On the other hand, she was living through the war in Britain and realized just how little the people had and how much they were suffering.

Gazing out the window of the Baltimore & Ohio passenger train, she saw the passing countryside still rich with late fall leaves from the hardwood forests that extended hundreds of miles to the west. Practically speaking, it meant that you couldn't really see anything from the passenger window except an endless corridor of trees as the train worked its way through New Jersey, Pennsylvania, and Maryland. It was so different from the wide open landscapes of Arizona.

"I also liked the sky in New York," she said.

"The sky?"

"As we walked through Central Park the sky was bright, clear, and blue. And the wind was crisp and fresh. The days are so often overcast in England. I guess I didn't realize how much I miss a clear sky."

Philip scooted closer and took her hand. "Thank you for coming with me to England. I know it's often hard on you. But I have so many obligations there."

Claire smiled. "I don't mind, really. The old saying really is true that home is where the heart is. And my heart is with you."

"Next stop, Pennsylvania Station near the Capitol. End of the line!" Philip and Claire looked up at the conductor who had just made this announcement.

"And now the White House." She looked at Philip sternly. "It's a darn good thing I like you, because I wouldn't go through this for anyone else."

He smiled and kissed her on the cheek.

Chapter Fifteen

NORTHBOUND
TO GERMANY

Bari, Italy—October 1943

"Schnell!" The German pointed his rifle at Michael and lifted the barrel a couple of times to indicate that he should stand up. Michael did so as quickly as his stiff limbs would let him. In nearly ten days of total isolation, he'd grown weak from inactivity, even though he forced himself to exercise at least once each day. With his watch taken from him and no hint of natural light to guide him, it was easy to mix daylight and darkness, particularly since the lonesome little bulb burned constantly through the period, so he wasn't exactly sure of when each day had passed.

At first Michael had resented the light bulb, but eventually came to think of it as a friend. He started talking to it on occasion, mostly as a passive listener as he tried to pass the hours. But on one occasion he'd tried to engage it in dialogue, asking about its family history back to Edison. It was a joke, of course, but when he realized that he was the only one to laugh, he started feeling a bit creepy to think he had come to that point. So he stopped talking to the light bulb and instead began rehearsing the various military protocols for the handling of his motor torpedo boat, the displacement of the engine, the top speed, the recommended maneuvers for various situations, and so forth. He was surprised at how much he could recall when not distracted by other concerns and came to relish the privacy—at least some of the time.

But most of the time he wondered why he was being left alone and when the next interrogation would come. He lived in dread of it, both for fear that they would hurt him and also that Mantz would trick him into saying something that might have military value. He practiced time and again at ways to resist him. Now it seemed the time had arrived, and he gulped as he approached the guard at the door. But instead of being taken to the interrogation room, the guard directed him to an open door where the sunlight dazzled Michael. He winced in pain as his eyes tried to adjust to the sudden brightness, but the guard jammed his weapon in Michael's back as he goaded him outside. Once clear of the door, he was overwhelmed by the amazingly wonderful smell of fresh air, and in spite of his anxiety he felt an enormous sense of relief. Of course he hadn't been given the chance to take a bath or otherwise groom himself, and so he was very aware of how filthy he was. But at least he could breathe here, and it felt wonderful.

He wanted to shield his eyes from the glare, but the guard wouldn't let him, so he had to stumble forward with his eyes almost completely closed. Of course he had no idea where he was going, and for just a moment he had a feeling of panic come over him that maybe they were taking him out to shoot him. It was a wild thought, but he'd heard of the Germans doing that and worse in countries they had captured. Before he could really think through all of that, he found himself coming up to the back of an old truck, where the guard motioned Michael to get in. This created its own anxiety, but there was nothing to be done but to obey, so cautiously he raised the canvas curtain and stepped into the darkness.

"Watch the light, Carlyle! Don't you realize our eyes are sensitive from being in here more than half an hour waiting for you?"

"Jules? Is that you?"

"Always rather brilliant when taken by surprise, aren't you?"

"And always sarcastic no matter what the circumstance, Jules?"

Even though he couldn't see well because his eyes were still smarting from the brief trip in the sun, he followed the sound of Jules's voice and sat down next to his old friend. Before Jules could say anything, Michael said, "Go ahead and be sarcastic. Just to hear the sound of a human voice is consoling—even if it's yours."

"Nice . . . you one-up me at my own game."

Michael turned, his eyes now adjusted to the darkness. "Seriously, I'm glad you're okay. I've been alone all this time, and I couldn't help but worry that you'd died or something. As irritating as you are, I didn't want to be alone."

"I missed you too." Jules gave him a small punch on the arm.

Michael jumped as the tarp was opened, and another prisoner came tumbling in.

"Ouch," was the rather graceful expletive that accompanied this, followed by, "Who's there?"

"It's me, Jenkins. I'm here with Captain Ellington."

"Captain Carlyle? Is that you?" The relief in Jeremy Jenkins's voice was evident. "Are you all right, sir?"

"I'm all right. What about you?"

"It was hard. They interrogated me on four separate occasions. It got pretty rough, but I didn't tell them anything of value."

"I just don't understand," Michael said. "After our first meeting, I never went back. Captain Mantz acted as if they were going to pursue me, but nothing came of it. And yet they went after a junior officer." His words trailed off.

"It's because they were too busy with me," Jules said quietly. Michael turned and looked at him and for the first time noticed his black eyes and bruised face.

"Indeed they did. Are you all right? What about your arm?"

"They stitched it up without any anesthetic. I had the good sense to pass out when it started to get really horrible, so at least they couldn't weasel anything out of me during that episode. But it didn't stop them from trying the next ten or fifteen times."

Michael was silent. He somehow felt guilty for his easy treatment. "So how badly did they hurt you?"

"Worse than I expected, but better than my commando trainers prepared us for. Eventually I had to feed them some non-key information just to stay alive, but they weren't able to get anything meaningful. I think towards the end they realized they wouldn't but kept going just for the fun of it." His breathing had picked up at this point. "I mean how much is there to know? We're in the process of invading on multiple fronts, there are only so many places we can land troops, and it's obvious to anyone with a map where those places are. So they really didn't need me, yet still they disfigured me." Jules was silent for a time. "The sleep deprivation is the worst. I spent some interminable period of time sitting in just my underwear on a three-legged stool. Whenever I'd fall asleep and fall off the stool, they'd kick me until I woke up and climbed back on the stool. That came to an end when I was too woozy to balance on the stool."

"I'm sorry, Jules. I wish I could have done something."

The three of them sat quietly for a time, each pondering their own ordeals of the previous days. "I still don't understand why they left me alone . . ."

"It's because of your name, Michael. Mantz talked to me about it. It seems your parents made quite a favorable impression on him. Perhaps he left you alone out of deference to them."

"I hardly think so, Jules. No matter how much he liked my father, he would still go after me if he thought it would serve a purpose. I get the feeling he'd torture his own father if the Nazis asked him to."

Jules nodded. "Well then, there are a number of other possibilities. For example, perhaps it was insurance on Mantz's part. Your father is a cabinet minister, you know."

"What has that got to do with me?"

Jules laughed. "The Germans aren't naive. They can see that the Allies are on the Continent with ever-increasing strength. Perhaps our little rottenführer figures that if Germany loses the war, he doesn't want to be on record as having abused a prominent person."

"Rottenführer?"

"A minor official. It's my way of diminishing the captain's status. It was a game I played with myself while they were working me over. I thought of all the demeaning titles I could think of to reduce their importance. It was kind of fun to listen to what they said in German—things like, 'So where do you want to go to dinner when we're done?' and 'We're not going to get anything out of this fellow, you realize that?' Of course anything sounds ominous when spoken in German, so I'm sure they thought I was over there trembling in fear at the nefarious things they must be plotting to do to me."

"But you don't speak German." Michael was waiting for the punch line, whatever it was.

"Actually, I do. After our escape in France earlier in the war, my superiors decided I wasn't a lot of use to them with English as my only language, so they put me in an intensive German language training school. I couldn't do anything as complex as ordering German pastries, for example, but I recognize a handful of military terms and at least some general words of casual conversations."

Michael shook his head in wonderment. "You never cease to surprise, Jules. I guess I've never thought of the torturers. In some ways, you make them sound human. It's easier to think of them as monsters."

"That's just it, Michael. They *are* human—in so many ways, just like you and me. Yet they do such horrible things to people. I find it almost incomprehensible that they're able to treat the job of torture like any other sort of routine task, such as being a clerk or school teacher. Can you imagine what goes on in their minds? 'I'm getting hungry. I hope this fellow breaks pretty soon so I can get something to eat.' WHACK! 'I hope my wife isn't angry that I'm late getting home.' WHACK! 'I wish this Englishman would crack just enough to give us something useful.' WHACK, WHACK! 'Oh, well, another ten minutes or so, and he'll pass out from pain, and then I can get a bite to eat and go play cards with my friends.' WHACK and KICK, followed by screams from the victim. 'Good, maybe we're finally getting somewhere.' It's just amazing that they can be like that. Even worse to think that we might do the same thing if the roles were reversed."

Michael was stunned. He'd never experienced this side of Jules before. As he tried to absorb the enormity of what his friend had just said, he decided there was no answer. What was it in human beings that allowed them to be so abusive of another person? Certainly it had something to do with acting under authority, as if orders somehow exonerated the perpetrator and made it appropriate for them to behave that way. He hoped the British didn't treat their prisoners that way.

After a pause, he said quietly to Jules, "You said there was a third possibility as to why they didn't interrogate me further?"

"Ah, yes. Let's see, number one possibility is that they like your parents, number two is that our little commander wants to be treated well if we win the war. That leaves number three, all right."

"Which is?"

"Which is that you're simply too boring to waste time on. I mean, think about it: if you had your choice of beating information out of me or talking with you, what would you choose?"

Michael laughed. "After talking to myself the last ten days, I suspect I'd pick you. I even bored myself. And since you have an unparalleled skill for talking endlessly without saying anything of real importance, the Germans were probably fascinated by your thought process. Either that or they get paid by the number of words they get the prisoner to speak." Michael said this good naturedly but quickly became subdued when Jules didn't respond.

"I didn't mean to offend you, Jules. I know that what you went through was terrible."

"Don't worry—I was the one who teased you. But there's truth to what you say. I had this feeling that I was just an interesting diversion to these people. Just think of their situation. They've all been trained in all these great interrogation techniques and haven't ever had anyone to try them out on. Then we come along. It was probably the most exciting part of the war for them, and they didn't want to waste it all in one setting. Now I get to live with the consequences of their entertainment, perhaps for the rest of my life."

Michael realized that Jules was concerned about his face. It was possible that bones had been broken and that without proper medical attention they would never heal exactly right. Jules was a very good looking man who took pride in his appearance.

"Ah, well. It's over for now, and I lived through it. Unfortunately there's probably more coming." That left everyone feeling subdued and quiet for a time.

"Well, the practical value of my eavesdropping is to learn that the Germans are moving us up to a place called Foggia, where we'll be transferred to a railroad train of some kind to go to a prison camp in Germany. Towards the end I could sense the anxiety they felt at having British operations in this area. While the main brunt is being felt in western Italy, these guys are still going to have to hold their own over here, and without a lot of troops. I wish I could get to a radio to let my contacts know how precarious I think the Germans' position is." He sighed.

Michael didn't know what to say. In fact, he was worried that Jules had spoken too loudly and that perhaps the Germans were somehow listening in to see what they could pick up from casual conversation. Then, without warning, he was blinded yet again as the tarp was thrown open and yet another body came tumbling in. He could see well enough to recognize their Italian guide. This man looked far worse than even Jules. Apparently the Germans didn't take kindly to having an ally turn on them.

Michael waited for the tarp to be closed as before but was startled to see a German officer step into the opening. With the sun behind him, all they could make out was his silhouette. "Well, gentlemen," he said in broken English, "you're going to leave us now. For you the war is over. You have the honor of going to the Fatherland, where you'll sit out the days while we crush your comrades' advances. Then, after five or ten years at hard labor for espionage, you'll assume your role as noncitizens in the Third Reich. That's not really a great position to be in, by the way—a noncitizen. And of course all this assumes that you survive." The man laughed a humorless laugh. "None of this applies to this Italian swine. He'll only go as far as Bologna, where he'll be executed. Treason is not to be tolerated." The Italian groaned, and Michael found he felt very sorry for the man who had simply tried to help them.

"By the way, the Geneva Conventions do not apply to escaping prisoners, so I advise you not to try anything. It would be far too great a temptation for our guards to resist shooting you." This time he smiled a real smile. "Of course it's up to you." The man gave a smart salute and then closed the flap of the tarp.

There was dead silence in the truck for perhaps a minute or longer. "I've never been to Germany," Jenkins said dejectedly, finally breaking the silence. "And I think I never wanted to go."

"A nice country, Germany. Except that their politics leave a great deal to be desired." Michael tried to say this with as light a voice as possible, since they had to try to keep their morale up with such banter. But at the moment it was simply too much, and the four of them lapsed into an anxious sort of silence as the truck engine rumbled to life and they lurched forward with a jerk that nearly knocked them off their seats.

* * *

After a long and tedious ride to Bari, they were ordered off the truck and into a local gymnasium where they were given the chance to take a shower. While it was humiliating to shower in front of guards pointing rifles at them and laughing at their filthy condition, the water felt wonderful, and Michael was grateful to be clean. They were allowed to sleep on the ground in front of the building. While they shivered from the cold night air, it was still better than being cooped up in the back of the smelly old truck with its obnoxious diesel fumes and broken springs.

The next morning they were forced to wake up at dawn and board a train that would take them north to Germany. Michael's optimism of the previous evening evaporated as he responded to the guards' orders. He decided that it was the most powerless feeling in the world to be a prisoner. They couldn't do anything without permission. He couldn't get out and stretch his legs, couldn't use the bathroom until permission was given, couldn't get a drink of water for himself, and couldn't even speak when in the presence of the guards. And from all he'd heard, it would be even worse when he got to Germany.

"Schnell, schnell, schnell!" the German guards yelled at Michael and the three others in the party, sticking bayonets against their backs to hurry them along. Michael scrambled up into the boxcar first, and then he and Jeremy Jenkins did their best to help Jules and Marcio, their Italian guide, up and into the car. Since Jules was too weak to lift himself, they had to pull him up by his arms, which caused him excruciating pain. The Italian was in even worse shape and fainted as they dragged him into the door. Once all were safely onboard, Michael stood in the doorway, trying to absorb as much daylight as possible, knowing what was coming next. Sure enough, the guards

motioned for him to back away from the door, and then the
Germans pushed the heavy metal door on its casters until it
closed with a clank. There was the noise of a heavy metal chain
being dragged through the appropriate eyelets on the door and
in the exterior wall of the train car, and then a metal lock was
closed through the chain to prevent their escape. The fresh
outside air was quickly swamped by the stench of people held
captive in an enclosed space.

Quietly Michael turned around and surveyed the scene after
giving his eyes a moment to adjust to the darkness. They shared
the car with perhaps ten other men who lay sprawled about on
the floor and up against the walls of the boxcar. At first Michael
couldn't see any space that he and Jules could occupy. But then
he was pleased when Jenkins made a ruckus and forced a
number of people to scoot closer to one another so that Michael
and he could drag Jules and the Italian up against a side wall
where they could rest.

"Thank you, Jenkins."

"They don't show proper respect, sir. You're both officers,
and they should yield to you immediately." Michael was
surprised at the hostility in Jenkins's voice. He was pleased by it.
It meant that the young man was loyal.

"I doubt that any of them are British, so we can't really hold
that against them."

"Officers are officers no matter what uniform they're
wearing, and they deserve to be treated with respect."

Michael smiled, thinking that loyalty was good, but it might
also lead to some fights if Jenkins didn't watch himself.

"Let's find out, Jenkins. Are any of you British or American?"
Michael asked the group.

No one replied, which undoubtedly meant that they didn't
understand the question. Leaning down to the Italian guide,
Marcio, Michael asked him if he could talk with the other prisoners to find out something about them. The Italian obliged,

and in just a matter of moments, the room erupted in noisy and animated chatter. Michael noted that whenever he listened to foreigners speaking in an unfamiliar language, it always sounded like they were talking fast.

Just then there was a sharp rap on the side of the boxcar with what sounded like the butt end of a rifle, followed by some very angry German words. Michael didn't have to translate for Jenkins, since it was so obviously profanities attached to the phrase that they better quiet down or there would be trouble. Some things were more obvious by the way they were spoken than by what was said.

It was a testament to the Germans' authority that the room went immediately silent. Undoubtedly all of these men had experienced some of what Jules and Marcio had been through. Very quietly he leaned over to Marcio and asked what he had learned.

"They have all been accused of treason for helping the Allied cause in some fashion or another. Most are innocent. Apparently the Germans simply wanted to make an example so that when the British really do invade, they won't have mass defections on their hands. So they have engaged in some cruel acts. For example, that man over there." He gestured to the far end of the car.

"Yes," said Michael, "the older fellow."

"The Germans shot his two sons because they found a short-wave radio in their house. Apparently there's a presumption of guilt just from the act of possessing a radio. They've taken him prisoner and are sending him north to a labor camp. You can see that at his age and with his health, he won't last a month." Marcio shook his head in despair. "It's our own fault. We allowed Mussolini to make us allies of the Germans, and now we will pay the price."

"Hopefully your new allies will be successful and will quickly liberate your country."

Marcio looked up at him, his eyes filled with more than physical pain. "It's a much harder country to conquer than you imagine, my friend. As your drive pushes north, you will encounter not just Germans but mountains. Great snowy mountains that will give the Germans the advantage at every turn. No, it will take blood to liberate Italy, and much will be shed from people of all nations."

Michael could have asked more, but to what end? There was nothing he could do about it anyway. He settled back against the cold steel wall, his arms resting on his knees. There was an inhuman groaning noise from the cars ahead of them in the train as each metal coupler was jerked by the car in front of it, and the slack was taken out of the string. In a matter of moments their car jerked crazily and then started moving forward. It was a car filled with men forlorn of hope and despairing of the future.

Chapter Sixteen

THE WHITE HOUSE

The Oval Office in the West Wing was a small room compared to the offices of most corporate chief executive officers, but it had a marvelous view of the Rose Garden to the east and the South Lawn from the windows behind the president's desk. On the opposite wall was a fireplace, made famous by photos of presidents with world leaders.

It was into these conspicuous quarters that Philip Carlyle was invited late on an autumn afternoon. After his business meeting, he and Claire would join the president and Mrs. Roosevelt for dinner.

"Excuse me, Mr. President, but Lord Carlyle from the British Cabinet is here to see you."

The president thanked his private secretary and motioned for Philip to come in. "Please forgive me for not standing," President Roosevelt said as an aide wheeled him out from behind his desk in the wheelchair that most Americans were unaware of. "I had polio many years ago, and it's quite painful for me to stand with leg braces. The cursed things cut into the skin."

"No need to apologize, Mr. President. I'm very pleased to meet you."

Roosevelt motioned to a man standing to the side of his desk. "I've asked Henry Stimson to join us, our Secretary of War."

The two men exchanged greetings, and Roosevelt motioned for Philip and Stimson to be seated in some comfortable chairs near the fireplace while he was wheeled into position. "The prime minister speaks very highly of you, Lord Carlyle, and is anxious that we help you with the problems you've encountered in accommodating our troops."

"Thank you, sir. I'm a bit embarrassed to receive such a high level of attention to what is hopefully a very minor problem, but the prime minister was insistent." Philip then went on to explain the nature of the difficulties.

When he was finished, Roosevelt simply said, "Henry? What can you do?"

"I'm sure we can work this out rather easily. I'll go to work on it tomorrow. Does your schedule allow you to stop by my office, Lord Carlyle?"

"My schedule is entirely open, but I'm afraid I don't know where your office is."

"I'll send a car for you. Where are you staying?"

"At the Willard."

"Very convenient," Roosevelt said. "Are you going to join us for dinner, Henry?"

Stimson declined, but confirmed the time of his meeting with Philip the next day. Then Roosevelt called for his aide to take them to the main mansion by way of the west terrace that bordered the Rose Garden. Churchill was right in his assessment that the White House was a beautiful place, standing in the middle of the well-manicured grounds on each side. Number 10 Downing Street was in the heart of London down an ordinary street near Whitehall, the government office complex that had once been a royal palace. The front of Number 10 was hardly distinguishable from its neighbors, whereas the White House stood on the most prestigious estate in Washington, DC.

Once taken by elevator to the third floor apartment, they were joined by the indefatigable Mrs. Roosevelt and Claire, who had received a tour from the first lady while she waited for Philip to meet with the president. It was quickly obvious why

Eleanor Roosevelt was so highly regarded by the public, as her energy and drive quickly manifested itself. She was an articulate proponent of the rights of the underprivileged in American society, including the poor and racial minorities.

"Eleanor was telling me about a recent trip she made to visit soldiers in the South Pacific," Claire said as they sat down to a simple table.

When Philip raised an eyebrow, Mrs. Roosevelt stepped into the conversation on Claire's behalf. "I insisted she call me by my first name, Lord Carlyle. We are compatriots after all, and women should not put on airs with one another."

"Then you must call me Philip, madam. That's what I was known by when I lived in Salt Lake City for more than a decade. In fact, it seems quite refreshing to be here amongst American accents again."

"An American accent?" Roosevelt queried. "And we thought it was you British who had an accent."

"With all due respect, that's not really logical, is it, sir, since we British were the first to speak English? It only stands to reason that those who adapt the language are the ones with the accent."

Roosevelt laughed. "I suppose you're right. Still, we think we've got it right. Part of the American ego I suppose. So tell me about your time in Utah and what brought you here to America. It's not often that a British aristocrat chooses to live so far away from home, at least not in the United States instead of one of your Commonwealth countries."

"The story starts in France, where I happened across a wounded American soldier by the name of Dan O'Brian from Idaho. I was a chaplain in the British Army, and I intervened to rescue him . . ." Philip continued the story of Dan O'Brian recuperating at Carlyle Manor and their eventual trip to the United States—a trip that lasted ten years. It was in this fashion that they spent the next hour as the Roosevelts and the Carlyles got to know each other. At the end of a simple dinner, the president declared the evening a great success, venturing that Philip was undoubtedly entitled to some kind of medal or recognition from the Americans for saving their young soldier, which Philip declined, and then he excused himself.

After he'd left, his wife explained, "His health is really quite precarious. The natural optimism and ebullience that so endear him to the public come at great personal expense. When he contracted polio, his doctors advised us that he should retire to a private life without too much excitement or stress. We have enough money that he could have easily done that. But he was resolved to continue to indulge his passion for politics, and so he challenged himself to regain the ability to walk. He has spent much of his inherited fortune encouraging research on how polio victims can do that. His legs have no strength whatsoever, and he tires so easily. It concerns me deeply."

"But I've seen him stand to make speeches on a number of occasions," Claire said.

"I'm afraid that's a bit of trickery. You might notice that he always takes someone's arm when he stands or pretends to walk. It's often our son. To the public it looks like he's just steadying himself. But in reality he worked very hard to develop superb upper body muscle strength. When you see him standing, he's lifting himself by the sheer strength of his arms and chest muscles and holding himself up using the steel braces on his lower legs. The deception has worked for many years now, but I think the time is growing short that he can pull the trick off."

"Why doesn't he simply speak from the wheelchair?" Philip asked.

"He's convinced that the public would see him as too weak to lead and that it would harm him politically. There's a great deal of prejudice against handicapped people. That's why I travel so many thousands of miles each year on his behalf."

"That must be very tiring for you."

"It is hard work, traveling, Claire. But I don't mind because Franklin is such a remarkable man. He's giving everything he has to lead the country during desperate times, first through the Great Depression and now in this war against such awful tyranny. It's only fair that I do what I can to support him."

"It seems to me that you're a remarkable woman, as well," Philip said. "I've read much of your writing and find myself sharing your empathy for the common people. I'm sure that sounds odd coming from someone of my position in British society, but had my mother not insisted that I return to London when my father died, I would never have left America. I preferred living the life of an ordinary citizen—something I can never do back home. Now I do what I can from the Lords to influence policy in favor of issues that help the poor and contribute to the economic well-being of the country so that men have jobs with enough income for their families to meet life's necessities." He turned to look at Claire. "And my wife is even more involved than I am. She has opened our home to displaced war widows, has been active in dispensing food to those made homeless by the bombings, and has recently hosted numerous young American military men who are struggling with homesickness. So we both deeply appreciate all that you do to assist people from your position."

As she pondered what Philip had just said, she fixed her eyes on the couple and said, "I need to know more about you—both of you. It sounds as if we're allies in more than just our shared military response. Do you have the energy to stay a little later and share some of your thoughts and experiences with me? I write a weekly syndicated newspaper column, and I would love to devote a column to the work going on in England."

"We'd be honored," Claire said simply. Nearly two hours later they finally took their leave and, declining the offer of a ride, started the short walk from the White House to the Willard.

"Was that so bad?" Philip asked. "You certainly fretted about it in advance."

Claire looked at him with narrowed eyes. "You know perfectly well that it was a delightful evening, and it's not very gentlemanly of you to remind me of my earlier fears."

Philip laughed easily. "I do beg your pardon, madam." He bowed to her with a small flourish and then added more thoughtfully. "They really are something, aren't they? I can see why Churchill thinks so highly of President Roosevelt. It makes me feel that God Himself reserved these two for leadership at this vital time."

"Do you think it's possible that men can be foreordained to be political leaders? That perhaps God considers such roles worthy of His attention as well?"

"I'm not sure. Certainly there have been political leaders that I hope were not foreordained. If so, they failed miserably to live up to their callings. But in this case, I find it entirely plausible."

"Well, it was a remarkable evening no matter how you think of it. Thank you for bringing me with you."

"I doubt I'd have made even half the good impression had you not been there. So the British government finds itself in your debt, my dear."

"Good, perhaps they'll repay the debt by giving me a bit more time with my husband when we get home."

Philip smiled. "I'll raise the issue at the highest levels of government, I promise."

* * *

"So, how did your meeting with the secretary go?" Claire asked Philip as he walked in the door.

Claire had spent the morning walking from the Lincoln Memorial on one end of the Washington Mall to the Capitol at the other end while Philip had been in meetings with the Secretary of Defense.

When Philip didn't immediately reply but took time to hang his suit coat on a hanger, she sensed that something was wrong.

"Philip?"

He turned but still didn't make eye contact. "The meeting went well. I think we got all that we need in order to resolve the issues. A cable will be going out to London today authorizing General Eisenhower to make the adjustments at that end."

"Then if you got what you want, why are you so serious?"

Philip hesitated. "It's just that I received some disturbing news about the return voyage. It seems that German submarines have been very active in the trade routes, and the Americans think we should avoid returning by ocean liner."

"So does that mean we have to stay here until the trouble is mitigated? If so, perhaps I could take a few weeks to go out to Arizona to see Karrie and her family. It's been a long time since I've seen my sister."

When Philip didn't reply this time, Claire grew serious. "What aren't you telling me, Philip? Out with it."

"It's just that they want us to go by airplane. It's really quite urgent that I get back, as some issues have come up that require the full Cabinet's attention."

"Airplane! Did I just hear you say airplane?" Claire said in a raised voice.

Philip winced. This reaction was not unexpected since Claire had always exhibited a morbid fear of flying.

"That's what they recommend . . ." Philip's voice trailed off.

"That's it. You've worn out your welcome, Lord Carlyle. Ocean voyages during wartime, meetings with ambassadors in New York, and tête-à-têtes in the White House are bad enough, but now you want me to get on an airplane? How can you even ask such a thing?"

Philip attempted a quick retreat. "Don't worry. We can tell them we're going by ship regardless. I'm sure there are troop transports that we can travel on."

She lapsed into silence. Philip waited as long as he thought prudent. "I'm not entirely sure what to do," he said finally.

Claire inhaled deeply. "We'll have to go on the darn thing. I'm not going to make orphans out of Grace and Michael. But you're very likely to have claw marks on your arm from where I hold on in a death grip."

"I'll wear a thick shirt."

"What a terrible thought," she said.

"That I'd wear a thick shirt?"

"No, the thought that I just had. For the first time in my life I found myself regretting that I don't drink alcohol. If ever there was a time I'd like to numb my thoughts, this is it."

Philip laughed, knowing that the decision was made and that she'd be all right. "We'll find some way to maintain your integrity while controlling your fear. I promise."

"You better. Maybe just wallop me on the head in the lobby and wake me when we're on the ground in England."

Philip cleared his throat uneasily.

"What?"

"Well, it's just that an aircraft can't make it all the way to England, so we'll have to stop for fuel in Iceland. And since we'll be there anyway, the British Embassy here in Washington was hoping we could spend the day meeting with some of our military and political officers there . . ."

"Iceland!" Claire smoldered. "That means an additional landing and takeoff." She brooded some more. "Philip, I think you should go for a walk. I need to take a hot bath. And if you're smart, you'll find some kind of chocolate before you return."

Philip moved to hug her, but she put her hands up.

"In search of chocolate, then!" and he was quickly out the door.

Chapter Seventeen

AN UNEXPECTED
OPPORTUNITY

Italy—October 1943

Italy is bordered by the Tyrrhenian and Ligurian Seas on its long
west coast, the Ionian Sea on its south coast, and the Adriatic Sea
on its east. It was through the Ionian that Michael had originally
taken Jules on his ill-fated espionage expedition to Taranto. Now,
as their train clattered north from Bari, the prisoners occasionally
caught glimpses of the azure blue waters of the Adriatic through
the slats in the side of the railcar. In America it would have been
called a cattle car, and that's just what it was. On good days the
Germans allowed the prisoners to sweep out the soiled straw and
replace it with fresh. At least that gave the men something to
recline on that wasn't the hard wooden planks of the floor. The
straw soaked up some of the odor from their unwashed bodies.
On bad days they'd leave the doors locked for endless hours at a
time, which forced the men to relieve themselves in the corners,
giving rise to a putrid stench that left them feeling nauseated and
desperate.

The ever-present problem was finding the best place to sit or
stand. The exterior walls were highly desirable because one could
see out and get some fresh air. But in late October, the nights
were often cold, particularly if an ocean breeze was blowing, and
so then it was desirable to be more toward the center of the car
huddled against other men to share their body heat. At first it

was a free-for-all with a lot of angry outbursts, but eventually an informal command structure developed with Marcio in charge. He was given the nod, because Jules was the highest-ranking officer, and Marcio was seen as his spokesperson. Jules arranged it so that everyone rotated periodically to the various parts of the car. That way, no one could claim preferential treatment, and all shared equally in the cold, the fresh air, and the crowded center where there was no sense of privacy. Normally, the journey north would take just a few days at most, but with German soldiers streaming southward to reinforce the region of Apulia, the little prison train was often shunted onto sidings where it stood idle for hours on end as troop trains and supplies steamed past them at breakneck speed. It had now been more than ten days since they set out from Bari, and they were barely as far north as San Marino.

"We should be turning inland for a while to go to the switch yards at Bologna," Jules said quietly. "That's where we part company with Marcio and the Italians."

"In other words, that's where they're taken off to be shot."

Jules looked at Michael. "Unfortunately. After that we're on our own."

"Where exactly are they taking us?" Jenkins asked.

"We'll go northeast to Venice, then due north to Austria. In better circumstances, this would be considered a luxury vacation."

Michael laughed. "I don't know what you're complaining about. We have a straw tick to sleep on, an abundance of fresh air blowing through the walls, wonderful vistas through our windows, and plenty of time to savor it all without being interrupted by showers or brushing our teeth. You should learn to see the bright side of things, Jules."

Jules cocked his head to the side. "Indeed, I should. Why think of the itinerary—Venice, Salzburg, Munich, and Nuremburg. We'll be passing through some of the most beautiful country in Europe. If only I had a coat to better enjoy the winter weather."

Before Michael could protest, Jules added, "Ah, but there I go again being negative. I should be grateful . . ."

"What will it be like in a prison camp?" Jenkins asked anxiously.

"Never been in one," Michael said. "But I suspect it's mostly boring."

"That's pretty much a given if you're there," Jules said to Michael, who glowered at him for this remark. "I've been to a camp in Germany. It wasn't for Allied prisoners, though. There was this Jewish scientist that had some special kind of knowledge about a top secret explosive device the Germans are working on. The Germans know of his expertise but refuse to use it because he's a Jew. So, they sent him to a concentration camp. We decided he could do us a lot of good, so a couple of us were sent in to find him and figure a way to get him out. It was pretty nerve-wracking." Jules went quiet.

"So what happened?" Michael hated it when Jules did that—start some really intriguing story and then just stop as if no one was paying attention. It was his way of keeping control.

Jules shook his head. "Yes, well, didn't turn out so well. To get in we had to pose as German officers. That's why I had to take the crash course in German. They didn't really want me saying anything except in an emergency. Apparently German with an English accent is fairly easy to pick out. But the fellows I was traveling with were expert, and they managed to get us in. Once we identified our man, we managed to isolate him. But as we approached him to tell him why we were there, he mistook us for real German officers, and before we could stop him, he chomped on a cyanide pill that killed him. Apparently it was the one thing he'd managed to conceal from the Germans throughout his imprisonment."

"Why did he do that?" Jenkins asked with big eyes.

"Because he thought they were coming to take him back to work on the project. He was a man of integrity who apparently had decided that he would offer no aid or assistance to the Germans' plans. So we lost out too. So much for the virtue of a good disguise."

Michael shook his head again but didn't add anything.

"So what was the camp like?" Jenkins asked.

"The camp? Oh, yes, that's how we got started on this, isn't it?" Jules flashed a grin. Michael was happy that Jules was feeling strong enough to engage in some of his old banter. "Well, it was a terrible place. If you think it's crowded here, you have no idea how they treat their Jewish prisoners. It's simply deplorable. It broke my heart to see old men in tattered coats and threadbare trousers that had once been fine clothing. It was obvious that they were wealthy at one time but were now reduced to abject poverty. Everyone was emaciated, including the women and children. And if our suspicions are correct, they were all doomed to die."

"Doomed to die? What do you mean by that?"

Jules grew very serious. "We have reason to believe that the Jewish camps are death camps—that the Germans are carrying out mass extermination in an attempt to destroy every single Jew in Europe."

Michael was staggered by this. "You can't be serious. Not even the Germans would do something so heinous."

"There's no way to know for certain, but rumor is rampant, and just the brief glimpse I had suggests it's true. There was certainly no mercy being shown by the Germans to any of the prisoners. Of course, I was just at a staging area, so I can't say for sure."

Michael and Jenkins were stunned. As bad as the war was, it wasn't historically unusual. The Europeans had been fighting each other for thousands of years. But if what Jules said was true, then this represented an inexplicable turn that staggered and repulsed the imagination.

"*Despicable* is a better word," Michael said to himself.

"What was that?"

"Despicable," Michael said, looking up. "Whether everything you suspect is true or not, what you did see is despicable enough to condemn the Germans for their infamy. That they would arrest their own citizens and treat them that way for nothing more than their ethnicity is simply beyond imagination."

"It's not just the Jews, although they're certainly getting the worst of it. The Slavs and Muslims are treated much the same way, as they're forced into virtual slavery with no rights in their own country." Jules's face was hard. "This really is a cataclysmic battle of good versus evil, and in spite of our success of late, the ending still isn't assured." The fire in his voice died down. "And now we're out of it."

Jules stood up and stretched. "That's the worst of it, Jenkins. Our camp will be nothing like what those people endure. But sitting idly by as the war unfolds will be infuriating. I can't stand the thought of it." Apparently it bothered Jules enough that he wanted to be alone, so he excused himself and picked his way across the many bodies lying on the floor to find another corner for a time.

"We're going to be all right, aren't we, Captain?"

Michael smiled at him. "We'll be fine. If the Germans had wanted to make an example of us, they would have done it already." Jenkins did not look reassured. "I think I'll take a nap, now, Jenkins." What Michael really wanted was some quiet time with his own thoughts.

* * *

Even in his sleep, Michael was aware of the sound of airplanes at a distance. Four years of war had so conditioned him that he could discern the difference between friendly and hostile aircraft without even consciously thinking about it. Perhaps that's why he didn't wake up immediately. Obviously the approaching aircraft were British and therefore nothing to be concerned about.

Then he heard the first bomb detonation, and in a cold second he sat bolt upright in the darkness as he realized that in this instance British wasn't good. After all, they were behind enemy lines, and any Allied aircraft would be totally unaware of their presence. That's when the second bomb went off. This time there was no confusing the British intent since the train lurched crazily to a stop amid the tearing and shredding sound of metal on metal. From a few cars up they could hear men screaming in agony, apparently the result of a direct hit on the train.

"What is it?" Jenkins shouted out from somewhere to Michael's left. It was hard to hear him above the clamor of the Italians. Before he could answer, there was a third explosion. This time the interior of the car was lit up in a brilliant, blinding flash of light that preceded the blast wave by perhaps a second or two. Previous experience prepared Michael more than the others and he quickly covered his eyes and tucked himself into a ball in anticipation of the shock wave. When it struck, the wood slats on the opposite wall were shattered into a hundred thousand splinters that splayed out and into the bodies of the men who had not prepared themselves, causing an instant simultaneous wail of agony. For his part, Michael tucked even harder as the car rolled to its side with perhaps half a dozen men falling on top of him in a jumble. The next challenge was to create a pocket of air so he didn't suffocate as he tried to stand up and clear himself from the others. As he did so, blood dripped down on him and he had to fight hard to avoid the twisting, writhing pack of men wincing in their pain while trying to find a way out of the car.

As Michael gained some freedom, he realized that the majority of bodies he had to force his way through were inert—killed in an instant by the deadly shrapnel of metal and wood unleashed by the fury of the bomb. "Jules! Jenkins! Marcio!" He shouted at the top of his lungs.

"Over here!" he heard Jules's voice to his right.

"I'm right behind you!" he heard Jenkins cry out. But nothing from Marcio.

"Are you all right?" he shouted, still clawing and crawling his way to—he didn't really know where. Probably toward Jules's voice.

"I'm okay. But we've got to get out."

The aircraft were gone now, and darkness had reasserted itself so that the whole exercise was even more frustrating. The blast had restricted his pupils such that Michael couldn't see a thing. "Jenkins, hold your position until your eyesight returns. Then help me figure out the best way out."

"Yes, sir!"

As the seconds passed, Michael tried to figure out what had happened. His guess was that the Allies had wanted to shake up the Germans by showing them they could launch an air assault deep behind their lines. By this point the train should have been close to the rail yards at Bologna, so perhaps that was the target. Their little train held no strategic value so was probably just an unintended casualty of the bombing that was really directed at destroying the rails and switches that allowed the Germans to send supplies on the southbound line.

As his vision returned, Michael looked forward in the darkness and thought he recognized one of the men stirring. "Marcio! Marcio, is that you?" The person turned his head, and Michael could see it was Marcio.

"Marcio is alive!" he shouted to Jules.

"Good. Have you figured out a way to get us out?"

By now he could see well enough to know that the wall he'd been leaning against had been tipped to the ground and that's what he was standing on instead of the floor of the train. That meant that the roof of the rail car was now the wall, and what had formerly been the opposite wall was now above them. There wasn't a lot left of that.

Unfortunately, the doorway was below them, pinned firmly against the ground. "I think I can climb up the side," Jenkins said. "Maybe I can find an easier way out from up there."

"Go ahead. We've got to get out of this mess." All eyes turned to Jenkins as he tentatively found his way up the slick side of what had been the ceiling. He placed his hands and feet on small eye brackets that had been installed in the ceiling to hang feedbags from in the car's former use.

"The back of the car is fairly flattened, sir! If you go that way you should be able to get up and out rather easily."

"Did you hear that?" Michael called to Jules.

"Already on my way. Do you need help with Marcio?"

By this point Michael had crawled his way over to the Italian, who seemed to be regaining his wits. There was a long gash across his forehead, which probably meant he'd been blown across the car. "Can I help you, Marcio? Mr. Jenkins tells us that we can get out at the back of the car."

"Thank you," Marcio said quietly. It was obvious he was very weak and shaken, but for some reason Michael felt they had to hurry, so he did his best to both guide and propel Marcio toward the back. Once there, they found that Jenkins was waiting to offer them a hand as they climbed up the twisted metal of what had been the back of the rail car. After a bit of intense effort, Michael found himself clear of the car and able to jump to the ground. Jules had been closer to the back and so was already there. Once Jenkins and Marcio made it to the ground, the four men stumbled their way to the side of the track, where they scrambled to find some cover where they could hide until they figured out what to do.

"I haven't heard any Germans," Michael said.

"It's probably too much to hope that the bomb hit the guard's car. But the first bomb to hit did go off towards the front of the train, so perhaps they're in a bad way," Jules said.

Instinctively everyone turned their gaze toward the front of the train. There was a fire burning up there, and it looked like the second and third car had been hit pretty badly.

"Like watching rats leaving a sinking ship, isn't it?" Jules said. Prisoners were slinking away from the wreckage of the train in all directions. "They are the lucky ones," Jules continued, "since they're Italians who can easily slip into the general population. This attack saved their lives."

"But what about us?" Jenkins said. "We don't speak Italian."

"I do," Marcio said fiercely. "And I will help you. We can go into hiding until the Allies make it this far in their advance."

Before anyone could respond, they heard the sound of a German voice, and they instinctively huddled close together behind the small signals box they were hiding behind. In a matter of moments, a German soldier came stumbling past them, calling out into the darkness. Michael recognized that he was trying to find his comrades, and he hoped desperately that the fellow wouldn't turn their way.

While waiting for the German to pass beyond them, he was startled a moment later as Jules suddenly broke free and dashed out into the darkness in the direction of the German. He watched in unbelief as Jules came up behind the man and grabbed him around the neck. Even from this distance, they could hear the sound of cracking bones and saw the German's body suddenly slump in Jules's arms. In spite of the shock of it all, Michael stepped wordlessly out into the darkness and went over to help Jules drag the body away from the train and back toward their box. "Over there!" Jules whispered urgently. Michael turned to see a small switchman's shack that was dark inside. As fast as possible, they dragged the body to the shack, where Marcio and Jenkins quickly joined them.

"I've got an idea," Jules said quietly as they closed the door.

"I hope so, since you just insured our execution if we're caught with this corpse."

Jules ignored this. "Look here. You speak very decent German, Michael. And, as you now know, I've been taking lessons myself. Although I would be terrible in a complex conversation, I believe I could follow along well enough to act appropriately in the abbreviated conversations one would have while traveling. And Marcio is trilingual with English, Italian, and basic German. Besides, you speak French. With that many languages between us, we ought to be able to hide out and do some damage while we wait for our comrades to catch up to us as the invasion progresses."

When no one said anything, Jules pointed to the dead German. "This man was an officer, and with his papers you could go anywhere you want, Michael. It seems to me that we should move towards the west coast, where the heaviest fighting's going to take place. Perhaps we can join up with the Resistance."

"You want me to impersonate a German officer while we cross the entire width of Italy?" Michael was incredulous.

"It's something to think of," Jules replied. "What else are we going to do?"

This was a unique opportunity. But Michael wondered why Jules had mentioned his French language skills. "Why west? Why not go south to Rome or something? The Allies will certainly get there before long."

Jules looked at each of them carefully. "What I'm about to tell you is top secret. I won't tell you much so that in case you get caught you won't have anything of real value to give away. But for some time now, the Americans have been agitating for a second front when the Allies invade northern France next year. There's a tentative operation called 'Anvil' that would take place on the Riviera. If it's coordinated with the main invasion up north, it will split the German forces by making them defend two different regions in France. In essence, it would be a fourth front to add to Germany's woes. If we could make our way over there, we could join up with the French partisans to carry out acts of sabotage in preparation for the landing. That is, if it ever develops."

"If?"

Jules smiled. "Churchill hates the idea of diverting forces to southern France. He thinks we already have our hands full with a Russian front, Italian front, and hopefully an assault on northern France. He's taken to calling the whole operation 'Dragoon,' since he feels like he's being forced into it by the Americans."

The group was silent. The thought of making their way hundreds of miles behind enemy lines with no one in the group able to communicate in all the languages they were likely to encounter was preposterous. But as British officers, it was their duty to harass the enemy wherever possible.

"But how would we do it? I can probably fit in this fellow's uniform, but what about everyone else? Jenkins is still dressed in his navy uniform, and no one is going to miss seeing that. And won't the Germans realize that this guy is missing? What happens when his identification papers start showing up in unusual places?"

"I don't know," Jules replied. "I have to think about that. I mean I guess you could treat Jenkins and me as your prisoners, but you're right that it wouldn't make sense for you to be taking us west instead of north."

They were all quiet as they tried to figure out how to form a credible story. Finally it was Marcio who broke the silence. "Perhaps you could forge a set of transfer papers for the German officer requiring him to go to France. With all the trouble the Germans have now, I doubt they'll search the rubble of the train too thoroughly and will simply assume that it is Michael's body that was destroyed by the bomb. In other words, you'll switch identification papers. I'm sure the authorities will hurry to clear this mess up so they can reopen the track. And as for this fellow turning up in the wrong places, the western division is totally separate from the one where he came from. I honestly doubt anyone will even take time to question the phony orders, let alone seek verification."

Jules nodded. "That's good. But it still leaves open the question of what we do with me and Jenkins. If we can get our hands on another German uniform and set of identification papers, I can act as Michael's subordinate, and you can act as an assigned translator. It's perfectly believable to have a German officer with an Italian interpreter, but what about our English-only speaker? Besides, how would we forge the appropriate papers?"

"I have some relatives in Bologna. They hate the Germans as much as I do. If we can find them, they will hide us for a few days. I'm sure they'd help us find an effective forger. As to your young comrade, Jenkins could act as if he was assigned to help as an Italian specialist or something. All we need to do is steal some of the identities of the dead men over there to have one more Italian as part of the entourage.

"Me, an Italian?" Jenkins said with a bit of terror in his voice. "I don't know anything but English, and my teachers used to say I don't even know that very well."

"That *is* a problem," Jules said. He pondered for a time. "I'm afraid that you'll have to be both deaf and dumb, Jenkins. That's the only way we could account for your not communicating.

"It's much harder than you think. For you to pull this off, you'd have to ignore all sounds. If people think you can hear them, they would expect you to respond to Italian conversation, at least to recognize that it's being spoken. So you'll have to learn to ignore all sounds and to never speak at all if there's any possibility that strangers are near. Do you think you can do that?"

Jenkins was equally serious. "I'll have to. Perhaps you can help me practice while we're in hiding."

"Good. So the plan is that Michael will exchange clothes and identification papers with this German, and I'll try to find another German of subordinate rank. The two of you will do the same with two of the Italians who were killed. That way the Germans will think that we all perished in the bombing. We'll then go with Marcio to his relatives', where we'll practice our routine. From that point forward, Michael will be a German officer, and we'll be assigned to his staff. We'll have to concoct some kind of story to explain why we're moving to the west, hopefully one that sounds credible enough to get us past whatever checkpoints we encounter. Is everyone agreed?"

Jenkins assented reluctantly, Marcio was enthusiastic, and Michael was quiet, apparently lost in thought. "Is there a problem with the plan, Michael?"

"What?" He turned his head. "No, not really. I don't see what alternative we have. It's just that if the Germans decide to report to the Red Cross, they'll send out word to British authorities that we've all been killed. Each of our families will get that dreadful black telegram. After what happened to Dominic, it will be a terrible blow for my family." Then quietly to himself, "And then there's Karen."

Jules raised an eyebrow. "So she means more to you than you've let on."

Michael looked up. "Perhaps she does." He turned to Jenkins. "The same is true for your family. And for your parents, Jules. To make this work, we'll have to let them all go through the grief of receiving those telegrams."

That was sobering. But the other choice was to be listed missing in action, which was a lot worse, since the Germans would be actively searching for them. By leaving their identification papers to be discovered, it would take the pressure off to a remarkable degree.

After a moment's hesitation, Jenkins piped up with an artificial sort of cheer. "Think of the surprise it will be to my mum if she thinks I'm gone, and then one day I show up."

"That's the spirit," Jules said. "Besides, there's a lot of war left ahead of us. It's likely that we'll all get killed anyway, so we'll just save them the trouble later on."

Michael laughed. "Always able to see the bright side, aren't you, Jules?" He nodded as if to confirm his thoughts. "All right, then, let's do it. Let's make our way west and see how much havoc we can create for the Germans. It's a different kind of war than I expected to fight, but it's got to be better than being a prisoner of war."

"Righto! So, I've got to go find myself a dead German. Or make one. And as for you, Jenkins, you're about to become an Italian. Let's hurry and do it, then." With that, Jules, Jenkins, and Marcio moved out in the direction of their rail car. The sound of fire engines in the distance told them they didn't have a lot of time. Meanwhile, Michael began stripping the clothes off the dead German officer.

"And your family will think you're still alive," he said quietly, "only to find that you never come home. I'm truly sorry about that." But not so sorry that he didn't hasten to turn the German into a British naval officer by the name of Michael Carlyle. As he looked at the body, he tipped his head just a bit and said, "I'll miss you, Mr. Carlyle. You weren't the worst of fellows, in spite of what Commander Billingham seemed to think." The thought of his old nemesis made him grimace. "At least I won't be answering to him again!"

As he pulled the German's identification papers out of the fellow's shirt pocket, he discovered that he was to become Kolonel Karl Braun of the Wehrmacht. "Colonel is good," he said to the air. "A colonel can intimidate most of the people we're likely to encounter." He smiled and went out to check on his transformed friends. Jules came striding up in a lieutenant's uniform.

"*Mein Fuhrer,*" he said confidently in one of the worst German accents Michael had ever heard.

"Heaven help us if that's the best you can do!" Jules looked wounded, but the smile behind the act betrayed his excitement. They were off on a new adventure.

Chapter Eighteen

TELEGRAMS

London—November 1943

*We regret to inform you that your son, Lieutenant Michael
Carlyle, RN, has been reported missing in action. We will keep
you apprised as additional information becomes available.*

The problem with communication between enemies about
prisoners of war was that it was always delayed by the bureaucracy, since it was up to the International Red Cross to act as
liaison between the combatants. Thus, at approximately the
same time that Michael was feigning his death in Italy, the
Carlyles in England were just learning of his capture.

On this occasion Philip was not given prior warning that this
telegram was to be sent to Carlyle Manor. In fact, he was in
Liverpool working on sorting out an unintended glut of arriving
American troopships that had backed up in the harbor. It seemed
that two German U-boat wolf packs had managed to wreak so
much havoc on the previous two crossings that they had tangled
up the convoys to the point that it had taken several days to get
them reassembled and back underway. The result was that three
convoys showed up in Liverpool simultaneously, overwhelming
the ability of the port to efficiently disembark the troops. Some
ships had been sitting in the harbor for nearly a week and people

were getting restless. Although there wasn't a lot Philip could do to untangle the ships, just having a government minister on hand to interact with the various military and civilian officials had a calming effect and showed that the British government was concerned for the welfare of their American guests.

"Julia, could you please call Grace and ask her to come down?" Claire asked.

"Certainly, my lady. Are you all right, madam?" asked Julia, the housekeeper.

Fortunately, Claire was seated on a sofa when she opened the telegram. As it was, she felt faint, and Julia reacted to how pale her face had grown. "I'm . . . I'm not sure. But I definitely need my daughter." Claire dropped her head back against the cushion and closed her eyes.

"Certainly, madam. Right away." And Julia was off running.

When Grace arrived a few moments later, she was so startled by her mother's appearance that she feared she'd had a heart attack. "What is it, Mother? What's happened?"

Claire motioned for her to sit down and then handed her the telegram. It was so short and terse that Grace absorbed the whole thing in an instant, gasped, and then clasped her hands over her mouth. "Oh, no!" After waiting a moment to regain at least some degree of composure she asked, "But what exactly does it mean? How does a navy person go missing?"

"I don't know." Claire squeezed Grace's hand in an attempt to calm her own panic. "I just don't know." For the life of her she couldn't imagine how a seaman could be missing in action— was his ship sunk, and they couldn't find him in the water? Or was he somehow taken prisoner? It just didn't make sense.

"Does Papa know what happened?"

"I don't think he even knows Michael is missing. I'm sure he would call me if he did."

Grace was silent again. Claire felt her heart racing and her breathing getting shallow. She knew from prior experience that her reaction was a mistake but felt powerless to stop it. She was grateful when Grace finally spoke up again.

"Perhaps it means he's all right—he's just missing, not dead. Maybe he somehow got separated from his crew and is even now making his way back to his base. He was in the water before, you know, and they found him." There was a hint of hope in her voice.

It was an obvious thing to say that meant nothing—Michael was either all right or he wasn't, and nothing that they thought about it could change reality. But just hearing Grace's voice and knowing that she wanted to be helpful was soothing. "I think there's a very good chance it's something like that." There was not nearly as much conviction in Claire's voice as she had intended. She had hoped to reassure Grace. Instead, another silence followed.

"I should call Karen. She should know."

Claire stiffened. Somehow this helped her thinking start to clear. "No, we should go see her together. News like this should not come over a phone. But first I have to call Philip's office and figure out a way to get in touch with him. Since we're going into London, perhaps you could have the cook fix us some sandwiches."

"I'm not sure I could eat . . ."

Claire looked at her firmly. "But you will. Michael's situation is uncertain, and certainly this telegram is distressing. But it won't help things if we allow ourselves to get sick or malnourished. You have to help me be strong, Grace. Can you do that?"

"It's hard to be strong, Mama . . . but I will. I must."

Claire forced a smile. "Thank you." She took a deep breath to force air into her lungs and to calm her heart. She held her breath for a moment and then released it slowly. The pause helped. "Now, we have things to do." She squeezed her daughter's hand again. "But first, let's kneel and say a prayer for Michael, and for us."

* * *

As Philip looked out the train window, he shook his head. The call from Claire had taken him totally by surprise and made him desperate to return home. He'd wanted to return to London by military aircraft, but the weather precluded any possibility of flying, so he'd commissioned a private railroad engine and car to take him immediately.

It was A.V. Alexander, First Lord of the Admiralty, who suggested the private car. Apparently someone had notified the First Lord at almost the same moment that Claire was calling him. The operator had interrupted Philip's call with Claire to indicate that the First Lord's personal secretary was on the line, and naturally Philip had to end his call with Claire immediately in case there was a national emergency. But it was just A.V., his friend, calling to console him and, if necessary, to give him the bad news directly. Alexander was like that—somehow able to balance a hundred tasks at once, yet thoughtful enough to make a personal contact in times of tragedy.

"Oh, Michael—what has happened to you?" Philip asked quietly.

He picked up the confidential report he'd brought along and pretended to start reading it, but his heart wasn't in it. It seemed so unfair that when the news was good for the country it should be so sad for the Carlyles. He shook his head to clear his thoughts and was startled to see a motorcycle come racing up to a crossing just as the train arrived at the same spot. The motorcycle stopped just feet from the train, and the rider waved at him. In spite of himself, Philip waved back and smiled. Then he thought of Dominic on his motorcycle in North Africa, and he winced in emotional pain. The pain of Dominic's suicide was simply too hard to think about. Philip felt desperation rise within his breast. "Father, this is so hard. Please be with Michael. Please help him." *Please.*

* * *

Bologna—November 1943

"Peter managed to steal some bread," Marcio said breathlessly. It had been three weeks since the little group had moved in with Marcio's cousin Peter and his wife. Obviously the first thing they'd done after Peter had consented to house them was to hide the German uniforms. Jules and Jenkins had stayed inside the small apartment the entire time, not wanting to draw unwanted attention, but soon after their arrival, Michael had discovered that French and Italian were close enough that he could understand some of the things that were said, so he'd ventured out on a few occasions with Marcio.

The stolen bread was important because the Italians, like everyone else in Europe, were living on rationed food, and it was very difficult to feed six people on two rations. Fortunately, Peter worked in a bakery, so it was relatively easy for him to smuggle out some extras, particularly since people had started wearing winter clothing. A few loaves could easily fit inside the large overcoat that Peter wore. Still, their presence was a constant danger to Peter and his wife, and so it was fortunate that they'd received their forged papers earlier that day, enabling them to begin their westward migration that very night.

It was a major undertaking, as it turned out. At first their plan was to jump freight trains in the night so as to not draw attention to themselves. They had procured some nondescript topcoats that Michael and Jules could wear over their uniforms. Their original thinking was that if they ever came to a town where they'd need to go out in public, Michael was prepared to act the part of a German officer. At other times, they'd simply be shadows in the background. But as they practiced and talked about it, they decided that if anyone ever spotted them, it would be too late to change their disguise, let alone explain why two men dressed as German officers were jumping freight trains with two Italians, one of whom was deaf and dumb. It was just too implausible.

So reluctantly they decided that they'd have to play the part completely, using Colonel Braun's status to travel on passenger cars. But that was a game they couldn't play by themselves, so Marcio made contact with the Italian underground in Bologna and revealed their intentions. Marcio never told Jules and Michael whom he had met with or where, but after a few days of discussion, word came back that they would be supported in the plan with high-quality forged transfer papers, authentic railroad tickets and timetables, and the name of a contact in each of the cities on their itinerary. They'd never get the full list of contacts, since their capture could compromise everyone up and down the line. Rather, they'd be given the name of a contact in the next town they were going to and, once read, they would destroy the paper the message was written on. Then, after successfully connecting with that person, they'd get the name of the next one, and so on down the line. Because they'd have to make numerous transfers to get to their ultimate destination, it was felt they should disappear from public view periodically so that if anyone was trying to chase them down, they could more easily slip out of harm's way. The Italians had enough eyes and ears in each town that they could quickly tell if a manhunt was on.

There was only one exception to this rule. They were also given the names of two pseudo "German" officers, one in Toulon, France, as well as one in Bologna, who could be contacted by telegraph if anyone ever challenged their credentials. These two co-conspirators could then act as German officers to verify their orders. These officers were, of course, simply members of the Italian Resistance who worked at the military telegraph terminals and who were trained to recognize the call letters of the hypothetical German officers. That way if anyone decided to check on the group, the telegraphers would intercept the request and simply respond appropriately to confirm their credibility. It was a nice little detail that could save them should anyone become suspicious. It would also allow the telegraphers to alert the local contact to take them off the train and put them in hiding if anything threatening went out over the wire.

At one point Jules asked if they could forge new identity papers just in case the Germans were looking for Braun, but word came back that it was one thing to forge a set of transfer papers, but quite another to try to duplicate German credentials. That was simply too complex a task with the variety of seals and stamps that made them authentic. So they'd have to accept the risk. It had taken the better part of a month to get all the paperwork and tickets prepared.

The three British members of the group never met any members of the Resistance, which was probably a good thing. It increased the safety of the operation for everyone involved. Instead, all communication went through Marcio. For a time Michael worried that Marcio was in an ideal position to betray them, but then he realized that if Marcio had wanted to do that, he could have done so already, since the reward from the Germans would be significant. Besides, that Marcio was planning to travel with them meant that he would be at as much risk as the others. So Michael relaxed and placed his trust in the excitable young Italian who had such a passion for the freedom of his country. Still, Michael's heart beat rapidly each time he heard someone at the door for fear it was the Gestapo or SS.

But nothing bad happened, and soon it was time for them to catch a late-night train to Parma. Their papers listed their ultimate destination as Toulon, France, which would put them right where they wanted to be in case "Anvil" was executed. Even if Churchill prevailed, and the Allies decided to pass on a southern invasion, they resolved to make their way north toward Paris, where they could meet up with the French Resistance.

At 2000 hours, Peter turned out the lights in the house so they could step out into the street unobserved. As they reached the front door, Michael took Gina's and Peter's hands and thanked them for everyone in the group in the best Italian he could muster. Peter laughed and corrected one of the words he said, and then squeezed Michael's hand earnestly. "Good luck, my friends. Go to France and do as much damage to the Germans as you possibly can. Telegrams have gone out to the next town announcing your passage, so no one should be surprised by your arrival." It was an extra touch of authenticity that would hopefully make things easier.

Peter then gave his cousin Marcio an affectionate hug and told him to come back safely once the war was over. Michael was surprised at how emotional the good-bye was. For almost a month these people had sheltered and fed them at grave danger to themselves. Now they were leaving and would likely never see their Italian hosts again. It was an odd bond that had formed, but one that meant the world to him.

"Well, then, ciao!" Jules said with his usual nonchalant air, but Michael could hear the stress in his voice, which indicated Jules was feeling the emotion of the moment as well. With that they were out into the night air. Jules and Michael were wearing their topcoats to cover their German uniforms. The coats would come off at the train station just before they boarded. From then on Michael had no other recourse but to act as a German colonel traveling with his aide.

As they reached the railroad station they surrendered their coats to a wastebasket, and then the group stepped into the darkened station. Even though the Allies were still hundreds of miles to the south, the bombing of the tracks that had liberated them had also put the city into a mandatory blackout. The windows of the station were covered in blackout canvas, and the entrances to the terminals were cloaked by great sheets of fabric. Even inside there was a minimum amount of lighting, which worked to their advantage.

"Are you ready, Colonel?" Jules asked in his very best German. Michael decided that the Italian they'd all been listening to the previous month had improved Jules's German, perhaps because his accent wasn't quite so English sounding.

Turning to Marcio, Michael said, "You remember the various lines we've practiced. Should we encounter any Italians, I'll speak in an authoritative German tone, and you'll interpret in Italian. You'll then put your hands on Jenkins's shoulders and direct him, since no self-respecting German officer would condescend to touch an Italian of inferior rank."

Marcio rolled his eyes, but nodded his understanding. "It's a great act we're performing, and we all have to do our part." Then Marcio smiled. "I'm ready," he said with just a hint of nervousness in his voice. Because his German was not very complete, they'd rehearsed the most likely questions he'd be asked so he could respond from memory if nothing else. Of course it wasn't entirely implausible that an Italian interpreter assigned to a colonel wouldn't be entirely fluent in German, so that wasn't really too great a concern. The bigger risk was that there would be other Germans in the station who would want to engage in direct conversation about the country, the war, military procedures, or other such gossip, in which case the whole thing could come apart.

"All right then, gentlemen, let's go." Three of the group started forward, but Jenkins stayed right where he was, looking into the station. At first Michael was tempted to call to him, but then he realized that Jenkins had simply moved into character. He gestured to Marcio, whose face lit up in recognition, and he went back and twisted Jenkins's body to face his and then guided him out into the crowd. For better or for worse, the game was on.

* * *

London

> *We have been notified by the International Red Cross that your son, Lieutenant Michael Carlyle, RN, has been declared a prisoner of war by German authorities in Italy. We will keep you apprised as we learn more of his status.*

"He's alive!" Claire fairly danced, and Grace quickly joined her. They tried to draw Philip in, but his joy didn't bubble out in quite the same way. Grace didn't mind and laughed, wiping away an occasional tear. "He's alive!" Claire kept repeating the phrase, sometimes almost in a shout, sometimes very quietly to herself. "I just can't believe it."

"All right, my dears, perhaps you can slow down now," Philip said good naturedly, but the pace of their dancing had almost left him breathless. "I know we're too excited to finish our lunch, but perhaps a good walk would be helpful."

Claire laughed. "A good walk indeed. Perhaps the best walk of our lives!" It was raining outside, so they donned their rain slickers and stepped out into the London air. Their townhouse in the Queen Anne district put them within blocks of Parliament and the government complex at Whitehall, and within an easy walk of the Thames.

"Where should we go?" Philip asked.

"The river—I want to see the river," Grace replied instantly.

"To the east, then," Philip said, and they were off.

They walked for a time in silence, the intense emotion of getting the telegram now spent.

"What does it mean?"

Philip cast a sideward glance at Claire. "What does what mean?" he prompted.

"That he's a prisoner. Perhaps we shouldn't be so happy. Certainly this isn't the best outcome."

"Ah. No, it's not the best, but it's far superior to the worst. What it means is that he's likely to get roughed up a bit in his initial interrogation." When Philip heard his wife and daughter gasp, he quickly added, "But as an officer they'll treat him relatively decently. Once they're done trying to extract whatever information they can, he'll undoubtedly be transferred to a prison camp somewhere in Germany."

"Will he be safe there?" Grace asked urgently.

"He'll be safe from the Germans. My understanding is that they treat our prisoners relatively well. He'll be fed regularly, given time for exercise, and spend a lot of days being quite bored. That's the biggest challenge for our men. One day they're on active duty, and the next completely idle. But he'll be safe."

"Thank heavens," Claire said.

"You said our prisoners are treated well. Are others treated poorly?" Grace almost always picked up on things like this.

"We don't know full details, of course, but it seems that the Russians and Eastern Europeans who are taken prisoner are rather severely abused. The healthy ones are put into forced labor squads that amount to nothing more than slavery."

"Why do they get treated differently?"

"Racial prejudice. The Germans believe that the Slavic people come from inferior genetic stock and that they're meant to be subservient to the superior German people. If Hitler succeeds in winning the war, he will almost certainly create a new class, or perhaps many classes, of undesirables who live in society without the natural human rights that we believe in. For example, even people of Eastern European ancestry who were born in Germany have been stripped of their citizenship."

"So why does he treat our people better?"

"The reason that the Germans treat our prisoners better is that Hitler has always admired the British. He thinks that we represent part of the ruling elite. Had it not been for Churchill, Hitler's goal was to strike an armistice with England and allow us to continue our empire. Hitler and his adherents admire anyone who is strong and industrious." It was all so patently unfair and perverse that there was really nothing more to say. But it did cast a pall on their enthusiasm.

"But Michael will be all right?" Philip felt bad that Claire felt compelled to ask the question yet again.

"Yes, Michael will be all right. He's alive and out of the battle." Philip thought, but had the good judgment not to say, "If only he doesn't do anything foolish."

Chapter Nineteen

CAGING A LION

London—December 1943

"Philip, I'm afraid we have a really tough assignment for you this time."

Philip decided that being a minister without portfolio had its definite drawbacks. Just as soon as he became competent in one area, his assignment changed and he was off on some new task for which he was totally unsuited. Or so it always felt.

"Sir?" Philip was talking with Lord Halifax of the Cabinet.

"It's General Patton. We need someone to babysit him."

"General Patton? The American?"

Halifax smiled. "Yes, perhaps you've heard of his recent troubles in Palermo. He struck a soldier in a field hospital for complaining of shell shock. The American newspapers had a field day with that, and he was forced to apologize publicly."

"I know. For someone as proud as Patton, it had to be humiliating. Still, what's that got to do with me?"

"It turns out that the Americans are ready to throw Patton over. And they would if not for the fact that the Germans think he's their most brilliant general and so fear him the most."

"A bit of a puzzle, isn't it?" Philip laughed.

"A puzzle indeed. One that General Eisenhower is wise enough to capitalize on. What I'm about to tell you is completely top secret. I know that you don't share anything anyway, but I have to say that."

"You have my assurance."

"Eisenhower is allowing Patton to transfer here to England to form the American First Army Group. There will be a massive and fairly obvious buildup of tanks, landing craft, troopships, and support units all massing near the ports for a cross-channel invasion at the Pas de Calais."

"Calais? But I thought the crossing was scheduled for . . ." Philip checked himself. As a cabinet minister he knew that current plans called for an invasion of France at Normandy, far to the west of Calais. Normandy was an impractical choice in that it exposed the troops to the greatest time at sea as well as landing the troops far from the main battle front. But it had the element of surprise and would provide a great staging area once the Port of Cherbourg was captured and secured. Besides, it would take the Germans a fair amount of time to move rein-forcements into the area, which might prove the very margin needed to establish a successful beachhead.

Halifax smiled. "Oh, did I mention that Patton's First Army Group will consist of nothing more than plywood tanks, phony landing craft, empty tents, and imaginary soldiers?"

Philip shook his head. "I don't understand." When there was no response, he continued. "You'll have to forgive me, but I'm not really a military man. I was a chaplain in the last war, not a member of the infantry."

"Don't worry, Philip. A lot of people are befuddled by this. It seems that Eisenhower is going to create a fictional army to prey on the Germans' fears. To the Germans it will be perfectly logical that Patton is put in charge of the main invasion, and so they will believe the reports of their spies about the buildup of an army in the southeast to take advantage of the short crossing at Calais. Hopefully they will divert troops and reinforcements to that theatre while neglecting Normandy. Since Calais presents the shortest crossing and would place our armies several hundred miles closer to Germany, it's the most logical choice.

It's also the place where we're most likely to be driven back into the sea precisely because it is so convenient to the Germans. Hence the need for a ruse in that area. Patton's role is to make the bluff seem authentic."

"But why would he agree to such a thing? It seems to me that a man with his experience and credentials would sooner retire than play an imaginary role."

"It's part of his penance. My understanding is that Eisenhower is giving him the chance to redeem himself. If he plays the part well and stays out of trouble, then he'll be given a real command after the invasion."

Philip was quiet. All of this was interesting, but there was still no explanation as to why he'd been summoned.

He smiled. "Perhaps it's better if I don't know why I'm here, but I am curious."

"Really, Carlyle. To make the deception work we have to let Patton be seen with all the right people, including cabinet ministers. And since you're the only member who has lived in America, you're the natural candidate."

Philip shook his head ruefully. "So I'm to be part of the deception? A pretend minister creating a pretend army." Before Halifax could protest, Philip continued. "Don't worry, I'll do it. It's rather perfect for me. It would be a disaster to put me in charge of coordinating a genuine military operation, but perhaps even I can pull off a phony one."

"You know that this is serious. If the deception works, it could be the difference between success and failure for the real landing."

Philip sobered up. "I know. I'll go to work with a vengeance. While the props may be artificial, their usefulness is anything but that. Thank you for entrusting me with it."

"Oh, I doubt you'll be thanking me for long. Patton really can be insufferable, and he's going to tax your diplomatic skills to the limit. Just remember that you hold the upper hand. He has to be on his best behavior so he can win his way back into

Ike's heart. Help him succeed, and you may cause Hitler genuine grief when Patton gets a real command."

As Philip walked away from the interview he had to shake his head to clear his thoughts.

* * *

Philip was in an unusually good mood when he walked up the steps of his London townhouse. In spite of the weather, which was unseasonably cold, even for December, he felt a bit of Christmas cheer. He'd already had a preliminary meeting with some of General Patton's American staff, and they had managed to smuggle an assortment of Hershey chocolate bars out of their commissary and were kind enough to turn over an entire box to Philip to share with Grace and Claire. He knew they'd feel extremely guilty, since it was such a rare treasure that no ordinary civilians in the British Isles got to enjoy, but the Americans were insistent, and Philip was thrilled to think he could share this rare treat with the women he loved.

Claire had been out at Carlyle Manor meeting with a new group of American soldiers at the Deseret Academy, but she had promised to come into the city for the balance of the week. With Grace working in the city, Philip could surprise them that evening after supper.

As he walked up to the front door, he was met by their butler, who apparently was not having as successful a day as Philip, at least by the look on his face. Philip tried some cheerful banter but sobered up quickly when the response was, "There's a gentleman waiting to see you, sir. He's with Lady Carlyle in the parlor."

Rueing his naive happiness of the previous moment, Philip quickly handed over his coat, hat, and walking stick and said quietly, "Thank you, John," and then hurried across the hall into the parlor. Claire was seated on the couch, her face deathly pale. *But she's not crying,* he noted hopefully. Standing to the side was a senior naval officer—a captain.

"What is it?" Philip said quickly.

Claire looked up at him and then turned her gaze to the officer, who shifted uncomfortably as the focus turned to him.

"Lord Carlyle, my name is Geoffrey Locke. I'm assigned to the Admiralty, and I'm afraid I have some very bad news to deliver."

Philip turned to Claire, who dropped her gaze and raised a handkerchief to her eyes. Looking back at Captain Locke, he felt that what he wanted was for the man to just leave the house without giving them any news. Certainly that would be better than hearing what he had to say. Philip's mind tried to turn the clock back to the moment just before he entered the house when everything seemed right with the world, but he failed. As he prepared himself for whatever Locke had to tell them, he realized that quite unconsciously he was gripping the box of Hershey chocolate so tightly that he'd undoubtedly crushed a number of bars.

"I assume this has something to do with Michael?"

"I'm afraid so." Locke stepped over and handed him a telegram. "Perhaps it's best if you read this, sir."

Philip almost dropped the box as he reached for the paper, but caught himself in time to set it down on the table. He had a dreadful feeling of guilt in doing so, realizing that he'd been so happy about a stupid box of chocolates just a few moments earlier at the very same time that something was so terribly wrong that the Admiralty would send a personal envoy. His hands trembling, he reached out again and took the paper in his hands.

We regret to inform you that the International Red Cross has received reports that Lieutenant Michael Carlyle, RN, has been reported killed in action while in the custody of

German authorities. We have no independent means of veri-
fying this report, since Lieutenant Carlyle has been missing
in action and is reputed to be behind enemy lines. We will
keep you apprised should any additional information
become available. On behalf of His Majesty's Government,
please accept our deepest sympathy.

Philip staggered and readily consented to be helped to the davenport to sit next to Claire. As Philip fell into his seat, Captain Locke straightened up and said, "I'm very sorry, sir. Very sorry indeed."

Staggered as he was by what had just happened, Philip still managed to struggle to his feet in respect for the captain.

"Please stay seated, sir. I don't think it's wise for you to exert yourself just now."

Almost in a daze, Philip nodded and settled back into his seat. After the initial anxiety of learning that Michael was missing, they had received the second telegram reporting him a prisoner, which had acted like a great relief valve, and Philip had assumed he was safe. There had been nothing to prepare him for this shock. His hands were cold when Claire reached over and took his right hand in hers.

"But how can this be? He was reported to be a prisoner of war. The Germans certainly wouldn't kill him."

"Of course we don't know all the details," Locke started to say. At the sound of the captain's voice, Philip looked up and realized that the poor man was still standing above them.

"Please, Captain, pull up a chair and talk with us. Even if you don't know much, we'd like to know everything you do know." He took a couple of deep breaths to steady his voice. "Perhaps we just need someone to stay with us for a few moments."

"Of course. I'd be pleased to stay, sir." Locke moved over to a wingback chair next to the couch and moved it so that he was facing the Carlyles directly. Once he was seated, he took a deep breath. "Although reports out of that area are very spotty, the Red Cross did pass along some information that seems to bear on what might have occurred. I'm afraid that it might not ease your grief to know the details, however." His voice trailed off.

Philip turned and looked at Claire, his own anxiety rising in fear that perhaps Michael had been tortured or mistreated or that he was the victim of some other gruesome event at the hands of the Germans. He didn't want to proceed if Claire wasn't up to it, even though he knew he'd ask for details later. The look in her eyes told him that she wanted to know, however, so he turned back to Locke.

"Please tell us whatever you've heard, Captain."

Locke shifted uncomfortably in his seat. "Yes, sir. Well, it seems that your son and at least one or two other British lads were on a train heading north, presumably to a prison camp in Germany. At approximately the same time that they were scheduled to pass through Bologna in northeast Italy, the Royal Air Force attacked the rail yards there, and it may be that their train was hit by some of the bombs."

Philip's eyes widened. "You mean they were killed by British bombing?"

"Of course we don't know that for certain." Locke tried to look away, but Philip held his gaze. "But we do know that one of our raids took place at the time the Germans reported his death, so it's a distinct possibility."

"Oh, my," Claire said, the sound in her voice indicating the horror of what this implied.

Philip didn't do or say anything. He just sat next to Claire, not speaking. It seemed as if he was paralyzed.

Finally Philip looked up at the captain. "Thank you for coming to tell us personally. I'm sure this is a great burden for you."

Locke took this as his invitation to leave, so he stood up, as did Philip. "We do our best to visit every home when one of our boys loses his life. It's the least the country can do to honor their sacrifice."

Philip pursed his lips and nodded. More than anything he wanted to be alone. "I'll see you to the door."

"That won't be necessary, sir. I can find my way out. Please stay here with Lady Carlyle." Philip nodded, and the man made his way to the door of the room and left.

Once the room was clear, Philip breathed deeply for a few moments more and sat back down next to Claire. He was surprised to find how little emotion he felt. There was no panic like he felt when he learned that Dominic had died. There were no hysterics from either him or Claire, although that certainly remained a possibility. He felt numb. Numb and tired and cold.

When Claire started sobbing next to him, he put his arm around her but found he was unable to say anything to comfort her. He felt as if he should be crying too, but the shock was simply too great, and he just sat there as his wife expressed her grief.

* * *

It was three days since they'd received the dreadful telegram. Each day Philip had gotten himself up and off to the office very early and returned home late at night. He'd avoided talking to Grace and had said barely a few words to Claire. He would have done the same this morning except that he found Claire unexpectedly waiting for him in the breakfast room. He mumbled a stiff good morning and made as if he was going to leave, but Claire quite subtly blocked him. As he was forced to look up at her, he was shocked at her appearance. There was no color to her cheeks, and her eyes were red and puffy. It was as if life itself had been drained away like the sap out of a cut flower, and she simply drooped in pain.

"Philip, are you going to talk to me about this?"

Philip dropped his gaze. "What is there to say? We've lost our son. Just like that, he's gone. Our dark-haired boy with such great promise."

"We've lost them both," Claire replied quietly.

Philip nodded an acknowledgment. "I had so much hope that he was all right. He should be all right. But hope doesn't seem to do much these days." He was quiet for a moment. "Nor does prayer, for that matter." He glanced up with a look that conveyed both despair and defiance.

Claire turned and looked directly into Philip's eyes, trying to decide whether or not she should say what was on her mind. When she saw his eyes narrowed and brooding, she felt she must continue. The simple truth was that since Dominic's death, Philip had not displayed the same generosity of spirit he once had, and she sensed that if he didn't deal with his emotions at Michael's passing, things might get even worse. So in as even a voice as she could muster, she interrupted his silence. "I said we've lost both of them, Philip. I'm not sure you heard me."

Philip turned and looked at her. "I did hear you. Yes, we've lost them both. But Michael was heir, and he's the one we've just learned about. Perhaps we could have a moment to grieve for him."

"Perhaps that would be easier if you took time to reconcile your feelings about Dominic."

"I don't know what you mean. I've thought of Dominic many times in these awful months." Philip held his gaze down toward the carpet, even though he knew Claire wanted him to look at her.

"That's good to know. But we never talk about him." She looked at Philip searchingly. "Philip, do you realize that except for a few words when you first came home from Africa, you and I have never talked about him directly—about his life, about his death, or about the circumstances that drove him to end his life as he did. We didn't even have a memorial service."

"Somehow that seemed . . . problematic."

"Oh? Perhaps it would have been healing."

"Claire, it's very difficult for me to talk about such things. It's not that I don't have feelings, but it's *my* nature to keep my feelings to myself." He dropped his gaze even further.

"But that leaves Grace and me so lonely. Grace and I have had to rely on each other. There have been many tears shed for Dominic—for his frailty and for his grace, for the aggravation he caused and for the fear he must have felt. Philip, we've needed you to talk to us, but you've been so withdrawn. You might have answers to our questions. Perhaps if we can settle our feelings for Dominic, then we can work through this new tragedy that has befallen our family." Claire caught her breath, because she didn't want to cry.

Philip shook his head as if in despair. "I'm sorry you've had such trouble. I should be a help to you and offer comfort and support, but I honestly don't know what to say. I've tried countless times to reconcile myself to Dominic's death, but somehow my feelings never come into focus. Sometimes I grieve for him deeply and even miss him. He was so intelligent and witty. But other times I mourn the futility of his suicide, and I'm ashamed by his dereliction of duty." Philip resorted to his habit of chewing his bottom lip when distressed. "I'm embarrassed to admit that some of the time I even remain angry at him—even though he was kind to me in our last time together." He shook his head as he struggled to control his emotions. "That's the hardest thing of all, to acknowledge that I can still find it in my heart to be angry with him. I'm ashamed of that and so do my best to put him out of my mind." He looked up at Claire with pleading eyes. "And now I feel even more guilty at the thought that I probably will be able to grieve properly for Michael because he was easier to get along with, because he was more like me, perhaps. What kind of a man am I that I can feel that differently about my sons?"

Philip slumped next to her as he attempted to conceal his distress.

"My dear Philip. You remain the best man I have ever known. That's why I hate to see you suffer. My great fear is that if you don't deal with your tangled emotions about Dominic, you'll never make peace with yourself about either Dominic or Michael. And if you don't, part of you will die—the part that is capable of such great unselfish love and caring." She stroked his hair, hoping that he would look up, but he didn't. Perhaps he couldn't. "So I think you must face their deaths in turn and find peace with both of them."

Philip's breathing was fast and deep. Claire knew that she had exposed his feelings and that it was excruciatingly uncomfortable for him. At times like this, his natural reaction was to try to get away to be by himself rather than to argue or continue. It's why he had stayed away from England in the first place when he joined the Church, rather than return home to argue with his father. It was the way he'd dealt with many of his disappointments in public life—withdrawing from the social scene rather than forcing his way onto the stage. But she felt he must face up to his distress.

As predicted, he started to rise. "Perhaps we could talk of this later . . . when I've had a chance to compose myself."

Claire hated to make things hard for him but decided that she must be firm. This was the longest conversation they'd had about Dominic since his death, and she wanted it to continue. "Philip, I've lost both my sons just like you, and right now I need you." She waited, but Philip still didn't sit down. He didn't leave either. "Please . . ." At last Philip sat down, but he didn't look at her.

"Philip." Her voice was soft and calm, but still firm. "How much we have lost. I can't even comprehend it. But I've been thinking about this for some time, and I have a thought about why you've been so closed about Dominic. Would you like to know what I think?"

Philip shrugged, which she took as a chance to continue. "I believe that until you can forgive Dominic for causing you to feel guilty, you won't be able to heal emotionally, and in time you will become bitter and resentful."

"Forgive Dominic for making me feel guilty? I don't get angry at him for making me feel guilty. If anything I get mad that he was always so obstinate and provoking."

"I know it sounds odd, but hear me out. Consider for a moment that part of your distress is caused because Dominic's life—and death—make you feel as if you were a failure as a father. If so, it's quite natural that you don't like feeling that way, so instead you find more reasons to blame him. If you can make it his fault, then you don't have to feel guilty. Perhaps that's why you try not to think of him. But then as you blame him, you feel even more guilty. And so continues a bitter cycle of regret and remorse."

"But perhaps I am guilty! I was often impatient with him and disgusted by what I took to be his laziness and sarcasm. I should have reached out to him in love, but instead I was short with him and badgered him. Perhaps if I'd been kinder and more patient . . ."

"The truth, my dear, is that he was hard to get along with, particularly when he provoked you and Michael. What you take to be a personal failing was, in many respects, quite reasonable. I felt there were many times you tried to reach past his bravado to help him get his life in order, but he seldom let you in." She was wistful. "He seldom let anyone in."

"Charity suffereth long, charity is not puffed up, is not easily provoked . . . I've always treasured those words from the Apostle Paul. Yet, I didn't suffer long and I was often puffed up. Yes, I wanted to help Dominic lead a good life, but I also wanted him to conform, because his cheating and his poor grades reflected badly on the family. On me! So there were times when I was angry because he was embarrassing me. If that isn't being puffed up, I don't know what is. So you see, I *was* responsible—I made myself responsible by failing to act charitably towards him. And in the end, he felt himself all alone and so he took desperate action. And nothing I can do will bring him back." There was an anguished sound to Philip's voice, an almost strangled sound. "You say I should forgive Dominic? How can he ever forgive me? He's gone. And now Michael is gone as well, and I can never make it right. I couldn't protect either of them. All of this makes me far from the wonderful person everyone seems to think I am. What should I do?"

Philip stifled a sob and dropped his head into his hands, resting his elbows on his knees. The world was dark, and he was bereft.

Claire stroked his hair again and brought her right hand up to his cheek, where she cupped it in her hand. "Philip. The only thing you can do is forgive yourself and Dominic. Only then can you heal. And then, in time, your memories will be good, and we can live out our lives in peace, if not happiness. 'Of you it is required to forgive all men . . .' I think that includes yourself."

"I don't know. I know what you say is true, but I don't know how."

"Think of it this way. Whose purpose does guilt and blame like this serve? Heavenly Father's? I don't think so. So logically it must be something that Satan would find pleasure in. Particularly now that Dominic is gone. All your anguish can do is haunt his memory and leave your feelings forever unresolved. And the only known antidote for that condition is forgiveness."

Philip looked up weakly. "You should be the chaplain . . ." He paused, but Claire didn't mind the silence. It wasn't hostile now. In time, Philip said quietly, "I thought I had forgiven him. On that last night in North Africa I told him that the Savior loved him. I felt that deeply at the time. Doesn't that mean something?"

"Of course it does. It means that in his moment of greatest need you set aside your embarrassment and personal anxiety so that you could act on his behalf. And that was a magnificent gift that undoubtedly helped him. But as meaningful as the moment was, it probably doesn't make sense that you could let go of a lifetime of confusing feelings and emotions in a single moment, as much as you might like to. So now you're left with confusion. In a very real sense, you are in the same position he was on that fateful night."

"I don't know what you mean."

"What I mean is that you must accept the Savior's boundless charity in exactly the same way you told Dominic to accept it. You must turn all your unresolved emotions over to Christ and let Him be the judge. You must pray for the ability to forgive Dominic and to forgive yourself for not doing all the things you think you should have done. Philip, you have spent a lifetime loving the gospel and all it stands for. Isn't this the time to accept the Atonement for both you and your troubled boy? Isn't this the time to let the Savior heal you?"

"Can you help me?" Philip asked.

"I will. If you'll let me, I promise I will. And Christ will too."

"I hope so."

* * *

Later that evening Philip came down from his room. His eyes were red, but he wasn't crying. "Are you all right?" Claire asked gently.

"I guess I am, because I seem to have run out of moisture."

She tried to smile. "I'm sure there will be more. At least I've found myself capable of crying on more than one occasion, and usually at the most inopportune times."

"What about Grace? How is she doing? The news of Michael must be devastating for her."

"She's out taking a walk. She should be back soon."

"Good, because I've been thinking that perhaps when she returns, the three of us can sit and talk about the things we loved in Dominic and Michael. There really were good times with Dominic. He had a sensitive spirit that sometimes manifested itself so beautifully, as in his poetry. And I believe that had the war not thrust itself upon him, he may have turned a corner in New York City, where he could feel the joy of his accomplishments. He'd found a challenge that he was equal to. But then a more taxing one came along, and he became another casualty of war."

"I'm so glad you went to see him in Africa. Just imagine how terrible it would have been had he been there all alone."

"It was a gift from God that I could go, wasn't it?" Philip was lost in thought for a moment. "It was such a brief encounter, but so much was said in a few short words of reconciliation. Late that night, after he died, I felt wrapped in the Spirit of the Lord as if in a warm blanket of love. I missed that feeling when it was gone. My heart has gone cold."

"I think I feel the Spirit now, don't you?"

Philip smiled. "I do. It's something I have missed desperately." Philip drew his wife close to him and hugged her with all his might. It was the kind of hug he used to give. "Thank you for helping me face this. I'm sorry I left you and Grace alone."

Claire hugged him tight. "Perhaps we could plan a memorial service for both our boys. I think there are many who would like to come." Claire said this as positively as she could. She'd expected Philip to agree, and he started to, but before he could get the words out, she felt him start to sob again.

"We've lost both our boys, Love."

Chapter Twenty

A DANGEROUS
TURN OF EVENTS

Parma, Italy

"Whoa!" Jules muttered under his breath.

"What is it?" Michael asked anxiously.

Jules tipped his head slightly to the left and motioned with his eyes. Michael turned casually to see what danger had presented itself, and he felt his stomach lurch when he saw a group of about a dozen Germans in uniform. These were the first Germans they had seen since they had left Marcio's cousin's house nearly an hour earlier. They had managed to walk to the railroad station in relative obscurity, and only now were they in the full glare of public scrutiny.

Michael's throat suddenly went dry, but he turned his head slowly from side to side as if in casual conversation, just in case someone was watching them, and then said as quietly as he could under his breath, "Are there any officers?" It was an important question, because if the group consisted of only enlisted men, Michael could easily stride past them with nothing more than a salute. But if there were officers, particularly higher-ranking officers, then he could easily be drawn into a conversation that could prove disastrous.

"Afraid so." Jules smiled and looked down at his timetable. Marcio seemed frozen to the spot, and Jenkins, bless his heart, looked as serene and unconcerned as a milk cow grazing happily in the middle of a pasture on a warm August day. Except that it was December, and there was no reason to be serene—unless you were a common laborer who was deaf and dumb. For a moment, Michael wished he had drawn Jenkins's role.

"What are we going to do?" he said in a soft but natural voice. They had come to the realization earlier on that whispering drew more attention than speaking softly. Somehow the s in words stood out more noticeably when whispered, and the tilting of the head to hear a whisper always looked suspicious.

Jules sighed. "We're going to go to Placenza, rather than La Spezia."

"Placenza? But doesn't that take us even farther behind German lines and add extra time?" The change of destination took Michael so completely by surprise that he said this far too loudly.

Jules straightened up and stretched, doing his best to act unconcerned. Smiling, he said, "Yes, that's true. But Placenza boards from Platform Three, which is to our right, while La Spezia boards at Platform Seven, which is directly through those Germans. What would you choose?"

Michael recognized that Jules was correct, but the realization of this disappointing news caused him to shake his head ever so slightly, which wasn't at all what he wanted to convey to the people in the terminal. Worse, he saw one of the German enlisted men cast a glance in their direction. While the fellow didn't appear concerned, it was impossible to know, and Michael felt a rush of adrenaline hit his system as if his mind thought the entire group was about to come chasing after them.

Attempting to recover, he looked down at Jules's timetable, pointed, and said, in his very best German, "Platform Three." Jules responded perfectly, scowling with his very best stage face and then turning to Marcio, who quickly repeated the words in Italian. Jules nodded his head vigorously, and the group turned to the right. It had become second nature by now for Marcio to physically turn and motion for Jenkins to follow. Michael marveled at how perfectly Jenkins had mastered the role of playing deaf and dumb. In the previous two legs of the journey, there had been at least three occasions when someone spoke directly to Jenkins, or a loud noise had startled everyone else in the area, but Jenkins had never once reacted. Michael was impressed and knew that he never could have pulled it off as well.

As they approached the train, they had to pass by a couple of German noncommissioned officers who saluted crisply but made no attempt to stop them. Marcio proved himself a cool character, as well, as he brought out four first-class tickets from Parma to Placenza to replace the tickets to La Spezia. Obviously, his friends had thought of everything, and once more their thorough preparation had saved the day.

As they reached the platform, Jules motioned to the group to stand off to the side. He'd developed this strategy early on in the journey because it minimized the chance of someone onboard trying to engage them in idle conversation. In this case, it was something of a risk because if the first-class cabins filled up, there would be quite a scene as some Italian group was forced out to make room for a German officer and his entourage. Michael would have boarded early had he been in charge, but Jules had more experience at feeling entitled, and so he waited. And waited. And waited even after the final blast from the train whistle indicated the train was about to leave. Finally, Michael decided to take charge—he was a colonel after all—but his exasperated look made no impression on Jules. Just when Michael thought that Jules must have decided to purposely miss this train for some undisclosed reason, Jules made his move. The conductor was about to lift the small footstool that helped passengers reach the lowest step of the railcar when Jules strode forward confidently and called out in a loud voice, *"Nein!"* which meant that the fellow was to stop. The Italian conductor looked up with a furious glare on his face, but he blanched when he saw this apparently arrogant German officer shouting at him and immediately replaced the footstool. Jules charged up to the train brusquely, and Michael, acting in character, strode over at a more leisurely pace while Marcio and Jenkins scurried after him. After boarding the train, Marcio lingered a bit and Michael heard him say something under his breath to the Italian conductor, who smirked as he heard it. Although Michael was catching a number of Italian words at this point, Marcio had said it so fast that Michael hadn't understood a single word. But by the amused look on their faces, he figured it was some kind of an inside joke that Italians told each other when dealing with their occupiers. Nice touch.

Once onboard they were shown to a vacant first-class cabin. Italy followed the European convention of passenger trains in which each coach was divided into compartments shared by a limited number of guests, rather than the open seating common in America. By securing first-class passage, they had a sleeping berth with beds that folded down from the ceiling. In addition to having more comfortable seating than a regular compartment, the best part was that it meant that the four of them fully occupied the cabin so they didn't have to share with strangers. On an earlier leg of their journey, a day trip, they didn't have a sleeper and so had to have a number of guests ride with them. Michael and Jules were forced to make small talk in German to maintain the ruse, and by the end of the day, Michael's head ached from trying to maintain the charade. Meanwhile, the Italians were a very expressive people, with animated hand gestures and loud but cheerful voices. One of the passengers, a minor government official, talked so fast that it was hard for even Marcio to keep up. At one point Michael had decided to exercise his authority as a German officer and so asserted himself by insisting that everyone quiet down so he could have a nap. That had cast an immediate pall over the room, and for perhaps fifteen or twenty minutes things were much quieter. But when Michael really did fall asleep, the conversation picked up again with the usual gripes about the lack of food and basic necessities. Meanwhile, Jenkins sat there serenely acting as if he didn't understand a word—which, of course, he didn't since it was all spoken in Italian. Michael wondered if Jenkins would be as successful if the dialogue were in English and someone tried to surprise him with a question.

Approximately twenty minutes into the journey there was a knock at the door, causing Michael's heart to skip a beat, even though the knock was expected. Sure enough, a bored Italian official stood on the other side of the door requesting their travel documents. It was a well-practiced routine by this point for Marcio to collect their identification papers and to chat amiably with the official while he looked over the tickets and documentation. But this time Marcio hesitated, and in an instant they knew why. Standing behind the Italian was a German officer. When Michael saw that he was a colonel, no less, he realized that the man would not be intimidated by his rank. So he drew a deep breath and waited. In a minute or two it would very likely be up to him to maintain the safety of the group by performing well whatever response he was called on to make. At that moment he felt a great deal of gratitude to his father for insisting that the family members learn the major languages of the Continent, even though he had originally thought it a waste of time.

At first the German didn't say anything, even though he obviously saw Michael sitting there in his uniform. For their part, Michael and Jules acted as if the whole thing meant absolutely nothing to them. Finally, after perhaps ninety seconds or so, the Italian official shook his head and started to hand the papers back to Marcio. At that point the German reached out and took one of the passes away from him. After studying it for a minute, he said something in German. For a moment no one responded, even though both the Italian official and Marcio were supposed to know German. After what seemed an embarrassing pause, Michael opened his eyes and said something in a deep guttural voice that sounded totally unfamiliar to the others. The German responded in a tone that seemed challenging even to those who didn't understand. Michael fired back very quickly and very sharply.

The German hesitated for a moment then fired something at Michael in response, but Michael responded just as fast. At this point, Michael happened to glance sideways and saw that Jules was fingering the inside of his jacket where a small pistol had been sewn into a secret compartment. Michael hoped Jules would not overreact.

There was one more exchange, and just when it looked like all was lost, the German officer burst out laughing, and a broad grin came across Michael's face, and he stood up and shook the German's hand. Marcio and the Italian official both smiled as well. The German officer reached out and handed Michael his identification papers and then retreated to the hallway. With that, Michael sat back down and closed his eyes as Marcio pushed the door to the compartment closed, locking it as he did so.

Marcio sat down with a sigh and then laughed again. Jules and Jenkins sat there in silence, waiting for an explanation that never came. Obviously the conversation had gone too fast for Jules to follow. Finally, even though he knew Michael would somehow use it against him, he broke the silence.

"Well?"

"Well, what?" Michael said laconically, his eyes still closed.

"Well, what just happened? I couldn't go through my mental Deutsch–English dictionary fast enough to translate."

"What happened was that there was a little problem, and I handled it."

Jules narrowed his gaze. "You should know, Lieutenant Carlyle, that I have my hand on a loaded pistol. A moment ago I was prepared to use it on that German officer. I can just as easily use it on you."

Michael cocked his head and raised an eyebrow. "How dare you threaten a superior officer, Mr. Ellington. I'll put you on report for this."

"Get in line. In the meantime, I have the gun and you don't."

Michael shifted in his seat and opened both eyes. "Well, if you're going to be like that . . ." He grinned. "It seems that the German wanted to confirm where I was from. When I told him, he made a comment about the fact that Eva Braun is from the same city."

"Eva Braun?" Jenkins asked.

"Yes, Hitler's mistress. He asked if I knew her from Munich. There were two ways for me to take that, of course. The first was to respond to it seriously, which would have called for one response, the second to think of it as a bit of bait for gossip purposes. I chose the latter. So without really answering his question, I told an old joke about how Hitler is reputed to not like girls all that much, which makes Eva more window dressing than an actual mistress, and the fellow seemed to like the story. At least he laughed at all the right places. It was one of those authentic touches, you know. Something that we Germans share with each other, but a joke that if you told as a British officer would wind you up in front of a firing squad."

Jules shook his head in disbelief. "You told a stranger a joke about the *Führer*?"

"It was a very short joke."

"I can't believe it." Jules broke into a grin. "There may be hope for you yet, Carlyle. You may turn out to have a sense of humor after all." He slapped Michael on the back. "Good show!"

"It was a calculated risk—but one that paid off. I can promise you that this fellow thinks I'm as authentic as a good Bavarian beer."

"Not that you'd know a good Bavarian beer from a tub full of swamp water," Jules replied. He was thoughtful for a moment. "We're still here, and so far they haven't crashed through the door to shoot us all, so apparently it's all right to tell a joke about the supreme leader of the Thousand-Year Reich. My sincere congratulations."

"Ah, you flatterer, you. I guess I'll drop those insubordination charges after all. Why don't you let me buy you a drink in the dining car? It's a bit stuffy in here, don't you think?"

"You go out there if you like, but I'm staying right here. I thought I could play along in German, but I couldn't follow you two to save my life. I'd sooner starve than watch you play your bluff again. My heart can't take it."

Michael burst into a grin. "I've never thought of you as a worrier, Jules. This is such a nice role reversal. Oh, well, let's go, Marcio. Maybe we can strike up a card game or something. And if you're lucky, Jules, we'll bring you some food back when we return. That is, if we do return . . ." he said ominously.

Jules shook his head. "That's enough of that. If you're going to get us killed, I want to be there when it happens, not hiding here in the cabin. We'll all go. And there's a very good chance that my German will improve if I get good and drunk."

"If you get good and drunk, there's a very good chance that you'll blow our cover completely, so I'll be watching what you drink. And I am your superior officer . . ."

"You are not, you blaggard!" Jules said in too loud a voice. "I'm the commander, you're the lieutenant."

Michael smiled again. "But not in German uniforms, Herr Lieutenant. You should always do what your colonel tells you!" Jules shook his head in aggravation.

"What about you, Jenkins? Care to join us?"

"No thank you, sir. It's too hard on my brain to ignore everything going on. Particularly with these kind of antics. If it's all right, I'll try to catch some sleep."

* * *

"Jenkins! Wake up!"

Jenkins stirred in the sleeping berth and swatted at Jules. "Go away and leave me alone." Of course that was a dangerous thing to do to an officer, but Jenkins was asleep after all.

It had been a week since they'd taken the diversion to Placenza, and, after spending two days at a safe house there, they'd finally felt comfortable heading back down south to Genoa, where they could connect with a train that followed the coastline to Southern France and on to the Riviera. With more opportunities to use the language, Michael had experienced a growing sense of confidence in his German and had managed to bluff his way through several encounters with senior German officers, even going so far as to talk about some of the battles they had supposedly been in together.

Fortunately, he'd learned at the feet of the master, Jules Ellington, in a late-night conversation in their sleeper car. "You really just need to know how to get people talking, and soon enough you'll know exactly what to say to sound convincing. Remarkably, they'll tell you. There's really nothing you can't learn with a little flattery."

"And if flattery doesn't work?" Michael asked.

"But it always does work, at least for me." He cocked his head to the side. "Of course, you're different, not a natural flatterer at all." He shook his head. "So perhaps you do need another tactic. Try this. If you stumble across a really hard case who doesn't open up easily, just try some sincere curiosity. For you that would probably work even better." When Michael looked skeptical, Jules continued. "You see, Michael, people see and hear what they expect to see and hear. If these German fellows were on the lookout for British imposters posing as German officers, they'd be onto us in a moment. But when we pass through the cabin, they expect that we are legitimate, and so they immediately give us the benefit of the doubt. Any good confidence man knows that you just listen to what your mark is saying, and pretty soon he'll be telling you his life story and giving you everything you need to know to gain his confidence. Suppose someone tells you that he's from a village you should know. You reply, 'Ah, yes, I remember the mayor—what was his name?' to which the other fellow replies, 'You mean Mayor Schindelmacher?' You reply, just in case he's setting you up, 'Schindelmacher? For some reason I didn't remember it that way. Did he have brown hair or black hair?' 'Black hair!' the fellow replies. Now you know that Schindelmacher is a real person because he just gave you his hair color. So you finish with a triumphant, 'Oh, yes, Schindelmacher, he was really something wasn't he? What's your favorite Schindelmacher story?' And with that," Jules said with a sly grin, "he's running off at the mouth telling you every important detail about the village. All you have to do is nod appreciatively and laugh once in a while to encourage him." He sat back in his chair and smiled like a Cheshire cat. "It's really just that easy."

Michael said, "You are a scoundrel, Jules. A genuine, high-born scoundrel. It will catch up with you someday."

"Probably, but then I'll just charm the jailors like Joseph did in Egypt, and pretty soon I'll be running the jail!" They'd had a good laugh over that.

But Jules wasn't laughing now. "Jenkins," he repeated urgently, "you've got to wake up. We're in trouble!"

It worked, as Jenkins sat bolt upright in bed, hitting his head in the process, which prompted a curse. "What is it?" he said crossly.

"You and I have got to get off the train before we pull into the station. Michael and Marcio will do the same but from another door. We need to move quickly!"

At this point, Jenkins reached out to turn on the light, but Jules swatted his hand. "We need to stay in the dark."

"All right, Captain Ellington, I'm awake now, and you've got me scared. Can you tell me what's going on? And where are Lieutenant Carlyle and Marcio?"

"They're still in the dining car playing cards. An Italian fellow approached Marcio to tell him that the Germans have discovered that the officer whose identity Lieutenant Carlyle has stolen is dead. The Resistance became aware that they're looking for him and sent this fellow to warn us. Which is why we have to jump from the train. I left Michael and Marcio in the club car to maintain our deception, but they'll make their exit shortly."

"Jump!" There was a clear note of alarm in Jenkins's voice. "We're going to jump? But the train is still at full acceleration!" Now his heart really was racing.

"There's no time to talk. We've got to go right now."

Jenkins was frozen in place, and Jules softened his fear. "Listen, Jenkins. We don't know if the Germans think he's deserted or if they think his identity is being used. But we can be certain that they'll put an alert out and that the next station will be on the lookout for him. At the very least, the colonel that Michael joked with is almost certain to connect the dots once he gets the news. Now you see why we have to get off!"

"Let's go, then." Jenkins was off the bed in an instant, and he quickly grabbed the little bag that he always kept packed and ready for just such a moment. Without another word, they quietly opened the door to the hallway, which was dimly lit by a single bulb at each end. Looking both directions, Jules beckoned for Jenkins to follow. They made their way to the end of the car and stepped onto the platform that connected their car to the next car. Stepping down into the stairwell, Jules looked forward, where the full moon revealed the silhouette of a distant city, mostly blacked out as a hedge against air raids. Casting a glance back along the profile of the train as it raced through the moonlit night, he saw first one form leap from the train and tumble down the embankment, followed by another.

"Go ahead and jump, Jenkins, and I'll follow." But Jenkins was frozen in place.

"I don't think I can do it. You go. I'll just let them arrest me."

"Sorry, mate—can't take the risk. Just remember to tuck and roll when you hit, just like they taught you in Scotland, or wherever you were trained." With that he pushed Jenkins from the platform. The sound of Jenkins's terrified shriek was easily drowned out by the shrill turning of the metal wheels.

Chapter Twenty-one

GENERAL PATTON

London—January 1944

"Is he always so charming and considerate?"

Philip turned to Karen Demming with a surprised look on his face. Having accompanied General Patton to visit wounded soldiers in the hospital where Karen worked, Philip had moved off to the side of the action to stand next to her while the general moved from bed to bed with a reporter and cameraman in tow. Her question caught him off guard.

"Charming and considerate? I doubt many people have ever used that particular combination of words to describe General Patton. He's usually viewed as vain and egotistical—and often bellicose."

"But look at how tenderly he speaks to the injured men. He's got them laughing and trying to sit up at attention in their beds. That fellow he's talking with right now has been so morose that we've had him on a suicide watch, and yet General Patton has him positively glowing."

Philip considered her words. Having accompanied General George Patton to a variety of events in and around the London area, he'd come to realize that the general was far more complex than the newspapers liked to present him. Most British and American newspapers portrayed him as a bully and a braggart, as evidenced by the slapping incident in Sicily, with some even calling for his dismissal. The Germans, on the other hand, viewed him as America's most daring and skilled military tactician, which was why they were buying into the ruse that he was busy creating the First Army Group as the main invasion force to launch from southeast England toward Calais. The evidence of their acceptance was found in the large buildup of Axis troops in that region of France, while Normandy remained lightly defended. While not a constant companion, Philip's role was to provide authenticity to the deception by showing up at public appearances with the general to increase the chance that German spies would report back to Berlin that Patton was indeed well connected.

Responding to Karen's comments, Philip said, "I suppose it is possible that both views of the general are correct. Behind closed doors I've seen his fiery temper and heard his intemperate words. He has a real problem dealing with his superiors, perhaps because he considers his opinion of greater veracity than theirs. And he has no sense of decorum when it comes to politics. I'm sure you read about his comments that America and England are destined to win this war, while neglecting to include the Russians."

Karen nodded.

"Well, that was a huge gaffe that very nearly did get him fired."

"So he's more trouble than he's worth?"

Philip smiled. "Oh, no—otherwise why would he hold such a responsible position right now?" Of course Philip could not tell her that everything Patton was currently doing was phony since a single slip on either his part or hers could undo months of work in creating the deception. "But what I have learned as I've traveled with him is that the men assigned to his inner staff hold him in the highest regard. You'll notice, for example, that everyone in his entourage is impeccably groomed and well dressed, with General Patton setting the standard."

Karen laughed and agreed. "I don't think I've ever seen such a crisp crease in a pair of trousers. And his blouse is tailored perfectly to fit his frame."

"Not only that, but he's clear and decisive in his communication, assertive in his orders, and always concerned for the welfare of his men. Contrary to the popular perception, he had some of the lowest casualty rates in the campaigns he commanded in North Africa, Sicily, and Italy rather than the highest."

"So why are people so angry at him? I mean, I understand that it was wrong to slap the shell-shocked soldier, but just look at him with our lads."

Philip shook his head. "Patton loves heroes and despises cowards. Of course he's entitled to his own opinion about that, but unfortunately he doesn't seem to have any internal censoring mechanism to tell him that he should watch what he says in public. Because of that, he's always in hot water. In the case of these boys, he admires men who are wounded in battle and does everything in his power to honor their sacrifice."

Philip turned to Karen and smiled. "Just keep him away from any of the men who are in here for mental conditions. The last thing I need is more controversy right now."

"Well, I admire him for taking so much time to visit our hospital. Wouldn't that have been something if he could have been here when Michael was recuperating? I'm sure it would have bolstered his spirits to have an American general stop by his bed to cheer him up."

The color drained from Philip's face. At first he hadn't even wanted to come to this hospital, because he knew it would remind him of Michael. But visits like this had turned out to be among the best opportunities to take Patton into the public spotlight precisely for the reasons Karen had enumerated. Besides, Philip had wanted to see the young woman that had meant so much to Michael. But hearing his name was unnerving.

For her part, Karen's countenance immediately fell when she saw Philip's reaction. "I'm so sorry. I shouldn't have said that. I didn't mean to bring Michael's name up."

"No, no—it's all right. I'm glad you did. Michael was here, and you and the nurses treated him magnificently. In spite of what he was going through at the time, Claire and I consider this one of our best times with him because it was one of the few occasions when he didn't have to be studying for something. I enjoyed having time to just sit and talk with him. So please don't feel bad."

"Thank you." She looked up to see if he was just being polite but was reassured by Philip's smile. Karen was still working through her loss, too. Michael had meant so much to her.

"Well, then, Lord Carlyle, how did we do today?" General Patton came striding up to them, and Karen stepped back a bit.

"According to Miss Demming, here, the visit is a great success. She was just telling me what a remarkable effect you've had on some of our lads who were feeling a bit down before you came."

Patton turned and looked at Karen for the first time. As he did so, she noticed how powerfully built he was and yet how he had something of a thin face that was not at all remarkable in appearance. But his eyes were penetrating and dark and suggested the keen intellect for which he was known.

"Perhaps you'd introduce me to the young lady. I can use all the English friends I can get."

"Of course. May I present Miss Karen Demming, a volunteer here at the hospital and dear friend of my son who was killed in Italy last month."

Patton's countenance darkened immediately. "I'm sorry for both of you in losing him. I hope it's at least some comfort that he lost his life in a valiant and noble cause."

"Thank you," Philip said quietly.

"I believe that every man who loses his life in war deserves a hero's honor. After all, there is no greater sacrifice one can make." Philip thought about Dominic and wondered if Patton would extend this gracious sentiment to him.

"I suppose I should be off," Patton said. "I'm off to head-quarters. Are you required to be my muzzle on this leg of the journey as well?"

Philip laughed. "I think not. You seem to be quite temperate today. Besides, I wouldn't be any help whatsoever in your military planning and would probably just get in the way of the important matters you have to discuss with your staff." Patton winked at him and gave Karen a small salute, and then the general was off with a flourish.

"My goodness," Karen said after he'd passed through the portal at the end of the corridor. "That's one for my diary."

Philip smiled. "I'm so glad I got to see you today. We miss your visits to Carlyle Manor. Grace often remarks at how lonely it is without you."

"I'm sorry I haven't come out more often." Her voice caught as she said this, and Philip regretted having provoked her.

"We understand, Karen." Philip started to make preparations to leave. As he did so he turned to Karen. "I hope you don't mind if I tell you something."

"No, please tell me whatever you're thinking."

"It's just that my wife had to wake me up a bit right after we received word about Michael to get me to talk about my feelings. It was painfully uncomfortable for me. Perhaps if you did come by a little more often we could all talk about it together. I know that we'd love to have you, but only if you feel up to it."

At this point they'd reached the end of the corridor. Usually a crowded place, it was empty now.

"I will come out sometime. Perhaps it's just what I need. Could I ask you one more thing, Lord Carlyle?"

"Of course."

"Michael and I had a number of discussions about your religious beliefs. I know that at one point you were a chaplain in the established church. Can I ask why you decided to convert to a new religion?"

"Oh, my—that's rather a big question." He looked at her to try to understand what motivated the question. He'd become so careful about sharing his religious thoughts in the political realm that he often recognized after the fact that he'd missed opportunities to share the gospel with those who might be open to it. In this case he saw sincere interest in Karen's eyes.

"I really don't have time to tell you everything I'd like to right now. When I met a young American in France during the last war, I learned about his religion and recognized immediately that there was something dramatically different about it from other Christian religions. One of the books he carried with him purported itself to be another volume of scripture, a testament of Jesus Christ ministering in the New World after his death and resurrection in Jerusalem. At first it seemed quite preposterous to me, but as I read it my heart was filled with the most remarkable outpouring of the Holy Spirit that I had ever experienced. In time I came to recognize that the true gospel—perhaps a better way to say it is the complete gospel—had been restored to the earth. And that's why I went to Salt Lake City to see for myself firsthand if a modern prophet does indeed live on the earth."

"And does he?"

Philip bit his lower lip. He'd been so caught up in his cabinet duties and prosecuting this awful war that he hadn't had many occasions to bear his testimony. Now it seemed to well up from inside him like a great fountain, and he was grateful for this opportunity.

"Yes, he does. God has called a prophet in modern times. The heavens are open again."

"Would you tell me more another time?" Karen looked at Philip searchingly.

"It would be an honor. What has piqued your curiosity?"

Now it was she who bit her lip to stop it from trembling. "It's just that I've tried to make sense of why I'd met Michael and come to regard him so highly, only to have him taken from me. Then one day I was thinking about our conversations about your church and how much it meant to him, and the thought struck me that perhaps I met him for this purpose."

Philip's voice filled with emotion. After all that he had lost— including in some measure the association he'd had with the Lord in prayer, perhaps this was just what he needed as well. "I believe I do have the answers, Karen. And I would love to share what I know with you."

"Thank you. Perhaps this Sunday?"

"After we share Claire's famous supper?"

She agreed, and they both smiled and then parted. On his way home Philip thought how remarkable it was that a shared tragedy had brought them together, and yet his heart felt lighter than at any time since the cascade of bad news had overcome his family. He thought of Claire and how grateful he was that she had forced him to confront his emotions. Now there was this small bit of light in their world, and he found he couldn't wait to get home to tell Claire the news.

Chapter Twenty-two

CROSSING THE FRENCH BORDER

Genoa, Italy

"Signore Carlyle. Signore Carlyle! Where are you?"

"Over here," Michael called out.

There was a thrashing sound in the brush, and Michael was relieved to see Marcio come into view.

"Are you all right, Lieutenant?" Marcio said in English. They'd mixed up the three languages so much recently that he seldom even noticed which one Marcio was using until encountering a word he couldn't understand.

"I'm not so good. My neck . . ." Michael was lying on the ground in the same spot where he'd come to rest after tumbling from the train. Unfortunately, when he first tried to sit up, he'd let out a yelp from the excruciating pain in his neck. As he struggled to support his head, he thought it was appropriate that his neck get injured again while on one of Jules's adventures. While lying on the ground waiting for help, he'd thought about that first surreptitious mission inside occupied France where they'd gone to get the secret German codes from members of the French Resistance. It was then that he'd been in the life-or-death struggle with the German who had wrenched his neck and whom Michael had killed. Undoubtedly he'd killed many more people since that time, but that was the one that troubled him most. It was a feral struggle, and it bothered Michael each time he thought about it. It was much easier to fire a torpedo or shoot a handgun, where the consequence was safely at a distance.

But now he was here, safe for the moment, but clearly in trouble physically. "Can you move your limbs?" Marcio asked.

Michael lifted his right leg, then his left, and shook both his hands. "I can move." He wanted to jump up to celebrate his lack of injury. Since getting hurt the first time, his greatest fear was of being paralyzed and totally dependent on others for the rest of his life. He'd concluded early on that he'd prefer to die than to live like that. But he quickly came to realize what an insult that was to the men who did live decent and good lives paralyzed. Still, he was grateful that his neck wasn't broken.

"Do you mind if I try to help you lift your head?" Marcio said this with an unusual quietness in his voice that was at once soothing and urgent. Michael motioned for him to come close. Gently sliding his hand under Michael's head, Marcio started to gently lift it as Michael struggled to sit up. Michael winced in pain but followed through on the motion by lifting his torso. Tears of pain streamed down his face, but he managed to force himself to come to an upright position.

"Can you move your head at all?"

Michael indicated that Marcio should withdraw his hands so that he was supporting the full weight by himself. That seemed to work all right, so he rotated his head to the left, which surprisingly didn't cause any pain. But when he tried to turn it to the right, he winced again and cried out in pain.

"We will have to find some way to immobilize your neck as best we can so that we can be on our way to the city. Once the officials on the train discover that we're gone, they will immediately raise an alarm, and the Germans will quickly know that we are the men they were searching for."

Michael felt a wave of despair sweep over him. The worst thing he could imagine was slowing the group down and perhaps being the cause of their capture. For a moment he thought it might be better if he had been killed in the fall, but he pushed the thought from his mind.

He heard a tearing sound to his right and started to turn that way, only to be blocked by yet another wave of pain. Recalling his months of therapy, he instead twisted his body so that his neck could remain relatively motionless. When he completed the motion, he was startled to see Marcio tearing the entire sleeve off of his jacket. "I will create a brace for your neck," Marcio said in his lilting Italian.

"But you'll freeze to death!"

"Only my left arm," Marcio replied jokingly. "And I don't use it much anyway."

Michael marveled at how tenderly Marcio was able to wrap the sleeve around his neck a couple of times, being careful not to choke him while at the same time providing a remarkable amount of support for his head. The relief was immediate, and for the first time since jumping, Michael thought he might be able to get up and travel under his own power.

"How do you know how to do that?" Michael asked.

"I was trained as a medic, signore, and I took a special course in helping people whose necks, backs, and spines are injured."

"I thought I was going to be a helpless lump, but I may have a chance now."

"Good, then we should stand you up." In spite of Marcio's attempt to sound calm and unhurried, the urgency of their situation betrayed itself in his voice.

"Where the blazes have you two been?" Fortunately Jules was off to Michael's left side so that Michael's unexpected jerk in that direction wasn't totally disabling.

"We waited for you, only to find that you've been lollygagging around here!" Jules was clearly annoyed, but Michael decided not to respond.

"Signore Carlyle has a badly injured neck. We've just now got him to his feet. It will be very difficult for him."

Jules looked at Michael, spotting the makeshift brace. "Oh, sorry, Michael. I didn't know."

"I'm all right. But we better get going. I really do understand the urgency of our situation." He tried to bend down to pick up the small duffel bag that he'd jumped with, but the pain was too great, and he cried out in spite of himself.

"Not to worry, mate—I can get that for you." Jules's voice had a totally different quality to it now.

"Thanks." And with that they started their way into the underbrush moving on an angle away from the tracks, in the general direction of Genoa.

"Are you all right?" Jules asked a few minutes later. Michael grunted that he was, but even in the moonlight, Jules could see the remnant of tears on Michael's face and the grimace that proved he was anything but.

* * *

"What's the word on the street?"

"The Germans have been making life miserable for the city officials. They're convinced that we've been taken into hiding, and they're bound and determined to find us."

Jules shook his head. "But what makes them think that we're the ones who copped the German's name? They should have found our bodies among the other casualties. Why can't they imagine that Colonel Braun simply lost his sanity or something?" Of course Jules recognized the absurdity of the question even as he asked it, but it was so frustrating to know that a good many Italians up and down the line were in grave danger because of the German's suspicions.

"From what I can gather, the problem started when Braun's name began showing up on the manifest of westbound trains, rather than northbound. When they started asking questions, one of the Germans assigned to the burial detail said that he thought one of the British sailors they'd buried looked something like Braun. My guess is that they added all that together to conclude that we'd made an escape."

Jules pounded one fist into the other. "Well, it's maddening being bottled up here in this safe house, knowing that it's anything but safe for the people who are hiding us."

Marcio looked over at the Italian woman who was busy fixing a modest pasta dish for their dinner. She seemed oblivious to any danger. "What you need to understand, Signore Ellington, is that they do this because they want to. If we can get to France, you will be invaluable to our efforts there. So while it's frustrating to you, it's worth it to us, even if we get arrested for it."

"I had no idea you hated the Germans so much."

"You've never had your country occupied by them. They treat us like infants, always lording over us their supposed superiority." Marcio looked up fiercely. "Frankly you're the best thing to happen to our morale because it shows the arrogant Germans that in spite of their vaunted superiority, they can't keep control of even three British sailors."

Jules laughed. "I hope we're able to keep that last part true."

"Which is why you have to be patient," Marcio replied urgently. "We've developed a plan to get everyone out of the city two nights from now. But you've got to be willing to stay down in the cellar just in case this house is inspected. It's not beyond imagination that someone out there is aware that the people in this house are going in and out at odd times. Whenever you come up to the main living area like this, you put us all at risk."

Jules dropped his head. "I'm sorry. I'll go back down. It's just that Carlyle is a real barrel of fun to deal with since he sleeps most of the time, and poor Jenkins is going crazy. I guess I tend to get claustrophobic."

Marcio was less sympathetic toward Jules than he had been to Michael. "It's a small price to pay, considering what everyone else is doing on your behalf, don't you think?"

"Of course you're right. I'll just be off then." With that, he lifted the heavy trapdoor that separated the main floor from the dank cellar below. It was very hard to do, since the latch that normally made it very easy to lift had been taken out and replaced by a regular wooden plank so that when the trapdoor closed it looked like the rest of the floor. Once he backed his way onto the ladder going into the cellar, he reached up and took the bowl of spaghetti that his hostess offered him and then listened in dread as the door closed above him, followed by the sound of a heavy table being dragged on top of the trapdoor.

"How is Lieutenant Carlyle doing?" Jules asked.

"He's been sleeping again, but the good news is that I haven't heard him cry out as much as usual, even when he rolls over."

"I'm glad. You know it's my fault that his neck was hurt in the first place, don't you?"

"I didn't know that, sir. Perhaps you'd tell me the story. That is, if you have time."

"Time? It seems that time is the only thing I've got right now. And the chance to tell you a story may be the only thing to keep me from going completely insane."

Jenkins smiled. "I thought as much, sir."

* * *

Fortunately, the Germans were frustrated in their attempts at finding the escaped British group, although Marcio recounted a number of close calls that members of the Resistance had encountered. Still, on this night they'd managed to sneak out of their hiding place in the cellar, into the streets of Genoa, and into the back of a truck loaded with industrial supplies destined for the border town of Nice, France, some twenty miles east of the Italian border. Located on the Ligurian Sea, a cove in the larger Mediterranean, Nice was a principal city on the coastal area known as the French Riviera. In happier times people would be thrilled for the chance to visit the area, but in view of their circumstances, no one was thinking of it as a vacation destination. Travel by rail would have been much faster and easier, but in this situation it was felt to be too dangerous, even if they'd stayed off passenger trains in favor of jumping freight trains. So in no time they were being bounced on the uneven mountainous road that led along the steep coast. There were dozens of boxes piled up around the little nest that had been carved out for them at the front of the fully laden truck.

"How's your neck, Michael?"

Michael smiled in the artificial darkness. It was broad daylight outside the truck. "It's been better, but I'm all right. At least we're getting closer to France, where I can understand people. Somehow that seems encouraging."

"For you," Jules said in an unusually dejected voice. "I won't understand a thing. At least when we pretended to be Germans, I understood some of it."

"Seems to me it's better to understand nothing and be in France than understand everything and be in a German prison camp."

"When you put it like that, I guess I should have a better attitude."

They were quiet for a time. "How long have we been riding now? Do you have any sense at all about where we are?" Michael asked.

"My father used to get angry with me for asking that question when we'd go out to our country estate," Jules replied, noticeably more cheerful.

"My dad, too. Dominic and I used to fight in the backseat even though there was more than enough room for the two of us. It didn't matter which side I wanted to sit on. He always wanted that same spot, at least until I moved. Then he wanted my new place."

"It's always like that with little brothers, isn't it? Sometimes I wish I had a little brother to make my life miserable. Who knows, it might have made me a better person." Jules either didn't think about Dominic being gone, or chose not to focus on it. Either way, Michael became subdued at the thought of Dominic.

"Yes, well, my question remains unanswered. Do you have any idea where we are?"

Jules sighed. "About halfway through Hades, as far as I can tell."

"Your claustrophobia acting up?"

"That's really something, isn't it—intrepid British commando done in by a confined space."

"We each have our weaknesses, Jules. God made it that way so we'd have a reason to pray to Him for help."

Jules nodded appreciatively. "I envy your faith, Michael. It's a lot harder being a religious skeptic at times like these."

Michael laughed. "I'd be glad to say a prayer for you if you like."

Just as Jules was about to say that he'd like that very much, the truck ground to a halt. Even under the pile of boxes they could hear German words coming through the canvas sides of the truck. Instinctively they all went silent. There was little question where they were now. They'd reached the border. Michael strained to hear what was going on and managed to make out the words for "cargo manifest" and "destination." That was all normal enough, but when he heard "search for contraband and spies," his heart leaped in his chest, and he whispered very quietly to Jules what he'd heard. They both fingered the German weapons they'd managed to steal during their escape.

Before long they heard noises at the back of their truck and listened in growing alarm as containers were roughly shoved about and moved. The driver had told them, prior to hiding them under the mountain of boxes, that the sheer number of boxes generally discouraged detailed searches and that the Germans usually gave up after ten or fifteen. So at this point they remained hopeful that the border guards would be content with a random check that never reached their hiding place.

After another five minutes or so, their hope began to diminish as the unloading seemed to continue unabated. Apparently the Germans were very interested in finding something. The three of them prepared to fire at the first German to emerge and hopefully shoot their way out of the truck when the moment came. Marcio had traveled in the cab with the driver, pretending to be a member of the loading crew, so certainly he would know what to expect and would hopefully know to shield the Italians from the gunfire.

As the sound grew closer, Michael felt his heart come up in his throat as the fear energized him for action. As a ray of sunlight broke through the stirring boxes he lifted his revolver to fire when suddenly there was an explosion outside the truck. The shuffling of boxes stopped, and there were German curse words. They listened in relief as the men who had been riffling through the truck scrambled out the back. From outside they heard a series of shots ring out through the air, and then silence. Michael's anxiety was so high that he had to periodically remind himself to breathe.

Eventually Jules leaned over and whispered in his ear, "Do you think we should try to work ourselves outside to see what's going on? Perhaps we could slip into the brush and find our way across the border on foot."

Michael didn't think much of the idea, since three men slipping out of a truck in broad daylight would certainly be easy to spot. He counseled patience, which of course was not one of Jules's virtues, but his friend settled back and went quiet again. A few minutes later they were startled by the sound of boxes being moved behind them. Arching himself into a sitting position again, Michael inadvertently wrenched his neck, which hurt terribly. But at least the leather collar that Marcio had somehow secured in Genoa prevented him from doing any real injury. With revolvers drawn, Jules, Michael, and Jenkins prepared for the worst. But this time they heard, very quietly, the sound of Marcio's voice.

"Signores—some friends of ours saw our difficulty and created a diversion up ahead. The bulk of the Germans have chased after them, and the few guards who remain at the border checkpoint are very nervous. They are anxious to have us leave so have ordered me to get things put back together as soon as possible. You'll forgive me if I don't take time to talk."

"Oh, you're forgiven," Michael said quietly. "But please send a thousand thanks to your friends." A few minutes later they heard the sound of the old truck engine growl to life, and with a disconcerting lurch they started moving forward again, the truck laboring as it mounted a steep incline in the road. After another twenty minutes, they ground to a halt again, this time to check in with the border guards at Monaco, the small independent principality that sat on a rocky headland jutting out into the Mediterranean. Just five miles from the Italian border, its opulence stood in stark contrast to its easterly neighbor. Known throughout the world for its beautiful beaches and the casino district that formed the heart of the small principality, the lavish city Monte Carlo was considered the jewel of the Mediterranean. Even during war, the wealthy and notorious from Germany and France came to the clubs to show off their wealth and try their luck at the gaming tables. But while the town was a rather substantial temptation to Jules, who had at first argued that they should settle in there, they eventually agreed that the risk of detection was too high. How many world-savvy card dealers would recognize even the slightest trace of an English accent? Far better to go the additional nine miles to Nice.

Holding their breath once again, they waited to see if there would be a search, but this time the truck started moving almost immediately. Apparently even the Germans were more casual in this area. Although they didn't have a long way to travel, it still took them nearly an hour before the truck finally stopped. They heard the voices of Marcio and the driver chatter excitedly with a new set of voices, and then the voices disappeared for a time, leaving them in silence.

It wasn't much later that Marcio returned and called out that the coast was clear. In a few moments, the boxes had been cleared away, and the three Englishmen stood up on wobbly legs, having been kept in their cramped little crawl space since early that morning. Emerging from the back of the truck, Michael was startled to see that it was already quite dark outside.

"So what are we to do now?" Jules asked Marcio.

"I'm afraid that now you will be passed into the hands of the French Resistance, 'the Maquis,' and I will return to Italy. You have created some great debts for me to repay to Italian resisters up and down the line."

"You're leaving us?" Michael asked.

"I must, my friend. It makes logical sense for an Italian to bring goods into France, but little sense for him to stay. So now you must redeem all the effort it has taken on the part of the people who have brought you here by doing great harm to the Germans in preparation for what I hope will be a glorious invasion by the Allied forces. Perhaps in a year or so we can meet as free men!"

"I hope so," Michael said through a tightened voice. He was a bit overcome by the emotion of saying good-bye, as were Jules and Jenkins. "You've been a good friend and protector, Marcio. We owe our lives to you. Thank you."

Marcio smiled broadly and gave him a big hug, being careful not to hurt his neck. Michael returned the embrace, and then Marcio said good-bye to Jules and Jenkins in turn.

A moment later, the old truck roared to life, belching dark fumes, and moved out into the darkness. Michael and Jules turned and looked at each other, and then they turned to the lone Frenchman standing to their side.

"My name is Pierre Guererre. Welcome to France," Pierre said in French.

"You speak English?" Jules said hopefully. But Pierre looked back at him blankly. So Michael returned his greeting in an easy sort of French, which made Pierre smile back at him. There was nothing that a Frenchman liked more than to hear an Englishman who could speak fluent French.

"He wants us to go this way," Michael said to the others. With a final glance back toward Italy, the three young men from England stepped out into the night air and into occupied France.

Part Two

INVASIONS OF FRANCE
Summer 1944

Chapter Twenty-three

THE MAQUIS

London—April 1944

"I find that I'm a little frightened."

"I think I understand, but you shouldn't be. I did this when I was eight years old and made it through. You can certainly do it at your age."

Karen turned to Grace. "At eight there wasn't nearly as much of you to put under the water. Besides, your family was excited for your baptism, I'm sure."

"I'm glad your parents have come, even if they're not excited. It will make it much easier for you to be a member of the Church if you have their acceptance. Some people who join the Church are completely disowned by their families. It's very sad."

"I am glad they're here. I don't think they would have been nearly so tolerant had they not known how devoted all of you are. My family has never been particularly involved in our church, other than on the holy days, so they're quite pleased for me to have found something that makes me happy. It's just that they're uncertain about how it will affect our friends and extended family. I'm sure you've experienced some of the misunderstanding that surrounds the LDS Church?"

Grace smiled at the question. "Oh, I think it's fair to say that I've experienced some of that. I don't know that I've ever been in a school where there were any other members besides me.

Inevitably when people learn about my religion, there are stares and questions. While most people haven't even heard of the Church, those who have seem to feel that it's a church for the lower classes, and they're surprised to think that we would belong. I've had to learn how to explain my way out of some potentially embarrassing moments."

"Well, perhaps you can help me be better prepared. The hospital staff attributes it all to Michael, so they don't probe much deeper than that. But the rest of my friends have no idea that I'm being baptized. I'm sure when they learn of it, things will change for me."

Grace helped Karen button up her dress and then handed her the white stockings she would wear under the white folds of the skirt. "I so wish Michael could be here. He would be thrilled to know that you've made this decision."

"There was always something special about Michael."

After just four months, it was still very touchy to bring up Michael's name, not because people were reluctant to talk about him, but rather because it might prompt an unexpected release of tears. But this was a happy day, and everyone sensed that Karen's baptism was something that would have been extremely gratifying to Michael, so Grace had resolved not to cry. And even if she did, they would be happy tears. Still, as she prepared to respond to Karen's last statement, she figured out very quickly that she couldn't possibly continue this conversation and keep her vow, so she changed the subject.

"There! You look perfect. And I know that Papa is thrilled that you asked him to perform the baptism. He will look so handsome in his white trousers and shirt."

"He is a wonderful teacher. I've loved listening to him in Sunday School each week. Somehow he opens the scriptures in a way I never thought possible."

"Part of that is his natural skill as a teacher, but a much bigger part is that you've been feeling the Spirit of the Lord."

Grace smiled. "It's wonderful to talk with you like this. I've had these things all my life and sometimes take them for granted. But as you talk, I realize how marvelous it is."

Karen turned to Grace one last time. "I want to thank you, Grace. I never had a sister and always wished I did. Feeling as if I've become part of your family is one of the most wonderful things ever to happen to me."

Grace was surprised that this prompted the very same response she was trying to avoid when she thought of Michael, so inhaling quickly to stave off a new attack of tears, she said simply, "I feel the same way, particularly now that I'm alone. I think it's time to go. I hear the music playing. Let me show you the way . . ."

* * *

East of Toulon, France—April 1944

Jules and Jenkins came running through the darkness, breathless as they raced around the large boulder that Michael was hiding behind. The gangly silhouette of the great stonework bridge stood out against the moonlit night like a giant insect temporarily at rest in the darkness, while the gentle sound of water flowing past them in the river created a different feeling altogether. The river gave a sense of serenity; the doomed bridge made the night feel menacing.

Jules grinned. "Just think of it. This bridge has probably been here for fifty or more years. The villagers never think twice about it. When they need to get to the other side of the river, they just drive their team or lorry up to the bridge, and in just a few moments they're across the wooden deck and on their way. But you're about to mess up their lives rather dramatically."

"Me? You're the one who set the charges."

"Ah, yes, but you're the one with his hand on the detonator. In a few moments you'll push with enough force to create an electric spark which will travel instantaneously through the wires we just laid so carefully, and kablam! No more bridge."

"And I'm to get the blame for that?"

"Only if we're captured by the Germans. We'll impress on them what a devious mastermind you are, ordering us to blow up bridges and railroad tracks. The Germans have a price on your head, you know. There's undoubtedly great lucre to be earned by turning you in."

Michael was having none of it. "Oh, don't worry. They'll take one look at the two of us and know in an instant that you're the commando, not me. After all, you're the one who always brags about your magnificent physique while making fun of the scrawny build of a naval officer."

"Hmm. You may be right, Carlyle. You and Jenkins are rather pathetic, aren't you?"

"Not me, sir. I'm an enlisted man—not an officer. We do the work of the boat, you know, so we're not scrawny." Jenkins thought he was very clever in saying this until he turned and caught the astonished look in Michael's eye. "That is, present officers excepted, of course."

Michael laughed. "We're going to have to work on your discipline, Mr. Jenkins, before we return to the navy. I'm afraid Captain Ellington has been a bad influence on you."

"Yes, sir!" Jenkins said.

"Yes, well, let's get on with it. I don't think there are any Germans within twenty miles of this place, but just in case, we should make sure we blow the thing to smithereens before they have a chance to stop us." Jules always pretended to be annoyed when the conversation turned away from him.

Michael dropped down into a crouching position behind the rock, as did Jules and Jenkins. Michael shoved the detonator with all his might. There was a pause of perhaps a second, and then the night sky lit up in a brilliant burst of light and color, followed a few seconds later by an ear-crushing blast of noise and fury that, in spite of the boulder, knocked the wind out of the three of them. From his new position on his back, Michael watched in fascination as the arms and legs of the great creature went billowing up into the air for perhaps a hundred feet or more before slowly reaching the zenith of their arc.

"Dive for cover!" he shouted as a great cascade of concrete, rock, and twisted railroad tracks started to rain down from the sky. The three of them cowered under the lee of their rock, hoping mightily to avoid being crushed by the debris. When the dust started to settle a minute or so later, Michael turned to Jules with narrowed eyes. "Do you think you might have gotten a little carried away on this one? Did you really think it would take that much explosive? It was just a local bridge you were blowing up, for crying out loud, not London Bridge!"

Jules peeked around the side of the rock and then looked back with a grin that stretched from ear to ear. "You can't be too careful! Judge for yourself—there's not a stick left of the old thing. That river is as free-flowing as it was a thousand years ago!"

Michael turned and saw Jenkins grinning every bit as wide as Jules. Michael shared their enthusiasm, so he returned the grin. But recognizing that they needed at least one adult in the group, he quickly added, "Well, if there weren't any Germans around here before now, there will be shortly. I suggest we find our way to safer ground."

"Right. Let's be off." Jules paused for a moment and then frowned. "Tell me if I'm wrong, but aren't we supposed to be on the other side of the river?" Michael's eyes widened, and then he punched Jules in the ribs.

* * *

Later the next afternoon when Michael woke up he found Jules staring at him. "What is it?" he asked.

"I think it's time, Michael."

"Time?"

"To use the radio."

A sick feeling came over Michael, and suddenly his stomach hurt. "But what if they want to arrest me? Commander Billingham was furious and promised to bring me up on charges."

"I know. That's why I've waited. But we have to let the Allies know that we're here so that we can start to send them intelligence. The things we've learned in the past three months will be invaluable to their planning if indeed they've decided to go ahead with the operation." Jules flashed one of his sardonic smiles. "Besides, even if Billingham learns that you're alive, he can't get to you while we're behind enemy lines—that is, unless he tells the Germans so they can take care of you on his behalf!"

Michael returned a weak smile. He knew Jules was trying to be reassuring, but he felt very anxious about it nonetheless. After a few moments, Michael took a deep breath and rested his head against the wall behind him. "There are our families to think about, too. They've probably made peace with the fact that we're dead. Now they'll have to deal with our being alive."

"That will probably be much harder on my family than yours," Jules said dryly.

Michael huffed. "It's not the coming back to life that's the problem, although I'm sure that will be the shock of a lifetime. It's that our chances of getting through this are still pretty remote. So there's a good chance we'll raise their spirits once again only to tear them down by getting killed—*again*—later."

Jules nodded and gave Michael a wink. "At least that way you won't have to face Commander Billingham."

Michael laughed and sighed. "Any chance the Germans will hear us transmit?"

"Of course! But it's all in code, and we'll be brief. You need to think of some little code that will let your family know it's you but that won't be obvious to any Germans who are snooping in on our conversation. It's got to be short. I'm not sure if we'll be picked up by the British or the Americans, but either way, they should recognize our unique code and identify us as British. Once they transmit the results to my unit, they'll know it's me from my preassigned code name."

Michael pulled out a pencil and piece of paper and started trying different combinations. Finally, after four or five minutes of trying, he handed Jules a piece of paper that read, "LMCMTBAOK."

Jules furrowed his brow and looked up at Michael, who gave no response. He looked up and down several more times and then let out an audible, "Ah—I get it. Very shrewd to mix British and American acronyms. I hope our boys are smart enough to figure it out."

"If they're like you, my identity will probably remain unknown clear to the end of the war. By the way, what is your code name that is so impregnable to German decoding?"

Jules got a conspiratorial look on his face, turned from side to side as if to make sure no one was listening, which of course they weren't since the Maquis had provided them an abandoned farmhouse in the middle of an empty field to live in, and then he said very quietly, "It had to be something that is so outrageous that the Germans would never connect it to a master spy."

"Yes?"

"The word is—please keep this to yourself—*humble*."

Even the threat of capture couldn't keep Michael from roaring with laughter at that one. Jules joined in, pleased at the perfectly brilliant irony of the word.

* * *

May 1944

Michael acknowledged the Frenchman and then turned and whispered to Jules. "He says that the train left the last station right on time. That gives us approximately ten minutes. Are you ready?"

Even Jules seemed a bit nervous this time, perhaps because the stakes were so high. "I've got enough explosives planted to sink an aircraft carrier, and we've checked the lines twice. The charges are close enough that if just one of them goes off, the others should fire in quick succession even if a line proves defective."

Michael nodded and passed the word back to their French counterpart. There were some more whispered words, which Michael confirmed with a shake of the head. Then he sat back and rested quietly.

"What did he say?"

Michael jerked at the sound of Jules's voice. "Just that there will be very serious reprisals as a result of this attack. You know that earlier in the war the Germans wiped out all the male citizens of a town over the age of twelve as punishment for a murdered German officer? What we've got planned goes so far beyond that act, so there's no telling what the consequences will be. I think he's just a little worried for his fellow citizens."

"It's a very dirty business—but this can make a real difference. I'm glad they're willing to take the risk."

Both lapsed into silence as they waited the interminable minutes for the train to approach. Michael gazed at the chasm through which the train had to pass on its westward journey to Marseille. One of the distinctive features of Europe was the range of mountains that ran north to south from the city of Chamonix in eastern France to the Mediterranean coast, where great rocky cliffs terminated the land in favor of the azure blue waters of the ocean. These cliffs gave rise to the spectacular views so often featured in postcards of the area, with houses climbing steeply up the sides of the cliffs as if stuck there by glue. Their present location was too steep even for houses, though, and the only sign of human habitation was the giant railroad trestle that spanned the mouth of the canyon as it opened up to the sea. With about a three-hundred-foot vertical drop, the trestle was an impressive structure by any measure. It was also extremely vulnerable to attack, as they soon would prove. Simply taking the span out would prove a major inconvenience to the Germans, since they'd have to switch to motorized convoys to move men and supplies into the area rather than using the far more efficient railroad. But their planning was even more ambitious than that.

"How many men do you suppose are on the train?" Michael asked.

"We've been over this—a typical car seats approximately fifty. If the train is pulling twenty cars, that gives you a thousand men. Of course all the cars may not be full, and the train may have fewer cars because of the grades it has to cross, but no matter what happens, it's going to be a lot of soldiers."

"And the Germans don't even guard the place."

"Well, except for the two guards that our Maquis friends dispatched to the next world earlier this afternoon. It was awfully lucky for the Maquis that you were there to respond in German to the guards' request for proof of clearance."

"Yes, I'm the one who set them all up to die."

It always irritated Jules when Michael talked like that. He preferred to keep the war impersonal—just a set of organized objectives and targets rather than people with names and faces. But he decided not to say anything since they'd plowed this ground before.

The Frenchman flashed a signal for them to be quiet, perhaps suggesting that he had heard something indicating the approach of the train. His job on the mission had been to identify the target, secure the explosives, and make sure that as many members of the Resistance as possible were seen in public places at the time of the attack. That would be their greatest safety in establishing alibis when people were rounded up. Better to use British commandos whom the local population had no knowledge of than local folk who could more easily be implicated.

The Frenchman's hearing was quickly vindicated when Jules stiffened and said, "All right, Michael, the train is in sight!" For some reason their little team had devolved into an organization where Jules was responsible for setting the munitions in place, based on his specialized training in explosives, with the help of Jenkins, and then Michael was the one to set off the charge. He wasn't sure he really liked that, but the fact was that with his injured neck he wasn't really very safe climbing around under bridges and trestles to place the heavy kegs of explosives.

At this point Michael held his breath.

"The engine is on the bridge," Jules said. "I'll give you the signal when it reaches the point where there's maximum exposure to the cars on the train." As if Michael didn't know that; they'd only rehearsed it about a hundred times while planning it. Still, people had to manage their anxiety one way or another— Michael's way was to hold his breath and Jules's to repeat the obvious. The objective was to blow the trestle at a time when the collapse in the center of the span would be sufficient to pull the cars that had already crossed that point back into the collapsing bridge while inevitably drawing all those that followed forward into the breach.

The anxiety was palpable as he waited, and Michael was tempted to push the plunger just to see if it worked. That was the problem with an operation of this type—they couldn't test the outcome without blowing up the bridge. So they had to set it up right and then hope that it worked. With thousands of feet of cable snaking out across the bridge, there was always the danger that the wind could whip up and disconnect the wire from the terminals, or that some German patrol would come out of nowhere and notice the cables, or that . . . well, the list of the things that could go wrong was fairly extensive. The worst thing that could go wrong was that Michael would lose his nerve and not push the plunger at the right time. At least that one was within his control, and he resolved to do his job in spite of the terrible consequences.

"Five seconds, four seconds, three, two, NOW!" The steam locomotive was more than loud enough to mask any noise that

Jules could make, so it really didn't matter that he shouted. In fact it was probably a good thing that he did, because it startled Michael so badly that he just reacted, shoving the plunger down with full force.

The pause that followed was undoubtedly more a function of the human mind distorting the time in which it expected a reaction and the time the reaction occured. It was just long enough for Michael to at first think the whole thing had failed. Then there was an amazingly small puff of dark smoke toward the center of the trestles which made Michael think that Jules must have been crazy, because certainly an explosion like that didn't stand a chance of bringing down several hundred tons of rock and rail. But of course what he saw was the effect of the blasting caps detonating. When the full explosion flashed, there was no delay whatsoever in the brilliance of the flare, which effectively blinded Michael even though it was broad daylight. To a casual observer it would look very much like the center of the superstructure had simply evaporated into thin air while the rest of the structure remained intact. Not a good sign. But of course the rest of the structure was totally dependent on the part that had now become liquefied from the heat and the displacement of the blast, and so the consequence was that the weight of the train would bring the whole thing down.

"Oh, my goodness . . ." Michael's voice trailed off as he watched the giant steam locomotive pause in its forward momentum. As the bridge started to sag in the middle, the cars that had started to fall into the chasm pulled back on the engine that, for a moment, looked as if it might win the battle against gravity. But it was not to be, of course, since the locomotive itself had not cleared the end of the bridge, assuring that the steel struts and infrastructure that supported it would quickly fail. Once the shock wave passed over their position, they were able to stick their heads up in time to watch first one car, and then another, and then half a dozen first tip to the side and then start their free fall into the chasm below. With a great tearing and ripping sound that to Michael sounded like the breaking up of one of the ships he'd witnessed sink in the English Channel, the tremendous combined materials of the bridge and the train that had been on top of it started to fall into each other as the whole mass fell to the ground. With great echoing crashes, the cars each landed in turn, mostly obscuring the sound of human voices screaming in terror, triumph, and surprise. But the greatest firework of all was reserved for when the locomotive hit the bottom. Weighing more than 300,000 pounds, it collapsed into the canyon with a great roar, followed by a final explosion as the superheated steam of the boiler exploded on impact. Even though the group was well back from the bridge, a shower of boiling water rained down on them, causing Jenkins in particular to cry out in pain. Even though the whole thing was over in less than a minute, it seemed to Michael as if it had taken an hour or more as his brain replayed the scene in slow motion.

"What have we done?" the Frenchman said in an awed voice. Michael didn't even realize it was spoken in French.

Michael said, "We have pricked the giant, and soon we shall hear his roar."

"I don't know what you two are saying, but I suggest we get the blazes out of here. Do you see the billow of smoke from that inferno?"

Michael looked up and was startled to see a black, acrid cloud extending perhaps a hundred and fifty feet into the air. A mixture of coal dust, burning wood, and melted paint, it would alert every German unit within at least twenty miles that something bad had happened.

"This way, *messieurs*," their French host said in English.

Their escape route took them down the steep cliffs to a small patch of beach where a small boat was waiting. The boat had been painted in neutral colors to match the rocky cliffs so that it would be harder for anyone to observe them. Tumbling into the boat,

Michael was gratified to hear the small motor sputter to life, and in an instant they were gaining speed as they maneuvered through the water, always holding close to the cliffs so that any shore-based observers looking down from above would fail to see them.

After approximately fifteen minutes, the driver slowed the boat and then turned off the motor. Michael found himself impatient with this until he heard the sound of air-raid sirens from far above them. "Do you suppose aircraft are really approaching?" he asked Jules.

"I suspect it's just the Germans alerting all units in the area to go on full alert."

"As well they should," the Frenchman said, looking at his pocket watch. "If my compatriots do not lose courage, the next round should begin shortly."

It did. Even from their distance they heard the dull thud of a great explosion. The Frenchman looked calmly to the northwest. He was as placid as if they'd been out on a luxury cruise and he was studying some odd bird that happened to fly by. That's one of the things Michael admired about the French. No matter how tense the situation, they always gave the appearance of indifference—so very much at odds with the excitability of the Italians. "Ah, there it is." The Frenchman pointed to a smudge that was rising above the horizon. "Hopefully a German ammunition depot that no longer exists."

Michael was impressed with his impassivity. This was one of the most exciting days of his life. The second attack had been planned to divert attention from the railroad attack. A third would soon follow right in the main motor pool of the Marseille garrison, where an extremely courageous French driver had parked a bogus German automobile loaded with explosives. The idea was that with multiple acts of sabotage going on in different areas of the coastal region, the Germans would feel compelled to leave their troops where they were, rather than rallying to the site of the original offense.

"Shall we be going?" Jules asked.

"Ah, yes, of course" the Frenchman replied.

Michael was convinced that they were both bluffing and that they were each as excited as he was. At least Jenkins had the common decency to whistle through his teeth and mutter, "This is proving to be a very bad day for the Germans."

"Indeed," Jules replied. "Let's hope we make it to safety before it turns into a very bad day for us."

* * *

London

"Philip, do you have a moment?"

Philip looked up to see A.V. Alexander, First Lord of the Admiralty.

"Of course." Philip walked over to Alexander, who beckoned to a small room off the Cabinet chamber. He expected that he'd be asked about his most recent encounters with General Patton, who had quite innocently created yet another press fury when he used a derogatory term to refer to the Russians. In this case Philip agreed that the whole thing was overblown, and he was prepared to say so.

Which is why he was taken by surprise when Alexander said, "We've put off asking you about this in hopes that we could decipher it ourselves. But we have a rather strange message that we can't quite make sense out of."

"A message?"

"Yes." Alexander looked at him seriously. "You might want to sit down before I share it with you." Of course this alarmed Philip, but he had no idea what they could bring to him now that could be any more destructive than the messages that had already been delivered in his life.

"It seems that our operatives in Corsica have started to receive some interesting but cryptic messages from mainland France."

"Yes?"

"Well, they've been able to identify that the originator is a young man whom you know, a certain naval commander named Ellington. You do know him?"

Since Philip was seated, he couldn't stagger. Instead the room seemed to waver as the blood drained from his face. "Yes, sir," he said weakly. "He was a friend of my son, Michael."

Alexander cleared his throat. "That's what we thought, which is why I've asked you to read this message. We've been able to decode all of it but one line. It isn't written in any standard code. We've finally concluded that it is simply a string of letters. Since you know him, perhaps you can intuit what he's saying?"

His hand trembling, Philip reached out for the paper that Alexander held in his hand. "This is the line in question," A.V. said, pointing to a single line of text mixed in with the rest of the message. *LMCMTBAOK.*

By this point Philip was shaking so badly that he could hardly focus on the line. But then he almost choked as he said, "Oh, dear heaven. Oh, my dear heaven."

"What is it?" A.V. asked quietly. "Is it what we think it is?"

Philip wiped his cheek with his hand. "It is indeed. It's my son Michael. He's alive." It wouldn't have mattered now what he did to suppress his reaction—he couldn't stifle a sob, and then he felt tears on his cheek. He looked up and tried to say, "I'm sorry," but he couldn't get any further than that.

"That's what I hoped it would mean. I thought it must mean that, given that Michael was on a mission with Ellington when he disappeared. But we simply couldn't decipher what he was trying to say. You're absolutely certain that this is what it means? I don't want you to get your hopes up if it's some other message that happens to mirror those letters."

"I'm positive," Philip said. "You see, when Michael was a little boy, he liked to use the phrase 'A-OK,' and went around the house saying it often. I'm sure he knew I'd recognize this."

Alexander smiled. "I'm very glad to hear it, Philip. More glad than you can possibly imagine. Congratulations."

Philip sat back in the chair. "I'm going to have to give that boy a good beating when he gets home."

"A beating! What on earth for?"

"I don't know if you remember this, A.V., but he was serving on the *Hood*. I was with you when it went down, and for the next four hours I thought he was on the *Hood* and killed. It was only after I got home that we received a telegram saying that he'd transferred off at the last moment before it sailed. For most of that dreadful day I thought we'd lost him then. Now he's done it to us again."

Alexander nodded. "I'd forgotten that. I think you're right— he does deserve to be throttled." Alexander put his hand to his cheek. "Rather like a cat with nine lives, isn't he?"

Philip smiled. "Or a Carlyle with nine lives. Thank you, A.V. You stood with me then, and you're with me now. It means the world."

"I'm glad it's good news, Philip. We're going to need a lot of it in the next few days with the invasion pending. I'm glad you've learned this now."

Philip stood up, suddenly anxious. "With your permission, I need to go home. I need to tell Claire and Grace about this."

"Of course. Do you need my car again?"

"No, I can drive myself this time." Fumbling with his papers, Philip reached into his pocket to make sure he had his keys. "I'll be off then."

Chapter Twenty-four

NORMANDY

London—June 10, 1944

"I can't stand this . . ." Patton paused and out of respect for Philip, deleted the rather intense profanity he'd planned to say. Even more upset that he couldn't give proper vent to his feelings, he finished the sentence with, "this charade!" Philip stood by quietly, knowing that the general needed to express his frustration. "Not any longer! The greatest military action in the history of the world is taking place in France, and I'm sitting on my rear here in England riding around in a chauffer-driven automobile *pretending* like I'm getting ready to invade. I should be there on the front lines of the blasted invasion!" Philip winced at the man's anger.

"It seems the German High Command agrees with you, General. From what I gather, they continue to hold precious resources in Calais in the belief that the main invasion is still about to launch under your command, even though four days have passed since the landing at Normandy, where our boys have established a beachhead. At least if you're going to be used as a bluff it seems good to know that you're a successful one."

Patton looked at Philip and nodded, though not in the least mollified. "You're a good fellow, Carlyle. At first it irritated me that I would have to endure you and the others on my various sight-seeing expeditions, but you've shown yourself to be a level-headed fellow who isn't all caught up in himself like . . ."

Philip completed the sentence mentally. *Like all the other arrogant aristocrats who fancy themselves militarily competent.* "It seems we're in the same boat, General. I'm part of the same ruse as you are, sent along to provide a veneer of authenticity. But unlike you, I'd be no good at the real work of command, so it's not such a pathetic waste of talent to use me in this fashion."

"I think you underestimate yourself, Carlyle. But no matter, we'll play out the hand and hope they deal me a new one shortly. I think I've been in the doghouse long enough."

"I certainly hope so. I can't wait to read your name in the paper for giving the Germans a good kick in their rear. I sincerely hope you're given a command, and sooner rather than later."

The car pulled up to Whitehall, and Philip prepared to exit. "I guess this is the last time I'll see you, General. Good luck, sir. I'm rooting for you."

"Maybe you'll let me buy you a drink after the war, Carlyle?"

"I'd be honored." And with that, General George S. Patton left Philip's life as abruptly as he'd entered it. As the car drove away, Philip reflected on the contradictions that make a man—the same passion that drove Patton to success on the battlefield was also his greatest liability. It seemed incongruous that a man with such self-discipline in his personal bearing and in the organization of his staff could be so lacking in common sense when it came to dealing with the press and with things that irritated him.

The invasion of Normandy was, indeed, the greatest event in the history of warfare. Over 156,000 American, British, and Canadian soldiers were landed on the gentle beaches of northern France in the first few days, to be followed by millions in the ensuing months. While the most difficult challenge was found at the cliffs at Pointe du Hoc, four miles west of Omaha Beach, where the Americans had to scale straight up the sides of the sandy soil directly into the fire of German defenders poised at the top, the rest of the beaches presented their own unique challenges.

But by this, the fourth day, it was established that the landing so far was proceeding generally as planned, and with each passing hour the Allies' foothold on the northern end of the Continent grew more secure. It was hopeful that there would be time to move far enough inland to establish a firm beachhead before the Germans fully reacted to the danger by freeing up the panzer tanks that had the potential to frustrate the landing and drive the Allies back into the sea, which was Hitler's standing demand to his beleaguered generals. That's where General Patton and his thousands of cardboard tanks had bought precious time, perhaps enough to secure the landing. At long last the Allies were on the Continent and could now take the fight directly to the Germans. The English Channel that had so effectively protected England to this point was now a bridge over which the liberators would start their march toward Berlin.

As Philip walked into Whitehall where he would take the secret entrance into the Cabinet War Rooms, he pondered the success of the massive planning that went into this grand event—hundreds of paratroopers, thousands of ships, tens of thousands of aircraft, hundreds of thousands of troops, and millions of pounds of food and supplies to support all of them. It was an unbelievable effort, and the thought that it might succeed was one of the greatest things he could possibly imagine. Even now, giant artificial piers were being floated into position to form a new harbor at Arromanches on Gold Beach, where the giant barges were to be flooded with water to sink them into position. Until the major port of Cherbourg could be liberated, this would provide a starting place for the weapons, food, and infrastructure needed to support the millions of troops flowing into France.

"You certainly seem lost in thought, Philip."

Philip looked up to see one of the members of the confidential staff drawing up next to him. "I just said good-bye to General Patton. I was thinking about the invasion."

"Ah, yes. They tell me you deserve combat pay for what you've been through."

Philip laughed. "It was a very positive experience to be with him. I certainly understand how he can rub people the wrong way, and I'm quite sure that he's neither as good a general as he thinks he is nor nearly as bad as others think him. But still, he has a warrior's heart." His companion smiled as they descended into the bowels of the great building.

* * *

Toulon

"Do you think we'll ever be able to come out of hiding?" The frustration in Michael's voice was evident. Since blowing up the railroad trestle, they had been under constant pressure from the Germans, who had indeed taken reprisal against many of the local citizens, including the constable of a nearby town who knew of their whereabouts. The man had personally brought them nearly a week's supply of food from stores he'd hidden in his basement. While the Germans had no direct evidence to implicate him, they chose him for his prominent position instead and executed him in the town center. While the constable could have easily betrayed the British group and perhaps saved his own life, Pierre told them that he had stood boldly in the town center and shouted, "Vive la France" before being cut down. He was only one of a number of the Maquis who lost their lives, but at least there had been no mass executions as earlier feared.

But Jules and the group were still not in the clear, since the Germans were also suspicious of the coded broadcasts that they'd intercepted. Enemy patrols continually scoured the countryside in search of the perpetrators. For this reason they'd spent nearly a week hiding under a rock outcrop while the few German planes that were available from the Luftwaffe searched for them.

"In answer to your question, I think our days of isolation will soon come to an end. Forces continue to build in France, and the Germans have to be aware of the probability of attack. They just don't know where," Jules said. "I'm sure that in spite of the terrible blow it was to their pride to lose a handful of bridges, they have much bigger worries on their minds right now."

"Our local contact tells me that the Germans are forcing local French laborers to rebuild a temporary railroad trestle. So aside from the men we killed when the train collapsed, our efforts won't make a huge difference," Michael said.

"You shouldn't feel that way, Michael. The fact is that anything that interrupts their operations makes a difference. It puts their people on edge, wondering when another attack will take place. Just keeping them tired and worried is worth more than you can imagine."

Michael nodded. He knew that, of course, but was still irritated by the inactivity.

"It's still frustrating sitting here. Why do you suppose we haven't heard anything yet about an invasion? About anything? They know we're here." Michael was usually the voice of reason in the group, but today he was unusually agitated.

"The Americans have acknowledged each of our reports. As things draw closer, I'm sure they'll start making unreasonable demands for information from us, and you can risk your life just as much as your like." This was Jules's way of telling him to give it up.

"Are the British to take part at all?"

"Apparently not, Jenkins. From what I gather, this will be mostly an American and French operation. I knew all along that Churchill was not a supporter, so perhaps he's reserved our lads for other theaters, like Italy or Greece."

"Meanwhile the invasion of France has taken place in Normandy, and we're stuck here camping out. Can you just imagine the action that's taking place up there? I'm sure that every MTB in the fleet is engaged with big fat targets everywhere."

"Temper, temper, Carlyle. We each have a role to play in this little drama, and you've done all right for yourself so far."

"Indeed—a naval officer without a ship. That makes a lot of sense, doesn't it?" Michael turned and looked at Jenkins, who was sitting rather sullenly. He instantly regretted his intemperate words. He was Jenkins's captain, and the young man deserved better than this. Michael debated whether to apologize, but decided that it would just add to their troubles.

"I think I'll stretch my legs. Care to go for a walk with me, Jenkins?"

Jenkins looked up, surprised. "Of course, sir."

Michael glanced at Jules, who just shrugged. "We'll hold close to the side. And if you don't mind, a good beef pot pie would be appreciated when we get back." Jules shook his head and glowered, knowing full well it would be another dinner composed of a small piece of cheese and perhaps a crust of rye bread.

A few minutes later, as they worked their way down to the seashore, Michael said quietly, "You've done very well for yourself, Jenkins. Circumstances have placed very unusual demands on you—far outside what's typically expected for a navy man."

"Thank you, sir. It has been unusual."

"Yes, well. I suppose I should apologize for being so defeatist back there. Not very proper on my part."

Jenkins kept walking without looking up. Michael had hoped for more but realized that this was as much as he could ask. "I think you've been magnificent, sir. I can't imagine all that you've had to do to cope, speaking German to native Jerries, now doing all the translating for us into French. Also you have to temper Captain Ellington's, uh, enthusiasm." Jenkins looked up, a bit alarmed, hoping that he hadn't crossed a line with the last remark.

Michael just laughed. "Perhaps you should be a diplomat after the war. That was extremely well said."

"Yes, well. It's all true."

"So, you're all right?"

"Oh, yes sir. It makes me a bit daft waiting, just like you. But I'm not as ambitious as you, so I don't mind so much."

Michael had never thought of himself as ambitious—just as one who did his duty. But on reflection he saw that Jenkins was probably right.

"So, if you don't mind my asking, what do you plan to do after the war? What lies in your future?"

"I hope to become a solicitor. My father has a practice in the West End, and he'd like me to go into business with him."

Michael nodded appreciatively. "I think you'd make a fine solicitor. You're very levelheaded, you're hardworking, and yet you don't take yourself too seriously. I think you've got great balance." He smiled. "I'd be pleased to have you as my lawyer should I ever need one."

Michael heard Jenkins catch his breath. "Thank you, sir. That means a great deal to me." He looked up and finally smiled. "Who knows, perhaps you will need my services someday. That would mean the world to a firm like ours, to have the business of a person in your position."

Michael wanted to say something like, "I may need a lawyer long before you are admitted to the practice," but decided against it. He was happy to have his young charge back in decent spirits again.

"Well, I suppose we should get back. You never know what Captain Ellington may have cooked up for us in our absence, and I don't mean food!" Michael was pleased to hear Jenkins respond with a laugh.

* * *

Carlyle Manor

"We have just one line of text. How shall we spend those fifteen words?"

"How about if we say, 'Your parents and your sister, as well as your ravishing friend Karen Demming, all send their very best wishes for your safety and for your safe return. And welcome back from the dead.'"

Philip shook his head and smiled. "Very good, Grace. And with that the Germans will have more than enough time to triangulate the poor boy's location as well as ample opportunity to dispatch a platoon or two to hunt him down."

"Well, it's what I'd like to say!" Grace said. She was strikingly attractive when defiant.

Of course, if one used that logic it would follow that she'd been beautiful at work a lot lately. So much so that she had actually been placed on report for being cheeky. "It's just that they could do things so much more efficiently at the factory if they'd just implement some of my suggestions," she had said moodily when sharing the story with Philip. "The matron is really nothing more than an old cow who thinks she knows everything while knowing nothing!"

"Grace!" her mother had said. "You know better than to talk about a person like that. I don't care what she's done to you. You should show respect."

Grace had not appeared repentant. "What exactly did you do to get written up?" Philip had asked warily. He should have followed his better instinct to let it alone.

Grace looked up and smiled easily. "I mooed shortly after she passed by while I was adjusting a particularly complex piece of my machine. Who'd have thought that she could hear a quiet little cow sound above all the racket of the mill? Apparently she has superhuman hearing."

Philip had laughed in spite of Claire's glare, but had ended the conversation by telling Grace that she deserved whatever she got and he would do nothing to protect her if she got laid off work. And then he hugged her.

After sharing the good news about Michael's escape, the military had given the family permission to send just one line of acknowledgment so that Michael would know that they had received and understood the coded message he'd sent them.

"How about just 'Love PCGK,'" Claire said helpfully.

"Perhaps love isn't exactly a word you send in a military telegram. Operators up and down the line would find that a bit too tempting to ignore when given the chance to gossip about it."

"You're not suggesting that men gossip, are you, Papa?"

Philip laughed again. "Call it what you like, dear—they will torment Michael if we were to use that language."

"All right, then what if we say 'Warm sheets and a hot bath await you—PCGK'?"

"I don't think I should be included in that message," Karen said with her face flushing.

Grace looked surprised and then burst out laughing.

"We need to come up with something that only Michael would understand but that wouldn't give the Germans any kind of hint that might reveal his identity," Philip said.

While this interchange had been going on, Claire had been diligently writing characters on her paper, occasionally pausing to scratch out a line. "How about this?" she asked while giving Philip the paper. "SLC2UK-HPYFRU-PCG&KD?"

It took Philip a moment to decipher the code. When he did, he smiled and nodded. "I think that will do nicely. Very nicely."

"What is it?" Grace asked. "I want to see." Philip handed her the paper and was rewarded with a broad smile when she too deciphered it. "We ought to write like this more often," Grace concluded as she passed the paper to Karen. "Just think of how much ink and paper it would save."

"Really? If that's the kind of suggestion you make at work, I can see why they'd be put off." Grace playfully slugged her father for that.

Chapter Twenty-five

THE ANVIL

The Mediterranean Coast west of Cannes, France—August 15, 1944

"Isn't that the most amazing sight you've ever beheld?" Michael had become accustomed to almost anything Jules might say. But the sound of sheer awe in his voice was surprising and refreshing. If anything could inspire a skeptic, this was it. The coastal scene that opened to their view *was* the most remarkable thing that Michael had ever laid his eyes on. The ocean was filled with more than eight hundred ships standing off the shore while what appeared to be a thousand landing craft were plying the beaches with men and transport. It was inspiring to see the organization involved in such a grand event. The landing was taking place on the beaches southwest of Cannes on the St. Tropez peninsula. In the course of the first three days, more than 150,000 soldiers waded ashore, with many more to follow as the Free French who had fled to North Africa early in the war returned to liberate their homeland.

"It looks like they're all American ships," Jenkins said. "I thought there'd be at least a few British ships out there to help them."

"Afraid we'll have to wait a while to see a British face. This is an American, French, and Canadian operation," Jules replied.

Michael was thoughtful. "Well, at least we're here to witness the whole thing on behalf of the British Empire. How many men do you think have ever been able to watch a spectacle like this?"

"It's sheer luck that we happened to be in the right spot in the first place," Jules responded. "The Germans certainly thought the invasion would come much farther to the west so that the Allies could more quickly go after the Port of Marseille. That's got to be their true objective."

"But apparently the Americans wanted to hit the Germans in the soft spot between their two main divisions. It's similar to the strategy in the north, where they landed in Normandy rather than at a more obvious spot closer to Germany. Given the light resistance they're encountering, it was probably a good decision. They'll be here to rescue us in no time." Michael then laughed a humorless laugh. "It may be better for me that we are picked up by the Americans rather than the British. It will delay my day of reckoning a bit longer."

"Now look, Carlyle. I've told you this before. Your actions very likely saved a national treasure—me—so no matter what you said to your Commander Windbag, they've got to give you credit for that." Turning to Jenkins he added, "If you look it up in the *Unabridged Oxford Dictionary*, I'm sure you'll find that the word *windbag* is a listed synonym for *Billingham*, so I'm certainly not being disrespectful here. You'll remember that at Carlyle's court-martial won't you?"

Jenkins scowled at him. Usually Jules was amusing, but Jenkins had very strong feelings about this and was not in the mood for a joke. "As far as I'm concerned, Captain Ellington, Lieutenant Carlyle acted heroically and deserves a medal, not censure. And if I'm given a chance to testify, I'll tell them that. You can count on that."

"You'll do nothing to put yourself in jeopardy, Jenkins. Do you understand that?"

Eventually Jenkins said, "It's still not fair, sir."

"I don't know why you're worried about this just now. A lot still has to happen before we hook up with the Royal Navy," Jules said in an attempt to divert the conversation.

"It's just that it's now growing closer by the minute. Do you realize it's been nearly a year since we've been on the run? And now it's about to come to an end." There was a deep pit in Michael's stomach, and if he weren't so hungry he felt as if he'd throw up. While the French had done their best to keep their three British saboteurs fed, it was very difficult for them, particularly since the Germans were always watching for any suspicious movements. Finally, their handlers had grown tired of keeping the group out in the country, so they had moved them into the city under the cover of darkness one night. Once in the city, they'd first stayed in an attic, whose door was hidden by a large armoire. At night members of the Maquis would slip in and pass them whatever food they could scrounge up, as well as vital information such as where German troops were deployed up and down the coast, the size of the various military units in a given area, and strategic locations of ammunition and fuel depots. Jules would then transmit this intelligence in short bursts to his contacts on Corsica. He had to be extremely careful not to broadcast for too long in any single broadcast, since the Germans could, by using three separate direction-finding receivers, hone in on the group's position with a fair amount of precision. That's why they'd been moved after just a few days in the first location, and had continued to shuffle about at least every few days thereafter. In their travels they'd been as far west as Marseille and as far east as the border of Monaco. It was all very nerve-wracking, and Michael yearned for the time when he'd be back on the deck of a ship where he didn't have to hide all the time.

But now they'd been allowed to come out into the daylight. When word was received that the invasion fleet had been spotted in the harbor, every German unit in the area had been activated and was now making its way to its preassigned defensive position. It was sickening to see the shore batteries firing on the Allied ships as they came in to drop off their precious human cargo.

"I understand that paratroopers landed behind us in the darkness after the American bombers pulled out," Michael said.

"Yes, and it didn't go very well for them from what I heard the French saying. The landscape is so confusing and uneven," Jules said.

There was a long period of silence after that. After all the time they'd spent together, they'd pretty much told every story they could think of and so had come to accept that periods of silence were a fine way to pass the time.

Suddenly there was the sound of footsteps on the rocks behind them, and in an instant they'd all whirled about and moved close to the walls of the small crevice in the rock that they'd been hiding in. With a raised pistol, Jules was prepared to fire when Pierre gave the two-part whistle that identified him as a friend.

"You scared us with that one," Michael said in French. He'd had so much occasion to use the language of late that it seemed almost as natural as English. There were even occasions when Jules or Jenkins would have to stop him and remind him to speak in English, since he'd launch into an explanation in what was unintelligible gibberish to them.

"Sorry," Pierre replied. "It's just that we think we've found a way for you to be useful. There are some American paratroopers not four miles from here, and none of them speak French. Can you imagine that?" Michael almost laughed at how incredulous Pierre was at this oversight but kept a straight face. The last thing he wanted to do was offend his host. "We urgently need you to help us coordinate with them. And my limited English is not doing at all well with their American English."

"But I thought the paratroopers dropped much farther inland."

"They were supposed to, but everything is all mixed up. This particular unit is supposed to work its way towards Le Muy, where they are to secure a German fuel depot. So you see how urgent it is?"

"Of course—let's be off." Michael immediately started gathering himself together for a quick departure.

"And were you ever planning to tell us what you just discussed? Or are you just off with your French friend here?" Jules said sharply.

"What?" Michael wheeled and looked at Jules and Jenkins, who both stood there with their mouths rather firmly set. "Oh, sorry. I forgot. All that took place in French, didn't it?" The glower that followed confirmed at least that fact. He quickly explained the situation, and Jules immediately collected his things.

As they started through the brush, Jules whispered furiously, "I can't wait to get there. At least we'll be with English speakers so that Jenkins and I won't be taken for granted quite so often!" He was thoughtful for a moment. "Not that they'll really speak English, of course. But it will be close enough that we can make it out."

"Oh, boo hoo!" Michael replied. "Sorry to have been such an inconvenience to you. I'm sure you'd have been far better off had I followed Billingham's order and left you to your own devices!"

Jules glowered again but made no reply. In spite of the tense words in their banter, everyone was very excited at the thought of escaping their isolation. Even Michael was able to forget his anxiety for a time.

The terrain was so difficult that it took more than two hours to make the rendezvous. When they did, they had to be very cautious so that the Americans didn't shoot them on the spot. After all, they were wearing local clothing and could very easily have been German spies. At first Pierre approached the Americans and did his best to explain the situation. Eventually he motioned for the three British to stand up with hands held high above their heads. It was quite disconcerting to have half a dozen rifles instantly pointed at them, but all three kept relatively calm and made no sudden movements. While standing there with his arms raised high in the air, Michael's neck started aching, in spite of his leather collar, and he hoped they would hurry things along. Jules very quietly said, as best he could without appearing to move his mouth, "I have to scratch the top of my head—terribly!"

Finally, after seemingly endless discussion amongst themselves, the Americans motioned for Michael, Jules, and Jenkins to come forward. As they started to walk, Michael's arms slumped a bit, which was a source of alarm to the Americans. The gestures with their rifles prompted Michael to sigh and then raise them back to full extension as he made his way across the rocky field. When they were about ten feet away from the paratroopers, their leader motioned for them to stop.

"What's the name of the leading soccer team in England?" the fellow barked out.

"That depends on which county you're from," Jules said.

"Don't get smart!" the fellow barked.

"That's not my intention," Jules replied calmly, "but I'm afraid we Englishmen are quite literal and find it almost impossible to answer an ambiguous question. But we'll try, honestly we will."

The American smiled. "That certainly sounds British. If you are a German you've got a darn good British accent."

"Perhaps our common friend from the Maquis has told you what we've been up to with the Germans of late. I seriously doubt that the Germans would claim us, other than as targets for a firing squad."

"He's not very easy to understand, but we've made out most of the story. But we're not entirely sure we can trust even him. Our leaders warned us to seek positive identification since there are Free French Forces of the Interior who are likely to act in sympathy with the Germans. So you'll forgive our caution."

"I'm afraid there's a problem with our papers. We had to plant our own papers on some dead German bodies so that they'd leave off chasing us. Most of the world thinks we're dead."

The American hesitated. "I'm not sure what to do in a case like this."

"If I may," Michael said evenly, "perhaps I can help move things along."

"Give it your best shot, buddy. We want to get on with our mission, and all this talk is wasting valuable time."

"My name is Lieutenant Michael Carlyle, Royal Navy. But I'm an American by birth and spent the first ten years of my life living in Salt Lake City, Utah. It's been a long time, but I think I could answer some pretty detailed questions about your country that a German isn't likely to know. Perhaps you could test me?"

"Salt Lake City? Are you a Mormon?"

Michael inhaled deeply, taken totally by surprise. Since he never knew what kind of a response this would prompt, he paused for just a moment, but then said evenly, "I am."

The fellow smiled. "Then I think we can establish the authenticity of your claim rather quickly. Who's the president of the Church? And who are his counselors?"

In a totally unexpected reaction, Michael felt a rush of emotion sweep over his whole body, and he felt a lump come into his throat. Only another member could ask a question like this—most people had no idea that the Church had a president, let alone two counselors.

"You must be a member." After spending his entire adult life without the companionship of other members of the Church, Michael was simply overwhelmed to think that in this extreme place he would be blessed to encounter someone who shared his faith.

"You didn't answer my questions." The smile was gone, and the fellow looked at him very seriously.

"Heber J. Grant is president of the Church, and J. Reuben Clark and David O. McKay are his counselors."

The American nodded. "Yes, you're right." The fellow motioned to his companions to put down the muzzles of their guns. "It's all right. He's who he says he is." The other Americans drifted off and returned to the work they'd been doing.

Instead of hazing them anymore, the American indicated they should drop their arms and then he walked over to Michael with hand outstretched. "I'm sorry, I didn't mean to be so rough. We have to be sure of these things.

"My name is Lieutenant Patrick Fenton. And you're Lieutenant Carlyle?"

Michael looked at him and smiled. "That's right. You've got a good memory."

"It tends to be sharper when you might be introducing yourself to a German spy. Who are your friends?"

Michael turned and looked at Jules and Jenkins, who both had rather puzzled looks on their faces. "This is Sublieutenant Jeremy Jenkins of the Royal Navy and a member of my crew. In normal circumstances we'd be onboard a motor torpedo boat, but our capture ended all of that. Jenkins is an extremely reliable fellow with whom I'm very proud to serve." Jenkins beamed and accepted Fenton's salute.

"And this is Commander Jules Ellington. He's a scoundrel and a knave, and you should probably shoot him where he stands." Michael was pleased by Fenton's astonished look. "He's a British commando and a very good friend of mine. But if you have a girlfriend, I wouldn't introduce her to him. He's a rogue that way."

"That's rather cheeky of a subordinate officer, don't you think, Lieutenant Fenton? Would that be considered insubordination in the American armed forces?"

Fenton laughed. "Listen, we'll have plenty of time to talk later. You're the first member of the Church I've seen in three years, so we have a lot to catch up on. But right now we have to get moving. Do you fellows have any weapons?"

"Just handguns, I'm afraid."

"That will have to do for now. The Frenchman indicated that you've blown up a bridge or something?"

Jules nodded.

"Well, it's good that we met up with you, then, because our demolitions expert broke his leg during his landing and isn't up to much, so perhaps you'd join us. Our task is to make our way to Le Muy, where we hope to take control of a German fuel depot. If that fails, we'll blow it up. The goal is to do as little damage as possible so that we can convert it to use by our Army group when they penetrate this far inland. If you've rested enough, maybe we can get going?"

Michael started forward but was a bit bothered when Fenton continued looking at him with concern.

"Is something bothering you, Lieutenant?" Michael asked.

"Your neck. You have that brace on. Are you all right to travel?"

Once again Michael was taken by surprise. He pretty much took the collar for granted now and wasn't really aware that he was wearing it, a lot like eyeglasses for those who wear them every day. "Thank you for noticing. Yes, I'm all right. I got hurt in a similar type of mission in northern France while wrestling with a German. About the only thing that really makes my neck hurt these days is when I'm ordered to hold my hands high above my head."

"What?" Fenton got that same startled look on his face he had earlier. "Oh, sorry about that. We'll have to make sure that doesn't happen again." Fenton moved confidently toward his men. "Johnson, you stay with Keller. The French have agreed to help you find a safe place to stay until more Allied troops catch up with you."

The look on Johnson's face made it very clear that he didn't want to stay, but it was also clear that the discussion had already taken place and that Johnson had lost. Grudgingly he stood up and helped Fenton put on his pack. As he did so, Michael heard Fenton whisper, "Thank you, Johnson. You know we never leave a man behind. We'll make it up to you later." Johnson smiled and saluted his leader, and then Fenton gave the order to form up.

As they started hiking through the hills, Jules came up and started walking beside Michael. "It's rather amazing, don't you think?"

"What?"

"How quickly you took on an American accent."

"What?" Michael stopped and turned to look directly at him. "Have you started imagining things? I did not take on an American accent."

"Oh, calm down. It's kind of charming. And I'm very glad that you managed to hook up with someone from your church. He appears to be a very competent leader. I think I'll like working with him."

They walked in silence awhile before Michael motioned for Jules to stop. "Listen, we may not get a chance to be by ourselves again. I just want to say thanks for getting us through all this. I make jokes every now and then, but the fact is that you're really good at what you do. It's an honor to serve with you."

Jules nodded slowly and then decided to reply seriously. "I feel the same way, Michael. You've handled everything that's been thrown at you, particularly with all the languages you've had to deal with. It really is remarkable that we've made it this far. You're a good friend." Jules saluted Michael, who returned it crisply. They started walking again to catch up to the group.

"Of course I still think you'll end up liking the Americans best, and Jenkins and I will become old news . . ."

Michael shook his head as his eyes narrowed. "You're certainly making it easier, Jules."

* * *

"Hit the deck!"

Instinctively Michael threw himself to the ground, which was not a good thing to do to his neck. But when he heard a bullet ricochet off a nearby rock, he decided it was well worth the trouble.

"Looks like we've found the Germans." Fenton motioned for his men to scatter and start working themselves into positions to put up a fight. They'd been hiking for nearly six hours, and it was getting close to dusk. Michael had hoped they could find a place to get a little sleep before making their assault on the fuel depot, but that wasn't to be.

"Did you ever see any cowboy and Indian movies?" Fenton asked Michael.

"Loads of them," Michael replied.

Fenton grinned. "I never thought I'd be in one. Here we are hiding behind a bunch of boulders, while the Germans are in position to ambush us. It's lucky that one of them fired prematurely, or we would have all been goners."

"The Germans in this area haven't seen a lot of action, probably many of them since the start of the war. I can imagine that they felt themselves pretty lucky to be assigned to the French Riviera, far away from the invasion of Normandy and the fighting in Italy. So it's not at all unreasonable that they would be less than combat ready."

Fenton motioned for two of his men to come over. Talking very quietly, he made a number of motions with his hands, and then the two went off quickly, gathering a couple of other fellows as they went. "Our job is to make them pay for their inexperience. I know you only have a handgun, but could you create some covering fire so I can move over there. It will make it easier for me to direct the battle."

"Sure!" When Fenton gave the signal, Michael raised his head slightly above the lip of the rock that was sheltering him and started firing at the Germans. With his self-loading pistol, he was able to lay down a quick pattern that didn't totally prevent a German response but at least made it so that they didn't stick their heads up to get off any accurate shots. Fenton raced out into the opening and then quickly dove for cover at his chosen position. Michael dropped down behind his rock when Fenton gave him a thumbs-up.

Even though Michael knew nothing of Army tactics, he was certainly smart enough to know that the Germans had given up a number of potential advantages. At this point the Germans were on higher ground, so they should have been laying down a withering barrage of fire to hold the Americans in place. But instead they just waited. Meanwhile, it was pretty obvious that Lieutenant Fenton had previous combat experience, because he was expertly moving his men into something of a crescent position, where they could close up on the Germans with fire ultimately pouring in on them from three sides.

Once Fenton had everyone in position, he gave the signal, and the Americans rushed the German position, weapons blazing in a barrage of automatic fire. The three British men joined in, and Michael felt a rush of adrenaline as he ran forward in a crouching position, getting off shots whenever a target presented itself. As he ran, he heard a man fall to his left side, but he just kept running. Everyone in the group was shouting, and in a matter of moments they reached the German position. As the Germans stood up to meet them, guns blazed on both sides and there was the sound of men screaming as they got hit. In short order, whatever advantage the Germans had at the outset quickly evaporated, and the withering fire of the Americans' automatic weaponry started mowing them down all across the landscape. Michael fired at one fellow who was about to shoot him and watched as the man fell backward.

What happened next was so fast that he couldn't quite process it. Without warning, he felt himself slammed from the right side, which sent him tumbling to the ground. Next he heard a yelp, followed by rapid gunfire, and he looked up to see Jenkins tumble to the ground beside him, with Jules firing quickly right behind. Following the line of fire he saw another German fall to the ground. Obviously this man had held Michael in his sights and would have killed him had not Jenkins knocked him out of the way. But clearly Jenkins had paid a price for it. In a panic Michael crawled over to Jenkins as fast as he could. "Jenkins! Jenkins! Are you hit badly? Where did they get you?"

"I think I got hit in my shoulder."

"Let me take a look." He rolled Jenkins to his back and saw a dark stain spreading on the top of his shoulder. "Let me help you!" he called out urgently as Jenkins's eyes rolled back. "Stay with me, Jenkins! Help me, Jules. He's been hit!"

Jules crawled over and said, "You stay with him, Michael. We've got to secure this thing, or we'll all be dead. I've got to help them." With that Jules got up on his knees and started advancing toward the German position, firing carefully each time a target presented itself. The only time he interrupted the firing was when he'd lie flat on his back to reload his gun.

"You're going to be okay, Jenkins. Let me get your shirt off, and we'll stop the bleeding."

"Thank you, sir," Jenkins said weakly.

By the time Michael got his shirt pulled open, he could see that the bullet had entered from the back at the top of his shoulder and exited out the front. As gruesome as that was, it was probably good that the bullet hadn't remained inside to cause an infection. As gently as he could, Michael forced his handkerchief into the wound to staunch the bleeding. Jenkins winced at this and went silent. "It's all right to faint," Michael said softly. "It will make it easier." At first the handkerchief turned a brilliant crimson as it soaked up the blood, but as Michael pushed harder, the flow started to slow. Eventually he felt as if he'd stabilized the wound enough that he could take a moment to pour some sulfa powder into the open wound before putting in another gob of bandage. Again, the material turned red, but it was clear that the bullet had missed any major arteries. Michael checked Jenkins's breathing and was relieved that his breaths were steady and deep. In spite of the fact that Jenkins had lost consciousness, Michael continued to speak to him in soothing tones. "You're going to be all right, Jenkins. You'll make it."

He looked up and was pleased to see Jules and the Americans all standing upright now, their weapons pointed forward at a group of perhaps half a dozen German soldiers who had their hands held high above their heads. Jules moved in expertly and started disarming each of them, as did a couple of the Americans. Fenton sent some of his men out to reconnoiter the area to make sure they were clear of any other hostile forces. Eventually the men returned and indicated that they were all clear.

At this point, Fenton noticed Michael crouching over Jenkins and came over. "Is he alive?"

"He took a shot in the shoulder, but I've got the bleeding stopped, and he's breathing evenly. He passed out from the pain, but I think he's going to be okay."

"That's good," Fenton said distractedly. "I better check on my men."

Jules came back over then, the Germans having been forced to lie down on their stomachs, arms fully extended out in front of them, while two of the American paratroopers stood above them with machine guns.

Jules made a quick report. "We came out of it pretty well. It looks like only one of the Americans was killed, with three wounded, besides Jenkins. That's a very high casualty rate for a group this size, but the Germans came off much worse. We killed at least six of them, and it looks to me like two more will die of their wounds very shortly. It's going to be a lot tougher going forward now with prisoners, but I don't know what else to do."

"I guess it's not really our problem, is it?" Michael replied.

"No, this is the Americans' show. But we did our part. How's Jenkins?"

"I think he'll live. The bullet went all the way through, but there's a lot of smashed bone right at the socket. He needs real medical attention as soon as possible."

Jules frowned. "I don't know where we're going to get it out here. We're a good fifteen kilometers from the nearest beach, and there's undoubtedly other roving bands of Germans like this."

"Then we'll just go forward with the Americans until we meet up with other units," Michael said. "There's no other choice."

"Bad luck, Jenkins getting hit. He's a good lad."

"He saved my life, didn't he?"

Jules looked at Michael seriously. "Just as you'd have saved his if the circumstances were reversed."

Michael sighed. "I still don't think I like your hand-to-hand combat. Much nicer to fire at the enemy from a distance."

"And I don't think I like the thought of fighting a battle where you can drown. So I guess we each chose the right service, didn't we?"

* * *

By the time the group reached Le Muy, they found that a number of other paratrooper units had already secured the ammunition depot. The Germans had tried to destroy it, but quick action on the part of the Americans had stopped them from setting off the charges that would have sent the whole thing up in smoke. The task for the paratroopers now was to hold the position until regular forces advanced to their position from the sea. Fortunately, the little town had a small hospital where Jenkins and other wounded had been taken for basic care. The local French doctor had abandoned the town, and the lone American medic threw his hands in the air over how to help Jenkins with anything other than controlling the bleeding.

"He really needs to get to a doctor," the man had said to Lieutenant Fenton.

Given the number of wounded, it was determined that they needed to get the most seriously injured out as quickly as possible. There was a lone truck in the community that they quickly commandeered for that purpose. Checking by radio with the troops who had established the beachhead, they felt like they could risk working their way through the back roads that led to the beaches. Once there, they could get the men in a landing craft and out to one of the destroyers anchored in the harbor, where a real doctor could help them. The various leaders of the paratrooper units drew straws, and it fell to Fenton to lead the group back. When he called for volunteers, Michael raised his hand. He wanted to go with Jenkins. But he noticed that Jules did not raise his. Fenton accepted Michael and two other men to tend the wounded and two others to ride as guards. They agreed to wait until the next morning before attempting the evacuation.

At 0600 the patients were loaded into the back of the truck on mattresses confiscated from the hospital. After a quick bite of breakfast, Fenton indicated they were ready to leave.

"I guess this is it, then," Michael said to Jules.

"This is what I'm trained to do. The Germans have been beaten back temporarily, but they can send reinforcements down from Grenoble if they want, so the whole thing is still quite precarious. I think this is where I should stay—at least for the time being."

"I understand. But my place is with Jenkins. He's a member of my crew."

"Of course."

The two men stood and embraced. "All sarcasm aside," Michael said, "you are the best friend I have. So I hope you don't do anything stupid like getting yourself killed."

"I told you a long time ago, Michael, that I'm out to kill the Germans, not the other way round."

"Good! Then I'll see you in London when the war is over. My treat at the Travellers Club."

Jules pretended to fumble in his pockets. "I was just going to check my calendar to make sure I have time, but somehow I've misplaced the thing."

Michael smiled and slugged him in the shoulder. Then he went over to Pierre and embraced him as well. "Thank you for protecting us, feeding us, and sheltering us. I'm sorry for the men who lost their lives."

"Fortunes of war. It was an honor to serve with you. Good luck to you and Mr. Jenkins."

Michael felt a lump in his throat but dealt with it by quickly climbing into the front seat of the truck with Patrick Fenton. He didn't turn to look back as the truck pulled away. But Jules watched the truck until it was out of sight.

Chapter Twenty-six

A CHANGE OF FORTUNES

St. Tropez—August 1944

"Do you mind if I ask how it is that you're an American who is serving in the British Navy?" Fenton asked.

Michael started to reply, but the truck hit a deep rut in the dirt road and he was thrown so hard that he hit his head on the glass window. He laughed. "I will if you'll drive a little slower."

"Sorry, that was probably pretty rough on the wounded in the back." The truck decelerated, and Fenton shifted to a lower gear. "I'm just so nervous driving through here for fear the Germans will attack us or worse—that our own aircraft will mistake us for Germans and fire on us. I just want to get to the beach."

Michael acknowledged this sentiment and then proceeded to explain how Philip had come to America at the end of World War I, joined the Church, and then married Claire. "I think my father would have been content to stay in Salt Lake City for the rest of his life, but when my grandfather died, duty called him back to England. And the one thing no Englishman can resist is duty."

"So I've heard. So which are you, American or English?"

Michael sighed. "I still ask myself that question sometimes. I thought I'd decided that I was English. But in just the short time I've been with you guys, I somehow find myself homesick for America. At the very least I'd like to go back there someday for a visit."

They drove in silence for a while. "So, what's it like being a member of the Church in England? I've never lived outside of Utah myself, until the war broke out. And since leaving home for basic training, I haven't met a single member of the Church until you."

"In most ways I think being a member is the same wherever you live—we go to priesthood meeting early on Sunday, then come home for breakfast, followed by a return to the chapel for Sunday School with my mom and sister joining us. Then a long afternoon with the family, and sacrament meeting at 5:00 PM." He furrowed his brow. "Except when we're at our home out in the country. Sometimes they hold Sunday School and sacrament meeting next to each other since it is difficult and expensive for some of the poorer members to travel so far."

"Are there a lot of members?"

Michael laughed. "Not like in Utah. I was only ten years old when we moved, but I still remember how there was an LDS chapel every couple of blocks.

"I was the only member of the Church at the school I attended, except for my brother. And there just weren't that many members my own age, even in London. And so far the number has been zero in the navy. So, I'm in the same boat you are as far as having been out of touch with the Church since coming to this theater. It feels good to have someone to talk to."

Their discussion was interrupted by someone pounding on the window behind them. Fenton eased the truck to the side of the road, and he and Michael got out. "What's the matter?" Fenton asked since nothing seemed out of order.

"We're in need of the latrine, sir. Perhaps you officers never need to go, but it's getting quite desperate back here."

"Sorry, Lewis. I'm just so focused on getting through all this. Let me help you with the injured." And with that, Michael and Fenton assisted the wounded men who could get out of the truck to the side of the road. Those who couldn't used a makeshift bedpan. When they were all resettled, some light food was distributed, and Fenton and Michael climbed back in the cab.

"I notice you have a wedding ring," Michael said.

Fenton smiled. "I do. I married my high school sweetheart shortly after the war broke out. We thought about it a lot since there's such a high risk that I might not come home, but my wife said she didn't want us to live our lives in fear, so we should do what our hearts told us." He nodded his head at the memory. "So we got married two and a half years ago, and I've been gone for almost two years. And in spite of her brave words, we've both been afraid."

"I can't imagine going through that."

Fenton glanced over at Michael. "Harder on her than me. She was able to come stay with me during my advanced training, but it was the hardest thing I ever had to do to put her on the bus and send her back to Salt Lake City when it finally came time for me to ship out. Particularly since she was pregnant . . ." His voice trailed off.

"So you're a father?"

Fenton smiled. "I am. I have a little boy named Matthew. My wife likes biblical names. I've never met him."

"I can't imagine going through that."

"They tell me that it will be pretty hard on him when I come home, since he'll have to share his mother for the first time. But I'll win him over."

They drove in silence awhile. "So do you have a girl?" Fenton asked.

Michael didn't answer for a moment. Nodding his head slightly, he said, "Yes, I do. I'm very good friends with a really wonderful girl. I probably wasn't as smart as you since I didn't ask her to marry me. I wanted to wait for the war to end. Just in case. I probably missed out."

"Is she a member of the Church?"

Michael shook his head. "No. But I think she's interested. I hope so."

Fenton sensed the tension in Michael's voice, so he changed the subject. "We're going to get to the beaches very soon." Michael nodded.

Suddenly a knot grew in Michael's stomach when he realized that he could be to his court-martial fairly soon now that he was back among Allied troops.

"What's wrong, Carlyle?" Fenton asked.

Michael turned and faced him directly, even though Fenton had to keep his eyes forward while driving. "It's just that I disobeyed a direct order, and I very likely will be brought up on charges when I get back to the British sector. When I'm found guilty, I will go to prison."

Fenton caught his breath. "Oh. I'm sorry to hear that," he replied, clearly flustered. He didn't add that criminal disobedience was the last thing he'd expect of a fellow member of the Church, although that's what he was thinking. Finally, after a bit of uncomfortable silence, he said, "Maybe you can tell me about it if you want to. Sometimes we're really not very good judges of ourselves. Not that I can judge you, but if you want to talk . . . or not."

Michael took a deep breath. He'd spent so much time avoiding thinking about what was coming that he didn't know if he could even tell the story. He was still angry at Billingham, but also frightened. Finally, though, he felt as if he must face it, so he said, "Well, it can't hurt. I'll have to tell it to a court-martial soon enough. Maybe some practice would be good for me." He smiled weakly, but Fenton quite wisely remained silent. So Michael told the tale of Billingham ordering him to leave Jules behind, of his defiance, and of their capture and abandonment. At times during the retelling there was suppressed fury in his voice and at others the sound of despair. Finally, when he brought the story up to the present, he was spent and could say no more.

"I don't know what's right and wrong here, particularly since I don't understand the British military. But I can tell you that I would have done the same thing," Fenton said.

"Then you'd be in the same trouble I am."

"Yes, I would. But either way, Jules would still be alive. Let the consequences follow."

Michael nodded and then he rested his head on the window as the truck rumbled along the road.

* * *

Although it wasn't a terribly long distance to the beaches, it took nearly six hours to reach the main Allied force. Surprisingly they weren't accosted by any Germans along the way. Apparently all the Germans in the area had been ordered west to try to staunch the Allied invasion from advancing northwest of Toulon. But they did have two harrowing incidents when Allied fighters flew overhead in a threatening pattern. On the first pass, one of the American paratroopers in the back had displayed the good sense to stand up and wave their unit flag high above his head. Fortunately the pilot recognized it and tipped his wings before flying north. On the second, they had all gotten out of the truck for another break when the pilot fired off a burst of rounds that tore up the bed on the back of the truck. When on the second pass he saw the injured as well as their protectors waving and gesturing wildly to indicate they were Allies, he must have felt guilty, because he flew on by without any acknowledgment. Fortunately, his shells had missed the engine and tires, so they were able to move ahead. But acknowledging the danger of not being recognized, they posted one of the Americans to sit on the front of the hood, holding his flag prominently as they pulled into the area where the Americans had taken control of the beach.

Once there, some medics immediately came up and helped the wounded off the truck. Michael then identified himself as British and asked permission to accompany Jenkins to whatever ship he was to be taken to.

Fenton took his hand, then pulled him into an embrace.

"I'm glad God brought us together." They broke the embrace and stepped back from each other.

"Well, I better go."

"Of course," Fenton said.

Michael turned to leave.

"Wait a minute!" Michael turned to see Fenton fumbling inside his jacket. Finally he pulled a very small book out, the smallest Michael had ever seen. "Do you have one of these?"

"What is it?"

"A serviceman's copy of the Book of Mormon. The First Presidency had it printed for everyone who goes into the military. The printing is miniscule, but you can still make it out. Do you have one?"

"No, I don't."

"Well, I want you to have this one. As a gift."

Michael's eyes grew wide. "But you need it. I couldn't take it from you."

"I think you'll need it more than me. Besides, I still have the New Testament. I'll start reading that now." He looked at Michael searchingly. "Please take it. I want you to have it." He held the book out.

Michael hesitated but then reached out and took it from Fenton's outstretched hand. It was a very small book, but the leather cover felt warm in his hand, and he felt a thrill as he thought about having the scriptures with him. Leafing through the pages, he saw that Fenton had made some very small notes and highlighted various passages. "This is the best gift I've ever received. Thank you. And God bless you!"

"He has. Now you better get going."

With that, Fenton stepped out into the sunlight and motioned to where Michael should go to catch the landing craft that would carry him and Jenkins out to a destroyer where Jenkins could be cared for.

* * *

British Naval Headquarters—the Island of Corsica

"Admiral Chadwick will see you now."

Michael, who had finally had the chance to take a real bath and don a new uniform, nervously adjusted his tie and stood up. After they had reached the American destroyer, the doctors had determined that Jenkins's condition, while stable, required more than they could give even there. The damaged bone in his shoulder was a mess. So the two had been transferred to a ship heading back to Corsica for resupply. There was a British infirmary there, as well as a command unit for the British ships assigned to support the invasion and other Mediterranean operations. As soon as Michael saw Jenkins successfully transferred to the hospital, he reported to headquarters, promising that he'd come back to visit him. It was a promise he hoped he could fulfill.

Once he reached headquarters and identified himself to the officer of the day, he was surprised that they didn't arrest him on the spot. Instead, the fellow indicated that there was a note in their files that he should report directly to the admiral. Apparently Billingham had gone straight to the top in his complaints. *At least Chadwick's fair—he'll let me tell my side of the story.* But he knew that it was a fairly open-and-shut case. Billingham had given an order, and Michael had disobeyed it. There wasn't a lot to dispute.

"Ah, Lieutenant Carlyle, come in." Michael snapped to attention as soon as he cleared the door and saluted the admiral. Chadwick looked older than he'd remembered. Weathered.

Chadwick returned his salute and then invited him to sit down.

"Begging your pardon, sir," Michael said, "but I'm a bit too nervous to sit down. It's my understanding that Commander Billingham was putting me on report." Perhaps it wasn't too smart to self-identify his problem, but he simply couldn't go through a bunch of pleasantries before finding out his fate.

Chadwick sighed. "He did, indeed. But I'm feeling rather old today and would like to sit down to talk with you, and it simply wouldn't be comfortable with you standing above me." He motioned to one of the two side chairs in front of his desk, and Michael sat down.

"I'm sorry I disobeyed an order," Michael started to say. "It's just that . . ."

Chadwick held up his hand. "I'll be glad to hear your version of events, Lieutenant, but before I do, you should know that Commander Billingham has retired from the service and is no longer on active duty."

"Retired?" There was a sound of disbelief in Michael's voice.

"Retired. Not entirely by his choice, I'm afraid, but at least he was able to keep his pension that way."

"I don't understand, sir."

Chadwick smiled wearily. "You wouldn't. You were off starting your little resistance effort in Italy and France. But let me tell you the story. Perhaps it will set your mind at ease."

Michael had to shake his head a bit to clear his thoughts. This was taking such a different turn than he'd anticipated.

"It seems that after you went ashore against the commander's order, he chose to leave you and your comrades rather than stay and defend you against the German gunboat."

"Yes, sir. We saw them leave."

"Well, it seems that your first officer took great exception to that and almost committed his own mutiny, but Billingham pointed a pistol at him, forcing him to comply under protest. Lieutenant Coleman nearly broke into tears when he told me about it later. He feels very guilty that he left you."

"He would feel like that. But he was in an impossible situation. Of course I harbor no ill feelings towards Lieutenant Coleman. He had no choice but to follow orders."

"So he should follow orders but not you?"

Michael dropped his head but said nothing.

"Well at any rate, as your boat withdrew from the battle scene, it was soon joined by Lieutenant Smith and the third boat. Of course they knew nothing of your action. Approximately halfway home, the group was attacked by German aircraft. This time your boat took some hits, as did Lieutenant Smith's. But it was the third boat that was in real trouble. On one of the strafing runs, the Germans hit one of its deck fuel tanks, which started a fire that doomed the boat. Thank heavens we use diesel fuel rather than gasoline like the Americans, otherwise everyone onboard would have been killed. When Smith turned to rescue the survivors, Commander Billingham ordered a retreat. Smith refused rather angrily and turned about to help the sinking boat anyway. Thus there were now two of you who disobeyed his orders."

"Good old Jeff Smith. It would be like him to rescue the other fellows even if he was in mortal danger."

"Which he was—the Germans hadn't entirely called off their attack and had returned for some more strafing runs. Fortunately, one of Smith's gunners hit one of the blaggards and down it went. That was enough to send the other one packing for home. At that point, Smith completed the rescue of all surviving crew members. Only half survived, including their captain. He was severely burned and in great pain."

"And what of my boat? Did they help, too?"

Chadwick was gray and drawn at this. "No, they abandoned this scene as well."

"Oh, I see." Of course Michael didn't see, but it seemed the best thing to say in the circumstance. He couldn't imagine how a man could act like Billingham. Was he that much of a coward, or did he think their departure served some greater purpose?

Chadwick reached across his desk and picked up a pipe that had been smoldering in an ashtray. Taking a few puffs seemed to calm him down a bit.

"So what happened next, sir?"

"Well, Billingham got back to base first, where he requested an urgent meeting with me. He accused you of mutiny, as you might expect, and started to say how your first officer was insubordinate. Of course I knew there was more to the story than that, but I couldn't get Billingham to calm down. It was then that Lieutenant Smith burst into the room, along with Mr. Coleman. Smith started to shout at Billingham that he was a coward and a disgrace, which of course infuriated the commander. Eventually I had to threaten all of them with a court-martial if they didn't shut up and sit down."

Michael smiled. "It sounds like pure mayhem."

"It was disgusting, is what it was, Lieutenant Carlyle. It made for a pretty mess indeed that I resolved to sort out quietly. The truth is, I didn't know who to bring up on charges. Clearly Lieutenant Smith was insubordinate, as were you and Coleman. But in my opinion, Commander Billingham was guilty of a far greater crime: abandoning those for whom he was responsible in battle." Chadwick was distressed at this point, as evidenced by the deep drags he took on his pipe.

"May I ask how it sorted itself all out and where I stand?"

Chadwick looked up. "Of course—I should have told you that first. In the end we decided that it was in the best interest of the service to keep Billingham from a court-martial. It would be very bad for morale as well as cause a formal inquiry on the part of Whitehall. Besides, it would have exposed you and Smith to greater danger should Billingham be exonerated. We just didn't have time for all that. Instead, he was given the chance to resign so that he could preserve his pension, as long as he promised to never speak publicly of these events. Of course it's doubtful that he would speak of them, since his own cowardice would be revealed. I know it must seem extremely unfair to you that he got off so easily, but I can promise you that for a man like Billingham, the blemish on his reputation will gall him for the rest of his life. He will die an embittered old man."

"Yes, sir, I can see that." Michael thought of Billingham's impeccably pressed uniforms and the care that he took for naval pomp and formality. It would indeed be excruciating for him to lose all that.

"As to your fate, we can't simply overlook your willful disobedience when given a direct order, so we have placed a letter of reprimand in your file. Should another incident occur, you would very likely be subject to court-martial for insubordination."

"Yes, sir." Michael dropped his head. Compared with what might have happened, this was great news. Still, a letter like that would certainly ruin his career and any further chance of advancement, particularly since the true circumstances regarding the event would never be public knowledge.

"Of course there were those of us who argued for leniency."

Michael looked up. Chadwick smiled. "Obviously we had to put the same letter in Lieutenant Smith's file, but since we didn't want to keep him out of combat, we tried to avoid making it a permanent blight. So we wrote in the reprimands that if there were no further incidents within a one-year period, the letter would be removed with no record kept of it."

"A year," Michael repeated, his eyes growing wide.

"A year." Chadwick stood up and walked over to his desk, where he picked up a file. Opening it, he pulled out a sheet of paper. "This is the letter that has been sitting in your file. As I look at the date on the letter, it seems that we're very close to the year."

"Yes, sir." There was hope in Michael's voice.

"Why don't you read it, so you see what the complaint is against you."

Michael took the paper and felt his face burn as he read. To be accused of defying a direct order was very serious business indeed. And even though it was embarrassing, and even though there were certainly extenuating circumstances, he still felt that the exhortations to more closely observe naval protocol were well deserved. When he finished it, he handed it back to Admiral Chadwick. The admiral rose from his seat, and Michael followed.

"Do you accept the terms as outlined in the letter, Lieutenant Carlyle?"

"Yes, sir, I do."

"Do you have anything else to add to the record?" The tone in Chadwick's voice conveyed the impression that he hoped the answer was no.

"No, sir."

"Then in accordance with my authority as area commander, I declare this action complete." With that, he held the piece of paper out in front of him and tore it into pieces.

Michael caught his breath as the paper tore. After a year of agony and worry, it was suddenly over. He thought of all the times he'd imagined how humiliating it would be for his father to have his oldest son disgraced in a court-martial and of the dread he'd felt at facing the scorn of his classmates from the Naval College when they learned about it. The scene had replayed itself over and over in his mind, filling him with dread and misery. And now suddenly it was over. The feeling of relief was so overwhelming, he didn't know exactly how to describe it. He'd never felt happier.

"Thank you, sir. I promise I will live up to your expectations."

Chadwick smiled. "I've been reading the report of your activities of the last year. Bridges and trains sent tumbling into canyons and rivers. That's not normally the type of action a naval officer gets to take part in."

Michael smiled. "No, sir. I certainly didn't expect to do such things."

"What I'm trying to say is that it seems to me you've already exceeded my expectations. In fact, would you consider joining me and my staff for dinner tomorrow night to tell us of your exploits with Captain Ellington and Sublieutenant Jenkins? It would make an interesting change of pace from our usual conversations."

"Of course, sir. I'd be delighted to join you."

"Good." Chadwick started walking to the door. As Michael stepped into the doorway to leave, he paused.

"Excuse me, sir, but do you know where I might be posted? Now that I'm in the clear, I'm a bit anxious to get back into the real navy. I'd love to join up with my old crew, perhaps see Lieutenant Smith and the others."

Chadwick paused. "Unfortunately, that's not in the cards for you. Lieutenant Coleman was promoted in your absence and now commands your boat."

"Oh, I see." He did his best to mask the disappointment he felt for himself. "But of course that's great news for David. I'm sure he's doing a good job."

"A very fine job indeed. But as for you, I'm afraid we don't have any boats, since our presence in this theater is going to naturally decline now that we've established a beachhead here in Southern France." Chadwick looked at Michael for a moment. "I see you're still wearing your leather collar."

Instinctively, Michael put his hand up to his neck, suddenly feeling very self-conscious. "Yes, sir, but only as a precautionary measure."

Chadwick smiled. "It's all right, Lieutenant. Your body has suffered a great deal as a result of this war."

"Sir?"

"We're sending you home, Michael. You're going back to England, where we want you to be an instructor at the naval training facility at Folkestone. I arranged it as soon as I heard you were coming. We still have a need for motor torpedo boats in the Channel to support continuing operations there. And the young men who are coming of age need good teachers to prepare them. I have the feeling you'll be an excellent instructor."

"An instructor? You mean I'm out of the war?"

"It takes many different people filling a variety of roles to make a war, Lieutenant. So I'd hardly say you're out of it. Could you have done the things you've done without the benefit of instructors?"

"Of course not, but . . . I'm still young and able. To be taken off the front lines . . ."

"Mr. Carlyle—you are young and certainly very capable. But after four years on the front lines, don't you think maybe you've done your part? Or do you think you are so indispensable that the fate of the war depends on your being in action?"

Michael debated whether to argue or not. He didn't feel ready to give up active duty. *When you enter a fight, you should stay in it to the end.* But the truth was that his neck really was a problem, and it was also obvious that the admiral was rather firm in his decision. So Michael decided to defer to the judgment of his betters.

"No, sir, I don't presume anything of the kind. I'd be honored to be an instructor." He looked up and smiled. "Thank you, Admiral Chadwick."

Chadwick returned the smile. "You won't forget tomorrow night?"

"Of course not, sir." Michael gave the admiral another crisp salute and then left the room. As he passed by the solemn young aide at the door of the building, he also gave him a crisp salute, doing his best to keep a straight face and maintain proper military decorum. But once clear of the building, he could no longer suppress the grin that forced its way to his face. Michael threw his hat up into the air and let out a cheer.

Chapter Twenty-seven

RETURN TO FRANCE

Number 10 Downing Street—May 1945

"Philip, we need your service again."

"Of course, Prime Minister. What can I do?"

Churchill motioned for him to take a seat. Lighting a cigar, Churchill came around the desk and sat in a chair opposite him. "I'd like you to go to Paris. I need a cabinet minister to interact with the Allied military authorities and the French civil leaders to get a sense of the problems we're going to encounter and your thoughts on how to proceed. I think you're the right man for the job."

"Thank you, sir. But who should I see?"

"I'd start with General DeGaulle. If he'll see you, meet with our generals, and meet with anyone else who you think is important. The main thing is to come back with impressions—I have plenty of facts, but I need to know how it feels there."

"Of course, sir. When shall I leave?"

"Tomorrow, if you can."

"Tomorrow?" Philip tried to think of all that would involve. Then he shook his head. "I don't see why not. But can I make a rather strange request?" Churchill raised an eyebrow. "Would it be possible for me to take my wife and daughter along? Grace lost her job in the munitions factory a month ago, and I've promised them a trip."

"This isn't a pleasure trip. There's still fighting in Germany."

"No, of course. But it strikes me that taking my family along will send a positive message to the people there: that we're opening ourselves up to travel again and that we have confidence in our position. It's just an idea, of course."

Churchill scowled as he puffed on his cigar, so much so that Philip was about to withdraw the request. Then the prime minister spoke up. "I like the idea, Philip, if you're not uncomfortable putting them in that circumstance. Perhaps it will open doors that might otherwise be closed. I can imagine that you'll be invited into people's homes for a meal and conversations with their families. Certainly the French have seen enough military men. It might be nice for them to connect at a female level as well."

Philip stood. "Naturally I'll leave it up to Claire and Grace to decide. But I think that they'll be eager to go."

"I don't have much time, Philip. Events are moving quickly. I need your report in two weeks at the latest."

"We'll be off immediately then."

* * *

Paris

Claire laughed. After five years of German occupation, the citizens of Paris couldn't seem to find enough ways to show their joy at liberation. The cafés were bustling, and the avenues along the Seine crowded with traffic as the trees started to bud.

"I know the schedule is full, but would we have time to visit any of the galleries or museums if they're open?" Grace asked.

"I'm not sure the museums are open yet," Philip said. "I doubt that much art was created during the occupation, but if I know the Parisians, they will quickly recover and start producing paintings and statuary with a vengeance. It's hard to repress such a creative people."

"They do love their art, don't they?" said Grace.

"And food and *amour* as well," Philip said playfully.

"Not that the second applies to me," Grace replied darkly. "I'm okay with the food, but so far I'm not doing so well in the love department."

"Didn't mean to raise a sore issue," Philip replied.

She looked at him and smiled. "Don't worry. There's nothing you could do to dampen my enthusiasm at this point. But you didn't answer Mama's question about the museums. Can we go?"

"Did you know that Hitler ordered that all the main bridges of Paris, as well as the most prominent museums and art galleries, be blown up before the Nazis left the city?"

"What? That's outrageous! Why would he do such a thing?"

"Pure spite. Fortunately, the commanding general, General von Choltitz, refused to give the order. The explosive charges were even set under the bridges, the Louvre, and other significant sites. Had he given the order, all of it would have been destroyed."

"What constrained him?"

"Realism, I think. In the end I think he decided he did not want to go down in history as the man who destroyed one of the world's greatest centers of art. It had to be obvious that Germany would be routed, so he spared the city.

"It's also the reason that I think it better not to go to the museums. There are bomb squads still inspecting the major facilities to make sure they've successfully discovered and disarmed all the bombs that were placed. But perhaps we can find a private gallery."

"At the very least perhaps you could buy us lunch. I'm a bit famished," Claire said. "And it's been years since I've enjoyed French bread. I didn't think I could stop myself this morning."

Philip laughed. "Lunch it is. My treat. We need to enjoy our next two nights here since we drive to Belgium the day after tomorrow so we can return to England with my report."

"So soon?" Grace asked.

When Philip's face clouded she quickly added, "It's all right, Papa. I know you have important things to do. It will be fine."

* * *

Belleau Wood in Eastern France

"Driver," Philip said in fluent French, "what is that large building over there?"

"It's the chapel at the Aisne-Marne American Cemetery."

"An *American* cemetery?"

"Yes, sir, from the Great War. This is where the Americans fought one of their first major battles."

Philip sat back in the car seat, and Claire felt his breathing quicken.

"We're very near the trenches, aren't we?"

"Yes, sir. There are still many remnants. It's been just twenty-five years."

"Are you all right, Philip?"

He shook his head. "It's just that this is very near where I served. Saint-Mihiel is only twenty or thirty kilometers from here. It's where I spent those interminable years of the First World War, and where I met Dan O'Brian."

Claire squeezed his hand. It was just a few days since Jonathon Richards had cabled them that Dan O'Brian had passed away in Salt Lake City. She knew that Philip ached for the loss of his friend. "Bad memories, I'm sure."

"Terrible memories. But wonderful ones too. Had I not met Dan, I would have never joined the Church, and then I never would have met you. Instead I would very likely have ended up an old, unhappy bachelor." In spite of his attempt to put a good face on it, Claire could tell that he was deeply emotional coming back to this place. She put her hand on Grace's knee when she started to speak.

"Would you mind?" Philip said haltingly. "Driver, could we stop over at that cemetery? I'd like to spend a few minutes there."

"Of course, sir. Whatever you like."

"You don't mind, do you, Claire? I won't be long."

"Of course not. I would love to see it myself, to honor those who died here. Perhaps you forgot for a moment that I'm an American. These are my kinsmen."

Philip smiled and squeezed her hand.

The cemetery was in an extremely isolated place, far from any cities or towns. In fact, they were driving through farmers' fields. The sun and rain had turned the fields a brilliant green, and the trees on the small hill behind the cemetery were starting to bud, though very young.

"Is this all right, sir?"

"Yes, this is fine. Thank you." The driver opened Claire's door while Philip got out on the passenger side. Grace quickly followed. They had stopped in front of a small rock building with glazed windows. As they started in the direction of the cemetery, a small man approximately Philip's age stepped out of the building.

"Welcome to Belleau Wood," he said in a thick Brooklyn accent.

"You're American?" Claire responded, the surprise showing in her voice.

"I am. These grounds are maintained by the American Battle Monuments Commission. This ground has been deeded to the United States by the French people in gratitude for our service in the Great War."

"I see. Is it all right for us to look around?"

"Of course. It's only been a few weeks since I got back here. I have to apologize for the grounds, since the Nazis allowed it to fall into disrepair. But at least they didn't deface it in any way."

"That's very good," Philip said distractedly. The fellow clearly wanted to talk more, but Philip felt very anxious for some reason.

As he looked at the hill behind the cemetery, he recalled that it had been completely denuded of trees in the furious battle that had taken place here in 1918. The landscape then was an ugly brown mud that had been churned up by the fierce artillery barrages. Even now he could hear the blasts of the great guns in his mind, and he recalled the screams of the injured. As a chaplain, he had been asked to provide comfort to the men in the field, but as often as not, he'd helped the medics evacuate the wounded from the battleground. Many died on their way to the ambulance, comforted by Philip's words of encouragement and faith along the way.

As they reached the end of the small driveway, Philip heard Grace catch her breath as she saw the great arcs of white crosses extended in both directions almost as far as the eye could see. The graves were arranged in a great semi-circle that faced the hill of Belleau Wood, rather than in the more traditional straight rows characteristic of most cemeteries. The effect was dazzling, particularly when the sun burst through a cloud and illuminated each of the white crosses.

"Do you want to climb the steps with me to enter the memorial?" Grace asked.

"I'll be there in a moment, sweetheart. I want to spend a few minutes here among the dead."

"I understand, Papa." And with that, Grace walked quietly to the steps of the memorial.

As Philip walked through the rows, he paused to read the names on the crosses. They each bore the name of the person interred, their date of birth and date of death, and their military rank. He realized that each had a story to tell and that somewhere back in America a family had grieved, perhaps still grieved, for a fallen son, brother, or father. Lost in thought as he was, he almost walked past a cross that was perhaps six rows in. But something in his mind registered, and he paused for a moment. Looking back, he read the inscription. As he did so he let out a small groan as a wave of emotion flooded over him.

Claire, who had been wandering a few rows away, was startled and called out urgently, "Philip? Are you all right?"

"Oh, Claire, come here quickly, please." Philip's voice was choked with emotion, and Claire ran to join him. When she did, she found him swooning dizzily and helped him to sit down on the jumbled grass.

"What is it Philip? What's wrong?"

Philip just pointed to the cross, his eyes brimming. "Look who it is."

Claire turned and read the inscription, and then she too gasped. It read simply, "Trevor Richards, Lieutenant U.S. Army. 1895–1918."

"Is it Jonathon and Margaret's Trevor?"

Philip nodded, too overcome to speak.

"Do you suppose the Richards have ever visited here?"

Philip shook his head miserably. "Jonathon talked to me about it in London several years ago. He said that at first they were too overcome with grief to come, and then the Depression hit, which left them with rather strained finances. They felt too poor to take time off from work. And then the new war broke out. He felt terrible that he'd never been here."

"Oh, my," Claire said. It was very difficult to focus her thoughts. "It suddenly makes all these other crosses take on more meaning, doesn't it? To think that this is someone who was such an important part of the lives of people we love."

Philip shook his head sadly. "Dan O'Brian was so heartbroken when Trevor died. I think he wanted to die along with him. I've never seen a man mourn the death of a friend so deeply."

"I knew they were close."

"They called each other brothers. Dan had a very hard life until he met the Richards. They in essence adopted him, and he told me that it made all the difference in the world to his happiness. That's why he was so heartbroken when Trevor's airplane was shot down—more so because Trevor was coming to visit Dan."

"And you met because Dan was wounded the same day. You saved him by dragging him from the battlefield."

"And he saved me by introducing me to the gospel."

"Oh, Philip. I'm so sorry for all that you've seen in your life. For two vicious wars, for your friends, and for our sons."

Philip simply nodded. He was at once grateful to find this spot, and yet overwhelmed at all it represented.

"Philip?" He looked up at Claire. She spoke very quietly, almost reverently. "Do you suppose this grave was ever dedicated?"

Philip felt a new emotion as the thought of what she was suggesting impressed itself on his mind. "No, I'm quite certain it wasn't."

"Is that something you could do, right now?"

Philip's emotions revealed themselves again in his voice. "I'd like that, Claire. I think it's a fine idea. It's the very least we can do for this man."

"Let me go and get Grace. I'm sure she'll want to be part of it when she understands who it is."

While waiting for his wife and daughter to join him, a new thought struck Philip. A thought that filled his heart with hope and joy. "Oh, Dan. Perhaps you two brothers are together now. I hope that you have finally joined hands again and embraced." He smiled at the thought. "And will you please seek out my boy and help him? He could certainly use some friends."

And then Philip wept.

Chapter Twenty-eight

REUNITED

London—June 1945

The war in Europe ended on May 8, 1945, with Germany's unconditional surrender. London had been in a state of almost constant celebration in the three weeks since. It would take time, of course, to muster all those serving in the military back into civilian life, but it was far easier to obtain a weekend pass than it had been during the war.

"Would you please pass another piece of bread?" Since returning home, Michael seemed to never be able to get enough of his mother's cooking, and he always looked forward to the Sundays when he could come home for a visit. Karen reached out and passed the plate of bread and then handed him the bowl of honey. She knew Michael well enough that he didn't even have to ask.

"So," Claire said anxiously, "when do you think this marriage will take place?"

Michael blushed. "We don't know, Mother. I just proposed last night."

"I think it should happen later in the summer," Grace said. "London is beautiful when the flowers are out, and you could have an outdoor reception." Michael turned and flashed her a look that clearly said, "Mind your own business," but she ignored him. "Don't you think that would be nice, Karen?"

"It seems rather soon, with all that has to be planned and arranged," Karen said quietly. "And Michael and I need to talk. But it really is a beautiful time of the year if we could get things planned." She turned and smiled shyly at Michael, who melted very much like the honey on his warm bread.

"Can I look at your ring again?" Grace asked.

Karen looked at her and smiled. "It's really beautiful, isn't it? I'm still a bit overwhelmed that Michael would use a family heirloom like this, but the diamond is lovely."

"That ring belonged to my grandmother," Philip said simply. "I'm sure that she'd be happy to know that it will be a continuing symbol of love rather than a relic to sit in a jewelry box. Besides, Michael loved her a great deal and she wanted him to have it. She only lived a few years after we got to England, but she and Michael became great friends in that time."

"Well, I'm very grateful." She looked up and smiled. "And still a bit nervous about all of this. I've never been through this kind of experience before."

Claire laughed. "Neither have we, but at least it's all happening with a person we deeply love. For our part, we couldn't be happier for the two of you. It will be wonderful to have you as part of the family."

"Certainly this is the best decision you've ever made," Philip said to Michael.

At last Michael smiled. "It is indeed. I should have been smart enough to make it before going off to the Mediterranean, but I've always been a bit slow in some things." He turned and looked at Karen. "But at least you were good enough to wait for me."

"Who said I waited?" Karen said breezily. "For all you know, I dated dozens of men while you were gone. You encouraged me to do that, after all."

Michael blushed again. "I was a fool—a genuine fool."

Grace laughed. "I think she's pulling your leg. I'm not aware of any dates while you were gone, and we spent a lot of time together."

"Oh, you hush," Karen said. "He deserves to suffer, at least a little." Then turning to Michael, she added, "But not too much."

"I'm glad you helped Karen learn about the Church. That's the best surprise of all. Now we can be sealed in the temple someday."

"Speaking of which," Philip said, "after learning about this earlier this morning, your mother and I talked about it and we wondered if you'd like our wedding present to be a trip to America so you two can be sealed. Of course, Karen's British citizenship makes it advisable that you get married here first, but then you could make the voyage as soon as civilian passage becomes available again."

Before they could answer, Grace spoke up. "Could I go too, Papa?" When she saw his surprised look, she said, "Not on the honeymoon, of course. But to America to be there when they get sealed. Perhaps we could all go. You did promise me a trip when the war is over."

"I promised you Rome or Florence or somewhere like that. Are you saying you'd give that up for a humdrum return to Salt Lake City—or wherever they decide to be sealed?"

"They could go to Hawaii," Grace said cheerfully. "That would be nice."

"We're not going to Hawaii," Michael said firmly. "At least not to get sealed. We'd most likely go to Salt Lake City." He caught himself and quickly turned to Karen. "That is, unless you'd prefer to go to some other temple."

"I think Salt Lake City is perfect. The pictures I've seen of the temple are wonderful, and you have friends there."

"I think you're rushing them, Philip. He really did propose just last night, and they need time to think all of this through."

"No, it's all right, Mother. Karen and I did talk about the temple, and a trip would be the perfect wedding gift."

"And we'd certainly like all of you there," Karen added.

Grace laughed. "This is just about the best day, isn't it?"

"Here, here," Philip said, and he held up his glass of water. Each of them held their glasses up as well. "To Salt Lake City, then, whenever Michael and Karen decide. And in the meantime, here's to Michael and Karen!"

Michael tipped his glass with the others and said, "To a glorious future, free from fear and war."

AUTHOR'S NOTE

On my first visit to Washington, DC, more than a decade ago, I took time to visit the Vietnam War Memorial on the Mall. I grew up during that era, and so it was a sobering and reverential experience to see row after row of names that were etched in the black granite wall of the memorial—more than 50,000 in all—soldiers who had died in that conflict. In an attempt to capture the feeling, I took a couple of random photos, mostly to capture the image of the American Flag reflected on the highly polished surface of the granite.

A couple of weeks later, I was at a monthly planning meeting at the home of my boss, where some of my business associates asked to see the photos of the trip. As the pictures were being handed from one to another, my boss suddenly jumped up and started for the stairs, calling urgently to his wife, "Marion, Marion! You're not going to believe this."

It was shocking, and I had no idea what had happened. A few minutes later, he came down the stairs, and it was clear he had been weeping. He then pointed to a specific name on the memorial wall in the picture, and said quietly, "Marion and I went to high school with this man, and we didn't know that he'd been killed there."

It was such a profound moment that it burned forever in my heart the price that is paid by those who serve in the military to protect the freedom we enjoy as Americans.

Perhaps it was with this experience in mind that I wrote the scene of Philip Carlyle at the Belleau Wood cemetery in France, where he happens across the grave of Trevor Richards. I understood the emotion he would feel on such an occasion because of my earlier experience with my friends. I have been to the Aisne-Marne cemetery in France and felt my heart overflow with grief to see the seemingly endless arcs of white crosses that mark the final resting spot of young men who died far away from home in World War I. They are mostly forgotten now and the cemetery is often deserted, except for the caretaker. The truth is that I wept as I wrote this scene, because good fiction should capture the emotions that are felt in real life. And war brings out every human emotion as if in a crucible.

Home Again at Last ends the 1,600-page saga that started with *'Til the Boys Come Home*. I have been pleased to hear from readers as this series has unfolded. My deepest desire is that in writing these books I have paid proper tribute to the real men and women who fought in these two great wars. Words are certainly inadequate, but they're all I have.

I started my writing career helping three great men tell their true life stories. Much of my thinking about World War II and Vietnam came from the hundreds of hours of conversations I shared with Rudi Wobbe, the young German who tells the story of *Three Against Hitler*, Joe Banks, whose marvelous spiritual experiences related in *A Distant Prayer* have inspired hundreds of thousands of readers, and Bernie Fisher, recipient of the Congressional Medal of Honor for valor as he placed his life in peril to save a fellow aviator. His story is told in *Beyond the Call of Duty*.

What an honor and blessing it has been to write all of these stories. I am so grateful to my many readers who have shared the experience with me. Thank you.

Jerry Borrowman
February 2008

British
Commando
French Resistance

SWITZERLAND

Mila

FRANCE

Cannes

Marseille

Ligurian Sea

CORSICA

SARDINIA

Mediterrane

Bizerte

Algiers

Constantine

ALGERIA

TUNIS